Deadly Dance

D1518140

Darville Knowles, M.D.

Milligan Books   **California**

Published and Distributed by:
Milligan Books, Inc.
An imprint of Professional Business Consultants

Cover Design by
Clint D. Johnson

Formatting by
Alpha Desktop Publishing

First Printing, January 2003
10987654321

ISBN 0-9719749-8-5

Publisher's note

Darville Knowles, M.D.
E-mail: oncall36@aol.com

Milligan Books, Inc.
1425 W. Manchester Ave., Suite C
Los Angeles, California 90047
www.milliganbooks.com
(323) 750-3592

About The Author

Darville Knowles, M.D. was born in Miami, Florida. He received his B.S. Degree from Howard University and his Medical Degree from Stanford University. He has been practicing medicine in Las Vegas for twenty years, where he resides with his wife Kyle.

Acknowledgments

Thanks to my wife Kyle, for her tremendous and unconditional support.

Special thanks to the Milligan Publishing family and Maxine Thompson for making this book happen.

Prologue

Blood had splattered everywhere—on the sheets, on the ceiling, on the drapes. An arc of blood even smeared the wall.

The sun streaming through the windows splashed upon the floor and was reflected in rivulets of thick, slippery blood. The stench of blood filled his nostrils, reminding him of the smells in a slaughterhouse he'd visited as a young boy.

Suddenly a putrid taste soured his mouth. He knew he would be blamed. His clothes, his shoes and his glasses were drenched with blood. No one would ever believe him. What could he do? But this was not his fault.

He hoped he wouldn't have to pay too dearly for this.

Chapter One

"**D**r. Hitchcock says it's urgent," Ms. Kennedy announced, rushing into Dr. Evander Parker's high-rise office. Her voice sounded terse as she took long strides across the plush champagne carpet. Without warning, she flung a slip of paper into the doctor's hands, reminding him of that old childhood game of "hot potato." Reared back on bowed legs, Ms. Kennedy's, eyes squinted as though studying the doctor's reactions.

Dr. Parker's gaze dropped to the telephone message. "Dr. Parker. Please come to the hospital labor and delivery room. STAT." He hadn't received a stat call in years. The ultimate emergency call. He knew he had to get moving.

He took a deep breath—something he always did when faced with a crisis. Although he raised his eyebrows and twisted his mouth to the side, he didn't comment. He clasped the message to his chest, trying to calm his heart's loud ka-thump. He hoped Ms. Kennedy wouldn't notice how nervous he was.

He could see how his secretary's nose practically twitched with curiosity, wanting to know the details. She seemed totally oblivious to Dr. Parker's current patient, whose session she had just interrupted. She wanted to know what was going on.

Dr. Parker stepped from behind his antique cherrywood desk and addressed her in a calm, even tone. "Thanks, Ms. Kennedy. You can leave now."

Ms. Kennedy paused, then left the room, slamming the heavy oak door behind her.

Suddenly, Parker's palms felt sweaty. What was going on? Dr. Emerson Hitchcock, his colleague and best friend, seldom called for his assistance. Whatever it was, it had to be serious.

As a psychiatrist, he didn't get many emergency calls to the hospital. In fact, that was one of the main reasons Dr. Evander Parker had returned to residency training and changed his specialty from Internal Medicine to Psychiatry.

"Excuse me," he said to his current patient, Heather. "I have an emergency at the hospital."

Heather looked disappointed, but nodded her head, lips trembling.

In a flurry of motion, Dr. Parker grabbed his coat, his Hospital Identification Badge and rushed through the office. He stopped long enough to turn to Ms. Kennedy. "Cancel the rest of the day's appointments." Ms. Kennedy bobbed her steel-gray head.

With that, Dr. Parker darted down the corridor to the bank of elevators and pounded the buttons. When an elevator didn't show up in a nanosecond, he bounded down the stairs two at a time.

Fortunately, Dr. Parker's office was conveniently located in one of three high-rises owned by the hospital and it was easier for him to run the two short blocks to the hospital than to retrieve his car from the doctors' parking lot, drive the two blocks and look for another parking space. Sprinting at a steady pace, colonnades of palm trees and lengthening shadows from the high-rises passed him in a blur.

As he bolted through the oversized glass front doors of the hospital, he noticed a few tired-looking people sitting in the main lobby. He continued jogging through the antiseptic corridors to the Labor and Delivery Room on the first floor. He pushed a brass-plated disc on the wall, opening the automatic doors, and dashed into the delivery suites.

"I'm Dr. Parker." Between ragged breaths, he identified himself to a young female nurse who was sitting at the desk of the surgical pavilion. "Where's Dr. Hitchcock?"

She kept the phone's receiver cupped to her ear and pointed an index finger tipped with brilliant red nail polish at the second door on the right.

Before entering the suite, Dr. Parker slipped into a faded green operating scrubsuit and wriggled paper covers over his shoes. He sterilized his hands and arms up to his elbows at the operative sink, then put on a face mask, along with protective eye wear and a surgical cap. As he was about to enter Labor and Delivery suite B, he bumped into Dr. Emerson Hitchcock, or "Hitch," as everyone called him.

Hitch's operating garb matched Dr. Parker's, except for a multi-colored surgical cap, the newest rage among the surgeons. Even in drab surgical attire, Hitch cut an impressive figure. He was just over six-foot two with a slender athletic physique. A stark contrast to a pasty-complexioned Parker who at five feet seven, brown hair and brown eyes with an average build starting to soften, blended into a room full of people like paint.

High cheekbones and piercing green eyes were the most salient of Hitch's features. At the age of forty-eight, three years older than Parker, his dark brown hair was just beginning to gray at the temples. He resembled the actor Jeff Chandler as Dr. Kildare, Dr. Parker always thought.

"What's the problem?" Dr. Parker asked, still gasping for breath. "This better be a real emergency," he said as he removed the mask and protective eyewear.

Glowering, Hitch's nostrils flared, air rushing out of them. Parker knew then, whatever it was, it was critical.

Finally, Hitch spoke, his words tumbling out fervently. "I have a young girl in suite B, who's having a difficult delivery. To begin with she's anemic, her platelet count is low enough to start affecting her and the baby's clotting ability, and if we don't get it corrected I'm afraid we'll lose them both."

"Well, if her platelets are low, give her some platelets."

"Thanks for the advice," Hitch said sarcastically. "If things were that simple I wouldn't have sent for you."

"Why exactly did you send for me?" asked a puzzled Parker.

"Because of her family's religious beliefs, I can't get permission to give her any blood products, including platelets, to help stop the bleeding."

"And?" Dr. Parker broke in.

Hitch held up his hands in an imploring fashion. "For God's sake, her parents are in the waiting room and I thought you might be able to talk to them." He let out a deep sigh.

"This is a little late," Dr. Parker replied, a bit irritated. "Why didn't you talk to them earlier about this possibility?"

Hitch glared at him, his green eyes becoming pinpoints of frustration mixed with fury.

"I would have, Doctor," Hitch replied sarcastically, "but this is a walk-in from the Emergency Room. She's had no prenatal care, and I never saw the patient or her parents until this very moment."

"Alright, alright."

Dr. Parker gently touched Hitch's shoulder.

"Calm down. I'll see what I can do. Where are they?"

"In the Delivery waiting room."

Dr. Parker took a deep breath and hastened to the small Labor and Delivery waiting area, mentally preparing what he would say to the girl's parents. It wasn't hard to spot them, as there were no other people in the silent waiting room.

Although he hadn't asked Hitch the girl's age, judging from her parents' appearance, she had to be very young.

Neither of her parents could have been older than thirty-five. Both were dressed in the all-white flowing robes of a religious sect that was familiar to everyone in Southern Florida. Their unlined ebony complexions stood in stark contrast to their white robes. The couple appeared to be meditating, with their hands intertwined, but stopped and looked up as Dr. Parker approached them.

The mother was almost completely covered from head to toe. The small part of her face that was visible seemed very pleasant. Although young, the father had a stern demeanor. Dr. Parker noticed that the father's face had the shadow of a beginning beard. That's when he realized he was going to have a difficult, if not impossible, task. The members of this sect all wore heavy beards and with this new growth, it was obvious the father was a relatively new convert. As with all new converts, they were the staunchest defenders of the faith.

Parker sat directly across from them and observed that they still held hands. He introduced himself and assured them that their daughter was doing fine—thus far. Just to be doubly sure, he asked if they were members of the religion that he had previously assumed and they both assured him that they were. The parents introduced themselves as Mr. and Mrs. Ahmed Farouk.

"How long have you been members?" He asked.

The father's austere mien hardened even more before he spoke. "It's not the duration of someone's faith that's important," he said, "but the depth of their commitment and convictions."

Exactly the answer Parker was hoping not to get.

The parents reiterated that, according to their religious beliefs, it was not acceptable for them to give or to receive blood or blood products.

"Have you thought about the possible consequences of this course of action?" Parker looked at both of them somberly.

"We are willing to accept whatever happens."The un-wavering young father's voice was steady, resolved.

Although Mr. Farouk did all of the talking and his wife often nodded her head in agreement, Dr. Parker noticed some apprehension in her moist eyes.

Parker gently reminded them that their decision not only affected the life of their daughter, but also that of the unborn child.

"Both of their chances of survival would be enhanced by a transfusion," Parker continued, "if Dr. Hitchcock thought it was necessary."

The father seemed to be genuinely pondering what Dr. Parker had said, when the worst of all possible things happened. A group of about twelve people of both sexes entered the dimly-lit waiting room. They were all dressed identically to the young girl's parents.

"Brother Farouk, we're here for you."

"It's in Yahweh's hands."

"Be strong in the faith."

The young husband stood up immediately and pro-claimed his faith—in what seemed like rehearsed verses—for all to hear. "It is now up to Yahweh," he said in conclusion.

Mr. Farouk then looked at each member of the group for their approval, which he received in the form of silent nods. At that moment Dr. Parker knew that there was no chance of convincing the parents to reconsider unless he could talk to them alone. The problem now was how to isolate them from their fellow members and what to say to convince them that all of the teachings they had recently embraced were not advan-tageous to the situation at hand.

His mind was racing furiously when a nurse rushed, panting, into the now crowded waiting room. Flailing her arms, she beckoned him to her. Her eyes literally danced in her face, they were so animated.

For the second time that day, Dr. Parker apologetically excused himself and calmly walked as fast as he could to her side. Grabbing him by the arm and pulling him out of earshot of the waiting room occupants, she gave him an urgent update on the progress of the patient in suite B. She informed him that not only had the girl's coagulation problems worsened, but her platelet counts were starting to fall precipitously.

"Dr. Hitchcock told me to come and get you," she said, gasping between long breaths. "He said we're going to need every set of hands available. He also told me to tell you that if you are going to be of any help to him at all in the Labor and Delivery room, to please try and remember when you were a real doctor. His words, not mine." She smiled wanly.

As soon as they were far enough down the corridor not to be seen from the waiting room, they both flew to Labor and Delivery.

He scrubbed his hands and arms again at the now familiar sink outside the suite. The nurse who was sent to summon him—later, he found out her name was Christy—assisted him into a gown, which covered his scubs. Again he donned gloves, mask and protective eyewear. Bursting through the swinging doors and into the suite, he knew from the nurse's constant mopping of Hitch's forehead that they were in for a long siege.

"Over here, Evander," Hitch shouted when he saw his friend.

The nurse who had been wiping Dr. Hitchcock's forehead retreated to let Dr. Parker stand by Hitch's side at the feet of the young patient. She was lying on her back in a lithotomy position with her legs placed in the metal stirrups of the operating table.

"Give me a quick assessment," Parker requested.

"She appears to have an extreme type of toxemia. She's hypertensive, her liver counts are elevated and her platelet count is now down to a critical stage, which naturally includes the baby. I just told the anesthesiologist to administer general anesthesia."

Parker nodded.

Hitch turned to Parker with pleading eyes. "What did her parents say?"

"No luck," Parker replied.

"Dammit!" Hitch spoke between clenched teeth. "I had her typed and crossed and had the blood bank place some fresh frozen plasma and platelets on standby just in case you were successful."

"You know," Parker said, "since she's having a baby she can sign as an adult. Did you think of that?"

Sweating profusely, his hands between the young mother's legs, trying to determine the dilatation of the birth canal, Hitch spoke brusquely. "I talked to her about it after I got nowhere with her parents. She had tears in her eyes and said that by getting pregnant she was a huge disappointment to them both and she had no intention of going against their wishes now. Even if it meant she would die, which she has a damn good chance of doing." Hitch's brow furrowed in worry.

Surveying the others in the room, Parker noticed an anesthesiologist—that he knew vaguely—at the head of the operating table. Parker knew the nurses had nicknamed him Dr. Cool because of his demeanor. Between Dr. Cool and the door stood a circulating nurse whose job was to get anything needed from outside the operating room. A surgical intern whom he had seen in the hospital hallways stood in the general vicinity of the patient's abdomen.

The scrub nurse, whose job was to give whatever instruments that were called for to the doctors and to keep count of all the gauze, sutures, cotton balls etc., so that none would be left in the patient at the conclusion of the procedure, darted in and out between Hitch and Parker with ballet-like agility. She dabbed the perspiration from his forehead when needed so that both of his hands were free for the task before him.

"Pressure's starting to drop," Dr. Cool said dispassionately.

"Increase her fluids and run that IV wide open," yelled Hitch with high-pitched fervor.

"You got it," Dr. Cool replied.

The nurse whom Dr. Parker had first spoken to at the desk stuck her masked face into the suite. "Reports from the lab are back. Hemoglobin and hematocrit are both decreased. Platelet count is down to thirty thousand. Coagulation panel has deteriorated. They want to know what you want to do with the platelets, fresh frozen plasma, and the four units of packed cells you ordered."

"Hold them," Parker shouted. He hoped he would still be able to have her parents reverse their decision.

"Fetal heart rate is increasing," this from Dr. Cool, who Parker could swear was chewing gum under his face mask.

Still checking the birth canal, Hitch suddenly pulled his hands from between the girl's legs and looked at Parker with a face engraved with unadulterated agony.

"The baby's leg is hanging out of her vagina," he said sotto voce to Parker. "Baby's breech," he called out loud enough for everyone to hear.

"Starting general anesthesia," Dr. Cool responded.

"Parker, help me get her legs out of the stirrups and lie her flat on the table. I'm going to tilt her away from me. You get on the side of the table opposite me with Anderson," said Hitch.

Dr. Evander Parker made a mental note. Anderson. He would try to remember Dr. Cool's real name whenever he saw him again. He wondered if Anderson was his first or surname. Nervously Dr. Parker surveyed the room again and positioned himself on the opposite side of the operating table facing Dr. Hitchcock. The patient's abdomen was now tilted slightly

15

towards him and Anderson. He thought of his name again to help him remember.

"We're going to do a C section." Hitch spoke loudly enough again for everyone to hear.

"Gonna do a bikini cut?" Dr. Cool sounded like he was trying to be facetious. Talk about gallows humor, Parker thought.

"No," snapped Hitch. "I'm going to do a vertical cut. It's faster and it causes less blood loss."

"If she lives, she's gonna be mad you didn't give her a bikini cut," sang out Dr. Cool, who Parker now was convinced had consumed too much anesthesia of one kind or another, himself.

Hitch did not reply or even look toward the head of the table.

"Scalpel!" he barked with his hand extended.

He received it from the scrub nurse who pressed the handle firmly into the palm of his hand. He wrapped his size nine hand around the handle and made a vertical incision from the umbilicus to the pubic ramus. After deftly cutting through the skin, fascia, adventitia and peritoneum, then separating the layers carefully with his fingers, he cut through the abdominal muscles, exposing the uterus. Placing a retractor between the bladder and the womb, Hitch then made a transverse incision into the uterus.

As he inserted his hand into the incision, he spoke to Parker. "I've got both feet now. When I tell you to push, I want you to push right below her sternum ... pushing the baby down towards me."

Holding both tiny feet in one hand, Hitch extracted the feet and hips first, then the thorax and shoulders.

"Now push," he said to Parker as he began to pull the head through the incision. The infant's head was large and round. Unlike most newborns, the head wasn't cone shaped because it had never passed through the birth canal. Unfortunately, though, as Hitch removed the baby from the uterus, the head ruptured both uterine arteries. Pulsating torrents of bright red blood spewed from the torn arteries, showering Parker and drenching everything within a three-foot radius. It was as though they had hit a geyser with a non-ending source.

Parker noticed blood was everywhere. The surgical table and drapes, the ceiling, and most of all the floor. HE WAS COVERED WITH BLOOD.

"Forceps!" Parker yelled, receiving them instantaneously from the scrub nurse.

He adroitly clamped the arteries as Hitch cut and tied the cord, before handing the baby, who was beginning to hemorrhage from the umbilical cord, to the pediatric nurse. She quickly wrapped the infant in a blanket before placing it on an adjoining surgical table. She then began a methodical physical examination of the eerily silent infant.

Ruptured uterine arteries are not uncommon or insurmountable problems with a Cesarean section, but with an anemic mother, a plummeting platelet count and abnormal clotting factors, they were now facing an imminent catastrophe. Less than two minutes had expired from the time of Dr. Hitchcock's initial incision to the time he handed the infant to Ms. Grinner, the Pediatric Nurse.

"Pressure's still dropping and the mother's heart rate is increasing," chimed in the anesthesiologist.

"The baby's not breathing," the Pediatric Nurse called out as she began cardiopulmonary resuscitation on the infant, who while continuing to hemorrhage from the umbilical cord was now bleeding profusely from his mouth and nose. "Probably a cerebral hemorrhage," she shrieked.

Parker rushed over to see what he could do to help, momentarily losing his footing on the bloody floor. As he and

the Pediatric Nurse tried to manipulate life into the exsanguin-
ating infant, he became saturated in what seemed like the
baby's entire blood volume.

"Patient's exhibiting cardiac arrhythmia," said Dr. Cool
dryly. "Giving her three hundred milligrams of amiodorone,
I.V." he exclaimed loudly so the nurse could now record the
medicines given and the time and route of administration.

"Isolated premature ventricular contractions," he continued ..." now couplets ... triplets ... ventricular tachycardia ...
full cardiac arrest.

Parker rushed from the moribund infant to the crash cart,
where the circulating nurse had already removed the defibrillator and had applied electrogel to the shiny metal surfaces of
the paddles.

"Maximum wattage!" Parker yelled as he applied the
cold slippery surfaces to the naked chest of the young girl who
would not be a mother this day. He wanted to give her another
chance.

"Stand clear," he shouted as he looked around to be sure
no one was in contact with the metal operating table. He stood
back himself as he depressed the buttons on each paddle
simultaneously. The young body jolted as the current of four
hundred watt seconds surged through it.

"No change," Dr. Cool droned in a monotone. "Drawing
a set of blood gases and giving one milligram of epinephrine
I.V. push."

Dr. Parker held the paddles toward the nurse for another
application of gel while the defibrillator was recharging. He
rubbed the metal surfaces against one another to spread the gel
evenly. Again he applied the paddles to her chest that was now
slippery from the gel and burned from the current, emitting the
odor of charred flesh.

"Stand clear," he repeated as he looked around the table
and pressed the buttons with his thumbs.

Once again, her frail body jolted and seared in response to the electrical current.

"Still no cardiac activity." Dr. Cool sounded bored.

Dr. Parker handed the defibrillator paddles to someone standing near him and gave the slick, scorched chest a hard thump with his fist. The young body shook almost as much as it had with the defibrillation. Pressing the heels of his hands into her sternum, he started external cardiac massage in concert with the anesthesiologist who was continuing artificial respiration. He counted aloud as he pressed downward onto her chest.

"One, two, three, four, five, breathe. One, two, three, four, five, breathe."

Periodically, his hands would slide across her slippery torso and the nurse would wipe a clean towel across the girl's chest. Suddenly Parker realized he didn't know the young girl's name.

"One, two, three, four, five, breathe …. One, two, three, four, five, breathe …. One, two, three, four, five, breathe …."

With all the marvels of modern medicine, all they were able to accomplish in two hours was a doubly disastrous result.

Since Dr. Hitchcock had requested his presence, Parker felt it was his duty to tell the parents what had happened.

In despair, he cleaned himself at the sink outside the operating suite and changed into fresh scrubs. As he soldiered down the corridor to the waiting area, he tried to think of what he would say.

The waiting room was now occupied by more than thirty people who were all similarly attired. The women had moved the half dozen or more chairs so that they formed a semicircle facing a solitary seated figure that he recognized as the mother of the now-deceased girl. Since there were not enough chairs to accommodate them all, some sat two or three to a chair and some sat on the carpeted section of the floor.

The men were standing silently in a circle holding hands. Mr. Farouk stood in the center of the human ring, his head bowed and his hands clasped to his forehead. The women, who were talking when Parker entered, stopped abruptly, causing the silent men to look in his direction.

"Will you excuse us, please?" Parker asked the rest of the group as he escorted both parents to an anteroom where they would not be disturbed.

After seating them both, Dr. Parker remained standing.

"We did our best," he began, "but we experienced a series of unfortunate complications that we could not overcome." Trying not to burden them with guilt, he continued. "It isn't even certain that receiving a transfusion of blood or blood products would have prevented the circumstances that led to the demise of your daughter and her child."

"So they're both dead?" asked the mother softly. Parker could see that she hoped she misunderstood him.

"Yes," he replied somberly.

Burying her face in her hands, the mother wept silently but unashamedly. The father, who seemed very much in control, stood and slowly approached Dr. Parker.

"Did she have a boy or a girl?" Mr. Farouk stood directly in front of Parker.

"Beg your pardon?" Parker fully understood the question but was stalling for time to think.

"The baby," the father said. "Was it a boy or a girl?"

"I'm embarrassed to tell you this," Parker replied, "but with so much going on at the time I really don't know."

Looking at the ground and shaking his head slowly, the deceased girl's father continued. "I guess it really doesn't matter at this point."

As quick as a thought, the small-built black man knocked him flat to the floor, fell on top of him and began to batter him into unconsciousness.

"You will pay! You will pay!" He screamed over and over.

20

* * *

Dr. Evander Parker awakened on a stretcher in the emergency room. The black face of the nurse standing over him was slowly coming into focus.

"What happened?" he asked, unconsciously rubbing his swollen face.

"Hospital security had to pull a deranged maniac off you," she whispered. "They just now handed him over to the city police."

The police, he thought. Permanent fixtures in all emergency rooms. Not for security, but because of the natural affinity between policeman and Emergency Room nurses. "Maybe I can write a paper on that," he mumbled to himself.

"What did you say?" asked the nurse whose badge identified her as Nurse Marshall.

"Oh, nothing," Parker replied.

"Security said he told them he was going to get you good for what you did to him and his family. And he said what he did to you today was just the beginning," she said.

All of a sudden a nice malpractice suit didn't sound so bad. At least it didn't sound terminal.

He was still lying on his back, propped up on his elbows, when he saw the police lead his attacker toward the exit. Mr. Farouk's hands were cuffed behind his back and he was sandwiched between two beefy Dade County police officers. As he passed, he looked casually over his shoulder and inadvertently turned his head toward Parker's cubicle. Their eyes met briefly and he immediately became animated.

"Your family will suffer ten times as much as mine!" he shouted. "And your heart will be ten times heavier with sorrow!" he screamed as the officers manhandled him roughly through the automatic door.

* * *

21

Parker eased his throbbing head back onto the stretcher and tried to imagine what his wife Cassie would say when she saw him. His lips curved into a smile, but the pain in his face changed his smile into a grimace.

Chapter
Two

Pregnant rain clouds dappled the tropical island sky surrounding Jamaica. It was almost time for the late afternoon shower. During this time of year, the only variation was how severe the rainfall would be. The rain could vary from a short tropical shower to a long and steady monsoon-like deluge that would send man and beast scurrying for shelter. In spite of the inclement weather, the sun would continue to shine brightly and warmly through either extreme.

The temperature was ninety-four degrees with the identical percentage of humidity. One could smell the curious mixture of ozone, combined with various flowers such as bougainvilleas, jasmine, bird-of-paradise, and vegetation such as sugar cane, breadfruit and aki in various stages of bloom and decay.

The climate was uncomfortable for the natives of the country, but the weather would have been unbearable to anyone not born to this land. Even though its natural beauty was still unsurpassed at this time of year, no tourists blundered over the landscape, even though hotel rooms could be had for one third of the price of the high season.

Walking slowly down Cemetery Road, two lean and lanky figures, dark as silhouettes, solemnly emerged from the shadows onto the brightly-lit path flanked on both sides by dense foliage. Without a word, the young men headed for the shoreline where they could meditate by the ocean and map out their futures.

Noel and Chandler Christian, the only children of Cyril and Hortense Christian, had just buried their father, who like most people on this island had died a premature death. Both brothers wrote their own epitaphs for their father in their heads.

Here lies Cyril Christian. Too much alcohol, too few opportunities.

Here lies the economy. Too many imports, too few jobs.

Here lies the Government. Too many bureaucrats, too few ideas.

Here lies our country. Too many problems, too few solutions.

The two men were quiet until they reached the ocean. The beach was empty, save for a few vendors. Their lack of business was a sore reminder of the state of the economy in their land.

"Papa was a good man," Noel said to his younger brother, matter-of-factly.

"Yeah, mon." Chandler stared at the ground as they strolled toward the beach area of the island.

"It's up to us to provide for Mama now," Noel continued.

"How're we going to do that?" Chandler sounded annoyed. "Papa only left a small amount of money from the store, which has barely been meeting its own expenses."

"Invest it, man. That's the smart way," his older brother said. "We got to start us up some kinda business."

"Yeah, start a business on this pitiful island. Even the government is broke. If we stay around here, that money will be long gone in a short time. We gotta get out of here."

"That's a good idea, but where?"

"The States, man, the States."

Chandler looked at his brother as if he were from another planet.

"Okay, but the States a big place. Where you thinking about going?"

24

"Me, I'm California dreaming." Chandler skipped a rock across the azure water.

"Too far." Noel, although the older of the two by only eleven months, was always the practical one.

"New York then." Chandler gazed out to sea as a gull dived on the gold horizon.

"You crazy, boy? It's too cold there. We need a place with opportunity and some place where we can blend in."

They stopped walking.

Still looking down, Chandler began to draw small circles in the sand with the toe of his right shoe as he drifted deeply into contemplation. He had done this since he was a small child, but usually in his bare feet. Right now he wanted to take his shoes off. He seemed to think better with his shoes off.

Noel did quite the opposite. He clasped his hands behind his neck, closed his eyes and looked toward the heavens as if for divine guidance.

As Noel lowered his head, his eyes met Chandler's who was raising his. They stared at one another for a brief moment before they both broke into wide smiles.

"Miami!" they shouted simultaneously.

Chapter Three

"Oh my gosh!" Cassie exclaimed, her hand over her heart, as her husband walked through the door of their high-rise condominium. "What happened to you? Were you mugged?"

"No." Dr. Parker held his hand up, trying to calm his wife down.

She tried to touch his bruised face and nearly swollen shut black eye. Grimacing in pain, he pushed her hand away. "Then it must have been one of those crazies in your office that attacked you. I told you that you should have stayed in Internal Medicine. But would you listen? Noooooo."

Parker shook his head. "It was not one of the patients in the office and I wish you would please stop referring to them as crazies."

"Then it must have happened at the police station. I know you get some kind of satisfaction from volunteering your time there, but counseling police officers can be very dangerous. I read an article where their mentality is the same as that of a criminal's, and—"

"It didn't happen at the police station either," he interrupted, walking to the master bathroom. "If you will give me a chance to gather myself together I'll tell you what happened."

Washing his face, Evander Parker related the whole episode to his wife. He told her he'd decided not to press charges against his attacker, Mr. Ahmed Farouk.

Cassie Parker, now seated on the edge of the bathtub, held her head in her hands, rhythmically shaking her head in disbelief the entire time her husband talked.

"So let me get this straight. And please correct me if I'm wrong." She stood up, placing her delicate hands on her slender hips. "You left your office, where you had scheduled appointments with paying patients, to help Hitch with an indigent, nonpaying patient." Her voice began to rise to a high soprano. "The patient's family refused to follow any of your recommendations and the patient and her baby died. The father of the patient attacks you in the hospital and now he may sue you both for malpractice." She pursed her lips, cocked her head to the side, and then suddenly let the words burst from her. "Evander, are you friggin' crazy?"

Parker heaved a deep sigh, holding up his palms in surrender. "Everything you've said is true but that's not the point."

With Cassie close on his heels, Parker walked out the bathroom to his bedroom closet and changed into a well-worn brown cotton bathrobe.

"Then please tell me what the point is." Cassie scowled.

"The point is ..." Parker turned and faced her, enunciating each word carefully, "that you are doing your best to try and help someone in need. Sometimes you are able to help and sometimes you are not."

"You know I hate it when you speak to me like that." Cassie sucked her teeth. "But in any case, you're the one who will be held accountable."

"Maybe."

Dr. Parker limped into the living room and slumped into a taupe ultrasuede loveseat. Picking up one of two remote controls from an overstuffed matching ottoman, he first turned the wide screen TV to the sports channel where some contest was always being waged, then pushed the mute button. He then picked up the other remote to bring his stereo unit to life which was already tuned to his favorite soft jazz station. The saffron-colored room had a large floor to ceiling window that faced the waterfront, and a small balcony with two diminutive patio chairs and several potted plants desperately in need of attention. The room was very soothing. His wife's voice was not.

"No maybe's in it, honey." Cassie sat next to him. Suddenly, she smacked her palm against her forehead as if struck by an idea. "When they haul you and Hitch in front of a jury and tell them how you two very well-trained and supposedly competent doctors let a teenaged mother and her baby die, you'll be lucky to walk out of there with your shirts on."

"But our hands were tied ...."

"Yes, they were. And when you walk out of that courtroom the rope won't be around your hands. It'll be around your ... well, let's just say your necks."

"But when the jury hears the evidence I'm sure—"

"Look, dear, I'm just trying to point out the fact that when it comes to malpractice suits, the evidence has no bearing on the outcome of the trial. I'm well aware that juries are supposed to weigh the evidence carefully and decide in your favor if you practice what they call a standard of medicine, which means that in the same situation, ninety percent of competent doctors would have done the same thing. But it doesn't matter."

"Cassie, please!" Parker leaned his throbbing head back against the loveseat's cushion.

Cassie was on a roll. "When the plaintiffs bring out a deformed baby or tell of the death of a baby, the average juror just wants somebody to pay. They figure that's what you rich doctors have insurance for. So they hand out the money. And if you think the judge will overturn the decision because it was based on sympathy and not facts, you better think again."

"Will you give it a break!" Parker peered up through blood-shot eyes. "I know you never liked Hitch, anyhow."

28

Cassie persisted. "Be that as it may, why do you think Hitch's wife has been after him for years to stop delivering babies? It's not only the hours or stress of the job. It's because if he delivers a baby that has a birth defect, they are going to have to pay. If the settlement is larger than the insurance covers, it will come out of their pockets."

"But, honey..."

"Let me finish. Lawyers use malpractice suits as a lottery system. They figure if they sue enough doctors, then one day they'll hit it big. Now I'm finished."

"Sounds like I am too," he said softly.

His willingness to admit his poor judgment seemed to disarm Cassie. She opened her mouth to say something, then closed it. Suddenly they both smiled. Before he knew it, she switched gears on him.

"You look terrible. Does your head ache?" Cassie ran her hand gently through his hair. Suddenly, her voice took on a cooing quality.

"Yes, but now I don't know if it was caused by the big guy at the hospital or the little lady in the house."

"Can I get anything for you?"

"Yes," her husband answered. "A new job and some aspirin. Not necessarily in that order."

"Do you want me to stay in with you this evening?" Cassie got up to look for some aspirin.

"What do you mean?" Parker was talking to her back.

"I mean do you feel well enough for me to go out?" she replied over her shoulder, walking into the powder room to search the medicine cabinet.

"Oh ... right. You planned to go to the movies this evening."

"I can stay if you want me to." Cassie looked peevish after lambasting him for doing his duty as a doctor.

"No. You go ahead. I know how much you enjoy being the first to see the new releases just so that you can tell everyone how bad they are."

29

"I do not."

"Do, too," Parker said. "Go on and have a good time," he added. He wanted to spend time alone with his thoughts. He was in a moral quandary.

Cassie kissed her husband lovingly on his swollen cheek and led him back into the master bedroom of their two-bedroom condominium. She then set two aspirin and a glass of water on the night stand, tucked him in and sashayed out of the door into the hallway of the building.

She really loved the building in which their condo was built. Located in one of the most desirable neighborhoods in the city of Miami, it was an early twentieth-century building refurbished in the original art deco style. By just walking through the halls, she always felt as if she were living in a more elegant and innocent time.

Upholstered with light beige silk, the corridor walls relaxed her. She'd always found that particular shade of beige soothing and had been looking for a jacket in that color for two years. Beautiful oil paintings and bright watercolors, although not originals, had been carefully selected to complement the large marble consoles, which this week held festive arrangements of exotic fresh calla lilies. Oriental carpets decoratively covered the marble floors, which were polished to a high gloss. The elevator that would carry her from the ninth floor to the lobby had suede paneling, parquet flooring and a small antique bench.

Her spirits were particularly uplifted when she exited or entered the building because the lobby was a showplace of period furniture and original art work.

Fortunately, Evan had inherited some money from his parents, otherwise they would not have been able to afford this life style. They could never acquire such a property on the money he was making practicing Internal Medicine, and certainly not as a psychiatrist. Before she married Evan, Cassie assumed that all doctors made a lot of money. And now, with the onset of managed health care with its low reimbursements and HMO's with their low monthly payment fees, their income was sure to become even more eroded. She was grateful that he'd bought their home, although to do so had exhausted most of his inheritance.

Shortly after they married, Cassie learned that Evan had never been particularly interested in trying to make a lot of money. He always seemed more concerned with gaining recognition from his peers and doing community service—a euphemism for "volunteer work."

The exhilaration she usually felt when entering the lobby of her building quickly dissipated when she stepped into the streets. It was a nice enough area of town, but there was a short supply of elegance. Innocence was nonexistent.

The short block on which their building was located contained many other structures in various states of disrepair and rehabilitation. To Cassie it seemed as if the work was taking forever and she wasn't naïve enough to think that muggings couldn't take place in her neighborhood, even though there hadn't been one in over a year now.

"Have a good evening, Mrs. Parker," Cecile, the doorman, said, opening the gilded and etched glass door for her as he touched the highly polished black brim of his bright red cap.

The ever-present humidity greeted her as she stepped outside and onto the sidewalk. She stopped momentarily to adjust a hooded windbreaker she was carrying over her shoulder bag. In Miami, showers were never unexpected, just unprepared for. She could feel sweat beads forming around her hairline.

She strode purposely down her familiar and once trendy street which had now been forsaken for the current trendy area of Ocean Drive, approximately ten blocks away. Saddened by the nearly deserted sidewalk restaurants and shops at what should be their busiest time, Cassie continued toward the movie theater.

She stopped by the travel office where she and Evander had made their honeymoon reservations. A sense of melancholy washed over her. It had closed recently. Gazing at soon-to-be discarded posters showing exotic lands and fun-filled vacation packages, she lingered for a while. She sighed longingly.

Two years had passed since she and Evander had taken a nice holiday. They had traveled to several of his medical conferences together before she told him how much she hated them and refused to go to any more. Although he always said that he was too busy—either on the verge of making a break-through in his practice, or writing a paper—she knew the truth was he just couldn't afford to take time off to go on a vacation.

Too much overhead. She paused to look in the window of a small antique store and listened to the words reverberate in her mind.

"If only he would listen to me," she thought. Counting on her fingers, she continued her solitary conversation. "There's the condo, and the office, and malpractice insurance, and his secretary Ms. Kennedy and ... and me." She broke into a wide grin when she included herself. She knew she was as much a liability as an asset.

With the decline in her husband's income and earning capacity, Cassie had offered to return to work, but her husband thought it was more important for her to continue her social and charitable activities. They did not have any children, and for this she was grateful. And as long as birth control pills could be purchased in the United States of America, she would make certain they would continue to be childless. She smiled at the thought. Evander thought she couldn't have children.

Resuming her stroll, she made a right turn and was immediately awash in the light from the marquee of the Canterbury Theater. A small playhouse that had been con-verted into a movie theater over ten years ago, and whose management prided itself on showing the latest releases, the

Canterbury was one of the few remaining constants of the neighborhood. Although she would never admit it, she truly enjoyed seeing the films first and reviewing them before her friends at their socials. Usually negatively, she thought smiling.

She approached the theater, reading the marquee which spelled out the name of the film she already knew would be playing. There was no line at the ticket booth. An elderly couple holding hands brushed by her as they exited the theater. She paid her admission and walked through the revolving glass door into the lobby. Cassie Parker had been in this lobby countless times in the past ten years. Casually, she glanced around and headed to her right. In keeping with the British decor of the theater, the antique rotary phones were housed in old English phone booths. She dialed a familiar number slowly, savoring each turn of the dial.

"Hello?" a male voice queried.

"Hi, it's me," Cassie replied.

"Wonderful. I was wondering if you would call."

"Don't I always?"

"Where are you?"

"At the usual place."

"I'll be there in ten minutes."

Cassie knew the routine. She knew to be outside in ten minutes or less. He would pick her up as he had for the past two years. He was the most punctual person she had ever known. She put on her jacket, raised the hood and went outside to wait.

About a half block from the theater entrance, a familiar car with darkly tinted windows pulled to the curb. Quickly, she opened the door and slipped in. A short, gentle kiss was exchanged and the car entered the sparse traffic.

"Did you see the movie?" He asked.

"Yes, I have the video here in my purse. I would like to know just how on earth you get copies of newly released movies on video?"

"Can't tell you all of my secrets." He laughed. "But sometimes you can get them even before they are released to the theaters."

"We don't have much time." Cassie sounded urgent. "The feature ends at nine, so I should be home by nine-thirty."

"I know," he said. "I already checked the movie schedule in the paper. Next time we have to find a theater where 'Gone with the Wind' is playing."

"Yes, either that or wait for the film adaptation of the Kentucky Cycle," Cassie said, smiling.

When she entered from the bath, he was lying in bed half covered. She was totally nude. Momentarily, she stood in the doorway separating the two rooms. Although they had been intimate for more than two years, Cassie could see how his eyes lit up, it was as if he was seeing her for the first time.

Cassie was almost five feet four inches tall. Her dark brown hair shimmered in a swingy, bobbed haircut and her light brown eyes communicated fortitude and intensity. She had a petite curvaceous frame that looked deceptively soft, but from their serious and playful lovemaking he knew her to be physically strong. Tonight he was not playing. This was more than just "stolen moments." He knew he was in love.

As she approached the bed, he held the sheet up, patting the mattress, inviting her close to him. He loved to have her near him. He loved her smell, the way she felt, and most of all, her touch. Her touch was delicate, but firm, and he could get aroused just thinking of it. She knew just how and where to touch him, which was exactly what she was doing now in a most exquisite manner.

She never failed to excite him and their lovemaking, while brief on this occasion, was no less passionate. It didn't matter that he already had a wife.

Cassie sauntered through the doors of the condominium at exactly nine-thirty. As she tiptoed her way to the master bathroom, she peeked over at Evan, curled on his side of the bed, sound asleep. She showered quietly. Putting on a knee-length, white cotton nightshirt covered with red hearts, she slipped into bed.

"How was the movie?" Evan asked groggily as he turned to face his wife.

"It was okay." She turned her back to him. "I'll tell you all about it in the morning. How do you feel?"

"Much better."

"So do I," she whispered sleepily into her king-sized, down-filled pillow as she snuggled deeper into its softness. "So do I."

Chapter Four

Vinny Roselli was twenty years old and considered himself a man of the streets—the streets of New York City. At six feet tall, he possessed a wiry athletic build, straight light brown hair, a fair complexion and hazel-colored eyes. These traits were inherited from his mother's side of the family, who were from Stressa in the North of Italy. His father's Sicilian family was quite the opposite. They possessed powerfully-built bodies, swarthy complexions and dark curly hair. Vinny's maternal family opposed the marriage between his parents; his grandparents were both first-generation Italian Americans. They wondered what their daughter saw in this family of—what Northern Italians commonly referred to as—North Africans.

Vinny ran with a rough crowd and always thought that he could handle himself if push came to shove. Fortunately for him, though, the occasion never presented itself. At this moment, Vinny sat in his father's small living room, hands clasped together, trying not to shake with fear. He wished he could simply disappear.

His father, Joseph Roselli, paced the floor angrily. Every so often he'd pound his fist into his palm. The veins in his neck, which were already very prominent, protruded like cords, even though he had not uttered a word. His chest heaved up and down although he had not physically exerted himself.

At this time, Joseph Roselli was trying hard—trying very hard—not to physically attack his only son. Beads of sweat popped on his upper lip and spittle formed in the corners of his mouth. Finally he walked as close to Vinny as he would allow himself and spoke.

"Vinny, that does it." He drew a line in the air above his perspiration-soaked forehead. "I've had it with you up to here. Your mother and I have tried everything. We've given you every chance to try and make something outta yourself. First you drop outta high school and then you mess up three jobs in one year—all of which I found for you, I might add.

"But the final straw is this stupid heist you and your bonehead friends try to pull off. The three of you got the combined I.Q. of a salad and now all of a sudden you're high-jack artists. If you wasn't my son, I woulda broke your arm myself. If I didn't have a coupla people downtown who owe me, you'd be looking at some hard time right about now."

"But Pop—" Vinny interrupted.

His father raised his hand and came within two inches of bringing it down on Vinny's head. He looked apoplectic as he enunciated each word.

"Don't say nothin' to me. If you open your mouth to me again, I swear I'll smack you one. Your mother would die if she knew the kind of trouble you've gotten yourself into. She's got a weak heart as it is, which, by the way, she got carrying you. I don't see no way to keep you around up here.

"You're stupid and aggressive. Which is always a fatal combination. I'm gonna send you to stay with my only brother, your Uncle Sal. He hasn't seen you since you were a small kid so maybe you got a shot at staying with him. I want you to go into your room and pack your bags right now. You're going to Miami."

Chapter Five

U nlike his son, Joseph Roselli had an impeccable reputation on the streets of New York. It was said that he could clean any stain from any garment. If a car splashed mud on your cashmere overcoat, "See Joe." If your girlfriend got lipstick on the white shirt your wife bought you, "See Joe." If you got blood from who knows where, on who knows what, "See Joe."

Joe could also be counted on to be thorough and fast. Even better, he could be counted on to be discreet.

A guy who could remove telltale lipstick from collars and handkerchiefs, or wine stains from your clothes when you were supposed to be out bowling, was a valuable guy. A guy who would do this while you waited was a jewel. A guy who didn't mind waking up in the middle of the night and who would usually say, "No charge," was a saint.

In real terms, Joe probably wielded more power than any Mafia chieftain. If Joe wanted to have it done, he could have an entire borough put to sleep.

Joe's shop was considered neutral territory and he did work for many different Mafia families. Joe and his wife Bianca lived above their cleaning establishment with his two spinster sisters Gabrielle and Magdalene. The wise, and not so wise, guys never insulted Joe by giving him money for special jobs, but they made sure that he, his wife and his two sisters had all of the creature comforts.

His wife and sisters all wore designer clothes, handmade shoes and fur coats for all occasions. Prime meats, imported wines ... Joe had it all.

He even had a satellite dish and a computer system that not only ran his business efficiently, but could have helped to launch the space shuttle. Most importantly Joe did not have the biggest worry of most shop owners—armed robbery. Word on the street was that if anybody, even another wise guy, ever looked cross-eyed at Joe, no one could save them. Not even Joe himself. This was a matter of pride and respect. Joe removed their spots for them and if the occasion ever arose, they would remove a spot for him.

Joe, his wife Bianca, and his sisters, had always lived and worked together in the cleaners. Joe had promised his parents to always take care of his sisters and that is what he did. He always thought that his sisters never got married because he overprotected them and indulged them as best he could. The truth was that they were too homely and had nothing with which to compensate for it. They were far from rich, they were not particularly smart and there were no "family" connections.

Joe never questioned any of his patrons about what the stains were on their clothes or how they got there. He only asked to see the garment and asked when they wanted it back. Of course, if some guy was standing there barebacked handing you his shirt, you could assume that he wanted it right away. Joe did often wonder why they even bothered to have some of their things cleaned, but he always assumed it was for sentimental reasons. Joe was a very sentimental person himself.

What Joe was not was superstitious. That being the case, he would not have guessed in a million years that a wise guy had to have on his "lucky pants" for a particular job, or "his lucky tie" for another. It really didn't matter because Joe never asked questions.

Superstition ruled many of Joe's clients. Some guys thought that if they wore the wrong hat to a heist the logical consequence was jail. The thought never occurred to them that committing a crime was the causal factor.

39

Joe was blessed with a peculiar ability to see and to not see. Oh, he could see the various stains on clothing that were presented to him and he certainly had to know what they were to remove them, but he had a remarkable ability not to see beyond the immediacy of the moment. He did not see what caused the stain, or even imagine what had occurred surrounding the event. He did not see one minute past his job or think of the consequences of removing this small bit of what in many cases would be considered vital evidence. No, not Joe. He could see and not see. He also had a small nose (kept out of people's business) and a closed mouth, which carried him a long way as an entrepreneur.

Joe had a special relationship with a character named Luigi Carboneri, also known as Luigi Carbone, a.k.a. Luigi Carp, a.k.a. Louis Carp, a.k.a. Louie the Chop, a.k.a., behind his back, Chop Louie.

Louie was the stand-up guy of the neighborhood. He was six-foot four, up, down and around. His neck was the size of most men's biceps, his biceps the size of most men's thighs and his thighs the size of most men. The best word to describe him would be "jukeboxish."

Lou worked his way up the ranks by being the toughest, meanest, most ruthless guy in his or any other gang. His heroics or stupidity—depending on who you talked to were—legendary. His savagery, however, was unquestioned. Louie wasn't afraid of anyone or anything. Except his wife Rosie and her sisters Selaine and Jorvanna.

Lou had never loved Rosie in a traditional sense. He married her because he thought it would be a good career move. Rosie's father was second-in-command in one of the leading crime families of New York, so how could marrying her be anything but good for him?

How could he know the idiot would go off and get himself killed almost immediately after the wedding? So after marrying Rosie, he still had the same job description.

Dispenser of mayhem. Which in a way was okay with him. Lou did feel he had been short-changed on the whole deal; he had the same job and now a wife he was scared to death of.

If he had been thinking, he would have known better than to marry anyone named Rosie. All Rosies were killers. Rose Kennedy ... what a tough old broad she was. Even the men named Rosie were killers; Rosie Grier, Slapsy Maxy "Rosie" Rosenbloom. If he had been thinking right, he would have known not to get involved with her at all.

In all of Lou's work and deeds he prided himself on never having a scar or bruise on him. He always thought of himself as a guy who could dish it out and take it, although in reality he really never took much. That is, until one evening at the dinner table, just as politely as you please, Rosie brought up the fact that she had heard that he had a girlfriend under wraps in another part of town.

Despite the fact that it was true, or perhaps because it was true, Lou was totally outraged. He went into a rampage that would have sent half the neighborhood to the airport to buy one-way tickets. Rosie wasn't fazed in the least. Her father was a tough guy who had five girls. He wanted boys but felt this was his fate, so he raised some very tough girls.

Lou's massive chest was testing the limits of the buttons holding his shirt closed.

"I'll kill anyone for starting or even repeating such a rumor!" he shouted. No matter that it was true, he grew belligerent and irate.

Lou finally calmed down. He settled back in his seat.

"Rosie, never mention anything like that to me again."

She gave him her best smile, seconds before she pinned his hand to the table with the meat fork.

41

Although she didn't speak, there was a "Take That!" glare blazing in her eyes. She pursed her lips in a way that said she meant business.

That was the moment that he realized that the back of his hand wasn't as tough as he had imagined. He let out a piercing animal-like howl that almost put a woman in labor to shame.

In addition, he decided that this would be the first and last scar he would receive and that he would stop cheating on Rosie for the good of their marriage and for his own well-being.

With his hand awkwardly wrapped in a blue and white checkered dishtowel, the rest of the evening progressed as if nothing had happened.

"This is one crazy bitch," he thought. He wondered how a person got to be like that. Sure he had done a lot of things, but he at least had to have a drink or go out with the fellows to wind down. Here she had skewered his hand and now seemed to be completely oblivious to the fact that anything had occurred. She would be a very scary wise guy.

Maybe she had seen that scene in the "Godfather" where the guys stabbed Luca Brazzi through the hand in that bar. But then he remembered that her father would never have let her see any gangster movies. He then thought that she may have read it in a book, but she never read anything but the *National Enquirer*. When Louie finally came to the conclusion that she had come up with this on her own, a cold chill like he had never known swept over him. All other humans on the planet would have recognized this as stark terror.

It was said that because they really never had a mother, and their father was overindulgent, Rosie and her sisters grew up like wild animals. Rosie's mom was committed to an alcohol abuse clinic so long ago that nobody even remembered when it was. In fact, they were called sanitariums then. The girls were never even allowed to see their mother because their father considered alcoholism a weakness, rather than a disease.

After Lou married Rosie, he discovered that Rosie and her sisters were known as the "wolf pack."

It was even joked that there had been another child, the youngest and by default the toughest, but that the older girls ate her. The way he felt now, he wouldn't doubt it.

After his unfortunate run-in with the serving fork, Lou really tried to be faithful. All he had to do to remind him of Rosie was to look at the two, now well-healed, puncture wounds on the back of his hand. Fate, however, has a way of derailing even the best of intentions.

Several months later, Lou was out at one of his late night haunts, when at the end of the bar, he heard this girl tell her boyfriend, fiancé, husband or whatever, to take a flying leap, or something to that effect, and she didn't care if she had to walk home in the rain.

It was obvious from looking at the pair of them that her male friend had just persuaded her to return to the bar. The couple were both soaked from head to toe. Ever the gallant gentleman, Lou offered the young lady a ride home and had every intention of doing just that and no more. He was in no hurry to get home and Rosie never questioned him about staying out late—the one bit of etiquette she learned from her father since he was in the same line of work.

Lou thought it might just be nice to be around someone of the opposite sex that he wasn't afraid of. Maybe she could carry on a decent conversation.

At first, he never noticed that she was dressed seductively. He never noticed what a great body she had even with her wet dress clinging to her. He never noticed that she had a perfect face and a very vulnerable look, with some of her make up washed away. He never noticed any of this until they were in the back seat of his car.

What a night! She was all over him. Maybe she was getting even with her boyfriend, fiancé, whoever. Maybe she even liked him. Who cared? She was only twenty-two years old. How could any guy turn down a twenty-two year old, even if she was only half as good looking as this girl was.

After he walked her to her door, she spoke to him for the first time, since she had gotten into his car and given him her address. That is, if you don't count all the things she asked "Big Daddy" to do to her in the back seat.

"I don't know what came over me," she said. "I've never done anything like that before."

Coulda fooled me, Lou thought as they stood in the doorway.

"I hope you don't take this the wrong way, but I've decided to go back to Steve."

Lou gave her a vacant stare.

"Steve's my fiancé. That's who I was with at the bar."

"Poor Steve," Lou said to himself as he turned to leave.

As he was descending the stairs of the brownstone, on the way back to his car, that annoying chill began to make its presence felt again.

Lou stopped by an all-night joint to check himself out in the bathroom mirror and came to a great understanding of what a paralyzing entity fear can be. When he saw the lipstick and make-up stains on his clothes, he almost couldn't move. "Almost" being the "relative" word. But move he did. To Joe's.

As usual, Joe was cordial even though it was two in the morning. When he saw Lou, he could not help but laugh out loud.

Lou was standing in a puddle he had made in the small customer service area of Joe's cleaners. The brim of his hat was turned down all the way around from the rain. His overcoat was soaked and when Lou turned down the overcoat's collar and opened the front, Joe immediately saw what concerns his friend had. Joe thought he looked like a six foot four, three hundred pound Bassett Hound. Lou's face conveyed a mixture of fear, sadness and anxiety.

Eventually, Lou's rigor mortis loosened enough for him to smile. He stripped down to his undershorts and Joe gave him a flannel robe that barely covered Lou's upper arms and only reached as far as his mid-thigh. They had some small talk and coffee as Joe performed his wizardry.

The events of the next few minutes earned Joe his moniker, "Santa Giuseppe," as opposed to "Joe the Chink," as in Chinese laundry. As Lou stood when he handed him his clothes back, Joe spotted a small area of lipstick on the fly of Lou's undershorts. Lou saw that the spot was infinitesimal, to be sure, but large enough for Rosie to see. Joe immediately went upstairs to get Lou a large towel to help cover a soon-to-be-exposed area that the robe had no chance of shielding.

Joe hand-washed and dried Lou's undershorts and reinspected them twice to make sure they passed "muster."

From that moment forth, Joe was to be referred to as "Saint Joe."

Behind their backs, they were known as "Joe the Chink" and "Chop Louie."

Louie tiptoed around his house for the next few days, especially when Rosie had any sharp object in her hand.

"Oh, I'll carve that for you, honey," he would say.

"Let me have those shears. I have to use them in the basement."

After a week had passed, Lou figured that Joe had not only probably saved his life, but had also prevented him from having a new moniker. He knew they called him "Chop Louie" and actually kind of liked it. If not for Joe, however, he would have forever been known as "Poor Louie." As in poor Louie, "his wife Rosie and her sisters tied him up while he was sleeping and stabbed him about a thousand times in the ass with a serving fork." Or "As in poor Louie, I heard he can't take a bath now because his wife and her sisters turned his butt into a sponge and now when he sits in a tub of water his ass soaks up all of the water."

Once a month, the regular guys would meet in their social club for a game of poker. It was usually a lot of fun and it served a useful function of letting guys blow off steam, which sometimes stopped things from reaching a dangerous level. There were many subtleties to this life. Insults, real and imagined, had to be resolved.

Territorial disputes had to be mediated, debts had to be finalized and the details gone over in front of witnesses, who could verify the statements of the parties. Nothing was ever written down, or heaven forbid, tape-recorded. Trustworthy witnesses were needed though, as people tended to have selective memories.

The club itself was nothing more than a storefront. Inside, there were round cafe tables with straight-backed wooden chairs and a small bar and grill. There was a small back room which was separated from the front with ceiling to floor black drapes. It contained a banquette but nobody ever used it because it made you look suspicious.

The aroma inside the club was the scent curious to most bars—a mixture of smoke, grease, liquor and old. Old carpeting, old wallpaper, old paint, old people.

It was during one of these meetings that Lou told everyone what happened and how Joe had saved his life. He further pontificated that from now on, Joe was to be called "Saint Joe" or "Santa Giuseppe." His description of that infamous evening's events had everyone in the place laughing. It was also during this meeting that Lou professed his undying devotion to Joe and his entire family.

Lou told everyone present that Joe was now under his personal protection and that if anyone messed with Joe that they would have to answer to him. Also, if anyone knew who had wronged Joe in any way, they were to tell him because he wanted to take care of it personally. In addition, he would kill anyone who deprived him of this opportunity. Lou then went into the most excruciating details, describing what he would do to the unfortunate victim.

For good measure Lou added, "And when I finally decide to whack the guy, Ima make sure the victim ask Joe to drop his trousers and bend over so that he can kiss his ass and thank him for now letting me put an end to his suffering."

This time no one laughed.

Chapter Six

"Dr. Parker, Ms. Fine is here," Ms. Kennedy said into the intercom.

"I'll be right with her. Give me about five minutes," Evander replied.

Heather Fine, thought Dr. Parker. A very pathetic girl from an affluent but dysfunctional family. He only had to review his notes briefly from Heather's last session. He knew her social history well.

Heather's father was a self-made millionaire. An ex-hippie doper who made money inadvertently in real estate when he used the money scored in a dope deal to purchase some property in Northern California. Property which he thought would be perfect for a commune ... property that ten years later developers thought was perfect for a business center. Her mother was a very self-conscious girl, who met Heather's father on that commune. She was attracted to him because she had very low self-esteem and he was attracted to her because she had low self-esteem. Heather's parents, Ryan Dawson and Myrtle Peterson, a.k.a. Mud Dog and Starflower, were married on the commune in an elaborate but legal ceremony.

Always the egotistical opportunist, Heather's father made a seamless transition from laid-back hippie to consummate yuppie, when yuppies became held in higher regard.

After becoming prosperous, Heather's father immersed himself thoroughly into corporate America. Suburban estate,

three-piece suits, a Mercedes convertible and his own real
estate company, where he arrived no later than seven a. m.
each morning, including weekends. Heather's father never
acknowledged the fact that he made his money by accident and
Mud Dog, now Ryan Dawson, was totally convinced of his
business acumen. He was never irresolute in his expectation
that he could parlay his small fortune into a large one. His
premise was wrong and within five years he was soon as
impoverished as he had ever been. Returning to his former
drug-abusing ways, Ryan Dawson abandoned Heather and her
mother and vanished.

With the money she managed to squirrel away, Heather's
mother moved to Santa Gorda, California, where she opened
a small, but moderately successful flower shop. With an
adequate income, she was able to shelter herself and her
daughter from most of the unpleasantness of the world. In fact,
she sheltered Heather and herself from most of the world,
entirely. Her life revolved around Heather and she made sure
that Heather's life revolved around her.

Myrtle's biggest fear was that her daughter would leave
her and she sabotaged every attempt Heather made to mature.
Heather's mother even went as far as to change the family
name from Dawson to Fine, in the hope that they would be
ostracized in the small community of Santa Gorda as Jewish.
It was surely one of the rare times, if not the only time in
history, that someone changed their name with the hope of
being shunned by the general community.

Despite the fact, or maybe because of the fact, that her
mother constantly reinforced the idea that Heather would leave
her and go to college if she did well in high school, Heather
was a brilliant student.

Heather attended San Diego State College on a full
academic scholarship where she majored in English Literature.
There were numerous attempts at making friends and Heather
even had kind of a date once, but the damage was already

done. She had such an inadequate personality that she could not form any successful relationships. She returned home briefly, after graduating in three years, but had come to realize that her alliance with her mother was an unhealthy one.

It was odd, but her lack of developmental maturity reminded Dr. Parker of the polio epidemics of the forties. By and large, polio was a disease of the well-to-do, because most middle-class infants were not allowed to frolic in the dirt like poor kids and thus were not exposed to the virus early in life. Without early exposure of their immune systems, they were susceptible to the effects of the virus. Therefore, the well-to-do kids, when exposed to the virus later in life, contracted the disease whereas poor kids had developed an immunity.

Heather had not been exposed to society and now could not deal with it. She might even die from it. Just as people who were physically constrained in an iron lung could not function in society normally, her mental iron lung placed the same restrictions on her.

Fortunately for Heather, her father had set up a small trust fund for her before he disappeared, which now allowed her to support herself modestly without a job.

She justifiably blamed her mother for many of her problems and had not spoken to her in years. She often thought very lovingly of the father she barely knew, who had taken the care to set aside some money for her. The truth was that it was done by his accountant as a way to pay fewer taxes and, during his lean years, her father would have taken every cent if he could have found an adequate loophole.

Heather fantasized about meeting her father, who, ultimately, had saved her from homelessness, because there certainly weren't any jobs for English Literature majors, and she would rather starve than depend on her mother who had crippled her so.

After her graduation from college, and the resolution to leave Santa Gorda, there was the search for a job that was nonexistent, the part-time dead-end jobs while she pursued an advanced degree, and now the latest phase of trying to find herself ... psychoanalysis. The problem was that there was no one who had developed sufficiently inside this woman's body to find.

Heather even thought for a while that her problems might have come from the fact that she was suppressing her homosexuality, but she discovered that she was not gay. When she filled out her profile for Dr. Parker, it read like this:

She wasn't gay. She wasn't straight.
She wasn't dumb. She wasn't smart.
She wasn't ugly. She wasn't pretty.
She wasn't rich. She wasn't poor.
She wasn't tall. She wasn't short.
Her life was full of "was nots," but not many "was's."

She finally settled in Miami, because it was as far as she could be from her mother in Santa Gorda and still be in the continental United States.

Heather had been an interesting patient right from the beginning. When she first came to see Dr. Parker, she always dressed in black, which made her make-up-free, pale skin look more ghoulish. She wore her black hair pulled back in a severe knot at the nape of her thin neck, which made her look even more unattractive. An anorexic size zero, she was almost transparent.

She was shy to the point of embarrassment and when she spoke, it was barely audible. She never looked anyone straight in the eye, had never had a positive relationship with any human being, and had attempted to commit suicide on three occasions. After treating Heather for 16 months, twice a week for an hour each session, only one thing had changed. She had now attempted suicide for the fourth time.

51

Shortly after this last, nearly successful suicide attempt, Dr. Parker became resolved to make some inroads into Heather's self-destructive behavior. He cancelled all of his patients for the day and had her scheduled as his only patient.

After she was seated on the leather sofa in his office and he was comfortably seated across from her, he spoke.

"Well, Ms. Fine, this time you came closer to succeeding than any of your previous attempts."

"I wish I had succeeded," she said quietly.

"Why do you want to end your life so badly?" he asked.

"You don't know how I feel."

"No, I probably don't. But can you help me to understand?"

She hesitated. "I'll try .... Have you ever been depressed, Dr. Parker?"

"I'm certain I have, and so has everyone to some extent."

"I don't mean to some extent. I mean totally and absolutely depressed."

"No. I guess I haven't. Could you tell me what it's like?"

Heather cleared her throat before she spoke. "It feels like you are in a dark room .... A very dark room .... An absolutely dark room that is not only dark but is surrounded by darkness that stretches into eternity.

"The darkness and the blackness of the room are palpable and they have a weight to them that is exerting pressure on your body from all sides. The weight of the darkness is unbearable and you cannot escape it .... In fact you cannot move because of it. Then, when it seems as if the weight of the darkness of the depression cannot become any worse ... it does. You feel as if you are sinking into a bottomless pit and all of the darkness of the universe is being heaped upon you."

"Sort of like a black hole?" Dr. Parker probed, trying to understand.

"Oh, you wish it were a black hole," smirked Heather. "Black holes, because of their heavy gravitational pull, do

52

attract light, but the hole into which you are sinking does not. Since you made the reference to a black hole, maybe this analogy may help you to understand. The feeling is like a star that has exploded and is now collapsing upon itself.

"You feel as if the implosion is at the very center of your being ... your spirit or your soul, so to speak. You cannot move ... you cannot speak ... you cannot think. But you can feel. And you feel the heaviness of this dark universe concentrated not over your whole body but pinpointed on your very soul.

"You want desperately to stop the pain ... this ... this otherworldly pain. You reason that if you kill your body, then the soul can be released of the pain. Suicide, at that time, seems a very rational decision. You believe that any physical pain experienced in order to relieve your spirit of this monumental suffering would only be a minor distraction."

The completion of the exhausting, marathon, one-on-one session with Ms. Heather Fine had accomplished two things. One was that Dr. Evander Parker had a better understanding of clinical depression and two, he almost wanted to kill himself.

Needless to say, Heather's problems were well-entrenched. Dr. Parker was desperate to find a way to help her. Help for them both arrived when Dr. Parker attended a seminar in Los Angeles on child abuse. Every year he attended at least six seminars and was always enthusiastic to find out about new treatment modalities. He loved to hear his colleagues tell about breakthroughs in treatment, ongoing research, or diagnostic tips. He longed with all of his heart to be able to deliver a speech to such a group. He often imagined that he was the only person from his medical school class that had no national import.

It was during a small section on child interaction that the idea came to him. This section showed how children often responded to role playing with dolls, when they would not respond to adults. Heather was, of course, much too old for dolls, but maybe—just maybe—if he played the roles himself, he could make some headway with her case and also make a reputation for himself. He didn't know why not. He had done some acting in school and had even gotten a few good reviews.

With his theory worked out in his head, all that was left was to see if it worked in practical application. During the first session, Heather was very apprehensive and he began to think that maybe this wasn't such a good idea.

Toward the end of the session, however, Heather had become more relaxed and Dr. Parker had become more confident. He had Heather close her eyes, and he spoke to her as he imagined her father would. Even trying to recreate her father's Midwestern accent.

"HEATHER."

"YES."

"YES, WHO?" ASKED PARKER.

"YES, DADDY," SHE REPLIED.

"YOU KNOW I'VE MISSED YOU A LOT."

"I WAS HOPING THAT YOU DID. DO YOU LOVE ME, DADDY?"

"ALWAYS, MY DARLING.........ALWAYS."

When he portrayed her mother, he was very pleased with the falsetto voice he was able to achieve after only a few days of practice.

Gradually, Heather spoke to him freely as if he were her parents and indeed he was able to gain insight into her problems. What was even more astonishing was that she began to adhere to his advice on certain matters.

Soon Heather had abandoned the black clothes and had actually gotten herself quite an attractive bob haircut. After six months of this role playing, Dr. Parker and Heather both thought that progress was being made. Her conversation was almost normal at times and she had not tried to kill herself recently, which Dr. Parker thought was a relatively good sign.

He meticulously documented his procedures and her progress. If she made significant strides, he would be able to present this at one of the local meetings and hopefully at a national meeting.

During these sessions, Dr. Parker portrayed Heather's parents as he imagined she would respond best to him. He therefore had a rigid and selfish mother image and a kind and caring father. Dr. Parker thought that Heather's progress was secondary to her wanting to please her father, but a curious development occurred.

After months of therapy, Heather had a difficult time separating Dr. Parker from the father he portrayed, or the friends he wanted her to have. He became everything to her. He was the father she never knew, the boyfriend and lover she never had and the son she had always wanted. In her eyes, he was the holy trinity, the Father, the Son and the unrequited love. She had never heard of the word "transference," and even if she had, she wouldn't have related it to what was happening to her.

But what did she know about him? Her doctor, her father, her lover, her son, ... her God. She made up her mind that she had to find out everything about him.

Chapter
Seven

Vinny's Uncle Salvatore had already told him that he wouldn't be able to meet him at the airport. Vinny had never met the person that he was told would pick him up. All that he knew was that the guy worked for his uncle and they called him "Jimmy the Swan."

Waiting for his bags, it only took Vinny one minute to look out into the crowd of people waiting for arrivals and pick him out. He had to be the guy with his head sitting on his shoulders. "Jimmy the Swan" had no neck to speak of. He was about five feet seven inches tall and weighed close to two hundred thirty pounds. No fat. He had an olive complexion and had to shave twice a day just to maintain a perpetual five o'clock shadow.

Vinny saw that Jimmy was dressed in a short sleeve shirt that hung over his pants, like the Puerto Rican guys in New York or the guys that played the Hispanics on "Miami Vice." Jimmy's full head of black hair was either slicked back with grease or sweat from the humidity, which had to be at least two hundred percent. Vinny thought Jimmy was quite a comical sight. His neck was so short that his collar touched both his ear lobes.

If Vinny had been a religious person, he might have said that if God did not give Jimmy something as basic and uncomplicated as a neck, he was sure he wasn't blessed to have anything as complicated as a brain. What Vinny did say to himself was "that no-neck fool must be dumber'n hell."

After the cursory introductions, they drove off to his uncle's place.

Being in Miami was already better than Vinny had imagined. Just thinking of it, he was blown away. A muscle-bound goon called "Jimmy the Swan" had met him at the airport, carried his bags and had even opened the car door for him.

Since he had gotten off the plane, almost everything was better than Vinny had imagined. If it had been a limo, it would have been too much to believe. But Vinny did wish it was a limousine and on the drive to his uncle's house he began to feel angry that he hadn't sent a limo. After all, he was his only brother's son and he hadn't seen him in over a dozen years.

"Yeah," said Vinny to himself, "he could have at least sent a limo. Even if he had to rent one ... the cheap prick."

Vinny had heard that his uncle controlled a lot of action, down in this banana town, so he better make up for not sending a limo by giving him a piece of the action. After all, he was a blood relative, for Chrissake.

After passing through the gates leading to his uncle's estate, they drove another hundred yards or so before reaching the circular driveway at the front of the house.

The exterior of the house was distinctly Mediterranean and could not be seen from the main street. The number of video cameras Vinny saw, driving up to the house and on the house, made him think that McGyver, the television action hero, would have a hard time breaking in here.

"Break" being the key word. The whole house looked as if it were made of glass. "Jimmy the Swan" told Vinny that the only privately-owned building that had more glass per square foot than his uncle's house was the Crystal Cathedral in California which belonged to a guy named Robert Schuller. *Damn*, Vinny thought. *If this guy Schuller was doing better than his uncle, he must really have some racket going.* In fact, if he ever got to California, he was going to look him up.

The interior of the house could best be described as a mixture of Italian Renaissance, Miami Vice and Surrealism. This was due entirely to the free rein his uncle gave to his live-in girlfriend. Although everyone knew her given name was Patty, she liked to be called "Patrice."

Sal Roselli had never divorced his wife, Jenny, but they had an agreement they could both live with. She would stay as far away from him as humanly possible and he would send her ten thousand dollars a month, tax-free. They never had any kids, which everyone said was a blessing, since all of Sal's associates said they, as a couple, reminded them of Ernest Borgnine and Ethel Merman, except they were even less attractive, possessed bad personalities and had no talent.

Patrice, or Patty, on the other hand, was drop-dead gorgeous. She was put together as if she had picked out all of the parts herself. To start with, she was about five feet, ten inches tall, with hair the color of burnt sugar with glints of amber streaking through it and eyes the color of steel. Her eyes were not blue-grey, green-grey or any other grey but pure grey.

They did not seem to change in the light, but would often change with her mood, which was pretty often. Her breasts were firm, pointy, and noticeable. She always wore something to accentuate that feature. Her legs were muscular in appearance, and had an athletic quality as a result of the daily exercise regimen she did in the specially-equipped gym Sal had built for her.

With all of that going for her, the thing that attracted most men to her was her mouth. Perfect teeth, enclosed in full pouty lips. It was enough to make any man melt ... and she had melted plenty in her day. And she was only twenty-six, her last three birthdays.

When Swan introduced Vinny to his Uncle Sal, he immediately thought of his father, who was himself a short, balding bastard who also wouldn't have sent a limo to save his life.

"Hi, Uncle Sal. Great to see you," Vinny said.

"Great to see you, too," Sal responded dryly, and with about as much enthusiasm as one would greet an undertaker. "You've grown quite a bit since I saw you last," Sal added, trying to make small talk.

"Yeah, I know." Vinny hissed through his nose, he was becoming so bored.

Vinny's gaze traveled over to Patrice. *What a beautiful girl*, he thought. *What eyes, what a body and those lips.* He was mesmerized by her lips. She could probably suck a garbage truck sideways through a lead pipe, he thought.

"Vinny, this here's Patrice." Sal pointed half-heartedly towards Vinny. "Patrice, this here is Vinny, my only nephew."

"Nice to meet you, Patrice." Vinny shook hands, but he was really thinking of the introduction his uncle had just given him. Why did he have to say his only nephew, as if that was the only reason he would be in his presence. He said it as if he had any other nephews, he wouldn't waste a second on him, thought Vinny. He was really beginning to hate this guy.

In the foyer, Vinny's uncle was cordial, but abrupt and to the point. He kissed Patrice on the cheek, and as if by some silent understanding, she disappeared up a flight of stairs. They both watched her gently dance up the stairs until she was completely out of sight.

"Follow me into the library." Sal waved his hand towards the large room at the end of the corridor.

"This is more like it," Vinny thought. "Now he's going to make up for not keeping in touch with me when I was a little kid or for not sending me stuff at Christmas. Or for not sending a limo. Maybe this bastard would turn out to be alright after all."

Sal's library carried over the general theme of the house. Custom-made mahogany bookshelves, filled with leather-bound books embossed with raised gold lettering, bordered the four high-ceilinged walls. Most of them looked as if they had never been opened. They hadn't.

Because he watched a lot of television, Vinny knew that these were those books that you ordered from an 800 number, where you got whole sets of books distributed by "Time Life" or "Readers' Digest." He vaguely remembered the commentator's words. "Order the greatest literature of the western world" or "Call now to order the complete works of ...."

Vinny thought this was the stupidest thing he had ever seen and a big waste of money. He had never read anything himself, and now he was going to do okay. Why did his uncle have to put on this whole show? What a phony.

When I get my piece of the action, Vinny thought, I'm going to fill my library with something useful. Like video games.

Sal sat behind an oversized desk that was too large even for his immense library. The desk was Napoleonic in style with ormolu embellishments on the legs and a large ormolu medalion in the center of the modesty panel. The chair behind the desk was a marbleized rendition of a Recaro chair with stereo speakers in the headrest.

Vinny hoped that they were turned off for this solemn occasion when he would be told what his share of his uncle's empire was to be.

Vinny sat in one of two low-backed chairs that faced the desk. Animal skins in leopard print covered the chairs. Vinny could not tell if they were real or fake. He was so filled with anticipation that he wouldn't have cared if they were live animals he was sitting on.

After getting a cigar from an unseen drawer, Sal reared back in his chair. He clipped one end off with a gold plated object that captured Vinny's attention for an instant. He then held a match about a half-inch from the tip of the cigar, drawing the flame slowly to it by inhaling through the cigar in well rehearsed motions.

This would probably have been impressive to many people, but not to Vinny who was about to wet his pants in anticipation. This guy was really starting to make him mad.

With the cigar stuffed in the corner of his mouth, Uncle Sal said something that was unintelligible to Vinny.

A more considerate person would have said, "Excuse me, but I was unable to hear what you just said. It must have been my fault. Would you mind repeating it for me?"

Vinny said, "Huh?"

Again, Sal mumbled something that was uninterpretable, but Vinny was sure the last part of the sentence sounded like "make you some kinda rich."

Once more, a now obviously annoyed Vinny said, "Huh?" but he could feel his heart pounding noticeably in his chest.

Sal crushed the cigar into a sterling silver ashtray and lumbered around the monstrous desk to where Vinny was sitting. He lifted Vinny's chair, with Vinny in it, and turned it ninety degrees. Sal then positioned the other chair so that he and Vinny were now facing each other, their knees almost touching.

Sal now leaned over as far as he could and, in a voice barely louder than a whisper, said, "You remind me a lot of your father. My older and only brother ... and that makes you as dumb as piss."

Vinny's jaw dropped to the basement. That is, if houses in Miami had basements.

Sal continued. "You think that somebody I haven't seen in just about their whole life is gonna fly down from New York and walk into my organization and sit pretty. I don't know anything about you except that 'I want everything' look in your eyes. I seen how you was looking at Patrice too. No respect."

As Sal got more excited, his speech slipped deeper into the vernacular.

"When I left New York and came to Miami, I wasn't much older than you are right now. And believe me, boy, nobody gave me jack. I worked hard and did every kinda dirty job that nobody else would do. I was known to be a stand-up guy who did what was necessary and didn't take nothin' from nobody. And let me tell you, buddy boy, this didn't all come naturally. I did some things that are repulsive to me, even today. I have surrounded myself with the same type of person I was.

"I have even tried to educate myself. I took some home courses, had tutors and even got me a correspondence degree in Economics and Literature. What do you think all them books are for? In addition ...."

Vinny thought his head would pop as his uncle's voice droned on and on, like a drier in a laundromat. This was the same "this-is-how-I-did-it" crap his father would preach to him every time he was caught making some small error in judgment. He wasn't expecting this at all. His own father was head of the household from an early age and tried to do everything right as an example to his younger brother Sal and their two sisters, Magdalene and Gabrielle.

How dare Uncle Sal say his father was "dumb as piss!" His father could not afford much of an education after high school, but he built quite a good business. The laundry business. That's why the guys in the old neighborhood called him "Joe the Chink."

That business kept him close to some of his old childhood friends, who had not been as legitimate in their pursuit of financial stability. His father knew that some of them even admired him for "making it legit."

He expected this from his father, and his aunts often heard the story about how his father worked so hard for all of them. But from Sal? Give me a break! Here was a guy, preaching to him, that the FBI would probably love to put away and who had done things that he just admitted even made him sick.

Vinny wasn't paying much attention anymore, but he knew Sal was rambling on, because his lips were still moving. He was like his father's evil twin or something. It was like in the Superman funny books, that guy who was like Superman, but was bad. What did they call him .... Bizarro superman.

Yeah, that was it. He was now in the room with his Bizarro father.

Vinny wasn't paying attention at all now and was thinking about his next move, when he heard Sal say, "But what I am going to do for you is show you the ropes in the smallest corner of the smallest action I got going."

With all the enthusiasm he could muster, Vinny hoarsely whispered, "Thank you."

"And also," Sal said, as he got up to leave the room, "after tonight you gotta find somewhere else to live."

Chapter
Eight

Vinny clambered out of the mahogany four-poster bed, showered and dressed about an hour ahead of his usual schedule. It was eleven o'clock in the morning.

He rushed downstairs and found Sal sitting in the breakfast atrium of the kitchen. He had his hands folded on the marble tabletop, thumbs twiddling in circles. He gave Vinny a baleful stare.

"What's for breakfast?" Vinny asked cheerfully.

"Breakfast is over." Sal scowled. "Has been for more than three hours. Have a seat." Sal pulled out a chair. "I'm going to introduce you to Midge who will teach you everything you need to get started. Midge and I go way back and we even used to live together, but now our transactions are carried on in a more professional manner."

Must be one of Uncle's old flames, Vinny thought immediately. The wheels began to churn in his mind. *And now that I'm in the picture, he's going to try and use me as an excuse for seeing her. I'll just turn the tables on him. I'll win her over with my smooth lines and big-city charm and get her on my side. She better be good looking though because I can't be seen around a new place with some homely broad. It would be just like Uncle Sal to hook me up with some old worn-out, tired broad and keep Patrice for himself. I hate this guy.*

Sal drove Vinny two hours to an economically depressed section of Miami known as "Little Jamaica."

"We're going to meet Midge in a restaurant over here," Sal said, as he drove. The streets swirled with people from different ethnic groups. Graffiti graced the cinder block walls. The smell of garbage wafted in the air and trash swirled in the breeze. Liquor bottles and squashed beer cans hugged the curbs around the broken sidewalks. Dilapidated buildings peppered the neighborhood.

Looking at the area Vinny became angrier. *I hope she's not one of those immigrant chicks*, he thought. *But even if she looks halfway decent ... hell, even if she's ugly, I'm going to get her, just to get back at Sal. Cheap bastard didn't send a limo.*

When they entered the restaurant and Sal introduced Vinny to Midge, Vinny was astounded.

"Midge, this here's Vinny. Vinny, this here's Midge."

Vinny froze where he stood. He saw Midge's dark brown hair and dark piercing eyes first. He also took in Midge's expensive navy jacket and contrasting slacks. He saw each piece of Midge's carefully selected jewelry. Vinny also saw that Midge was probably the shortest grown man that he had ever met. Vinny figured that "Midge" had to be short for "midget" and almost burst out laughing. First "Swan" and now "Midge."

Nobody had better give him one of those stupid names. He wondered how many people you had to kill around here so that you got a real name, at least to your face. He began to wonder what name they had come up with for his Uncle Sal. *Cheap bastard* immediately came to mind, but that was too long.

Midge was almost five-feet tall. He was in his early forties and had a boyish face. Vinny felt two things ... extreme disappointment in that this was surely not the girl of his dreams ... and immediate contempt for this dwarf.

If Vinny were a more scientific person, he would have pondered the mental prowess of one whose cranium was in such close proximity to the terminal portion of his alimentary canal. What Vinny thought was that short guy has to be retarded because his brain is too close to his asshole.

Vinny wanted to say something smart to Midge, but Midge's reptilian eyes said, "Try me. Make my day." Midge had the kind of gaze that would freeze you on the spot. He seemed to have the ability to look right though you and right now he was looking straight through Vinny. Vinny could feel it. He felt that if this guy looked at you long enough, you could probably get bone cancer or something. Vinny wondered if you were born with that kind of intimidating glare or whether you could practice and learn it. Anyway, he would put that on his list of things to do.

Midge was a piece of work in his own right. Sal had met him shortly after moving to Miami. Midge was the typical short guy, who wanted to impress everyone. Luckily, Midge still had a young face and for this he was grateful, because there was something freakish about a small youngish-looking body with an old face hung on it. He had a good body too—the kind that constant workouts and pride can achieve. With his compact, strong physique he had inflicted quite a few dents, lacerations and scars on a number of people. His weapons of choice being number one his fists, and number two, a tire iron. He preferred the vintage models that resembled a crowbar.

The tire iron thing came about during the early days when a young Carmine Aluppi, which was Midge's real name, had an altercation with some goon over something that Midge took very personally. So after beating the guy and knocking him cold, he decided to give him something to remember him by—permanently.

Being a spur of the moment thing, the only weapon he could readily get his hands on was the tire iron from the trunk of his car. So he got the tire iron and really flattened this "buffoon" with it. More accurately he depressed a portion of his skull. Which is how the X-ray report read. "A depression of the occiput of the skull." Midge knew this since he waited in the emergency room after taking the guy there. He was that kind of person. He would do grievous injury and wanted to know exactly what he had done.

So that night, two things became part of Midge's make-up. The use of a tire iron, which he found very satisfying, and his saying that he really wanted to "depress" someone when he was angered.

The talk around town was that Midge was probably the only guy in Miami, and possibly the world, who drove around with two or three tire irons in his car, because occasionally he would leave them like calling cards.

Midge could have moved up "the family's corporate ladder," as Sal had, but he really lacked drive and ambition. He never wanted to be rich, just comfortable. And when he reached his comfort level, he settled in.

Where he settled, was running a large section of the city's immigrants for Sal. The usual stuff. Protection, drugs, loan sharking, overseeing prostitution and illegal gambling. Another and maybe more important factor which hindered Midge from really being his own man, had been his abrupt and often violent behavior. This was okay in its place, but Midge always acted as if he had something to prove and you couldn't leave decisions that were important to a person with that kind of attitude. Even Midge knew he was compensating for his short stature, but he couldn't help himself.

People are always trying to compensate for what they perceive as inadequacies—whether these are actual or false perceptions. That is what the shrink told him. It was like the guy in a Ferrari who never speeds. But on the highway, it's always some jerk in a '57 Plymouth station wagon who is trying to show you what a fast and agile car he has. Yeah, that shrink had helped him to understand a lot of things. Now he understood that he didn't have to prove to every one that he was a tough guy, and many situations that would have sent someone to the hospital a few years ago didn't even bother him now. Now he felt more in control than ever. He would just depress the people now that really deserved it.

Although he fought tooth and nail not to go, he was glad he went to see that shrink. The only reason he went was that his wife told him she was going to leave him if he didn't get his act together. This was after he had struck their oldest son for not instantly doing what he was told.

After he began his sessions, Midge got to the root of his problem with his son—the fact that his son had grown taller than Midge.

The truth was Midge really was afraid of going to see a psychiatrist, but not as afraid as living without Valerie. She had been the only girl in school who took him seriously. They had been married since they were teenagers and he had never once been unfaithful to her. He didn't see how he could make it without her, so he told her to find a shrink and he would go.

Sal was explaining the operational details of this part of his organization to Vinny, who was really trying very hard to look as if he was paying attention.

For the life of him, Vinny could not understand how you could get anywhere at all, or make any money, if you took every cent these immigrant monkeys had. Here he had dreams of an easy life and material things like you saw on reruns of *Miami Vice* and now his uncle had him down here in the jungle. If he had to wait a hundred years, his Uncle was going to regret treating him this way. Knowing he wanted revenge, Vince tried to dissemble his face muscles into bland acceptance.

"So it's all settled," Sal said. "Midge will get you a car and find you a place to live. Then he'll show you how to work a few angles. Starting with this one block. And if you do alright, then we'll see if you can handle something bigger."

Midge never protested; nor was he threatened at all by this whole process because he understood two things. One, was that oftentimes, you had to do things for your family and two, he could see this kid was a loser.

Chapter Nine

"What a day. What a damn lousy day," Sal said, as Swan opened the car door at the house. "I can't believe that, at my age, I'm saddled with a retarded kid who wants me to hand over my organization to him. If he wasn't family, I swear I'd drop him out of a plane about a hundred miles out in the Atlantic."

Sal paused for a moment, a light coming on in his head.

"If Midge can manage to keep him out of what hair I have left, I might double his take."

Settled in bed, Patrice turned a sympathetic smile to Sal. She arched her back and gave her willowy frame a feline stretch.

"Everything alright? I hope you had a good day," she said, kissing him softly on the neck.

His back was turned to her. She gently massaged his shoulders, then his neck. She pressed her pink nipples into his back, as she reached around to his stomach and worked her hand slowly downward.

Suddenly, Sal bolted straight up and turned around, facing Patrice. "What the hell are you doing?" He said, through clenched teeth. His pupils narrowed into slits of anger.

"You know exactly what the hell I'm doing or trying to do ... you bastard," Patrice said, now sitting up in the bed. "Something better start happening in here, besides snoring, and

I mean soon. If you don't get your act together, I'm going to leave you."

Sal and Patrice had played this scene out many times before. They really hadn't made love in over a year. She always threatened to leave him, but Miami was a very expensive place. Especially to live in the manner to which she was now accustomed. He would always tell her to get herself a boyfriend, but she knew he didn't really mean that. She also knew better than to tell anyone about Sal's problem. He always encouraged her to get out of the house and get some fresh air, which in her case, usually meant shopping in Bal Harbour. The longer she was out, the more peace he could have.

The shops were closed now, but Sal fell back on his same line. "Why don't you get up and get some fresh air?"

Pouting, she got up, snatched his grey Polo robe from a wicker chair, which she intentionally knocked over in the process, and stomped out the door.

Letting out a deep sigh, Sal got out of bed and shuffled to the small bedroom balcony that overlooked the ocean. He couldn't understand why his life was so messed up. Here he was, firmly established in the position he had worked so hard for. Important people respected or feared him. He owned a mansion on the waterfront and, just a few moments ago, he was lying in bed next to a beautiful woman and he couldn't get it up. This was getting too serious. Tomorrow he was going to ask Midge to give him the name of that shrink he saw. If the Doc could help that psychotic, sawed-off bastard, he should be able to help anyone.

71

Chapter Ten

Getting into Miami illegally proved much easier than Noel or Chandler had imagined. They had given themselves a planned schedule of a year but were able to accomplish their goal in six months. Working in their father's small store had introduced them to some very interesting souls. If it were not for the fact that their family had been in Port Ann since the first slave ship arrived from the West Coast of Africa, and subsequently knew everyone in the area, they were sure that some of their regular customers would have gladly murdered them for the small amount of money in their till. Like many of the storekeepers, the family kept most of their money hidden in a box under the store.

As it turned out, the person who arranged for them to get into Florida, without going through immigration, was the one they would have thought least able to help them in such a matter. Wesley Kinton was the only person in the whole township who had actually gone to college in the states. He engaged in this, and other, illegal activity to save enough money, so that he would not have to remain in Jamaica and in his words, "waste his education on a bunch of backward-thinking ignoramuses."

What he planned to do in Jamaica or in the states with a major in Japanese history would remain a mystery to Noel and Chandler forever.

After selling the store and giving their mother Hortense most of the money, Noel and Chandler set out for America to find their fortune as millions had done before them.

*   *   *

The day the Christian brothers arrived at Miami Inter-national Airport was the kind of overcast and humid day when the Jamaican women back home would take the clothes off the line—even if they weren't dry. It was just impossible to tell if it would rain or not.

This was their first day in America and after their plane landed, they caught a cab from the airport, asking to be taken to Little Jamaica as they had been instructed.

"From here on, boys, you're on your own," the cab driver said as they each took one suitcase from the vehicle. "Good luck to you," he added earnestly, looking at them in the rear view mirror as he drove off. "You'll need it."

For a moment, the two brothers stood still. The wide streets, the skyscrapers in the distance, and the ear-piercing cacophony of noise both intimidated and awed them. They had never seen so many trucks, cars, and campers passing by, and the blaring horns were deafening. Although they were used to a humid climate, Florida's weather seemed more oppressive.

Noel's heart pounded so loud that he was afraid Chandler would hear it. Finally he forced himself to get moving. "Let's get something to eat," Noel snapped at his brother. He felt uncomfortable for being afraid like a little boy, so it made him irritable. He shivered, trying to swallow his fear. Here they stood, on an unfamiliar corner in a new land.

As if reading his thoughts, Chandler said, "We're in America."

Noel temporarily ignored his younger brother as he in-haled his new reality.

"Even in America we have to eat," Chandler said.

"Where's a good place to eat?" Chandler asked of a few people passing by. Finally, someone pointed up the street.

73

This indifferent welcome brought them and their suit-cases to a small diner, "Bucky's," which served excellent Caribbean food. Small wonder in that ninety percent of the people in the neighborhood were West Indians.

The current owner, Wendell Johnson, had made a half-hearted attempt to give the place atmosphere, but at least it was clean. The place reeked of familiar smells and accents and for a moment they both were homesick. But they knew they had to get about the business of making their fortune. They wanted to hide the fact that they were new to the area and the country, but this was as obvious as the fact that this had once been a traditional diner in a traditional neighborhood. That they walked into the restaurant carrying suitcases was also a subtle hint.

Chandler and Noel slid into a small booth which had gray duct tape covering several rips in the well-worn leatherette upholstery. They assumed the menu that graced the worn Formica counters was handwritten because it was cheapest to reproduce, not because the menu changed daily. Judging from the frayed edges of the menu, the bill of fare here hadn't changed for a number of years.

"What're you having?" Noel asked.

"Not a big choice," Chandler said as they both studied the menu. "They have rice and beans, curry goat, ox tails, jerk chicken and fried fish."

Red Stripe Beer and fresh squeezed lemonade were the only cold beverages offered.

They both ordered the same thing: rice and beans, jerk chicken and a Red Stripe.

Before leaving the island, they had converted some of their money to US currency. On the black market, of course. That was where you got the best exchange rate. They could only take a chance on changing a small portion of their money since anyone exchanging large amounts of currency would immediately be suspected of trying to leave the country or dealing in drugs. In either case, you didn't want the police looking into it because then you would have to pay them off. "Ahhhhh, what a good meal." Chandler belched and plopped his just emptied bottle of Red Stripe on the table a bit too forcefully, causing a few heads to turn in their direction. "What now, big brother?" he whispered, trying to make amends.

Reaching into his pants pocket, Noel, a great one for making lists, laid out his carefully planned agenda to see what was next. "After a good meal, we find a place to live," he said.

Noel had even written down a price range of places they should be able to afford.

After searching the neighborhood for eight hours, they both realized that what they had budgeted for a month's rent would only last a fortnight at most ... and not in the best of accommodations.

By the end of the day, the space they finally rented was in a small and relatively clean rooming house, which housed primarily young immigrants like themselves. Most of the occupants were from the West Indies, but some were from Ethiopia, or Nigeria, and there were a couple of American Blacks. The rent was exorbitant and they had to pay in advance because it seemed that everyone was aware of their illegal status.

"This place is a dump," Chandler whined. "We're paying way too much money for this."

"I know," replied his brother calmly, "but this is where we want to be."

"This isn't where I want to be. We only have one room, with two single beds and a small closet. The kitchen and the bathroom's down the hall. The closest phone is...."

"I mean the States, little brother," Noel cut him off.

"Oh yeah, right." Chandler seemed to perk up.

"I think it would be best if we just kept to ourselves at first." Noel gave Chandler a solemn look to let him know he was serious. "Just feel things out, nice and easy. Not bring any attention to ourselves."

"Oh yeah, right." Chandler nodded.

They would soon discover that the whole building population was illegal and the two Americans were hiding from the police.

During the next two days, they discovered that the next item on their agenda would be the hardest—finding a job.

They had figured that two able-bodied, intelligent young men like themselves would have little or no problem finding work. The reality was that there were at least twenty people for every decent job opening they could find. The only thing in their favor was that there were some jobs that were wanted neither by Americans, nor illegals who had been in the country for a while.

That is how it came to be that the masters of their fate got a job in one of those famous crab houses, cracking stone crab claws ten hours a day on the graveyard shift.

Other than the fact that they were known illegals and were therefore paid less than minimum wage, the worst part of their job was the fact that they went home smelling like crabs. The odor was relentless and pervasive. It was as if in their death throes, the crabs, who were robbed of their precious claws, were determined to make someone pay. And in the United States, as in all countries, it was always those who could least afford it that had to pay.

"What kind of satan crab do these people have here in the States where you have to use a hammer to break the claw? Never saw anything like this back home," Chandler grumbled bitterly.

"I read an article a while back about this type of crab," Noel said. "These crabs are caught and their claws pulled off and they are tossed back into the sea to regenerate another. I also read that only ten percent of them lived after that. The scientists thought it was because they could no longer defend themselves from the other crabs."

"Sort of like the situation we're in." Chandler snickered.

Noel laughed nervously and silently prayed that they would be in the surviving ten percent.

Each day was pretty much the same: getting up in the early afternoon, looking for a better job; getting turned down, going back home; getting ready for work, hating it; getting something from the diner, loving it; getting to work on time on the night shift, cracking crab claws until early in the morning; getting tired, back home for a shower and sleep. Getting nowhere. Seeing a Miami Dolphins' game or frequenting a hot nightspot was out of the question. They had no time for frivolous pastimes.

They both knew how to cook, but their cramped quarters had no facilities for that. One of the Ethiopian guys had gotten thrown out for using a hot plate. A common kitchen on the floor of their rooming house served as a food pantry, more or less, but it was always too dirty to use and the tenants were always stealing each other's food from the refrigerator. They heard that two years earlier one tenant had killed another over a leftover potpie. Noel and Chandler both thought it would be stupid to risk your life for a potpie, even it if weren't leftover.

The diner's food was cheap enough, and occasionally the owner of the crab house would get drunk enough to actually give them some of the tips that they heard the customers say to give to the boys in the back.

"Time to go to Bucky's," became Chandler's nightly liturgy, signaling that he was hungry and was ready to go to their favorite, and only, dining spot. "Why you think they call it Bucky's?" he asked his older brother.

"Probably because that's the name that's displayed in large neon lights on the roof over the door." Noel broke into a smile.

"You know what I mean." Chandler smiled back. "You know there are no West Indians named Bucky."

"Things are different here in America," Noel commented. "If a poor man can be president and wealthy people can walk around in tattered clothes, a West Indian can certainly be addressed as Bucky if he wishes. Especially if he can't afford to have the sign from the previous owner replaced."

Chapter
Eleven

Eight months later, Sal and Midge were lounging alone, on the patio, poolside. A balmy breeze blew through the bowing palm trees wrapped around Sal's estate. The landscaping in the back rivaled the beauty of Parisian gardens. Midge inhaled the redolent fragrance of jacaranda, oleander and lilac.

"How's the kid working out?" Sal snorted through his nose, his distaste for his nephew obvious.

"Tell you the truth, Sal, it's only been eight months and he's starting to catch on. Why just the other day he ..."

"Cut the crap, Midge. Is he working out or not?"

Midge wanted to give Sal an answer that would not paint too rosy a picture of the kid's progress, because they both knew that he was dumb. Midge was just banking that Sal didn't know just how dumb. He wanted to keep the kid around for personal reasons. If there was a little shortage with the money or if some items got, shall we say misplaced, or if in the future he needed a patsy, Vinny was perfect.

"Honestly, Sal, the kid's catchin' on, but I do have to go over things a coupla times ... which I don't mind. But once he got it, he don't forget." The furrow on Sal's brow began to re-lax. Midge felt relieved. He knew his answer was satisfactory.

"Good," Sal said. "Let's take a dip and then run over to the jungle and see how the kid is doing. I want to put at least a little time in with him. Being family and all."

"By the way," Sal asked offhandedly, "what was the name of that headshrinker you went to see?"

Midge was a little caught off guard at first, but did not question Sal. Besides, he was sure he wanted the name for that loony nephew of his.

"Parker," Midge said, "Dr. Evander Parker."

Sal and Midge slowly cruised through the section of the city of Miami known as "Little Jamaica," or to them, "The Jungle."

"Stop the car," Sal shouted suddenly. "I don't believe it. I just don't believe it!"

Midge pulled the car to the curb and focused his attention on what Sal had been yelling about. In the window of Bucky's Diner, oblivious to any and everything, sat Vinny eating dinner.

In a calmer voice, Sal turned to Midge. "You did tell him about this sort of thing, didn't you?"

"Yeah, sure," Midge replied, "but like I said, he has to be told a coupla times before it sinks in. You know how easily kids forget." Midge tried to appease his boss.

Midge and Sal strode into Bucky's, and abruptly squeezed next to Vinny, in the dilapidated horseshoe-shaped, red vinyl banquette.

Unmistakably irritated, Sal blurted out, "What are you doing?"

Startled by his newfound companions, Vinny exclaimed, "Uncle Sal! Midge! What are you doing here?"

"No," Sal said. "What the hell are you doing here?"

"Well, Uncle Sal," Vinny said, "I heard the jerk chicken was real good, so I thought I'd try it."

"Listen to the bright guy," Sal scoffed. "He thought he might try the jerk chicken. Well, the chicken isn't the only jerk in here. Didn't Midge tell you never to eat in a place that is paying us protection?"

"Yes, but ...."

"No buts," Sal said. "When Midge tells you somethin', that's it."

Vinny tried to speak. "I didn't see any harm …."

"Get a grip. Now you listen to me," Sal said, now so furious that he would have struck Vinny if it wouldn't have drawn too much attention. "You don't eat in a place that we're shaking down. Number one, you don't want the owner to think you're getting too chummy with him. He feeds you and the next thing he asks is if he can pay you next week. There is also a matter of respect. We know we're taking money from the guy, but it's rubbing his face in it to also take his livelihood, which in this case is food.

"Maybe he thinks you're being mean and arrogant. Maybe he gets mad enough so that he doesn't want to pay at all. So now you have to do something to get him back in line. Maybe you have to do something so drastic that you lose a good paying customer." Sal clenched his teeth, trying to contain his temper. "Maybe he gets mad enough to put somethin' in the food of a dumb fool who can't seem to unnerstan' plain friggin' English.

"Tell you what, Vinny," Sal continued. "Your meal is over. You pay for the food and leave a nice tip."

Having had his say, Sal scanned the restaurant, as he had in his early days. Old habits die hard. Suddenly, eagle-like, something caught his attention. He seemed to take a particular interest in two guys sitting in a booth, at the far end of the diner.

"Another good meal at Bucky's," Noel said, wiping his mouth with the paper napkin.

"Yes, it was," Chandler replied, "but every time I think of that name I have to laugh."

"Yes." Noel nodded. "They have a ridiculous name, but a damn good cook. Fortunately for us he's Jamaican. Can you imagine," Noel continued, "some people here in the States think all West Indian food is the same?"

"It's all good." Chandler smiled. "But we know which is the best. I'll order some Blue Mountain coffee and we can get down to business."

"We're doing pretty good," said Noel as he began to peel money from a roll he had removed from his pocket. He felt as comfortable and secure at Bucky's as he had in their small store at home. "We may be able to get a better place soon. Even after sending money home to Mother, we have a decent profit.

"I only wish we didn't have to carry every cent of it around with us," Chandler said, looking around suspiciously.

"No choice." Noel shrugged. "Could you imagine leaving it where we live? And putting it in a bank is out of the question. I hear they ask a lot of questions about you, if you want to open a bank account. Besides, we don't have the proper identification ... yet ..." he smiled. "Soon come," he said, "soon come."

"We haven't even been able to change our native currency." Chandler sounded discouraged.

"Yes," Noel said. "I hear they have government agents to investigate anyone who changes foreign currency. I don't necessarily think this is true, but we can't take the chance."

"How about if we get some Travelers' Cheques?" Chandler raised his eyebrows, hopefully.

"I thought about that." Noel lowered his voice. "And I don't think getting them would be too difficult, but when we tried to cash them is when we might encounter problems. I'm sure they would want to see three forms of identification and a note from our Mother. Why, just the other day, I heard that there is an illegal alien from Jamaica, who made it big here in the States and put over a hundred thousand dollars in Travelers' Cheques. Story goes that he died a beggar on the streets, because he couldn't prove who he was to get them cashed."

A few moments of silence passed, before they both broke out in raucous laughter which ended only when Chandler knocked over his coffee cup, spilling coffee over their entire life savings.

"Look at what you did," Noel scolded, trying to be angry. "You shouldn't be so clumsy."

"Oh yeah," Chandler quipped, "and you shouldn't be so funny."

"Did you see that?" Sal asked.

"I saw," Midge replied.

"Reminds you of the old days—huh?" Sal rubbed his palms together and tilted his head to the side in a silent signal.

"Sure does."

Sal spoke to Vinny. "Did you notice anything unusual—in this restaurant?"

"Yes," Vinny said. "I'm hungry and I'm sitting in front of a plate full of food I can't eat."

Sal just shook his head. This kid must really have pus for brains, he thought. One more wise crack from him, and I might borrow one of those tire irons from Midge and have a look.

"Vinny," Sal said as if he were talking to a child. "You always have to be aware of your surroundings. There may be danger or there may be a golden opportunity. You see those two monkeys at the far booth over there?" Sal went on to explain what had transpired.

When Sal called the two black men monkeys, Midge recalled one of his sessions with his psychiatrist, Dr. Parker, wherein he'd informed Midge that this type of behavior was unacceptable and really stemmed from his own feelings of insecurity.

The doctor had gone on to explain that this unfortunately was common behavior, and a way of one group dehumanizing

83

another so that the initial group would not feel badly about committing reprehensible acts against the other. By the end of his therapy Midge had gained a lot of respect for the Doc and he had to admit that the Doc had certainly helped him with his basic problem, which was his temper.

But there were certain things that Doc didn't know jack about. Midge always felt the same whether he was beating the crap out of a black, African American, nigger, wop, spick, cracker, chink, Asian or whatever. It gave him a sense of power and it felt good. That was something all the therapy in the world couldn't take from him.

"So you see, Vinny," Sal said. "There are two guys over there with money, who probably can't even go to the police if you take it from them. Chances are that if they are living in this area they are almost guaranteed to be illegals or criminals. Besides, even if they are legals and have no criminal record, they are probably afraid of the police. People in those banana countries don't go running to the police for every little thing like they do here. The police there have really earned the fear of the population."

Sal could feel himself getting excited, just thinking about strong-arming these guys.

Vinny could feel himself getting depressed, just thinking of his Uncle Sal rolling those two bums for a couple of dollars. The cheap bastard.

Midge didn't feel anything.

But the more Sal thought about it, the more excited he became. He even thought that he felt the onset of a slight erection. Hot damn, he thought to himself, *I'm really going to do this*.

Sal leaned over closer to Midge and spoke softly. "You got your piece with you?" He knew the answer, since this was like asking if he had a tire iron in his trunk.

Midge looked at Sal, raised his thick eyebrows and said, "Whatta you think?"

In the old days, Sal would do all of the intimidating while Midge would act as a seldom used, but effective, backup. They rarely had to use a gun, but things had changed over the years. Sal was still in good shape, but these days you had to be extra cautious. In Miami, anyone over the age of ten might have a piece. They were finding weapons in grade schools. *What was this city coming to, for crying out loud?* Sal thought.

Even if they didn't have a gun, these West Indians could still be trouble in a fight. They were almost always poor and had worked hard all of their lives. Working in those cane fields, or wherever the hell they worked, gave them muscles where you had never seen muscles before and they had the endurance of oxen.

Sal often said that if they were not all so stupid, that he might have employed some of them. Midge agreed with Sal on all of the above and once had mentioned to Dr. Parker that he held the belief that all blacks were stupid. Midge thought about what the doctor told him—that he was perpetuating stereotypes by this type of statement and behavior.

The doctor then asked Midge if he thought it was a fair statement to say that all the Italians that Midge knew were criminals? He'd never forget the quizzical look on the doctor's face when he said, "Yes, they are."

Sal and Midge were confident they would remember each other's moves. It would be like riding a bicycle. It was almost genetic.

Midge slipped the gun under the table to Sal and took Vinny outside with him. Midge didn't mind giving his weapon to Sal. He didn't even mind if Sal had to use it. He was confident Sal wouldn't leave it behind with any prints on it and the gun itself couldn't be traced back to him or anyone else with a pulse.

However, if Sal asked him to loan his piece to Vinny, he would have wiped it off before he handed it to him. Probably at the end of a stick. But that wouldn't matter, because he was sure that in a pinch, Vinny would rat them out and Midge hated turncoats more than anything else.

The two guys Sal watched took an inordinate amount of time getting up from the table, but Sal was very patient. The Big House was full of impatient guys. Guys who were transformed from being free citizens into inmates because of haste. Thinking of the Big House reminded Sal of a nickname given to him earlier in his illustrious career. Salvatore "Little House" Roselli. He was given that name because, although he had been booked into the county and city jails innumerable times, he had never gone to the penitentiary or Big House. He intended to keep it that way.

Finally, Noel and Chandler got up from the table and walked out of the restaurant, headed for home. Sal followed them from a reasonable distance, waiting for an opportune moment. He, in turn, was shadowed by Midge, who had Vinny in tow. The moment presented itself when Noel and Chandler approached a small dead-end alleyway. Sal rushed up behind them, pushing them both into the alley. Vinny and Midge remained in the front end of the alley as "look-outs."

"What's going on? What are you doing?" The two brothers cried out as they turned to see who was shoving them.

Eyes wide open with alarm, they turned to their assailant and came face-to-face with a deadly serious man displaying what looked like a huge gun.

"What have we done to you?" Noel pleaded, flinching in apprehension, his eyes glued to the barrel of the gun.

"Your money in my hands, or your blood in the street," Sal said, a predatory gleam in his eye.

This was a line Sal was famous for, what seemed a hundred years ago, and at the time it seemed quite clever. As he heard himself say it now, he had to keep himself from laughing.

Noel and Chandler weren't laughing. They were barely breathing. Their fear was palpable, and sensing it, Sal became even more aroused. This time he was sure about it. He had a magnificent erection.

Noel reached in one of his pockets, cautiously eased the money out and gave it to their assailant. Sal snatched it without taking his eyes off Noel and Chandler, then stuffed it in his own pocket. He knew there was more money in this guy's other pockets but that wasn't his focus as in the old days. It gave him great pleasure and excitement to know that he had overpowered and outsmarted his victims.

"Face that wall and don't come out this alley for fifteen minutes ... if you want to stay alive."

Sal knew Midge would be along with the car any time now and he would be gone in two minutes, but he always gave himself a little breathing room. He could take his time today, because Noel and Chandler had no intention of moving for at least a week.

Sal waited until he arrived safely back in his library to empty his pocket and to see exactly how much money he had taken. When he looked in his hand, he erupted with laughter.

"I'll be damned." He chuckled to himself. "I went hunting in the jungle and returned with a pocketful of monkey money. Not one U.S. bill in the pile. Not only that, it has something spilled all over it. I wonder if this crap is worth the paper it's printed on."

He took the money upstairs to the bedroom, replaying the evening's actions over and over in his mind. He stopped to put the money in a three-foot tall, standing floor safe which he never locked. He didn't have to. Everyone knew that it was strictly off limits, with capital punishment a likely penalty. It was very satisfying for his ego.

By the time Patrice sashayed up the stairs leading to the bedroom, Sal was in a very heightened state of arousal. He had monitored her movements from the time she entered the property via his security cameras.

As she exited her car and stood at the front door fumbling for her keys, he had a good opportunity to regard her. She was wearing an outfit that was more like a slip than a dress. He hadn't seen her when she left this morning, and the cameras only projected images in black and white so he could not tell what color dress she had on earlier, or the color of her make up. Sal made a mental note to have all the cameras replaced with color ones. He believed she was intelligent enough and fearful enough of him not to have an affair, but intelligent and fearful people often did unexpected things. It had been too long since he really celebrated her beauty ... or anything else she had to offer.

Studying the black and white monitor, he was reminded of long-forgotten screen goddesses he had longed for as a boy. He savored her flowing hair, heart-shaped face, sensuous bow-shaped lips, long supple arched neck and full breasts. That was as much as the camera lens would permit him to see.

He now longed to see much more.

As she walked through the bedroom door, she deposited two large shopping bags, which was her usual m.o. The look on her face said she was surprised to see Sal in bed at this time of day. With genuine concern she approached the bed.

"You O.K., Sal?"

"Tell you the truth, I feel better right now, than I have for years."

As he said this, Sal pulled the sheet aside to flaunt what Patrice had longed for for so long.

"Ooooo, baby," she cooed, and immediately began to put her perfect mouth to work, in a perfect way.

Her slip dress, which Sal could now see was pale blue, would soon be ripped and thrown in the same corner of the bedroom as the shopping bags. He closed his eyes and enjoyed the ride.

Suddenly Sal pulled Patrice up, hovered over and climbed on top of her, taking her forcefully. It was as if he were trying to make up for two years in one moment. Patrice could not believe what was happening. Sal gave her the opportunity not to believe it more than once.

The next day Sal felt like a new man and Patrice felt like an old woman. There were no complaints.

Sal thought about his newfound sexual prowess and wondered how long it would last. He hoped he wouldn't have to rob someone every night.

Chapter Twelve

Somewhat thankful that forty minutes ago a gunwielding maniac had only managed to take most of their money and not their lives, Noel and Chandler collapsed through the door of their small room. They both fell sideways across the nearest twin bed. Noel was lying on his back staring at the ceiling, while Chandler was on his stomach facing the floor.

"Noel, how are we going to get our money back?" Chandler asked. He bit the corner of his chapped lips, which turned down in a forlorn frown, reminding Noel of when they were children. He remembered the time Chandler was spanked in front of the entire school by the Headmaster, Mr. Wiggins, for a slight infraction.

"I don't have a notion. I'm just thankful to be alive right now. This is some country. We just got robbed and almost killed by an old white man. I don't believe it. You notice he didn't ask you for nothing? He must have been watching us. We're lucky that we didn't lose everything."

"Our U.S. identification should be ready soon. Maybe then we can apply for some better jobs," said Chandler, "and move to a better part of the city."

"Perhaps you haven't noticed, brother, but people living here all their lives can't find work."

"I just know if I have to keep working at the crab house, I am going to lose my mind."

"You mean to tell me you haven't lost it already?"

They both could only manage to generate weak smiles.

* * *

The 25th Precinct in Little Jamaica was frantic and chaotic on a good day. Today was not a good day. Confusion reigned supreme, with turmoil being second in command. This precinct had more felonies and murders annually than some countries. On casual inspection, it was difficult to determine if anything constructive was being achieved, but after careful evaluation of the situation, you were certain that it was not. It was into this arena that Noel and Chandler presented themselves.

"I don't like the police at all," Chandler said under his breath, "and I like police stations even less."

"Be cool, little brother," Noel hissed. "Nothing to fear. We are here to report a crime. We're the victims."

"Oh, no," Chandler replied. "We don't have a thing to worry about. We're just illegal aliens in this country, working without permits and carrying false identification. Why should I feel uncomfortable?"

"Quiet, you're making me nervous," Noel said.

"Thought we didn't have nothing to worry about," Chandler said.

"I'm not worried," Noel said, raising his voice slightly. "It's you that's making me nervous."

"Quite a difference."

"Good afternoon, " Noel enunciated carefully in his best American accent. "I'm wondering if you can assist us."

Wonderful, thought the desk sergeant, *two illegals want my help and I'm too busy to even help real people.* By real people, Sergeant Buntz meant United States Citizens.

"You boys see Detective Rolle," the Sergeant said through coffee-stained teeth, pointing to the rear of the building.

The term "boys" was not lost on them. Even though accep-table at home, they knew it was derogatory in the States. No matter the complaint, Sgt. Buntz always referred anyone he thought was an illegal or of West Indian origin to Detective

91

Livingstone Rolle. He thought that since they were his people, he ought to take care of them. What Buntz did not know, or care to know, was that Rolle's family had been in the Miami area for over four generations. Which was three generations longer than Buntz's family had been in the States.

At the turn of the century, Rolle's family had originally come from the Bahamas and settled in the area known as Coconut Grove, where Bahamian fisherman had originally settled. Now it had become trendy, so Rolle's family had long since had to move to a less expensive area, but he still enjoyed visiting the site of his family's start in this country.

Livingston Rolle was about 5'10," but his build made him look shorter. He was "tick," meaning thick as his Bahamian cousins would call him. He was powerfully built and many a criminal had unwittingly assumed all the bulk under his clothes was fat. He was as proud of his build as he was of his exceptionally dark skin.

Unlike many American-born Blacks, he had an ethnocentric pride in his color. His family had taught him that. He, in fact, was very vain about his dark skin. He was content in the fact that God may have created many men smarter, handsomer, or richer but none darker. He was very aware that Buntz referred all of the West Indians and illegals to him. But he didn't mind. That was Buntz's problem, not his.

"Have a seat, gentlemen," Rolle said.

"Gentlemen," thought Noel, "now we're getting somewhere."

"How may I help you?" Rolle, pen poised in his hand, whipped out a police report from his desk.

"We were robbed," said Chandler.

"At gunpoint," Noel added.

"Not unusual," Rolle thought. He said out loud, "Where did this happen?"

"Not far from Bucky's Restaurant. Do you know where that is?"

"Yes I do." Rolle began to write on his form. Still nothing new here. "Can you describe the perpetrator?"

"The what?" asked Noel.

"The person that robbed you."

"Yeah …. He was white, significantly under six feet, kind of muscle bound and about forty to forty-five years old. He had on a tan coat and carried a big gun."

"Did you say he was white?"

"Yes," said Noel.

Now that's unusual for this area, thought the Lieutenant. A white guy, well-dressed, robbing two illegals at gunpoint in the worst part of the city. Rolle wondered if these guys had been smoking too much of that Gunga, Jamaicans were famous for. He could tell right away they were Jamaicans. His job had made him an expert on accents.

"What did he take from you?" Leaning forward in his seat, Rolle's interest had shot up.

"He took our money from home," Chandler blurted out.

"He means he took some money that we brought from our house," said Noel as he kicked Chandler under the table.

"Yeah, I get it," said Rolle. He knew that their families back home often supported illegals until they could get a foothold in the States. Detective Rolle also knew that they must have been carrying a substantial amount of money or they wouldn't have taken a chance on coming to the station. Still, he had to ask for the report. "How much did he take?" Detective Rolle probed.

"It was quite a bit," said Noel.

"It was almost all of our money from home, I mean, our house," said Chandler, immediately correcting himself.

"Was it over five hundred dollars?" asked Rolle, trying to at least get an approximate figure.

"It was almost sixty thousand dollars," replied Chandler.

"Almost sixty thousand dollars," sputtered Rolle, trying to regain his composure.

"Sixty thousand Jamaican dollars," said Noel calmly. "They were Jamaican dollars. We had exchanged our American money for it so we could send it to our Mother back home. She's getting along in age now and we thought we would save her the trouble of going to the bank."

"Okay," said Rolle, "that would be approximately twelve hundred dollars U.S."

Rolle didn't ask why they had so much money on their person, in such a crime-ridden area, because he already knew the answer.

"Was there anything else unusual about the perpetra—" Rolle interrupted himself ... "the person who robbed you?"

"Yes," said Chandler. "He had an accent."

Rolle could hardly contain himself, but he didn't even smile. "What kind of accent?"

"I don't know," said Chandler, "but not like from around here."

Rolle deduced that he meant it wasn't a Southern or Hispanic accent. He could certainly rule out a Caribbean one. That still left a lot of territory, just in the States. He could imagine that it was some blond-haired surfer dude with a Valley accent that robbed them. This thought did bring a smile to his face.

"What's next?" Noel queried, fully expecting to have Detective Rolle call in an artist to make a drawing of the perpetrator. Noel was beginning to like that word, although he didn't care too much for the person it represented.

What Noel didn't realize is that forensic artists are only called in on high-priority cases and that this certainly wasn't one. He felt better, however, when detective Rolle ushered them over to the albums filled with mug shots.

Detective Rolle told them that these were albums with pictures of people most likely to have committed that type of crime in that area. There were dozens of books with several hundred pictures, to be sure, but he figured it wouldn't take them that long to look at the pictures of the white guys in them.

After they had completed the task, he told them that if they wanted there were other books that they could look at which had less likely candidates.

He eyed both brothers warily. Just to be sure, he asked, "You are both sure that this was a white man, not a light-skinned black or Hispanic?"

They both averted their gazes, studying Rolle out of the corners of their eyes. Their eyes were telling him that by being black, you knew the difference without even trying. Rolle, of course, knew this was true. But a well-dressed, white guy robbing two illegals in Little Jamaica? That was a puzzle. Every time he thought he had heard it all on this job, someone came up with a new one. Besides, the only thing they could truly describe in detail was the gun because that was where most of their attention was focused during the whole episode.

Noel and Chandler carefully studied every white face they saw in the first books Detective Rolle had given them. There was no mugshot of anyone who looked like the man who robbed them.

"What do we do now, Detective Rolle?" Chandler asked. Meaning what was Rolle going to do.

"I'll have to do some investigating myself and see if I can come up with any leads. I'll be in touch." Rolle put his pen down.

"Hell of a case," Rolle mumbled to himself after they left.

This case was full of surprises, not the least of which was that Sgt. Buntz had referred a case to him that actually fell within the parameters of his job description. "Hell of a case," he said to himself again.

Tomorrow he was going by Bucky's to take a look around.

Upon entering Bucky's, Lt. Livingston Rolle discovered what a leper must have felt like during biblical times. The isolation he felt was somewhat more complete, for people probably looked at lepers, if just out of curiosity. He was dressed in a short-sleeved white cotton knit shirt, which was opened at his eighteen inch neck, a pair of green khaki trousers and black canvas running shoes. He had removed his sunglasses upon entering the restaurant, inserting them into the pocket of his shirt. Rolle did not tell anyone he was a cop. He didn't have to. Everyone knew instinctively. Although he savored the pungent smells of Caribbean cooking, he felt strangely at odd with his surroundings.

Three spindly men, eating at the counter, hurriedly paid for their just finished meals and quickly exited. An obviously tense young couple in their early twenties decided that they weren't hungry anymore. They slid from their booth and followed the three men out. None of the patrons seemed to be enjoying their meals, with most staring into their plates and repeatedly stabbing their food without eating. No one in Bucky's restaurant even looked in his direction. In fact, they all made a concerted effort to avoid his gaze. He understood what the problem was, but that didn't make his job any easier. A Black policeman. A detective no less. He knew they all thought he must be utterly corrupt, an Uncle Tom, or worst of all, a Black cop that wished he were white and would do anything to prove to his white counterparts that he could treat Blacks more reprehensibly than any of them ever could.

He talked briefly to the owner, who denied even being in the city the week that the robbery took place. And this was the response from a person that was in the country legally.

He decided to save his energy and return to his unmarked car, so unmarked that little kids would often run beside him, as he cruised neighborhoods, yelling obscenities. Few people in this section of town or any other drove stripped-down Plymouths, with black wall tires.

As he approached the car, he could see his partner smiling that broad "I told you so smile" that he hated. The next words from Detective Roland Guttierrez were inevitable. "I told you, you weren't going to get anywhere."

They both then inspected the alleyway where the robbery occurred. After sifting through countless bottles, cans, papers, and one commercial dumpster, they decided to call it a wrap. They both thought that their best opportunity would occur if this person committed a second robbery.

After getting back in the car, Guttierrez was the first to speak. "I still think they were pulling your leg, hermano," Guttierrez said. "An older, well-dressed white guy, holding up two young illegals in this precinct. That's too way out. You know, Buntz may have put them up to it."

"I don't think so." Rolle shook his head. "If they were acting, they could get an Academy Award."

"Academy Award?" said Guttierrez. "I know felons who can lay down a story line so good, you want to adopt them."

"Yeah, I thought about that, but these guys seemed straight. And with our workload, Buntz wouldn't dare send us on a wild goose chase," said Rolle.

"That's exactly why he'd do it," replied Guttierrez emphatically. "He would love to get one in on a black guy, namely you, and a Hispanic, namely me, at the same time."

"I'll have a talk with him back at the station." Rolle rubbed his chin thoughtfully. "He better not be hanging me out. I've ignored a lot of stuff from him in the past, but this would be going too far. I have too much important work to do."

"That's probably why he did it. Because you've been letting him get away with stuff. I don't let him get away with nothing. I'm straight up in his face all the time."

"Then how come he's got you out here too?" asked Rolle.

"Only because I'm your partner, homey. Only because I'm your partner."

Returning to the station, Guttierrez had a seat and decided to see just how Rolle would confront Sgt. Buntz.

"Buntz, do you know anything about the case you referred to me?" Rolle asked.

"And what case would that be?" Buntz snapped. "Could you be a little more specific?"

"The case where two illegals were robbed at gunpoint by a white guy near Bucky's."

"That's really giving it to him," thought Guttierrez as he flashed Rolle a sarcastic look without saying a word, but because they knew each other so well as partners they could communicate telepathically.

"Just a minute," said Buntz. "Let me get this straight. Two Thirdworlders say a white person held them up in this ghetto. At gunpoint, no less."

As the image of what Rolle had just told him began to gel in his mind, Buntz started chuckling deep within his belly. What started out as a slight rumble, traveled up his esophagus, until he began to whoop and holler. By the time he was finished, he was coughing up spittle, which had covered his chin.

"I don't know about it," he gasped in between coughs, "but I really want you to tell me all about it."

Angrily, Rolle turned to Guttierrez. "Let's get out of here. This clown doesn't know anything."

"No, no, don't leave," Buntz yelled. "You gotta tell this to the Captain. He'll never believe me. Come back. Pleeease!"

Buntz, fighting back the crinkles threatening the corners of his mouth, looked up at the ceiling until the picture was refocused in his mind's eye. Then he began to laugh again.

"Don't gooooo ..." he yelled to Rolle, who was angrily exiting the building.

Chapter Thirteen

Over the next few weeks Sal found that he still could revitalize himself by reliving the events surrounding the robbery. Occasionally he would augment his recollection by going to his safe and fondling the money. The palpable currency seemed to reassure him that it was all very real. His performances over the next thirty days, while adequate, were nevertheless meager in comparison to what both he and Patrice had come to expect. But, unlike previously, he now knew what had to be done.

Peculiarly, the thought of repeating his strong arm tactic was neither stimulating nor desirable. He had already pitted his strength against that of two more physically superior men and had come out on top. The fact that he had a gun did not enter his thought process. It was now time for something riskier and more difficult. He needed bigger and better thrills to keep him pumped.

What should I do? He thought. *What can I do?*

He did not have to ponder too long for his answer.

ROBERTO MENDEZ.

This Columbian-born immigrant had been a thorn in Sal's side for a number of years now. He was aggravating— profesionally and personally. Usually Sal dealt with Robert by not dealing with him. He ignored him. There was also the problem that Roberto was very clever and, although Sal had his suspicions, proof was never forthcoming.

In the old days, Sal would have let Midge take care of Roberto, but now you couldn't just whack out an adversary, without good reason. There were certain rules that even Sal had to follow. One could not afford to have all the other "business men" aligned against him. The idea of getting rid of Roberto Mendez produced the desired sexual effect. Now he had to formulate a plan.

Roberto Mendez was from a well-to-do Columbian family. He had all the charm and grace expected of a person of means from that region of the world.

He was slightly over six feet tall, with the sculpted, muscular body of a professional dancer. There appeared to be no wasted motions in his movements, which were almost effeminately graceful. His eyes were dark and intense, connoting the presence of his considerable intelligence. His hair was black and wavy, with premature gray at the temples, which disturbed him when it first appeared, before his twentieth birthday. However, he now proudly brandished it as a hallmark of wisdom, now that he was close to thirty-five.

Roberto Mendez's family in general, and his father in particular, provided him with a life of privilege and opportunity. Roberto's largest character flaw, of which there were many, was that he was very eager to fully enjoy the power, status and most of all, the money of his father. He could never understand why his father would not indulge his every whim. He therefore dropped out of college after one semester, and did not indulge his father's dream of his becoming a decent and educated man. Subsequently his father had no choice but to disassociate himself and his family from his ungrateful son.

Cartahegna, Columbia, which was the family's home city, was, however, replete with people who relished being around a member of the influential Mendez family, disinherited or not. Many unsavory characters sought out Roberto's company and, in return, they treated him very well. Roberto soon became a trusted member of their inner circle, learning much about their illegal activities. Especially about cocaine.

His path to becoming a major player in the cocaine business started quite accidentally. Roberto asked an old family friend, who happened to be a judge, if he could intervene in a minor traffic offense, committed by one of his new-found friends. The traffic incident was minor, but this happened to be his friend's fourth alcohol-related charge. This meant the possibility of some jail time in Columbia. Something which even the most hardened criminals dread. Roberto was successful in his plea.

With the charge dismissed, his friend, in order to show his appreciation, gave Roberto a nice gift for the judge and a little something for himself. With his ties to influential family friends and colleagues in need of the occasional favor, it wasn't long before Roberto was a very important intermediary in the drug trade.

Like most respectable drug dealers from Columbia, he eventually settled in the city of Miami. His reception into the fabric of the city was quite different from his expectations. He had a good family background, exquisite manners, impeccable taste and a lot of money.

But the people of Miami only despised him as another immigrant Hispanic. These Americans, he thought bitterly, tend to group all Latin Americans into one category, "Hispanic," even though their cultures were very different and they seldom got along with one another. Their only common bond was that of language, which each group thought it spoke better than the other.

Roberto gradually accepted that he would never be accepted, and made a life that revolved around his associates in the trade in Miami. He occasionally entertained guests from Columbia, chased every skirt in the Northern Hemisphere, and made life as miserable for the gringo drug dealers as he could, especially Salvatore Roselli. His rationale being that it was all their fault that he was not accepted into polite society. Roselli epitomized what Roberto thought the obstacle was—a man with money and no breeding or couth.

He enjoyed sabotaging any of Sal's enterprises, legitimate or not. If Sal owned a restaurant, he would, through third parties, hire people to write to the Board of Health, prompting annoying inspections. He would have rumors spread on the streets that Sal's prostitutes all had the AIDS virus.

It wasn't even beyond him to destroy their drugs, if he found out where they were being stored. So what if they suspected him? They had no proof and could not "punish" him for their suspicions. In addition, he was very careful so that no accidents would befall him. His house was a fortress and his chauffeur-driven limousine was bullet proof. His bodyguards, gardeners, and house staff were all from Carteghena, so they would be harder to bribe. No outside help worked in or around his house.

Sal called Midge, at home, on a private line.

"Hello?" Midge answered.

"It's me," Sal replied, and hung up.

This was their total conversation. This was the total of all the conversations they ever had on Midge's private line. Midge knew to meet Sal at his home. This line had been in operation for some ten years now and, if the number of words spoken per phone bill were calculated, it would surely be the most expensive phone line in history.

Midge and Sal only discussed business outside Sal's home by the pool, with the fountains running and the music blaring loudly through the numerous speakers surrounding the grounds. They both felt, quite correctly, that it would be hard to overhear a conversation carried out in this manner. Midge was seated at a Brown Jordan patio table, which held an enormous turquoise umbrella. He sat with his back to the sun, under the shade of the umbrella. He was dressed in a bright tangerine Polo tee shirt and khaki pants, which were held up with a bright tangerine fabric belt. With white socks, white deck shoes and Rayban sunglasses, Midge thought he looked very stylish.

Sal sat opposite Midge, facing the pool, the ocean and the sun. He positioned his chair so that he was as close to Midge as possible, without being in the shade of the umbrella. He wore an oversized, white terry cloth robe over green Speedos, pale blue Gucci slippers and a Rolex Presidential watch. He had on custom-made sunglasses, with a tiny capital R, made of twenty-four carat gold, stamped on the lower outer quadrant of each lens. Sal imagined that he looked quite like Warren Beatty, in the movie "Bugsy." And he would have, if Warren Beatty were five foot seven, with a receding hairline and a face like a swarthy Broderick Crawford.

From his seat, Sal could see across the inlet to the Miami skyline. There was a zero clearance pool, which looked as if it flowed right into the ocean. There was also a forty-foot Bertram cabin cruiser, which he had proudly managed to use three times this year. Two more times than he used it all of last year.

Reflecting on the last month with Patrice, his financial success and the idea of eliminating Roberto Mendez, Sal wondered how Midge could be so content with the small niche he had carved out for himself. He was certainly capable of having more, but he never seemed to want it badly enough. Suddenly Sal felt sorry for Midge.

                                *   *   *

Midge looked past Sal to his boss's palatial home. He knew the view behind him, which contained the pool, fountains, ocean and boat. He thought of the front driveway that was home to six luxury cars the last time he counted. Sal had no wife to speak of, no kids and no close family. Midge wondered why Sal worked so hard for a house that was too large for two families, much less two people, and a boat he seldom used. A person can only drive one car at a time. Why did he need all this stuff? Midge felt sorry for Sal.

"I've decided to get rid of Roberto Mendez," Sal said, looking around out of habit as he spoke.

"I agree, he's a pain in the ass, but we can't have everyone in the cartel turn on us for blowing him away." Midge looked around to see what Sal was looking at.

"That's the beauty of it." Sal spit between his teeth. "That's gonna be the real beauty of it. Roberto will be taken care of and no one is gonna know who did it. "And," Sal said with a wide smile, "we're gonna do it personally."

"That's a tall order. Roberto is real insulated. How're you plannin' on doin' this?"

"I don't know just yet, but I am assuredly going to do this." Sal's voice was deliberate.

When Sal spoke slowly and used big words, Midge knew that his mind was made up.

"So what do you want me to do?" Midge tried to hide his trepidation.

"Just observe him for a while. Unnoticed, naturally. And report back to me."

Three weeks later Sal and Midge were again at poolside. "Sal," Midge said, "I been following this guy for three weeks now and what you're planning to do is gonna be real hard. I mean anyone can be taken out. But to do this guy and have nobody know it was us, is going to be tough. He never lets his guard down. He's always got two big goons with him. He always brings his broads to his house and if he eats out, it's in a very public place. You can't get inside his property, without being stopped at the gate. Those two goons even wash his car at home."

Midge was referring to a past hit, and a mobster who was so careful that he never left his car, even to have it washed. One of his enemies, however, had assassins pose as employees of the car wash, and a very clean car with a very dead guy came out the other end.

Midge also thought that if Sal wanted to solve two problems at one time, he could strap a bomb to his nephew and let him walk up to Roberto and have himself detonated. As dumb as Vinny was, Midge thought Vinny would probably want to know how they were going to pick him up afterwards. *With tweezers*, Midge smiled to himself. *With tweezers, Vinny.*

"Where does he get his car serviced?" Sal asked Midge.

"I think one of the bodyguards is a lightweight mechanic. I saw them buying oil and gas for the limo at the service station, about a mile from his house. They even pumped the gas and put the oil in themselves. Not much chance of getting under the hood," Midge continued. "I'm sure if there is a major mechanical problem, they check the car thoroughly before they take it back." Trying his best to discourage Sal, Midge put on a serious face and said once again, "This is gonna be tough. Maybe impossible."

Midge's protestations only had the opposite effect. The more problematical Midge made Sal's objectives, the more excited Sal became.

Yes, thought Sal, *I've got to beat him at his own game.* "Just keep watching him and I'll figure something out."

* * *

105

"Hello?"

"It's me."

In less than 40 minutes, Midge was poolside at Sal's.

"I think I got it figured out," said Sal, "but we're gonna need Vinny to help us."

Oh hell, thought Midge, *we're dead.*

"I want you to get Vinny a job working at that service station where those spics take Roberto's car."

"I already told you," Midge said, still agitated, thinking about the prospect of having to work with Vinny, "they don't let nobody near that damn car."

"That's alright." Sal decided to overlook Midge's attitude. "Nobody's goin' to have to get near it."

At least not at first, he thought.

It wasn't easy getting Vinny a job at the gas station. The first problem was that he didn't want to do it.

"Oh great," Vinny said after Midge told him that his uncle wanted him to work in the gas station. "I could have stayed in New York and done that," he protested. "First I'm muscling monkeys for tips in the worst section of the city and when I think things couldn't get any lower, you tell me that Sal wants me to work in a gas station."

That cheap bastard, he thought ... one day.

"Well, just tell him I ain't going to do it, no way, no how."

"Uh-uh, you tell him yourself," Midge said, knowing Vinny didn't have the balls to tell Sal.

The second problem was that there wasn't a job available. The easiest way to make a position available was to get rid of the kid that already worked there. That, however, might cause suspicion and then there was no guarantee that the owner would hire Vinny even after Midge helped him to fill out the application. Midge thought that the owner may have wanted to hire someone who didn't need ten additional I.Q. points to learn to bark. Besides, Midge wouldn't do anything to make Vinny's life easier.

The strategy was to have Vinny hang around the station and pretend to be stupid. Type casting was the way to go, thought Midge. He could take a bottle of glass cleaner and clean windows for tips or pump the gas for people who didn't want to do it. He would also clean up trash around the station and keep the general area tidy without ever asking for a salary. With a little patience, Midge was sure the owner would soon offer Vinny something in return.

It was Midge's responsibility to get Vinny to the station, just before it opened, every morning. He would pick Vinny up and drop him off approximately two miles from the station and let him walk to work. Midge did this in order not to draw attention to a scruffy kid being driven to work. One mile would have sufficed, but Midge enjoyed the fact that Vinny had to walk an extra mile every day.

After about a month, their perseverance paid off. The owner told Vinny that he couldn't give him a salary, but he would be glad to show him how to work on cars. Starting with small things like changing tires, fixing flats, changing oil, etc. The gopher at the shop was pleased, because now he had a gopher.

With Vinny comfortably, or uncomfortably in place, Sal started on phase two of his scheme.

It always amazed Sal that some of the people with whom he came into contact could perform very complex chemical tasks, without the benefit of any formal education. Indeed, there were, probably at this very moment, hundreds of individuals cooking up crack and methamphetamine, who literally could not read or write. No matter. He asked one of these uneducated chemists to prepare material that was essential for his program.

Roberto Mendez was a wary and resourceful man, but on the one and only occasion that Sal had been to his home, he did not see an oil refinery on his property and correctly concluded that from time to time Roberto had to purchase oil for his cars from an outside source. With a little luck, it would be the service station where Vinny was now working.

"It's amazing how these things work, isn't it?" said Sal, referring to the new style of can opener that removed the lid from a can the way it was put on originally at the factory. The gadget Sal was holding in his hand removed the whole top and rim ostensibly, so that no foreign matter would contaminate the food contained in the can while it was being opened. "I saw it demonstrated on one of those Infomercials."

"Info what?" Midge queried.

"You know," Sal said, "those shows where they always have the idiot guy and the pretty girl with some expert demonstrating the product to an audience that has more plants in it than Viscaya."

This tool was perfect for removing a lid, putting something into the can, and resealing it. Although it was doubtful that the inventors of the product had that purpose in mind.

Sal had Vinny write down a list of every type of oil the station carried and had Swan buy a case of each and bring them to the house. The oil that came in a plastic bottle was even easier to replace. After that, Vinny was given a description of Roberto's car and his drivers. All Vinny had to do was give them one of the special cans or bottles to replace any oil they ordered.

"Even if they ordered a case," Sal told Vinny, "just be sure it has one of our replacements in it."

Sal was a very patient man and sometimes a very lucky one, because in the next week, Roberto's limo—minus Roberto—was driven to the station. Two thickset men exited the car and while one pumped the gas, the other opened the hood and checked the oil. Discovering that the limo was a

108

quart low, he asked for a specific brand, which Vinny brought to him. As Vinny approached the car with the oil and a nozzle, the man near the front of the car snatched them from him and said to Vinny in a very thick accent that he would do it himself.

"Damn," Vinny said quietly, "I'm dealing with foreigners again. Isn't anybody around here from America?"

Vinny was also upset because he had the can and nozzle snatched from him. I hope there's a bomb in that can, he thought, not thinking of his proximity to any possible explosion.

Midge and Sal had also been very specific in telling Vinny to bring all the cans back, even the empty ones, when the deed was done.

After approximately three weeks, Sal's additive had the desired effect, as Roberto's limousine began to have problems that his chauffeur-bodyguard-mechanic could not remedy. The automobile was unceremoniously towed to the car dealership, where it was to be repaired.

"No, we don't need a loaner car," said the driver. His real first name was Caesar but, for reasons no one understood, was always called Mike.

Mike's constant companion, Ignacio, had followed him to the dealership in his own car. As Mike talked to the manager of the service department, Ignacio strolled through the showroom and admired the new model cars. With any luck, he would be able to afford one soon. He was a faithful employee of one of the richest and most influential men in South Florida. He was always thrifty and Mr. Mendez could be very generous.

Mike explained, as best as he could, what he thought the problem was with the car. "Just have it fixed as soon as you can," he said to the Service Manager with a scowl. "Come on, Nacho," he shouted into the showroom. "We're outta here."

With the limo now out of commission and surely to be stored in the dealership's garage, Sal was ready for part three.

Late that evening, Midge parked about a hundred yards from the dealership and called on the cellular phone to make sure everyone had left. On a moonless night, perfect for breaking and entering, Sal and Midge crouched near the door that led to the service bay. Sal was so excited that he could barely contain himself. *Patrice was dead meat tonight*, he thought.

"After the places we've broken into, this shop was a piece of cake," Sal said, once they were inside.

"I'm sure this is the first time we ever broke in a place and didn't plan to take nothing," replied Midge.

They both muffled their laughter.

"So what's the deal?" Midge said. He had been kept relatively in the dark until now.

Sal patiently explained to Midge what he had planned to do.

Midge was not overly impressed.

"I'm sure," Midge said, "that after Roberto gets his car back, his two men are going to detail it inside and out, and find whatever it is you got in that bag."

"Maybe and maybe not," said Sal.

Midge was headed for the front of the car, when Sal called out to him, "No, back here."

They carefully opened the trunk and Sal let Midge in on the final details of his program.

"Damn," Midge said. "You know, this might just work, and we'll be rid of that Colombian bastard for good."

"Did you get the car?" Roberto asked.

"Si, I mean yes, boss," Caesar, a.k.a Mike, said.

Roberto never liked his men to speak to him in Spanish. It tended to remind him of his Latin background, which made him so unwelcome in this country.

"Did you check it?" Roberto asked.

"Inside and out, boss. Nothing unusual."

Roberto did not want any unsuspected items in his car, whether it was a wiretap from the law or an explosive device from his competitors.

"Okay, let's go."

Roberto stepped into the opened car door and told the driver to take him to Club Cabana, which was his favorite pick-up spot. He was always self-assured, knowing he could impress some beautiful woman with his looks, allure and refinement. And if that didn't work, he would use money. As Roberto often said, "Whatever it takes."

As Roberto settled back for his ride to the club, he felt very relaxed. With the exception of not having his limo for a few days, everything seemed well. All was not, however, going well for Roberto because Sal was putting the final phases of his operation into completion. All he needed now, for everything to fall into place, was a junkie. And finding a junkie in Miami was as easy as finding sand on the beach. The only difference was that there were probably more junkies than grains of sand.

Midge was able to find just such a person. One who would do just as he was told and not ask any questions in exchange for, what else? Some dope.

What a surprise, Midge thought to himself. "Junkies make very good helpers ... if you have some dope. Junkies do anything you ask ... if you have some dope. Junkies never ask questions ... if you have some dope. Junkies are even reliable if you have some dope.

Junkies are easy to get rid of ... if you have some pure dope."

Sal knew that the police often used informants and, with the information that this junkie was soon to have, he was going to be a very popular person in law enforcement.

Midge didn't even give the junkie a false name, or hide his face, because he knew he was talking to a dead man. The way Midge looked at it, this guy was going to die from dope anyway. He was just going to speed up the process.

The agreement was that this junkie, whose name was Vernon, would offer information to the police at a local precinct, in exchange for a few dollars. This type of deal was made all the time between police and informants, so it was not going to arouse any suspicion.

At first, the cops were really skeptical that a person as strung out as this one could have any useful information. But if he, indeed, overheard a conversation, telling where some goods might be found, it would be a feather in their cap.

There was genuine surprise, when the abandoned house did yield a small, but worthwhile, amount of drugs. They staked the place out for a few days, hoping to get an arrest, but no one showed up. They were surprised several times, in the next few weeks, with the accuracy of his information.

So that the police wouldn't think he had a pipeline, Midge gave him a few wrong tips also. When Sal and Midge thought the time was right, they told Vernon that he could tell the police that he could hand them a big fish. Based on his testimony and his past successes, law enforcement would issue a search warrant for the limo of one Roberto Mendez.

Vernon told the police that on his next visit to his favorite night spot, Roberto Mendez was going to be carrying a large amount of drugs in his car for a delivery.

The detectives waited patiently. After a few days, Mendez showed up at the club. He was very polite and very cocky, when they approached him as he was getting out of his limousine.

He never got within a mile of any drugs and he certainly never transported them in his car.

"These American police ... they must think I just fell off a banana boat," he said to Mike, as they both stood outside the limousine.

His lofty attitude and smile both vanished when the police, in front of at least a hundred onlookers, produced approximately two kilos of very pure cocaine from the inside of his spare tire.

At approximately the same time, Vernon was overdosing with ninety percent pure heroin that Midge had given him, poor Vernon naturally thought it was the same ten to fifteen percent crap he had used all of his addicted life.

"Hello?"

"It's me."

Again—at poolside—Midge and Sal were smiles all around.

"I told you," Sal said to Midge, "that no one checks the inside of their spare tire. Except, from now on, you and me."

They both had a good laugh, courtesy of Senior Roberto Mendez.

Sal and Midge began to discuss any loose ends.

"About that junkie, what is his name?"

"His name waaas Vernon," Midge said, emphasizing the word was. "Dead. I saw them cart his body out the next morning. You know, the place was crawling with junkies the next day. That's a sure sign that someone overdosed. They all come around, trying to find out where he got dope good enough to overdose on. They think there must be a new supplier trying to get a foothold, who is not cutting his stuff eighty percent. That is what they live ... and die for," laughed Midge, reaching an index finger under his sunglasses to wipe a tear.

Sal mentioned that it would be alright for Vinny to quit his job in about two more months, without arousing too much suspicion. After all, it had been almost six months since he started working at the service station.

This time, they both laughed until tears rolled down their faces.

* * *

Patrice thought that in the last few months Sal had undergone quite a change ... transformation ... metamorphosis ... yes, metamorphosis. That was the word. She had discovered this word from her new favorite pasttime of reading. It wasn't by choice, or for self-improvement, that Patrice had started reading extensively. It was because of Sal's metamorphosis.

In addition to his newfound sexual libido, Sal had gradually become very jealous and possessive. Patrice just couldn't figure it out for the life of her. When he was sexually malfunctioning, he did not care where she went, with whom she went or how long she stayed. As of late, he was concerned about all of these things. She became a virtual prisoner in the house, only being allowed to go out with him, which wasn't very often.

After the Roberto Mendez thing, as Sal liked to refer to his latest feat, he was at his sexual peak again. He felt like an adolescent. He even had a passing thought about getting himself a mistress, but this had come to be about more than sex. These contests were about his very being. It was now a matter of proving that he could hold his own in any situation, against any opponent.

Sal decided that it was time for him to pull off a masterpiece of ingenuity. This caper had to be so complicated in its scope, with such high stakes, that the mere thought of it would carry him well into his advanced years. But where could he find such an adversary?

He was better educated than all of his friends and most of the people with whom he came in contact. All this, with only a mail order degree from a second-rate correspondence school.

Sal did not want to spar with just an educated person. This had to be a man of distinction, who was not only educated by the best minds the country had to offer, but who had achieved status and acclaim in his chosen profession. But where and how could he come into intimate contact, with such a man? The answer slowly came to him. *DR. EVANDER PARKER.*

Yes, this was the man that was going to cure him of all of his ills. Sal was sure it would not be in the way the good doctor imagined.

Chapter Fourteen

"Hello ... Dade County Medical Society," a pleasant female voice answered.

"Yes ... Dr. Evander Parker is a member of the Medical Society," she replied.

"Yes, Dr. Parker is certified in the practice of Psychiatry. Incidentally, he is also certified in the field of Internal Medicine."

"Of course I can send you some information on Dr. Parker. He is one of our most distinguished members."

Several days later, Sal got the information that he had been waiting for. He had it sent to a mail drop he had acquired under an assumed name. He could not wait to get home to open it. He tore it open and read it, like a child receiving a note from Santa. His face was no less full of glee.

"Un huh, certified Psychiatry. Internal Medicine, Harvard Graduate, three books, dozens of publications, awards, citations, the whole nine yards." THIS WAS THE GUY!

"Dr. Parker's office. May I help you?" answered Ms. Kennedy. "Yes, Dr. Parker is still accepting new patients. Would you like an appointment? Certainly, Mr. McIlvane, I will be glad to make an appointment for you. It'll be just a moment, while I check the appointment book. Sorry to have kept you waiting. Our next available appointment is in two months. However, if this is an emergency, we can refer you to another physician. You'll take the next appointment? Very well, we'll see you in two months."

Sal was a very patient man.

"Dr. Parker, your next appointment is in ten minutes. It's a new patient, a Mr. John McIlvane. He didn't mention any specifics. He also stated that he would not be using his medical insurance, but would pay at the end of each session."

For reasons of privacy, Dr. Parker always had approximately twenty minutes between appointments to lessen the probability that patients would meet accidentally in the building corridors. Additionally, he had his office structured so that entering patients came in through the reception area and were able to leave through a rear exit.

Ms. Kennedy brought Sal from the reception area into the doctor's office and introduced him.

"Dr. Parker, Mr. McIlvane."

Sal quickly surveyed the office, as Dr. Parker was getting up from his desk, which was situated near the door in one corner of the rectangular room. At the far end of the room was a small grouping of furniture—two large dark brown leather chairs and a chestnut leather sofa, separated by a cherrywood Butler's table covered with magazines. A ficus plant graced the corner of the room. The room had soft ceiling lights which cast a solemn glow.

"How may I help you?" Dr. Parker got up and walked around his desk with his hand extended. It's been quite a while since I've seen a swarthy Irishman, he thought.

Ms. Kennedy politely excused herself and exited the room.

117

As Dr. Parker shook Sal's hand, he led him to the opposite end of the room and motioned for him to sit in one of the large dark brown chairs.

"Well, my man," Sal began, scooting his buttocks onto the leather seat.

Very little regard for authority figures, thought Parker.

"I've done a lot of wrong things in my life," Sal continued.

"And you feel guilty about them," Dr. Parker interrupted as he sat in the other chair.

"No, not at all. That is why I'm here. I think I should feel some guilt but I don't."

A true sociopath, thought Parker.

"Furthermore, the things I've done have brought me a degree of financial security."

Ah, a successful sociopath, thought Parker.

"So let me ask you a question," Parker said with a bemused smirk, "is it that you want to not do things that are wrong or do you just want to feel guilty about having done them?"

"I'm not sure what I want, Doc. It's just that I know the majority of the people in this country, or any other, would disapprove of the things I have done and continue to do. I am somewhat confused about how I can do them so easily, when other people wouldn't."

A true sociopath's dilemma, thought Parker.

"Before we go any further, Doc, let me ask you. How confidential are the things that I tell you?" Sal already knew the answer because Midge had told him. He thought this might create some bond between Dr. Parker and himself. Sharing intimate secrets and all.

"Everything is very confidential but I must report any confessions of murder or child molestation to the police."

"That's okay," Sal said, "since I have never molested any children and I have never exactly murdered anyone." He knew that phrase would not escape the doctor's attention and he noticed a little eyebrow raising but Dr. Parker remained silent.

"I really hope that you can help me, Doc."

"We really haven't established what it is you want help with."

"I really don't know. I think I just want to be normal."

Oh great, a sociopath, maybe a psychopath, who wants to be normal and accepted. Dr. Parker was getting somewhat bored during this session. Every new patient was a potential new paper or at least good for some anecdotes, but this McIlvane person, while certainly in need of help, was not very unusual. He had seen hundreds of patients like him, during his training at the locked ward of the County Hospital.

"Just what is it you would like from so-called normal society?" Dr. Parker asked, already anticipating the answer.

"Respect," Sal said.

They all said that, thought Parker. *Even a person who had just killed his own family or a room full of total strangers always wanted to be respected. His time at the county jail during his training had taught him that.*

"And how is it that you plan to get this respect from society?"

"Oh, I don't plan to get respect from people," Sal replied. "I already get it and plenty of it. From people in all walks of life."

"And exactly how is it that you do this, Mr. McIlvane?"

Dr. Parker seldom referred to his patients by their first name even if they requested him to do so.

"By just being like God."

"Like God?" Dr. Parker perked up, his curiosity piqued. He was becoming a bit more interested. *Hmm, a sociopath with a God-complex,* he thought. *Not unheard of, but not commonplace.*

"So you are God?"

119

"Oh no," Sal replied. "I think I might need some help, but not that much help. I meant like God commands respect in the Bible."

"And how is that?" Dr. Parker modulated his voice to sound non-judgmental.

"It goes like this," Sal leaned forward, "if you don't do what God wants you to do, then something bad happens to you."

"Actually, Mr. McIlvane, that is the Old Testament view of God."

"Well, that's the view I take."

"Do you base any of your other actions on the Bible?"

"Oh yes," Sal said.

"I suppose you like an eye for an eye?"

"Now you're talking."

How boring. How completely boring, thought Dr. Parker.

"So you pick and choose the parts of the Bible which you have use for and disregard the rest?"

"Pretty much." Sal gave him a deadpan stare.

"Well, that is about all of the time we have for our first session."

"Yeah, okay, thanks Doc. But before I go, I want to ask you one question. I came here for you to help me. Basically because the ideas of the world in which I live conflict with society in general. How can you help me, or really understand, if you have had virtually no contact with or experience in the world I live in?"

There may be a paper after all, thought Dr. Parker.

* * *

120

Chapter Fifteen

"Hello?"

"It's me."

Midge knew to get over to Sal's pronto. When he arrived, Swan escorted him back to the pool area.

"Do you ever do anything around this pool besides talk to me?" asked Midge.

"Very little," Sal said. "Tell me what is going on with Solly in North Miami."

"I think we gotta problem," Midge replied. "His receipts have been down for the past six months."

"What'd he say about it?"

"Said his action's down and he's taking some heavy hits with guys picking winners."

"Whatta you think?" Sal glowered.

"I think it's bullshit." Midge went straight to the heart of the matter.

"Why's that?"

"Cause I hung around outside for a few days and clocked the number of people going in his store, which is increased if anything. And you and I both know someone that's been around long as Solly knows to lay off some of the bets if he gets too much action on one event."

"What do you think we should do about it?" Sal asked earnestly.

"I think I should introduce him to one of the accessories that came with my car." Midge gave a toothy grin.

"No, no," said Sal. "I think I want to handle this another way."

"You don't want people to think you're getting soft, do you?" Midge's voice egged Sal on.

"Me, soft? I strong-armed two black guys in the middle of the jungle and got rid of Roberto Mendez personally. A soft guy couldn't do that."

"Didn't say you were soft. What I said was you don't want people to think you're soft. I know you ain't, and you know you ain't, but that don't count."

Patrice would not agree with that statement, thought Sal. Sometimes what you know about yourself counts for a lot. Oh shit, he was beginning to sound like the Doc. The past few months of therapy were starting to have some impact.

"Do you think M.C. could help us out?" Sal knitted his eyebrows together, forming a bridge over his Mediterranean nose.

"You mean FAO, don't you?" Midge laughed.

FAO was the nickname that Sal and Midge had privately given to Robert Benjamin, also known as M.C. They called him FAO because he was the first and only black person that Sal had employed personally or that Midge ever liked and even admired.

M.C. was a bonus, acquired when Roberto Mendez was manipulated out of the picture. When Roberto Mendez's spot in the Miami underworld was vacated, Sal was only too happy to take charge of Roberto's operations. Sal fully expected to take over the dope trade and bookie joints but was surprised that Roberto controlled a substantial part of Miami's illegal lottery known as Bolita, Policy, Cuba or simply, the numbers.

Mostly blacks in the Overtown or Liberty City area of the city played this form of gambling. Playing the numbers was very simple. The player picked out a number from one to one hundred and if his number was pulled or "came out," he was paid at the rate of 70 to one. You didn't have to be a math genius to know that the odds of winning were a hundred to one, so even when you won, you got cheated and the guy who took the bet expected a percentage. The lucky winning number was the last two numbers of the total bets as posted on the tote board at Hialeah Race Track. Double zero would represent the number one hundred. That way it at least had the appearance of some degree of honesty.

M.C. had been born Robert Benjamin in the Overtown section of Miami or, as it was called in those days, the Central Negro District. At an early age, he had moved with his family to the projects in Liberty City, which, even today was still a strange name, for there wasn't much liberty for coloreds then in a strictly segregated city. From his first days in school, Robert was recognized as being very gifted in math which is how he got his nickname, M.C. as in $E=mc2$.

Although he attended an all-black school with all-black teachers, he received a very good education and everyone expected him to go far. He always dreamed of going to Florida A&M College or one of the other black schools in Florida.

There was never a thought of going to a white school because they didn't accept any colored. Not even if you could play ball. There were no blacks to cheer for at any of the white schools in Florida. Not the University of Miami, not the University of Florida, not Florida State. None of them had a single black player on any team, in any sport. When Robert and his friends went to the football games with their Boy Scout troop, they were always seated in the last row of the bleachers, but on the "home" side of the field. The University of Miami fans never seemed to understand why they would always cheer for the opposing team.

A professor of mathematics at Florida A&M is what Robert's parents would tell everyone their son was going to be and, with Robert's ability, that goal was not unrealistic until it was all shattered when Robert was a victim of a drive-by shooting which left him permanently, absolutely and totally blind. After the incident, which occurred during his Junior year in High School, Robert refused to go to school and began to drink whenever he could persuade someone to get a bottle for him. Fortunately for him alcohol gave him headaches that were too intense for him to become an alcoholic.

With limited opportunities in his community for a blind person who happened to have a penchant for math, writing the numbers was a natural career choice. Most number writers, or runners as they are called, carried a small notebook with a piece of carbon paper. You told them what number you wanted and how much you wanted to bet or place on a number and it was entered into the notebook. You were then handed a copy, which was your proof of your bet, and you presented it to the runner the next day or, sometimes the same day, for your winnings.

Often times, small entrepreneurs would not work for anyone but would back their own numbers. Sometimes these small operators, rather than pay off, would skip town never to be seen again. However, if they were ever seen again, they would never be seen again.

M.C. was perfect for this line of work. With his mastery of numbers and photographic memory, he never had to write down a single wager. He was known all over Liberty City as being honest and paying his winners promptly. He never took a percentage of the winnings before he gave them to his customers, but waited for a gratuity. Best of all, the police would never suspect a blind man of being a numbers runner and, if they did search him, there were no telltale receipts.

M.C.'s only limitation was that of locale, because he could not go house to house in a neighborhood with which he was not familiar. His talent for figures did not go unnoticed and soon he was working in the counting room helping to reconcile the sheets for the day's wagers. Of course, someone had to read the figures to him but he could tally them as fast as they could be read. Eventually, Roberto Mendez would question the tallys of the calculators rather than M.C.'s.

When Salvatore Roselli took over Roberto Mendez's action, he decided that it would be easier to let the people who worked for Mendez stay in place rather than trying to replace them all with his people. He did send out the word that he expected loyalty and respect from those working for him and that if they decided they did not want to work for him, they could move on with no hard feelings.

Sal, of course, would put his people in as overseers of all operations. All of Roberto's operations were basically sound in their functions, but Sal changed the way some things were done, sometimes for no other reason than to establish who was in charge. Most things were as he and Midge expected, except for the black man in the counting room who seemed to have access to all of Roberto's dealings and accounts.

At first, Sal and Midge thought he was a janitor or at most a gopher, but when the others explained M.C.'s role, they could not believe it. To say the least, they were surprised by M.C.'s presence in the counting room, and astonished by the degree of responsibility he had. They were in awe when he displayed his talent.

Later, when they were alone, they discussed M.C.'s phenomenal talents.

"If I wouldn't have seen it myself, I wouldn't have believed it," Midge said.

"I saw it," Sal said, "but I still don't believe it. Do you think it might be some kind of trick?"

"We didn't like Roberto," Midge commented, "but he wouldn't have some colored checking his books if it was a trick. And if it is a trick, it is a damn good one." Midge cracked his knuckles, a habit he had whenever he was thinking. "Never seen nothing like it," he continued. "Most of the coloreds I run into can barely add. At least that's how they play it when it's time to pay up. 'Whatchu mean I owes you twenty dallahs?

When I add it up, it only come to fi'teen'." Midge did his best eye rolling, butt-scratching, teeth-showing, "colored" impersonation of buffonery.

"I don't know," Sal said. "I just never had one of those people working for me. However, a guy that can keep all of those numbers and stuff straight in his head could be valuable. Besides, if he messes up it can't be too hard to get rid of a blind colored guy."

Trusting M.C. came very slowly, but he clinched the deal after Sal and Midge decided to make a pay off of five thousand on the plus side. M.C. told them a mistake had been made and gave the extra cash back to them.

If Midge were more verbally skilled, he would have said that based on personal experience, it was genetically impossible for a person of African heritage to possess such mental skills.

He said, "M.C. must be some kind of freak of nature."

It was M.C. that Sal and Midge decided to send to Solly's to place some bets and get a feel for what was going on.

Solly's was located in a lower-middle-class area of North Miami. It was a hole-in-the-wall bar, a front for his illegal activities. Sal had paid the police so Solly had no worries of any intrusions that were unannounced. Sal had an underling rent M.C. an apartment near Solly's bar and showed him how to get around the neighborhood.

M.C. was a quick study and soon had no problems making his way to and from Solly's and to and from the places that were critical, like the grocery store. Sal could have had all of M. C.'s essentials delivered but it may have caused suspicion. A blind colored guy coming in to make bets was enough. Sal told M.C. to keep the bets relatively small so as to not draw attention to himself but to wager enough so that Solly wouldn't mind him hanging around all day.

At first, M.C. was an oddity, but after a few weeks he became a fixture. Solly, being very sure of the security of his surroundings, took the bets and made the pay-offs in public, unless privacy was requested. This was a rare event because every player wanted everyone to know when he was a winner and Solly made a big production of paying because it made him look like he was doing right by his customers.

M.C. took all the action in mentally and made notes of the day's wagers and pay outs when he went to his apartment late in the evening. He had a remarkably good memory, but no one could expect him to keep a running tab of weeks of bets without notes.

After two months, Sal and Midge decided to meet with M.C. at the North Miami apartment. Sal had the receipts and figures on the money which Solly had turned in during the last two months.

After he read the figures to M.C., Sal spoke. "Okay. Take your time and let's check the figures you have recorded against the ones I just gave you."

"Don't need any more time," M.C. said. "I can tell you right now that those figures do not jibe with what is going on in the bar. They are only about eighty-four percent of what I estimate your take should be. You understand that there is a probability of error of one percent which means ...."

"Time out," Sal said. "Enough mumbo-jumbo. How much is he cheating me out of?"

"Approximately four thousand dollars a week," said M.C.

"Four grand a week?" Sal screamed, eyes bulging from his sockets. "I had him figured for about a third of that. Are you sure?"

"Numbers don't lie," M.C. was adamant, "and neither do I."

Assured that Solly was stealing from him, Sal asked Midge to drive him home.

* * *

127

"Aren't you glad I told you to hire that guy?" Midge smiled broadly as he drove towards Sal's home.

"You told me to hire him?" Sal asked incredulously. "It was totally my idea. You hate coloreds."

"And you don't?" Midge raised his eyebrow.

"Not like him. He's different."

"Now that you're sure that Solly's stealing, what are you going to do about it?" Midge's voice carried the challenge of school kids when they would say, "Dare ya!"

"I've already decided what I'm going to do," Sal replied coolly, patting his foot. "I just have to figure out how I'm going to do it."

Later, Midge told M.C. to hang around Solly's for a few more days. Sal gave him some money to lose some rather substantial bets so it wouldn't arouse any suspicion when he left. It just made him look as if he was tapped out.

Chapter Sixteen

Heather posed and preened in her bedroom's floor-length mirror and was pleased with what she saw. *Dr. Parker was right,* she thought, *my hair does looks better cut short like this.* She had even applied a small amount of beige make up to her face. She wore a scarlet-colored dress, and, sweeping her hands over her newly-discovered curves, admired her reinvented self. Everything he said was true.

"I look *and* feel better," she said to herself. "It is just wondrous how marvelous he is. I do want to please him so. My transformation is nearly complete. I have been born again in the image he has created for me. I am reincarnated for him."

She turned from the mirror and looked around at her small apartment. Her environment stood in stark contrast to the picture she projected in the mirror. All was turmoil. Clothes were strewn everywhere. Furniture was overturned. Weeks-old dishes, vermin and food were in the sink and rotting garbage was piled in various corners of the apartment.

She returned to the mirror. "Yes, I must be perfect for him. I am perfect for him."

She did not, however, know very much about him outside of the office, she thought. This she was resolved to change. She wanted ... no, she needed to get to know more about him.

"Yes," Ms. Kennedy said, "I understand. I'll get him right away. I'll have to put you on hold for just a second."

She pressed the hold button and rang Dr. Parker's office. He picked up the phone on the fourth ring.

"Yes," he said curtly into the phone.

"I'm sorry to interrupt you," Ms. Kennedy said, "but you have an urgent call on line two."

Dr. Parker excused himself from his patient and stepped into Ms. Kennedy's area.

"It's Heather Fine," Ms. Kennedy said.

After her fourth and nearly successful suicide attempt, Dr. Parker had told Heather to call his office at anytime. Especially since he was making such great progress with her treatment and his treatise.

"Hello, Heather," Dr. Parker said, "I'm glad you called. How are you doing? Yes, I understand completely. I would like for you to come into the office immediately. I'll just finish with my current patient and I'll see you as soon as you come in."

Dr. Parker explained to his current patient that he would have to cut their session time because of an emergency, but assured him that he would make up for it during their next session.

A half-hour later, Dr. Parker was dictating some correspondence when Ms. Kennedy rang to let him know that Ms. Fine had arrived.

"Send her in," he said.

Ms. Kennedy escorted Heather Fine to the office. She sat on the edge of the large, brown leather sofa, with its innumerable fine cracks.

"How are we doing today?" Dr. Parker asked.

"We ... are doing terrible," Heather said sarcastically.

"What brought you to such a state of mind?" Dr. Parker asked. "Was it something that has been going on for a while or was it something that happened recently?"

"Actually it's both," she replied. "My life has been marching on inexorably for a while now and that's depressing enough.

But today I heard a very beautiful love song that was very popular when I was in high school."

"And it brought back some painful memories," Dr. Parker interjected.

"No, that was the problem," Heather said. "It didn't bring back any memories at all. It didn't remind me of any good times or bad times. You know, a beautiful love song should inspire some memories of a time, a place or a person. Most of all a person, but it didn't do any of those things. It made me think that, whenever that song played or any love song, that I would not have any reminiscences of anyone. But the worst part was ... that of the tens of thousands of love songs played tens of millions of times ... that no one on this planet was thinking of me."

"I am sure," said Dr. Parker in a reassuring tone, "that one day you will find that special person and you both will have a special song or many songs."

"I'm glad you feel so optimistic," Heather answered with a miffed frown, "because somehow I feel as if time is running out. I am now at an age when I'm still looking for my first love, but I'm too old to be anyone's first love. You know, Dr. Parker, everyone should be someone's first love."

At that moment, tears began to stream down her face. She walked over to his desk, plucked several tissues from a leatherette holder and returned to the sofa. This time she laid down and turned her back to him. Without warning, she began to shiver, tremble, and sob uncontrollably into the wad of crumpled tissues.

Dr. Parker wished that there was something he could do or say to make her feel better. He felt that he should comfort her in some way. He wanted to place his arms around her or at least pat her shoulder and tell her that everything would be alright, even though they both knew that it probably wouldn't. But that would be inappropriate for him to do, in these politically correct times. It might even make him liable for a lawsuit. So he did nothing, even though every cell in his body told him that would be the human thing to do.

Suddenly, he was overwhelmed with grief. He felt very sad for her. He felt very sad for himself.

Chapter Seventeen

"Dr. Parker, Mr. McIlvane is here."

"Thank you, Ms. Kennedy," Dr. Parker said.

Mr. McIlvane decided to keep his appointment, Dr. Parker thought. *And he's on time again. Maybe we are making some progress.*

"Hello, Dr. Parker," Sal said.

He called me Dr. Parker. This is almost a breakthrough.

"Hello, Mr. McIlvane. How are we today?" Dr. Parker said, motioning for Sal to be seated in the corner grouping. Once Sal complied, he followed right behind him.

"I don't know how we are," Sal sighed, taking a seat, "but I'm doing just fine." Pensively, Sal continued, "I've decided that this is my last visit."

"Your last visit, Mr. McIlvane? But I thought we were just beginning to get some insight into your problems," Dr. Parker sniffed in a bemused fashion as he settled into his chair.

"That's just it, Dr. Parker. I'm not sure that I have a problem and I don't know if you are the one that can convince me that the way I see things is wrong. As I said when I first came in here, I have lived in your 9-5 world and I understand a lot about it, but I don't know if I can accept the judgments of a person who has not experienced the world I come from."

"Someone who has not walked in your shoes, so to speak," Dr. Parker prompted.

"Exactly."

"There is going to be a problem finding someone who has walked in your shoes that holds a degree in psychiatry."

"I thought about that too and that's why I'm offering you a chance to hang around with me and see how things are."

This may be the opportunity I have been waiting for, thought Dr. Parker. *I will have insight into a world that few have studied with my credentials, and not just from the viewpoint of a common street criminal but from the standpoint of one who has some position of authority.*

"So what's it going to be, Dr. Parker?"

"The premise is intriguing, but first we have to set some ground rules."

Sal sat silently in wide-eyed anticipation.

"No one gets physically hurt," said Parker.

"Of course not," said Sal sincerely, as he pinched his eyebrows together.

"Either one of us may stop this experiment at any time."

"Not a problem." Sal waved a dismissive hand.

"I can use my experience from this to publish a paper. With the names changed, of course."

"Of course," Sal replied, smiling, his eyes hooded.

"I will also need a little time to get someone to cover my patients for me." He knew Cassie would understand.

"Understood," said Sal. "Will forty eight hours be enough time?"

"That's short notice but I am sure I can have everything arranged by then. How shall I contact you?" Dr. Parker said.

"I'll get in touch with you." Sal grinned as he closed the door behind him.

Heather was devastated when she received the call.

"Hello?" said Heather.

"Is this Ms. Heather Fine?"

"Yes, it is."

"Hello, Ms. Fine. This is Ms. Kennedy from Dr. Parker's office."

"Hello, Ms. Kennedy. How are you?"

"I'm fine."

"No," Heather said. "I'm Fine, you're Kennedy."

Heather had been trying to develop a sense of wit and humor lately. In fact, she had read two books on it. If she was going to become Ms. Evan Parker she would have to have a sense of cleverness and charm. After all, she was sure his friends were charming and witty and she wanted to blend in perfectly.

"Yes, of course," Ms. Kennedy replied tersely. "Dr. Parker apologizes but he has to cancel his appointments with you for the next six weeks."

Heather gripped the telephone receiver, feeling as if her heart had stopped. In fact, she was sure that it had stopped. "What have I done wrong?" she pleaded.

"You haven't done anything wrong, Ms. Fine. Dr. Parker is just taking an emergency leave. He has canceled all of his appointments for the next six weeks." She tried to comfort her, hearing the anxiety in Heather's voice. "Dr. Seaforth will be handling any emergencies for Dr. Parker. Do you have Dr. Seaforth's number?"

"Yes, I still have it," Heather answered. She had gotten Dr. Seaforth's number from Ms. Kennedy the last time Dr. Parker was out of town attending a conference. She had no idea where it was. She would not have been able to find the telephone, if it had not been ringing.

Heather knew she would hate Dr. Seaforth even though she had never met him.

"Is Dr. Parker in?" Heather asked.

"Yes," Ms. Kennedy answered, "but he's seeing his last patient now and then he will be gone for six weeks."

"Thank you," Heather said sweetly, waiting until Ms. Kennedy hung up before she slammed the receiver repeatedly into the phone.

135

She could not stand the thought of not seeing Dr. Parker for six weeks. She looked at her watch. It was three thirty-five. His last patient should keep him there until four. If he had a little paperwork to do ... if there was only light traffic ... and if she had a little luck, she could see him before he left. If only for a little while.

As she was driving to Dr. Parker's office, she was very careful not to exceed the speed limit. Now was not the time for a ticket or an accident. She had to see him. She was making very good time as she had started from her apartment before the four o'clock rush hour, which lasted well past 9 p.m. She had decided that if she were in an accident or if a policeman tried to pull her over, she would not stop. She would not let the police stop her from her divine mission, as the Centurions in Rome had tried to stop people from seeing Jesus.

She also decided that she would not have to talk with him in order to feel whole again. In fact, it would prove her faith if she knew she could be made whole by just his presence. If she were fortunate enough to get close to him, that would be excellent—"and she touched the hem of his garment and was made whole"—but even to see him from afar would suffice.

As Heather pulled up in front of Dr. Parker's office building, she suddenly had a severe attack of anxiety. What if he had come out of the building already? What if he was already in his car? Oh my gosh, she didn't even know what kind of car he drove. What if he had those really dark tinted windows that were so popular in Florida?

With a couple of deep breaths, she managed to calm herself down and position her car so that she could see the entrance of the medical building and also the exit of the doctors' parking lot.

There he is, her mind screamed.

She had spotted him in his car. It was a five-year old, plain-looking Chevrolet. She was delighted. It was the kind of car she expected him to have. Nothing too flashy or ostentatious like most of the other doctors. No, sirree, no Mercedes or Cadillac for Dr. Evander Parker. *The dear thing.* He was a simple man of simple pleasures, who wanted to identify with his flock. She imagined that his driving a Chevrolet was similar to riding an ass, in biblical times. The Chevrolet had more to do, however, with Dr. Parker's financial situation than any spiritual enlightenment.

Dr. Parker passed very close to her, but seemed pre-occupied and did not notice her. That was when she got the idea to follow him. By the time Dr. Parker turned onto the street where he lived, Heather had convinced herself that he would pull up in front of a manger. Instead, he turned into the private garage of a very fancy condominium complex. Heather was disappointed, but not for long. For had not Jesus gone into the temple of the moneychangers? Yes, that was it. Dr. Parker must tend to the spiritual needs of the rich and the poor. What a wonderful man.

She pulled her car to the curb and stared at the building. So many questions came to mind. On which floor did he live? Which condo was his? How was it furnished? Very sparsely, she thought.

Although he wore a wedding band, Heather did not want to believe that he was married. He might have worn the ring to discourage women that were not worthy of him. Maybe he was a widower. She had to find out if he was married.

Back in her apartment, Heather's heart was pounding so hard that it was making her head hurt. No matter what, she thought, this was what she had to do. A large red box, with the name of an exclusive store imprinted in gold letters, lay on the floor in front of her. She looked around her cluttered apartment for something to give weight to the box.

It was like she was seeing her apartment for the first time. She couldn't believe how much junk she had accumulated. Clothes of any and all descriptions, papers, magazines, books, catalogues, newspapers, half-eaten fast food containers.

Heather had convinced herself that she now had to eat fast foods for most of her meals, because she was busy fulfilling a higher purpose. The truth was that she could no longer squeeze herself into her small kitchen, because of all the rubble.

She finally decided that a coat that had been carpeting the floor for at least eight months would be perfect. She meticulously folded the coat into the box, placed the top on it and tied it very festively, with a gold ribbon with bright red trim. She checked her watch to be sure of the day and date. Fortunately for her, some time in her life, she had bought a perpetual calendar, day/date watch, because she never watched television, rarely listened to the radio and, despite the fact that her apartment was overflowing with yellowing newspapers, she never glanced at them. It was five p.m., Friday the 22nd. She planned to arrive at Dr. Parker's complex at approximately six-thirty p.m.

Heather parked her car about two blocks from Dr. Parker's condo and at six-thirty two p.m., Heather Fine, carrying the large box and dressed in a navy blue business suit, was admitted to the lobby by the doorman.

"May I help you, Miss?" he asked.

"Yes, please," she replied. "I have a package here for a Mrs. Parker."

"Exactly which Mrs. Parker?" the doorman asked. "We have two."

"I was afraid of that," she answered. "My department manager told me her full name but I have a date tonight and I must admit that with it being Friday and all, I didn't pay as close attention as I should have. Oh well, I guess she'll just have to wait until Monday to get her dress. Although my manager did say she wanted to wear it to a party this weekend."

She turned toward the door and although she was walking very slowly, her heart was beating very rapidly. She kept telling herself that she had to remain calm. She must maintain her composure. She was hopeful that the doorman would be helpful in anticipation of a gratuity, from whichever Mrs. Parker it eventually turned out to be.

"Pardon me, Miss, but do you think you might recognize the first name if you heard it again?" asked the doorman.

Allriiight, she thought cheerfully. She turned slowly toward the doorman, gave him her most innocent look and said charmingly, "I might."

"Good," he said. "We have a Mrs. Cassie Parker and a Mrs. Penelope Parker."

"No," she replied, "neither of them sound familiar."

She tried to look very disappointed.

She waited a few seconds and then said, "You know, I just thought of something. This purchase may have been made in her husband's name. It's not that unheard of for a woman to make a purchase using her husband's credit card." She smiled demurely.

What a clever person she was becoming, she thought.

"How true," said the doorman. "Then it wouldn't be Mrs. Penelope Parker, because she's a widow."

Although that wouldn't stop her, he thought sarcastically.

"Mrs. Cassie Parker would be Mrs. or Dr. Evander Parker."

"No, that still doesn't sound familiar," Heather said. "This is 3506 16th Street, isn't it?"

"No, it is not," the doorman replied, becoming annoyed, as he thought of his vanished gratuity. "This is 3206."

"Oh, how embarrassing," Heather said. "I must have been rushing more than I thought. As I told you, I have a date to-night and I'm already late. Thanks anyway," she said and turned to leave.

Her heart was not beating as fast now as when she heard the doorman say, "Mrs. Evander Parker." It was as if he had pulled it from her chest. She had to restrain herself from running from the building. She glanced briefly at the doorman prior to leaving.

After she was gone, the doorman felt ashamed for being so angry with her. He could plainly see that she was crying when she left.

Heather was still weeping when she re-entered her apartment. She no longer had the expensive-looking box, having thrown it out of the car somewhere on the causeway.

How could this be happening to her? All she ever wanted from life were some fleeting moments of happiness. Her sorrow and self-pity soon turned to anger. She became convinced that this Cassie person must have deceived her doctor into marrying her. Cassie could not be as worthy of his love as she was.

Lying in bed, she tried to sleep but could not. Her mind continued in overdrive. She concluded that Cassie Parker was trying to ruin her life.

"Bitch," she cried out into the dark silent room.

The light from the sun of the new day shone on a determined Heather Fine. She was now on a mission. What kind of a mission or what she hoped to accomplish was a mystery ... even to Heather. Heather knew that her doctor, father, son, and unrequited love was married to someone named Cassie who didn't deserve to even know him. She also knew where this Cassie person lived. She could not bear to call her Mrs. Parker or even Cassie Parker. Heather now needed to know what Cassie looked like.

From tidbits of information from Dr. Parker and Ms. Kennedy, gathered over many years of therapy, Heather correctly surmised that this Cassie was somewhat of a socialite. She decided to go to the library and research the local society column to see what she could turn up.

Heather had never been to the main library on Flagler Street or any library in the city of Miami. The old biddy in the reference department showed Heather how to search for old columns using the computer and microfilm. Heather's perverse determination paid off. She had the librarian copy the two-year old society column of the Miami Herald.

Heather finally had what she had been looking for. A picture of Cassie "what's-her-name." She probably had a copy of that very issue on her apartment floor.

On the way to her apartment, Heather stopped at Kinko's Copies on Brickell Avenue. She had two additional copies of the photo accompanying the article enlarged and laminated. It'll last longer that way, she thought.

After clearing a space on the small desk in her apartment, by pushing everything onto the floor, Heather turned on her reading lamp, which wasn't really a reading lamp, but just a table lamp without a shade on it. She then took the two laminated pictures out of a large plain manila envelope and arranged them neatly side by side on the desk. She looked back and forth from picture to picture, which wasn't really a pro-ductive stratagem since both pictures were identical.

The pictures showed three ladies sitting at a dais at a charity fundraiser for dyslexic children. According to the in-formation at the bottom of the picture, the ladies, were from left to right, Mrs. Beth Hitchcock, Mrs. Cassie Parker, and Mrs. Esther Wallace, co-chairpersons of the charity auction.

Putting the copied social column between the two identical pictures, Heather began to read silently. The article stated that it was the fifth year of the fundraiser and it had been a very big success, eclipsing the amount of money raised in the preceding year. It further stated that each chairperson was responsible for selling one hundred tickets and offering for auction one prized possession each.

Mrs. Beth Hitchcock, wife of Dr. Emerson Hitchcock, was going to part with an autograph from his collection of famous signatures. It was a letter signed by John F. Kennedy, thanking Dr. Hitchcock's father for his support during his campaign. Mrs. Esther Wallace, wife of Judge Theodore Wallace, was going to auction a small jade horse, which dated from the Ming Dynasty and had been in her family for generations. Mrs. Cassie Parker, wife of Dr. Evander Parker, was to auction an evening of dinner and backstage passes with a now famous rock star, who had once been her husband's patient before he became famous and drug-free.

The article mentioned other items that were up for bid that local companies had donated, but the items offered by the chairpersons were clearly to be the high point of the evening. The dinner and show with the celebrity were auctioned first and sold for a high bid of fifteen hundred dollars. The Kennedy autographed letter was next and brought in three thousand dollars. Heather wondered why someone would part with an autograph of such a wonderful person as John F. Kennedy.

Many of the guests were overwhelmed that Dr. Hitchcock would part with such a prize, not knowing that he did not get along well with his father and hated all Democrats, even dead ones. The small jade horse brought a high bid of fifty-two hundred dollars, which was bid by Mrs. Wallace herself so that it could remain in her family for many more generations. The final statement in the article declared that the fundraiser was a success and a good time was had by all.

After reading the article three times, Heather began to study the pictures in earnest. Heather wished that the picture had been in color. She started with Beth Hitchcock.

Beth Hitchcock appeared to be a woman in her early thirties. She had a so-so smile and was fairly plain looking. Her hair was shoulder length and worn with a slightly curly perm. She did not wear any jewelry other than gold band earrings. She wore a sequined camisole under a dark dinner jacket. Heather then concentrated her attention on the lady on the right, Esther Wallace. Mrs. Wallace appeared to be in her late fifties to early sixties. Her make up was somewhat garish and she wore a diamond choker which Heather suspected was real. To Heather, Mrs. Wallace had the Old World look. Old diamonds, old money, old face.

Now for Mrs. Cassie, she thought. Cassie Parker looked to be in her early thirties. She had a short, stylish haircut and just the right amount of make up. She had single pearl earrings and a single strand of pearls around her neck. Her dress appeared to be a sexy strapless black number, which showed just a peek of an ample décolletage. After looking at the pictures, Heather could not help but think of Goldilocks and the three bears.

Mrs. Hitchcock was too little, Mrs. Wallace was too much and Cassie was just right. As Heather continued to gaze no, stare at the picture of Cassie Parker, some of her anger was exchanged for curiosity. She began to wonder how Dr. Parker was attracted to her enough to marry her. Of course she was pretty, but she was sure that Dr. Parker was exposed to many pretty women in his lifetime. She was sure it was not for money, for if he had been interested in money he would not have been a psychiatrist.

Was it her intellect, her wit, her manner, her interests? It could have been one of a million things. Even more important, what had Cassie lost so that the perfect Dr. Parker now wanted her instead of his wife? What had come between them, so that Dr. Parker decided to create Heather into the perfect woman for him? She must know these things, because she did not ever want Dr. Parker to fall out of love with her.

"She must have done something pretty awful," she said, still staring at Cassie's picture, "because Dr. Parker is not a petty man."

At this moment she decided that she must meet Mrs. Cassie.

* * *

143

During any spare time that she had, Heather Fine was parked outside 3206. Being unemployed, and her therapy sessions temporarily canceled, she practically lived there.

After sitting outside the condo for a good part of three weeks, Heather assumed that Mrs. Cassie had either left town with her husband or didn't go out much. She carefully scrutinized each and every person that entered and left the building. She even bought a pair of high-power binoculars to help her in her holy quest. She not only observed the women but the men and even the pets. She got to know the routines of some of the occupants of the building.

At times, Heather amused herself by trying to guess who would be coming out of the door next or if the white poodle was going to get his scheduled walk. It helped to pass the time somewhat, but it wasn't what she was there for. Heather did not know how she would approach Mrs. Cassie, but she knew the answer would come to her when the opportunity presented itself.

If she were a private investigator being paid by the hour, she would have made a fortune by the time she got her first look at Cassie Parker. She wasn't very hard to spot really. She looked almost exactly like her picture. She wore the same haircut and perfect smile, which she flashed at the doorman as she was leaving. She was much shorter than Heather had imagined, but then who wasn't? Every movie star, rock star, television personality that she had ever seen in person was always shorter than she imagined.

Maybe because you expect so much from them, or you want them to be larger than life. No matter, she was there. All five-feet three inches of her. She had on a silk, short-sleeved designer blouse and a pair of expensive designer jeans, whose label Heather could read with her binoculars. Heather couldn't figure out why she was carrying a windbreaker, unless she was going to walk along the beach. It didn't look like rain.

Impulsively, Heather decided to get out of her car and follow Mrs. Cassie, knowing in her heart that she would get the chance to meet her. Heather jumped out of the car nervously, locked the doors and proceeded across the street. She then had to re-cross the street, unlock the door and put her binoculars in the car. She had never followed anyone before but thought it couldn't be too difficult.

It was now about seven in the evening and the street lights had just come on. The remaining small boutiques on the block had been closed for nearly an hour now. Cassie had stopped to look at some of the displays in the windows. The only places that were open were the restaurants and a small playhouse that had just opened recently.

The smell of food wafting from the restaurants reminded Heather that she had not eaten recently, and walking quickly down the street reminded her that she had to go to the little girl's room. Those things were of little consequence now that she was so close to the woman she had been trying to see all this time. She noticed that Cassie peered in at a store front for quite an unusual length of time. When Heather got to the establishment, she noticed that it was a travel agency. Had Cassie been thinking of her husband and his trip?

As they turned the corner, the street became brighter with the neon lights from the marquee of the theater. Cassie headed straight for the ticket booth.

Oh perfect, Heather thought, *I'll sit next to her in the theater and strike up a conversation. Very normal stuff.*

"One, please," Heather told the ticket attendant, panicking momentarily when she couldn't find her wallet in her purse. It was fortunate, Heather decided, that she wasn't going into one of those multiplex theaters, because after fumbling for her wallet, she would have certainly lost Cassie.

To her surprise, when she entered the lobby of the theater, she didn't have to look far for Cassie. Heather took a seat on one of several red NAUGAHYDE lobby benches and watched as Cassie Parker, at a pay phone, placed a brief call.

Could she be talking to Dr. Parker? Heather thought.

Heather stood, preparing to follow Cassie into the viewing room, when she became very confused. Cassie was turning to go out the door.

Maybe there was an emergency, Heather thought. *Was it Dr. Parker?* Her heart began to pound. She had to restrain herself from running up to Cassie and asking her what was wrong. Cassie put on her windbreaker and walked to the curb.

Heather watched her from inside the theater lobby.

Heather watched as a car pulled to the curb.

Heather watched as Cassie got into the car.

Heather watched as Cassie, and someone other than Dr. Evander Parker, sped off.

Sal was working out on the stairmaster in the exercise room of his home.

"Come on in, Vinny," Sal said. "How are things going?"

"Fine," Vinny said without any enthusiasm.

"Midge told me you've been doing pretty good." Sal, trying to be complimentary, was getting used to the idea of Vinny being around. "I got a special job for you."

Oh great, thought Vinny, *I'm still trying to get all the grease offa me from the last special job. What am I going to do this time, clean sewers?*

Before Vinny could speak, Sal continued. "I would normally work with Midge on this, but I can't for a number of reasons."

Why? Vinny thought. *Too dirty or too dangerous?*

Sal went on. "I'm going to be working with this doctor guy, see, and he might write a book about me or something like that. The thing is, I don't want him to know too much about me, not even my name. I want you to be my chauffeur and take the Doc places I might tell you to take him and make mental notes of what he talks about when I am not around, but most of all, don't tell him anything personal about me.

"When we're together you call me, 'Chief.' Never 'Sal' or 'Uncle Sal.' You got it? Your main job will be to chauffeur us around, listen to what's going on and be quiet."

Oh yeah, I got it, Vinny thought. *I have been moved up the ladder in the family from grease monkey to all-around flunky. It won't be hard to remember to call him Chief, because it sounds like cheap. The hard part will be not to add bastard to it.*

"Hey," Sal snapped. "Are you paying attention here?"

"Of course," said Vinny. "I got it down pat."

"Okay then. I'll see you here tomorrow."

"Right, Cheap."

"What?" Sal's voice rose indignantly.

"I said, 'right, Chief.' Just getting ready for tomorrow."

Vinny arrived at Sal's home at approximately 6 a.m. and found him dressed and waiting in the front courtyard. Vinny parked his car and walked over to where Sal was standing.

"We'll take the Lincoln Towncar," Sal said.

Good morning to you, too, Vinny thought. *I don't get to ride in the limo. I guess I don't even get to drive it.*

At 7 o'clock, Vinny pulled the Lincoln to the front of Dr. Parker's medical building. Dr. Parker was waiting downstairs as Sal had instructed him to do. Sal was sitting in the backseat and rolled the window down.

"Morning, Doc," Sal said through the rear window.

The pleasantries extended to the stranger were not lost on Vinny as he exited the car to open the rear door and usher Dr. Parker into the rear seat next to Sal.

147

"Today," Sal said, "we are going to look at parts of the city you probably have never seen."

Their first stop was at the Miami shipyards where Sal went into great detail about how unnamed criminals extorted money from each shipping company and every union that worked on the docks. He explained how payments had to be made for any goods to be delivered or exported. Sal was very careful in detailing the criminal activities of others but was just as careful in omitting all events in which he was a participant. He never mentioned that this was the same dock where he and his cartel brought in large amounts of illegal narcotics and exported illegal weapons.

The entire tour was of a similar nature, with Sal exposing the crimes of others as if they were his own. Dr. Parker was none the wiser and was very excited with this inside look at the underworld at work. He was sure that this vein of exposure would lead to quite an usual and sought-after treatise.

Late in the afternoon, Sal told Vinny to return to the medical building where they first met Dr. Parker. Sal whispered something to Parker as he was getting out of the car and told him that he would see him in the morning.

At seven the next morning, Vinny again drove Sal to Dr. Parker's building and was surprised to find Dr. Parker standing out front with a suitcase and garment bag.

"Slight change in plans," Sal announced to Vinny.

Vinny got out and put Dr. Parker's bags in the trunk. He then held the door for him to get into the rear seat. Sal then directed Vinny to an apartment that was located not too far from Solly's Bar and Grill. Vinny waited in the car as Sal and Dr. Parker got out. Sal led the way.

It was a newly renovated four-plex in an area of town in need of renovation. There was a small courtyard in the front that appeared to have been freshly planted. Sal walked up to the second floor with Dr. Parker following closely behind. Sal unlocked the door and the two men entered. It was a nicely furnished, two-bedroom apartment with two baths.

"All the comforts of home," a beaming Sal said. "This is a strictly turn-key operation here, as I told you, Doc. All you have to provide is your clothes and toothbrush. Maybe not even that."

Sal proudly showed him the kitchen, which was stocked with food. There were canned vegetables, bottled water and tuna in the small pantry. Soft drinks and two types of beer were in the refrigerator and a bright blue bowl full of fresh apples sat on a counter top in the galley style kitchen.

After a quick inspection, they both sat in the living room.

"As I told you yesterday afternoon, Doc, I thought you would get a better feel for things if you could really immerse yourself into it. This way, you will get to experience things first hand and not just have me tell you how things are. I told you before, I just provide things that people want and in an honest way. There is a bar and grill not far from here called Solly's. It's also a bookie joint. I want you to hang around and get the feel of the place. Put down a few bets and see if the clientele is happy or not. We'll do this first and then we'll move on to something more exciting."

Sal then reached into his pocket and pulled out a thick wad of money, which looked like it had been well-fingered and counted.

"Here's six thousand dollars. I want you to place some bets in the next few weeks on whatever you want. Don't worry about the money. I'll get it back from the royalties from your book. Who knows, you might even get lucky and win a few bucks."

What Sal did next was even more unexpected. He reached into his inside coat pocket, producing a small leather case. He opened it and showed it to Parker. Inside the velvet-lined case was a small caliber revolver.

"This is for you," Sal said, handing him the gun.

"I don't think so," Parker said, holding his pink palms up and shaking his head. "If the neighborhood is that dangerous, maybe I had better call this off."

Sal laughed out loud. "This is a good neighborhood but any place can be dangerous. This is just for precautions."

Sal extended his arms, moving the case closer to Parker. He looked like a priest offering communion.

"Go on, take it. It's not loaded." *Not yet*, he thought.

Dr. Parker took the revolver from the case. It was nickel plated with a pearl handle. If he knew anything about guns he would have known that it was a .25 caliber short-nosed Smith & Wesson. He didn't have to know anything about guns to know it looked expensive and deadly. Parker caressed the gun in his hand and even allowed himself to pull the trigger, before giving it back to Sal.

"I just don't think so." Parker was adamant.

"All right, Doc," Sal said. "It's your call."

Sal held out the case for Parker to place the weapon into it. He then closed the case and put it back into his coat pocket.

Changing the subject, Sal got up and walked slowly toward the door. "Come on, I'll walk you over to Solly's place."

The two men walked down the street for about two blocks before turning east. At the end of the street, Dr. Parker could make out the flashing neon sign that read "Solly's."

Vinny had followed them in the car and was now waiting at the curb.

"Okay," Sal said. "You are now officially on your own."

"What do I do?" Parker sounded like a little lost boy. "After all, this type of wagering is illegal."

Sal had to bite his lip to keep from laughing. "Yes, bookmaking is illegal, but I tell you it goes on every day and in the open. So you just go into Solly's, make yourself at home, and observe what is going on. This is now the beginning of your new life on the street."

My street life, thought Parker. He began to hear the song "Street Life" playing in his head. As he walked toward Solly's, he began to hum the tune the Crusaders and Randy Crawford made famous.

"Street life. You can run away from time.
Street life. For a nickel, for a dime.
Street life. There's a thousand parts to play.
Street life, until you play your life away."

When this episode was over, he was going to have to see if he could find that song at the record store. He wondered why they still called them record stores since they no longer sold records. Only compact discs and cassettes.

Solly's place was noisy and reeked of liquor and grease. Actually, Solly's was a bar and grill. Parker sat down and looked at a worn menu, which consisted entirely of sandwiches—most of which were variations of a hamburger. Number one was a plain hamburger with fries. Number two was a cheeseburger. Number three was a cheeseburger with lettuce and tomatoes and so on. In addition, you could also get a grilled sausage on a bun, or hot pastrami on rye.

After taking a seat on a barstool, Parker noticed patrons, one by one, going over to sit with a middle-aged guy at a black and red striped banquette near the rear of the restaurant and then returning to their seats.

This was Solly. A full head of tousled gray hair, medium build with a slight paunch. Sad doe-brown eyes and a wrinkled face that could no longer resist the pull of gravity. His clothes appeared two sizes too large and looked disheveled as if he had slept in them, which he oftentimes did in his small office behind the bar.

Soon Parker had a racing form in his hand and placed his first bet. He used his own money as he had not separated the wad of money Sal had given him. He wasn't naive enough to pull out that much money anywhere in the entire United States of America, much less this place.

The races were played through speakers at the tables, at which you could adjust the volume. Other sports activities could be watched on televisions which were more numerous than patrons today. Parker quickly figured that Solly had to have a satellite dish or two to get this much coverage.

After losing four races in a row, Parker decided to return to his new address. Making sure the door was locked, and then retreating to the bedroom, he took out the money that Sal had given him and counted it. He thought it would be offensive to have done that in front of Sal. He was right. Six thousand dollars exactly. John McIlvane seemed to be a man of his word.

Over the next several weeks, the transition from his daily routine as a practicing psychiatrist to that of a degenerate gambler was much easier than Dr. Parker had anticipated. It did not take him long to blend into the flow of things at Solly's. He would get up early, shower and dress casually, which meant no neck tie. A new phenomenon for him. He would then walk slowly to Solly's, sometimes taking the long way just to enjoy the morning. It had been many years since he had enjoyed the mornings.

Dr. Parker would arrive at Solly's with the early birds and they would all have coffee and bagels, while they studied the daily racing forms. Early morning was the time for studying the forms and swapping stories. Almost everyone had one about the day they couldn't lose a bet, or the years when they couldn't win one.

A common thread among the regulars was having to be in what they called "the action," yet being resigned to their fate as losers. Dr. Parker concluded that gamblers and farmers must be the most superstitious people on earth. Maybe it was because they had invested their lives totally in something over which they had very little control. If the regulars at Solly had little control over the outcome of events, Sal—still known as John McIlvane to Evan Parker—had quite a bit of control. He had given Dr. Parker three "hunches" of his to play one day last week and told him to bet only on those races.

Dr. Parker did just that and had three very big winners. All of which earned him the envy and respect of the regulars and the scorn of Solly. Parker and Solly even had an argument about it when Solly tried to lower the amount that Parker had placed on the second race. Solly had to give in when two of the regulars said they heard the bet being made.

Many of the old-timers admired how Parker stood up to Solly and insisted on his fair winnings, which he used to buy drinks and greasy sandwiches all around. With Sal's help that day, Evan Parker took home an extra sixteen hundred dollars.

Evan Parker never had any illusions about being a real player, because over the next few days he had managed to lose all of his winnings and a good portion of the six thousand. Dr. Parker was, however, very pleased with the research for his book. Many of the guys were pouring their hearts out to him. He became known as an easy touch. Subsequently, Parker learned not only about the degenerate gambling lifestyle of the regular patrons at Solly's, but soon saw the resultant tragedies of any friends or relatives unfortunate enough to care for or rely upon any of Solly's patrons.

Parker could never understand the animosity he had generated in Solly by having just one winning streak. He could not have known that Solly was in a tight squeeze between a pretty young girlfriend and some of his roughshod cohorts.

Later in the week, Sal came by with a few more hunches for Parker. Evan thought that it was wrong to take money from Solly if the races were fixed and he told Sal so. Sal said to do it just to get in close to the guys at the joint and if he felt so guilty about it, then just gamble it all back using his own infallible method for losing. They both laughed and Parker thought that this was fair.

This day held no amusement for Solly, when Parker's luck with large bets seemed to be beyond reproach. Parker made sure that there were witnesses to all of the betting and demanded his payments, which totaled more than twenty-two hundred dollars. He could have won much more, but he figured that this was about the amount he could easily lose in the time he had allotted himself for this phase of his research. Solly paid the money, but with much hostility, and Parker and Solly had to be separated by two of the regulars.

Dr. Parker had told his wife that he was going underground to do some research on a book but left it at that. He knew she trusted him totally and imagined that the whole mysterious episode would add a little excitement to their lives as he told her all of the stories later. He called her every few days to see how she was getting along.

She always seemed glad to hear from him and always seemed to be doing fine. He was pleased that he had chosen to marry such an independent person.

Although Dr. Parker was not a physical person and hadn't engaged in any physical altercations since grade school, he had to admit to himself that he got some perverse pleasure from taking Solly's money, which he reminded himself he had no intention of keeping. Dr. Parker went to bed rehearsing the next day's scenario, and how he could maximize his irritation of Solly.

"Solly? Where are you, Solly?" Dr. Parker singsonged. "I've got the bet today that's going to make you close shop. Either that or you'll have to turn it over to me."

Dr. Parker smiled to himself. The thought of a psychiatrist running a bookie shop was very amusing to him. I'll bet I could get a thesis out of that. He was excited by the very thought.

The early morning quiet of the shop was not unusual. Parker had been the first one there many times in the early a. m. to study the racing forms and to get his caffeine jump-start.

Solly always left the front door open because he didn't want to miss any players or potential players. After all, what should he be afraid of? The police were paid off and the common thugs on the street knew if they interfered with whatever was going on inside there would be a considerable price to pay.

What Evan Parker did not know was that Sal had his people put the word out on the street that the police would raid Solly's. Sal had done this in a way that he could never be traced as the source of the rumor.

"Solly," he continued to yell. "Come on out. What are you afraid of?"

He found Solly in his small cluttered office. Solly was sitting in a chair, facing the door, staring at him. The only telltale sign of injury was a small puncture wound in his forehead. Parker had seen gunshot wounds previously and was quite sure that this was one. He was also sure that Solly was dead. Solly was never going to be afraid of anything anymore.

A curious thing happens when the human mind encounters a horrific situation. There is an immediate suspension of belief. Although Dr. Parker had seen many corpses in his life, he had never seen one outside of a clinical setting.

IS THIS REAL? he thought.

The next thing he saw almost sent him into convulsions. A small shell casing. He was no expert but he knew it was from a small caliber weapon. Probably the same caliber as the gun McIlvane had shown him. Probably from the same gun McIlvane had shown him. The gun that McIlvane had asked if he wanted to keep. The gun that he had handled. The gun that he was sure still had his fingerprints all over it.

COULD THIS REALLY BE HAPPENING?

He backed out of the room. Slowly at first, but soon with more speed and deliberation. In fact, he backed out of the whole bar, knocking over two barstools and a table on the way out of the door. His eyes had not fully readjusted to the light as he stepped onto the sidewalk, but he walked briskly away from the bar, jostling two passersby as he fled. He could barely overcome his urge to run down the street. He could barely overcome his urge to scream at the top of his lungs.

WHAT TO DO? WHAT SHOULD HE DO? WHAT COULD HE DO? He eased back out of the shop, closing the door softly behind him.

His mind was racing furiously as he walked briskly and determinedly away from Solly's. He had no destination but he did have an objective and that was to put as much distance between him and Solly's as possible.

I must be walking too fast, he thought. I feel lightheaded and dizzy. He sat on a bench at a bus stop but his shortness of breath continued. He felt numbness in his arms and lips, and his chest began to hurt.

"Oh hell, I'm hyperventilating," he said to himself. He gulped slow deep breaths, put his head in his lap and tried to relax.

It must have been a set up from the beginning, he thought. But why? What possible reason would McIlvane have for doing this to him or to anyone? Had he been chosen at random or was he chosen specifically for some reason as yet unknown to him? There would hopefully be time to sort that out later, but now he needed short-term goals and solutions. Like where am I going to go now?

He surmised that it would not be logical to return to the apartment, his home or office. Since this was a set up in the first place, the police may have already been notified.

He was only partially correct. The North Miami police department would not receive an anonymous tip until later that afternoon.

The bus driver pulled over to pick up a well-dressed man sitting at the bus stop. He was only mildly surprised when the man waved him on. He had seen plenty on this route.

Dr. Parker got up and began to walk again. Maybe he should have gotten on the bus. He decided he would get on the next one. Meanwhile, he spotted a phone booth in the distance. He walked into the phone booth which had a stench of urine and alcohol. He only hoped the phone worked.

He didn't have the correct change and put three dimes into the pay phone. Ordinarily this would have bothered him. Today was anything but ordinary. He prayed that Cassie was at home.

The phone rang three times before the answering machine clicked on. The message was in Cassie's voice.

"Hello, this is the Parker residence. We are not able to come to the phone right now, but if you would leave your name and number, we will return your call as soon as possible."

"Cassie, pick up if you're there ...."

"Hello, Evan, I was wondering if you were going to call today, I wanted to tell you about ..."

"Cassie," he interrupted, "I have some bad news and I want you to listen carefully. I'm in trouble, big trouble ...."

"What happened?" Cassie asked.

"Just listen please," said Evan harshly. "This is hard enough without your interrupting me. I'm pretty sure I'm going to be blamed for a murder..."

"A murder!" Cassie screamed.

"Will you shut up for a minute," he responded in a tone that was unfamiliar but frightening to her.

"A murder which I did not commit. I have been framed in a most clever and complicated manner and I don't know why. I would turn myself in but the evidence against me would be overwhelming at this point. Therefore, I must try to unravel this by myself and try to make some sense of it all."

As he talked, his breathing became more rapid and shallow.

"I have to get some proof that I am totally innocent. I don't know when or if I can call you again. I'm sure the police will monitor all of your calls pretty soon."

"But what am I supposed to do?" Cassie cried, unable to control herself any longer. "I have very important friends now who may not understand that you are innocent. What am I supposed to do for money? You haven't worked for weeks now and the bank account is nearly empty. How am I supposed to live?"

He couldn't believe his ears.

"I always thought you were self-centered," he said evenly, "but I guess I didn't know the extent of it. I'm scared to death, standing in a filthy phone booth, telling you that I'm going to be accused of a capital crime and you're worried about what your friends are going to think. You're going to regret this selfishness. I can promise you that. I can't talk anymore. I see the bus coming."

Evan hung up the phone and stepped out of the phone booth, its sickening sweet odor lingering in his nostrils.

He flagged the bus and climbed the two steps to the seated driver. Again he discovered that he did not have the correct change as he handed the driver a five-dollar bill.

The driver wearily pointed to a sign above his head.

EXACT CHANGE ONLY.

He hadn't ridden a bus in years. Feeling too self-conscious to ask any of the passengers for change and risk bringing anymore unwanted attention to himself, he gave the five-dollar bill to the bus driver, a young Hispanic male in his twenties. Before the driver could respond, he told him to keep the change. As he calmly strolled to his seat, he noticed that the driver did not put any money into the change collector. Dr. Parker sat in an unoccupied row of seats by the window and released an audible sigh.

He tried to gather his thoughts and his nerves together as the bus lurched erratically from the curb. He could only surmise that his life and this bus ride were very similar, in that they both seemed out of control and were headed for some unknown destination.

The apathetic driver at the terminal awakened him.

"End of the line," shouted the driver as he shook Parker's shoulder.

Parker smiled feebly, wiped the sleep from his eyes and prayed that the driver's statement wasn't prophetic.

Evan Parker figured that the bus had taken him a good distance from where he started. And that was good. He figured that he was lost, but not hopelessly so. And that was not so bad. As he focused on his surroundings, he figured he was in a very rough part of the city. And that was bad.

He walked slowly out of the terminal in the direction of some brightly-lit buildings. It was now early evening and Parker correctly deduced that he must have ridden the entire bus route several times. He shuddered at the thought of passing Solly's.

He passed several colorful characters inside and outside of the terminal. Most of whom asked for money.

He felt very out of place, which in reality he was. Dr. Parker searched through his jacket pockets and, without looking at the items, put all of the contents into his front pants pockets. He decided that if he got rid of the jacket he would look less like a victim. Folding his jacket over his arm, he gave it to the next panhandler that approached him.

"Thanks for nothing, man," the panhandler shouted through rotted, yellow teeth. "I need some money, not a stupid coat. What am I supposed to do with this? Give me some money and you can have your coat back."

Evan did not respond, but continued to walk away from the stranger, who. angrily threw the coat to the pavement and leered at him until he was out of sight.

Evan Parker kept walking and did not stop until he reached the lobby of the Ambassador Hotel. He did not know how far he had walked but he was exhausted. He sat down in a threadbare orange velvet overstuffed chair in the hotel lobby. The chair reeked of years of cigarette smoke. It was covered with food stains and he hesitated to think of what else. The springs were worn out from time immemorial but it was the most comfortable chair he had ever sat in, in his life.

He would have fallen asleep again if not for the desk manager.

"No loitering here," he shouted from behind the safety of his screened-in cubicle. "This is a respectable place."

His voice startled Evan and he wondered if this dilapi-dated firetrap ever had a breath of respectability. If this ever were a respectable hotel, he thought, it had certainly fallen a considerable distance from grace. The parallels with his own life were too easy for a man of his intellect to waste time pondering. He pulled himself out of the chair and approached the desk clerk. As he approached the desk, the clerk's eyes widened and he retreated as far as possible in his small space.

"I don't want any trouble," he pleaded. "I was just telling you the rules."

Fred Winter was a mousy fellow with a receding hairline, half-veiled eyes and a small Hitlerish mustache. He wore a soiled long-sleeved white shirt and black pants, held up by black clip-on suspenders. A black tie hung loosely from his shirt which had the top two buttons unfastened. He wore a plaid vest that was too small, even for a man who weighed all of one hundred thirty pounds and was nearly six feet tall. This eclectic ensemble was topped off with a khaki cap with a green transparent visor.

Although he had not looked in a mirror since he left the apartment early in the day, Dr. Parker could only imagine what his appearance must be to frighten a desk clerk, who must have seen quite a lot in this transient hotel.

"I'd like a room, if one is available," Parker said in his most reassuring voice, trying to calm the desk clerk.

"Rooms are six dollars a night or forty dollars for the week," Fred said. "Payable in advance." His confidence was making a modest comeback.

Dr. Parker reached into his wallet, being careful not to show its entire contents, and handed the clerk forty dollars.

"I assume the rooms have private baths," Parker said.

"Of course," the clerk responded. "I told you, this is a respectable place."

"Of course," Parker said sarcastically. "And I'd like a receipt, please."

Frowning, the clerk scratched his balding head and began to search for the receipt book. After a few minutes, he produced an enormous worn ledger that looked as if it had not been opened since the hotel was built. In a sweeping motion, he wiped the dust from the cover with his shirt sleeve and turned the yellowed pages until he came to one that contained blank receipts.

"Who should I make it out to?" the clerk asked, smiling broadly, showing several missing and soon-to-be-missing teeth.

"John Smith," Parker said, caught totally off-guard. "That's Smyth with a 'y,' he said, trying to make a small recovery.

"Is that first name spelled 'J-O-H-N,' or 'J-O-N'?" the clerk asked, smiling to himself, just enough to let Parker see.

"J-O-H-N ," said Parker tediously.

"J-O-H-N S-M-Y-T-H," the clerk spelled slowly and deliberately.

"Here's your receipt, Mr. Smyth. And here is your room key. Your room number is 216. Second floor, third door on the right. Is there any luggage you'll be needing assistance with?" he asked, obviously enjoying himself at this point.

"No," Parker said. "I'll bring it up myself later."

161

"Naturally. Do enjoy your stay," he said, as he mockingly bowed from the waist.

After witnessing Fred's theatrics, Dr. Parker walked toward the ancient staircase, not trusting the ancient elevator. Fred returned his attention to a small black and white television which had a wire coat hanger for an antenna.

As he wearily climbed the stairs, Evan Parker became mildly depressed at the prospect of living in the Ambassador Hotel for a week. He turned the key and entered his room, becoming moderately depressed at his immediate surroundings.

Sparse would be an understatement.

A chair with three legs was propped against the far wall. A metal desk with more rust than paint, and a reading lamp that flickered for a full minute before going dark, were situated near the door. Opposite this area, a full three feet away, stood a four-drawer dresser of the same ilk as the desk, whose drawers were rusted and frozen in various degrees of open. There was a single bed covered with a chenille bedspread which was sprinkled with cigarette burns.

He walked to the bathroom which did not have a door and observed the toilet, which thankfully had a seat but no cover. There was a shower stall enclosed with a curtain that was heavy with mildew and a cracked mirror hung askew over a sink striped with rust stains.

As he looked in the mirror, he became profoundly depressed. The image reflected back to him was not his own. Small wonder that the desk clerk had been alarmed. His hair was unkempt as was his whole appearance. His clothes were not just soiled but dirty. His whole appearance was askew. It was as if he had his clothes on sideways.

The most disturbing feature was his face. The look in his eyes was familiar to him, but not on his own face. He had seen it many times in the faces of his patients. It was the look of an impending mental breakdown.

Sitting on the bed, he could not decide if he was more tired or hungry. He decided to lie down for awhile and then find a spot to get something to eat. He was fairly certain that the Ambassador Hotel did not have room service and he was definitely certain that if they did have it, he would not want it.

Not anticipating that his nap would become a coma, Evan Parker awakened ten hours later at nine o'clock in the morning. He decided that this would be a good time to take inventory of himself and of his possessions. Standing up and emptying his pockets onto the bed, he began to examine the items.

First, he picked up his leather key case, which contained the keys for his condominium, his car, his office, the apartment that Sal had rented for him and two keys that he had carried around for three years and had no idea what they were for. He then picked up his address book that contained all of his important phone numbers and addresses. He wondered how important or useful any of them would be to him now. He then fondled the bullet casing which he did not even remember picking up at Solly's. Deciding to keep it for now, he pushed it deeply between the mushy pillow and its tattered pillowcase.

Lastly, he examined his wallet. It contained one expired credit card, an auto club card, his driver's license and his license to practice medicine in the state of Florida. He looked at the date of issue and the date of expiration of his medical license and wondered if this would be his last medical license. He laughed to himself when he concluded that he might also be looking at his last driver's license.

Opening the billfold section of his wallet, he removed the receipt that the desk clerk had given him and approximately five thousand dollars, which was what was left of the money that Sal had given him to place wagers at Solly's. He hoped that five thousand dollars wouldn't have to last him the rest of his life. He also hoped that the rest of his life would outlast the five thousand dollars.

Dr. Evan Parker wearily stood up, took off his clothes and walked four steps from his bed into the shower.

The shower consisted of a shower head. Rusted.

One hot and one cold handle. Rusted.

A drain in the floor. Rusted.

A semicircular curtain rod. Rusted.

And lukewarm water. Rusted.

The Ambassador Hotel had supplied him with a small bar of soap, which he inspected for any foreign matter although it was wrapped and sealed. The hotel also supplied one bath towel and a washcloth. Both were so thin they were almost transparent. The hotel management had thoughtfully placed these items on the tank of the toilet.

As he showered he made a mental list of some of the necessities he would have to purchase. The first of which would be a pair of rubber thongs for his feet, because as he showered he swore that his feet would never touch that shower floor again, even if he had to wear his street shoes.

After disgusting himself, by putting on his soiled clothes again, Parker hit the streets.

He managed to locate a small corner store that looked as if it started life as a grocery store, but had gradually evolved to serve the needs of the neighborhood. In addition to groceries, one could purchase toiletries, underclothes, tools and even small appliances.

He then discovered a second-hand store where he bought several shirts, pants and even found a comfortable pair of loafers. On the way back to the hotel, he stopped at a small restaurant that he had passed earlier. He ordered a bowl of soup, a hamburger, fries and a slice of apple pie.

To his surprise the food wasn't bad. It was awful.

Entering the Ambassador Hotel, Evan Parker, laden with packages, heard a familiar but irritating voice.

"Good day, Mr. Smyth. Would you like some help with your luggage?"

Caught by surprise, it took Evan a few beats to realize to whom the desk clerk was speaking. "No, thank you," Parker said, "I can manage."

"As you wish," Fred replied, showing his now familiar Jack O'Lantern smile. "No cooking allowed," he shouted playfully after Parker, who was now halfway up the stairs. "Those are the rules."

Closing the door to his room, Evan began to talk aloud to himself. "If this is going to be my home and base of operation, I might as well make it as livable as possible."

He smiled to himself as he looked around the room. At first he wondered how a room could be rented at such a cheap rate. Now he was sure that Fred Winter was severely overcharging him.

Dr. Parker began to fill a small Styrofoam cooler with ice. He then placed a quart of orange juice, two one-liter bottles of spring water, and a package of assorted luncheon meats into the cooler before fitting the lid snugly into place. On the lid he set a small loaf of wheat bread and a half dozen apples.

Removing the threadbare, cigarette-tortured bedspread, he replaced it with one he had bought at the second-hand store. He then hung his shirts and pants on a coat hook that was attached to the entrance door to his room. He covered the top of the decaying desk with a sheet of aluminum foil before placing his newly acquired toilet articles on it. Evander Parker, M.D., then put on a pair of heavy gauge rubber gloves and proceeded to clean every surface of the room with Pine-Sol.

Hours later, with that unpleasant task completed, he decided to clean himself. Unable to find the rubber thongs he was searching for, he entered the shower with a pair of cheap sneakers. After this shower, he felt refreshed but was perplexed as to why he felt lightheaded and had a slight headache until his nose started to burn from the overpowering smell of pine. He cracked the door open that led to the hallway, having given up on trying to open the room's solitary window yesterday.

"Now to catch up on the news," he said aloud, trying to amuse himself as he unfolded the newspaper he bought. As he began to read, he could hear the voice of the clerk downstairs, through the cracked door. It reminded him of what Fred Winter had said. "No cooking." Who would be dumb enough to try and cook in this fire trap .... Tomorrow he was going to try to find a portable smoke alarm, if there was such a thing. He also made a mental note to look for an alarm clock radio.

It was somewhat comforting to see that at least he was not on the front page of the Miami Herald. Renewed interest in a scandal at City Hall and increased instability in the Middle East had rescued him from that honor. Thank heaven for corrupt politicians, he thought. The article that was written about him was not as far from the front page of the Herald as he would have wished. He would have preferred, for instance, the Peruvian Sentinel.

The picture accompanying the article had been three years old when he had given it to the Medical Society when he first applied for his Florida license. For that he was grateful, since he now only slightly resembled that picture—on a good day. And with respect to the kind of days he'd been having in the last forty-eight hours, he had almost no resemblance to that picture at all.

PROMINENT PHYSICIAN SOUGHT IN MURDER OF TAVERN OWNER.

THE MURDER SEEMS TO HAVE OCCURRED AS A RESULT OF A MONETARY DISPUTE.

The article went on to describe the crime scene with which he was all too familiar. The last sentence of the article left him shivering.

THE SUSPECT IS TO BE CONSIDERED ARMED AND DANGEROUS.

Evan Parker got up shakily and closed the door. He sat on the bed and held his head in his hands because it was spinning

166

furiously out of control. And this time it wasn't from the smell of pine.

He didn't remember falling asleep but remembered how badly he felt before he did. He raided the Styrofoam cooler for the bottle of orange juice and tried to think of what to do next.

"Ms. Kennedy," he said to himself.

He pulled out his address book and decided to call her. He was sure she had seen the article by now, but he was just as certain that she knew him well enough not to believe such a thing. Besides, he needed her help. She was the only other person to see the mysterious Mr. McIlvane. She could help to corroborate his story and possibly help him find the real bad actor in this play.

"Here it is," he said, looking at a dog-eared page in his simulated leather book. "Rita Kennedy."

Although they had worked together for almost fourteen years, Dr. Parker had only called Ms. Kennedy at her home on one other occasion. That was when he had lost his keys to the office and could not find the security guard. She was very obliging and came right over to help him even though it was late in the evening.

He apologized profusely, explaining that he needed to review some records for a deposition the following morning. She was quite pleasant and even stayed until he was finished. He was always grateful to her for that kindness.

The only things he knew about her life outside of the office had come from the conversation they had after she let him into the office. She had never been married, had worked in a secretarial pool for the government, and then retired. Six months after retiring, she decided to return to the work force and answered his advertisement for a receptionist.

She immediately impressed him with her professionalism and was hired, even though she was only the second person he interviewed. She also mentioned that she had a cousin named Vance, her only living relative, who lived in Fort Lauderdale.

Parker had written the name Vance in parentheses beside her name so that from time to time he could remember it and ask, "How is your cousin Vance?"

There was no phone in the room, so he walked into the dimly lit hallway to place his call. The area around this phone was not as foul as the last public phone he had used, but it was not better by much. The carpeting in the hall looked as if it had not been changed or cleaned since the hotel was constructed and it reeked of years of abuse. This time he had the correct change and dialed the number written in his book for Rita Kennedy.

"Hello?" a male voice answered.

"Uh, hello," Parker answered weakly, surprised at the sound of a man's voice.

Parker immediately decided that he must stop being put off balance so easily by unexpected developments during this surrealistic time in his life.

"Is this 555-3412?" Parker asked a little more authoritatively.

"Yes, it is," the man replied politely.

"May I speak with Rita Kennedy?" he asked.

"Can I tell her who's calling?"

"Yes. Tell her it's her cousin Vance," said Parker, now more poised and hoping Vance was still in Ft. Lauderdale.

"Just a minute," said the voice.

After a brief while, another male voice spoke into the phone.

"Hello?"

"Hello," said Parker, determined to hold his own.

"Is this Vance Kennedy?" the voice asked.

"Yes, it is," replied Parker, his confidence slowly growing.

"This is Lt. Baskins of the Miami Police Department. We were just about to give you a call. I'm afraid we have some bad news for you."

Parker did not reply.

"If you're in town, maybe you should come over so that I can speak to you in person. This is not the type of information people like to hear. Especially over the phone."

"Please tell me what you have to say," Parker said, now genuinely apprehensive and intrigued.

"Your cousin Rita has been murdered. It seems she was the victim of a burglar that she interrupted during the night. It appears that she was struck on the head with some sort of blunt instrument. Of course, that's not the final and official version yet, but that appears to be pretty much what's happened."

Parker could not believe his ears. If the phone had not been wedged between two walls at the end of the corridor, he would have crumpled onto the filthy floor.

He could not speak. He did hear the voice at the other end of the phone asking if he was alright and shouting hello over and over, but nothing mattered to him at that point. He managed to cradle the receiver and walked unsteadily back to his room.

The Police Department, in its superb efficiency, would not be puzzled when the real Vance Kennedy called two days later after reading about his cousin's death in the newspaper.

Evan decided that he had done enough investigating for the day and prepared a sandwich from his makeshift refrigerator.

He noted that he would have to replace his ice every twenty hours or so. As he lay in the bed, hoping for sleep to come, he felt tears well up in his eyes. He wasn't sure, however, if they were for Ms. Kennedy or for himself.

That night Evan Parker had a dream within a dream. In his dream, his life was very normal and nothing adverse had occurred. However, when he went to sleep in this dream, he dreamed of all the horrible things that had occurred. When the Evan Parker in the dream awakened everything was as perfect as it had ever been.

When the actual Evan Parker woke up that morning and appraised his immediate surroundings, he was electrified back to reality.

Sitting on the edge of the bed, Dr. Evan Parker concluded that Ms. Kennedy's demise was no accident and that if he was ever going to clear himself he had better try to retrieve the files on John McIlvane from his office. A task that he had been going to ask Ms. Kennedy to assist him with. He had the keys to the office, but was sure the building would be watched. He was not sure what he would do when he got to the building, but he felt that he must proceed with urgency.

The oversized T-shirt he used as a nightshirt was moist with perspiration. He usually slept in the nude, but he wanted as little of this room to come into contact with him as possible. He showered, washed the T-shirt and hung it in the bathroom to dry, put on his second set of clothes, and walked to the phone.

"Number for the Miami Transit Authority?" he asked of the information operator, assuming the phone directory would be missing. It was.

He called the city's public transportation system and got directions from where he was, to where he wanted to be. If all of the connections were on time, the trip would take a little less than two hours. One way.

While riding toward his office, Dr. Evander Parker, psychiatrist, tried to prepare himself for all possible variations on this tragic theme. What if the police had cordoned off his floor or changed the locks on the doors? What if the police questioned everyone going in the building? He decided to try and relax and deal with the situation that presented itself when he arrived at the office. He was determined not to let his fears get the better of him.

"The police can't question everyone going into a seven-story building," he said to himself, causing the two passengers riding in front of him to turn around.

Parker was trying desperately not to let his imagination run amok. One thing he was not concerned about was that anyone would recognize him as he hardly recognized himself when he looked in the mirror and he certainly knew who he was. His facial hair was starting to fill in and he purposely did not comb his hair.

He wore an extra large plaid flannel shirt outside a pair of threadbare jeans. He had tucked the jeans inside some knee-high horizontally striped red and white leg warmers that were rolled down to mid-calf. He also had on a pair of black army boots without laces which were wrapped at the top, ankle and toes with silver duct tape. He had the homeless look down-pat.

He got off the bus, two stops before necessary, and began to walk to his former office building. As he turned the corner to get his first view of the building that had been such a central part of his life, his deepest fears and his wildest imagination could not have prepared him for what he saw. He did not even try to approach the building. He just sat on the curb and stared in disbelief as long as he could, before he buried his face in his hands and began to shake uncontrollably.

The entire floor on which his suite was located was engulfed in flames. The fire department was already on the scene and was now trying to save the rest of the building and to protect the surrounding structures.

At least, he thought, *Mr. McIlvvane and his accomplices were kind enough to wait until the weekend when the building would not be fully occupied.*

"Do you need some help?" a petite woman in a nurse's uniform asked. She hovered over Parker who was still shaking, but now almost lying on the curbside. "I can help you to the hospital. It's not too far away," she said, thinking he was going through alcohol withdrawal or worse.

"No. No, thank you," he said, sitting upright on the curb. "I'll be alright."

The nurse, whom he now recognized as the young woman Hitch had sent to summon him from the waiting room area, then reached into her purse and put a folded dollar bill

171

into his shirt pocket before walking on. Evan Parker could not conceive of his life being any worse than this.

Unfortunately, before long, he would consider these the good old days.

Evan Parker, Ivy League graduate, did not remember how he got back to the Ambassador Hotel. He was just grateful that Fred Winter was nowhere in sight.

Closing the door to his room, he exhaled. "I'm glad to be home." He fell back onto the bed, which almost collapsed to the floor. Staring at the peeling ceiling, he wondered when he began to think of this room as home.

Evan Parker never smoked, rarely drank alcohol and never even tried marijuana in college. So it was hard for him to figure why he suddenly wanted some crack.

"Lighten up," he said to himself. "There's always light at the end of the tunnel. Even if it's a locomotive." He smiled for the first time in over forty-eight hours.

"No more thinking for this brain today," he said. He then picked up the only book in the room, which was a Gideon Bible. "Those Gideons must be very thorough and brave in-dividuals to have placed a Bible in this hotel."

He placed the Bible on the windowsill and thought it would be better for him if he did not try to find an explanation there for what was occurring in his life. If it were Divine Justice, he didn't want to spend the rest of the night trying to determine just what he had done to deserve such punishment ... and if it were a test, he was failing miserably.

He downed a salami sandwich, with a bottle of spring water, and fell into a restless sleep.

At four a.m. in the morning, Evan Parker was roused by the loud sounds of two people next door trying to kill each other. He was hoping that Fred would not have to call the police, if indeed Fred ever called the police.

The commotion stopped as suddenly as it had started.

Good, he thought. *A short violent exchange.*

172

Unable to sleep, Evan walked to the cramped bathroom and splashed cold water from the tap on his face. Returning to the bed Parker sat and reviewed his options. There weren't many. Again he pulled out his address book, stopping at the name of Lt. Livingston Rolle.

Riiiiing.

The phone's shrill ring pierced Detective Second Grade Livingston Rolle's sound sleep.

It was four o'clock in the morning, he had worked three overtime shifts in the last week, and had just completed two extra hours of paperwork on a repeat felon who was probably out of the precinct on bail before Lt. Rolle reached home.

Riiiiing.

No, make that before he reached his house. His wife and daughter were living in what he had always considered home. He knew the divorce was mostly his fault but at the present time that didn't make him feel any better.

Riiiiing.

It could only be the Department calling. What unthinkable crime had been committed to prompt this call? He tried to imagine what it could be. He said a silent prayer, before he picked up the receiver. He prayed that whoever was on the other end would have a heart attack and die before the phone rang again, so that he could go back to sleep.

Riiiiing.

Another unanswered prayer. Lt. Rolle always prided himself on being a professional. He thought carefully about what he would say when he answered the phone. He did not want to appear unprepared for any situation that might have arisen. He wanted to sound in control. He slowly and deliberately picked up the receiver and said, "Unhh..."

"Rolle. Wake up. It's me, Dr. Parker."

"Who?" Rolle said.

"It's me, Dr. Evander Parker."

"Dr. Parker," Rolle replied, now a little more awake and sitting up in bed. "Where are you?"

"Doesn't matter," replied Parker. "I need help."

"You aren't kidding," said Rolle. "You're up to your elbows in it."

"That bad, huh?"

"Worse," Rolle said.

"How worse? ... I mean, how bad?" Parker asked nervously.

"You had motive, opportunity and there is physical evidence."

"Motive? What motive could I have possibly had?" Parker asked incredulously.

"Several witnesses have already testified that you lost large amounts of money to Solly over the past few weeks, and that the two of you argued publicly. And, furthermore, you had to be physically restrained on at least one occasion."

"But it wasn't even my money!" Evan shrieked into the phone.

"And you think that makes it better that you lost someone else's money?" Rolle said.

"No, you don't understand. Listen to me."

"No, you listen," Rolle interrupted. "Your fingerprints are all over the murder weapon, which we found in a small apatment you rented in North Miami. I think you'd better turn yourself in. In fact I'm ordering you to turn yourself in."

"I just can't right now," replied Parker. "Look, I need someone to help me."

"I can better help you if you bring yourself down to the station," Rolle answered.

"Don't start that with me," Parker laughed anxiously. "I taught the class on crisis mediation. Remember?"

"Oh, yeah. Right," Rolle said.

"I'm innocent," Parker declared. "You have to believe me. You know me from the classes and the private sessions we had in the evenings. You can't believe I'm capable of doing something like that."

Detective Rolle thought about that for a minute. After all, Dr. Parker did teach classes at the Police Academy and he had surely helped him through more than a few personal crises. In fact, if it hadn't been for Parker he was sure he would have swallowed a round from his service revolver. And Dr. Parker never charged him for the sessions.

But then again, he knew cherubic fourteen-year olds that had mutilated their parents beyond recognition. He knew sweet little old ladies that poisoned their boarders for their pension checks. He knew doctors, that looked like Marcus Welby, who administered deadly drugs to their patients.

"I was there for you when you needed me," Dr. Parker said, interrupting Rolle's thoughts.

"So I owe you one, huh, Doc?"

"Of course not," Dr. Parker said. "I was glad to be able to help you when you needed help."

Parker knew that if he said Rolle owed him, Rolle would take that as an insult and arrest him at the first opportunity. With Rolle's strong sense of duty, Dr. Parker was not sure this is not what he would do anyway. To get Rolle to help him was a calculated risk but a real risk that Parker had to take. He knew he couldn't survive on the streets without help.

Finally, Rolle spoke. "I'm going to give you a name and a number. Don't call before tomorrow, give me a chance to let him know what's going on. And, Doc?"

"Yes," Parker said.

"This conversation never happened."

The late afternoon sun was very hot in Little Havana. The sights, sounds and smells of Cuba were everywhere. For an instant, Dr. Evander Parker was able to relax and ingest the beauty of his surroundings. The atmosphere was so imbued with the essence of the people that it was palpable. Two little girls in brightly-colored outfits brushed past him.

Almost costumes, he thought.

There was the unmistakable sound of Aldelberto Alvarez and Son 14 emanating from a jukebox in one of the restaurants. And that wasn't all that was coming from the restaurants. The smells of roasted pork, garlic, thyme and so many other savory aromas immediately made him hungry, although he had eaten a sandwich less than thirty minutes ago.

He was sitting on a bench in a small park, more like a plaza, with Latin America all around him. If he weren't a wanted felon, it would have been a very pleasant afternoon. He was sitting exactly where Taylor Nash, Private Investigator, whom he had spoken to earlier that day, had told him to sit. Nash had told him to be there at approximately two o'clock and to sit on the bench facing Primo Groceria.

It wouldn't take much of an investigator to recognize him, thought Parker, as his face had been on the television and newspaper almost daily. He only hoped no one else would recognize him. They had both agreed that Little Havana would be less of a risk.

Investigator Nash told Parker that he would be wearing red shoes. *Red shoes*, Parker thought. Emmett Kelly was the only man he could think of that could pull off wearing red shoes, and that was because he was a clown. Parker hoped that Nash wasn't a clown.

As a man in red shoes approached him, Evander Parker felt perspiration start to form on his forehead and run in rivulets down his face. As he took in the form and being of Taylor Nash, Parker was sure of his imminent arrest.

Nash looked too much like everyone's idea of a private investigator to be real. This had to be a set up. Parker thought about trying to run, but he knew that Nash would not be working alone. Plainclothesmen were probably all around him and sharpshooters had their weapons trained at his head.

Would they shoot to kill if he tried to escape, he wondered? Why not? came the immediate answer.

After all, he was a fugitive wanted for murder. And he was considered armed and dangerous. That's what was printed in the paper and that's what they said on the eleven o'clock news. The first time he heard it, he wondered who they were referring to. He would never get accustomed to anyone thinking of him as armed and dangerous.

Taylor Nash's figure enlarged with every graceful stride, reminding him of a black panther.

Parker figured him to be about thirty-eight years old, six-feet three inches tall, two hundred thirty pounds. Even under his Palm Beach sport coat you could tell this was a powerfully-built man. Nash wore a no-nonsense look. His eyes were a piercing brown and his face looked as if it had been chiseled from a solid piece of black granite. Jim Brown in sportswear, thought Parker, trying to amuse himself.

"Dr. Parker?" Nash asked rhetorically.

Parker could not move, he was afraid to stand or extend his hand. *NO SUDDEN MOVES OR YOU'RE A DEAD MAN,* he thought.

"Yes," he said weakly.

"I'm Taylor Nash. Come with me."

Come with me, Parker thought. He expected him to start the conversation with "You have the right to remain silent" or "on the ground, dirt bag."

"OK," said Parker. "Where are we going?"

"Right over here to this restaurant," Nash said, pointing. "I'm famished."

"Me, too," Parker said, resuming full breaths.

Fiona's Cuban Food stood off from the main street so Parker felt a little safer. He was so upset, he couldn't take in the Cuban decor of fishnets on the ceilings, bongos, and maracas strategically placed in the corners. Nash tried to make an obviously shaken Dr. Parker feel at ease.

"This is a very good restaurant," Nash said. "Have you eaten here before?"

Parker just shook his head as he stared listlessly at the menu, which was in Spanish and English.

"What looks good to you?" Nash asked.

"I don't know," Evan said. "I'm not too familiar with Cuban food."

How could anyone live in Miami and not be familiar with Cuban food, thought Taylor, *this guy must be a geek.*

"I'll order for us both," Nash said. "That okay with you?"

Parker nodded his head, folded the menu and placed it on the table.

When the waiter came over, Nash gave their order, in fluent if not perfect Spanish.

"So you speak Spanish," Parker said, trying to make small talk.

"I grew up in Miami," Nash said, "and my parents thought it would be dumb not to learn Spanish, since it was so prevalent. It has really come in handy more than once in my business."

"I wish I could speak another language," Parker said.

"Most people do." Nash eyed Parker suspicously.

The waiter brought out appetizers of grilled shrimp and fish. This was followed by Cuban sandwiches which consists of Swiss cheese, roast pork, country style ham and dill pickle slices on buttered French bread that is pressed dry cleaner style on a hot grill. The meal was accompanied by large glasses of guyrapo. And for dessert they both had flan.

His hunger sated, Nash looked directly at Parker. "Time for business."

Parker related the sequence of events, as they had occurred, from the time John McILvane walked into his office, until he discovered Solly's body. He then looked at Nash. "I didn't kill him."

Nash did not reply, but believed him instantly. No one could be that stupid and then make up such an unbelievable story. Not even this geeky doctor.

"What did you do after you found the body?" Nash asked.

"I did the only thing I could think of," Parker said. "I ran."

"Where did you run to?"

Behind that preposition, Parker was tempted to say, but he didn't think this was the time to correct Nash's English.

"The Ambassador Hotel," Parker replied.

"The Ambassador on Southwest 23rd?"

"The very same," Parker looked around suspiciously.

"Oh, man," Nash laughed. "You stood a better chance of getting killed in that place, than by the police or your Mr. McIlvane."

Nash continued to laugh."You must have a guardian angel."

"Yes," Parker said. "I should have guessed that by the way things have been going for me lately."

"Speaking of the way things are going for you lately. Have you seen today's paper?" Nash asked.

"No, I haven't."

With some effort, Nash slid his large frame out of the banquette and walked over to a man standing behind the cash register. They exchanged words in Spanish and the man reached under the counter, producing a well-read newspaper. Nash and the paper returned to the booth. This time he sat on the same side of the table as Evan Parker. Nash searched the paper briefly and then placed a folded section between Parker and himself.

The Headline read: SEARCH INTENSIFIES FOR FUGITIVE DOCTOR

Doctor Evan Parker, wanted for questioning in the slaying of tavern owner Solly Weinstein, is now a suspect in the murder of his former receptionist Rita Kennedy. Ms. Kennedy was found slain in her home four days ago and was at first

179

thought to be the victim of a robbery homicide. New evidence indicates that there was no robbery. Furthermore, Dr. Parker is being sought in connection with the arson fire of his office, which was leased in the Townsend Medical Building.

The fourth floor where Dr. Parker's office was located was completely destroyed. Intense smoke and heat and water damage to the rest of the building resulted in substantial property losses. No damage was sustained to any surrounding property. If anyone has any information regarding Dr. Parker's whereabouts, they are advised to contact the Miami Dade Police Dept. at 555-5555. All information is confidential, and persons submitting information may also call the Secret Witness Program at 555-2222. The general public is advised not to make contact with or try to apprehend Dr. Parker as he is considered armed and dangerous.

Dr. Parker read the article and heaved a heavy sigh.

"Still think I have a guardian angel?" he asked.

Nash paid the bill, and the two men walked outside into the bright sunlight. They sat on the same bench where Nash had first approached Parker.

"May I ask you a question?" Parker stared straight ahead.

"Sure," Nash replied, "but I may not answer it."

"Fair enough. How did you know who I was when you came into the park? Besides the fact that I was sitting where you asked me to sit. I certainly don't resemble the photograph in the paper. In fact I tried to be inconspicuous."

"It was easy," Nash said. "You didn't fit. Look at the people and surroundings. Of all the things in this park, you are the one thing that definitely does not fit in."

"That obvious?" Parker waved his hand wearily.

"That obvious."

"How long have you been doing this type of work?" Parker asked indifferently.

"What you really want to know is, if I'm any good and if I can help you."

Sheepishly, Parker nodded his head.

"I've been doing this work for quite a while now," Nash continued. "Since I injured my knee in college and had to drop out."

"I always thought that it was unfair for a school to take away an athlete's scholarship, if they got injured. I figured you for a football player the moment I saw you," Parker said.

Nash didn't respond for a minute. "I was on an academic scholarship. I injured my knee pledging a fraternity and I dropped out because my father was terminally ill. As for football, I never played an organized game in my life, because my mother was afraid I would get hurt."

Trying desperately to change the subject, Parker asked, "How do you know Detective Rolle?"

"When I dropped out of school to help my family, Rolle, who was a longtime family friend, introduced me to an old private eye, who was well known and well respected by the police department.

"This private investigator put out feelers that he wanted an off duty police officer to do some leg work for him. It was illegal for a policeman to do that, but Rolle introduced me to him and the rest is history. He taught me every thing I know about this line of work. He died about four years ago. It was like losing my father all over again."

"I'm sorry to hear that," Parker said. "It's good to have a mentor."

"Yes, it was," Nash said. "He taught me that there were only three basic rules of private investigation. One, observe what doesn't fit in. Two, see who protests too much. And three, notice who tells the first lie."

"I guess rule number one is how you found me," Parker said.

"Exactly," Nash said. "Now before I start to work on your case, we have to get you settled in somewhere safer to live, as in safe from the police and safe from the standpoint of your not getting killed. The Ambassador Hotel," he laughed. "I can't believe it."

"I have some things over at the Hotel," Parker said.

"Anything worth getting arrested or killed for?" Nash stared him directly in the eye.

"No." Parker didn't flinch a muscle.

"Then forget about it. What do you have on your person?" Nash asked.

"My wallet with my identification, an address book, some keys and about forty seven hundred dollars."

"You're walking around with your correct identification?" Nash sounded incredulous. "What if a policeman asks you for your identification because you're, say ... loitering?"

Before Parker could answer, Nash said, "We'll have to get rid of that."

Parker reached into his pocket to give Nash his wallet.

"Later," Nash said sternly. "Not now. Someone seeing you give me your wallet now might think I was robbing you. People have been known to make incorrect assumptions," he said with a smile.

"I'm glad you have some money," Nash went on. "I'm taking you on because I owe Rolle a lot and this will go a long way toward canceling some of those debts. But paying your way wasn't included."

"I have a small studio apartment, that I use as a safe house, not too far from here," Nash declared. "It's only a ten minute bus ride or about a half hour walk. I'll give you the address and directions to memorize, which you should be able to do, being a doctor and all."

He paused for a moment. "I don't want the police to find my address on you, if you get arrested between here and the apartment. I'll meet you there at eight tonight. Don't be late, because if you are, I'm going to assume that either you don't want my help or you got arrested. In either case there would be no reason for me to stick around. Here's a key."

Nash stood up abruptly and left. As Taylor Nash walked away, of all the things that had transpired since they met, Evan Parker could only think of one thing. Taylor Nash looked good in red shoes.

After a forty-minute walk, Dr. Parker was standing in front of the building that Taylor Nash had referred to as his apartment or safe house. It was actually a two-story duplex, with identical floor plans on the first and second floor. The small white building was located on the outer fringe of Little Havana in a low income, but well-kept, neighborhood. A three-foot chain link fence, whose gate was unlocked, surrounded the neatly manicured yard. Per Nash's instructions, Parker knew that he was to proceed to the second floor, via a staircase that ran along the north side of the narrow structure.

Staring at the door, Parker hesitated momentarily before turning the key that he had placed into the lock. As he entered the apartment, he quickly saw that the rooms were not much larger than those at the Ambassador Hotel.

The room where he stood held a leather reclining chair and an occasional table near the door. A full-sized bed was placed near the center of the room and a small dinette, with three Bentwood chairs with cane seats, was situated at the end of the room near a galley style kitchen. To his immediate right was a Lilliputian bathroom, with an enclosed shower stall, toilet, and a sink that was smaller than the one at the Ambassador. The rooms were immaculately clean.

He didn't know what he had expected, but this wasn't it. Maybe he thought that walking through the door would be similar to Alice's walking back through the looking glass and returning to normalcy.

Suddenly he felt his stomach muscles constrict as a wave of nausea washed over him. He took three hurried steps to the bathroom and delivered his housewarming gift of his after-noon's lunch into the commode. As he sat on the cool tile floor, he decided to stop feeling sorry for himself.

It was now six-thirty, the Florida sun had set somewhere in the west, and the air had begun to cool. Since Nash wouldn't be coming until eight, Evander Parker decided to take a short walk around his new neighborhood.

Nash was sitting on the bed as Parker reentered the apartment. He was pointing what Parker thought was the largest handgun in the world directly at him.

"What's going on?" Parker exclaimed excitedly.

"Just turn around. Slowly," Nash said grimly.

Parker did as he was told.

"Now back up towards me and put your hands on top of your head."

When Parker was about two feet in front of him Nash ordered him to stop. Nash then patted him down to be sure he did not have any weapons.

"You can turn around now," Nash said.

"What's gotten into you?" Parker asked. "What's this routine all about?"

"Have a seat," said Nash, putting the cannon into his shoulder holster. "If you know what I'm going to say, it's really bad for you and if you don't, then it's worse."

Nash paused a moment to study Dr. Parker's face.

"Tell me," Parker demanded. "After what I've been through, I can take anything."

Nash's next words changed his mind.

"Your wife has been murdered," Nash said flatly.

* * *

Parker's face turned an ashen gray, as if all the blood had been drained from the upper part of his head. Nash looked on with concern as Parker slid out of the chair and onto the floor. He then keeled over to his right, in a kind of slow motion. Parker had a dazed expression on his face the entire time, and his eyes were wide open.

Nash was hoping that he hadn't suffered a stroke. He had only seen someone look this bad once before, but that was because he had shot him a coupla times. But this guy hadn't been shot. At least not with a bullet.

When Evan Parker regained consciousness, he was lying in the bed and Nash was drinking a diet soda and staring at him.

"Man, I thought you had a stroke or something. If you hadn't started to stir around a bit, I was going to have you taken to the hospital."

Parker noticed that Nash didn't say that he was going to take him to the hospital.

"Did you say my wife had been killed?" Parker asked sadly, his eyes misting.

"No," Nash replied, "I said that she had been murdered. There's a big difference."

"How do you know this?"

"I have friends on the police department." Nash looked solemn. "Friends other than Lt. Rolle who probably doesn't know about the murder himself ... yet."

"When was she killed? I mean murdered?" Parker corrected himself.

"Sometime this evening, after I left you," Nash said. "I don't have all of the details yet, but I will."

"So that's why the whole scenario when I came in here. You thought that I might have done it."

"Anything is possible ...." Nash changed the subject. "By the way, where were you tonight?"

"I was out walking around, trying to clear my head. No offense, but these are fairly close quarters."

185

"I know the feeling. Look, I'm really sorry about your wife," Nash said genuinely.

"Thanks," Parker said."I just can't believe Cassie's gone."

"Needless to say, you can't go anywhere near your home or to the funeral," Nash said. "Everyone will be expecting you to be in the vicinity."

Dr. Evan Parker suddenly felt very alone. More so than he had ever experienced in his entire life. The realization that he could not attend the funeral only made him feel worse. He was helpless. He just wanted to sleep and that's exactly what he did.

Nash gave him some tablets to take. He didn't even bother to ask what they were.

Nash slept in the chair. After what he had seen, he thought he had better keep an eye on the doctor to be sure he was really okay.

If there was a person more deserving of compassion right now, Nash could not think of who it could be.

When he awakened the next afternoon, Dr. Parker observed a freshly-shaved and showered Nash sitting in the same chair, reading the newspaper.

Maybe this was his guardian angel, thought Parker.

Nash had just finished the financial section of the Miami Herald, when he heard Parker sit up on the side of the bed. He folded the paper meticulously before he stood up and stretched his large frame.

"How are you doing?" Nash asked.

"Fairly well, considering," Parker replied. "What's in the paper?"

"Unfortunately, you are."

This time Dr. Evander Parker had made the front page headlines.

ELUSIVE DOCTOR WANTED FOR QUESTIONING
IN THIRD HOMICIDE

Will this nightmare never end? he thought.

The article read that there were no witnesses to the brutal stabbing death of his young socialite wife. There were no other details of the murder in the article. It reported their marriage of eight years, that they had no children and outlined a brief history of Cassie's charitable work. He read the lead article quickly and did not bother to read the continuation on the following page. Disgusted, he folded the paper twice and threw it into a corner of the room.

Nash, who was still standing, slowly walked over and picked the paper up from the floor. He handed it back to Parker. "I'm afraid you'll have to continue. Page two," he said unemotionally.

What now? Parker thought as he apprehensively turned to page two.

It struck him like a splash of cold water or maybe more like a block of ice.

There he was, or more precisely, there his photo was. This was not like the previous photo but a recent, looks-just-like-him photo. He could not remember when it was taken, but he was sure it had been retrieved from the condo. This was bad, he thought. He looked sadly at Nash.

"Yeah, I know," Nash said.

Even with the recent stubbly beard and longer hair, this picture was *him.*

"You're gonna have to stay put. Close quarters or not. I'll go out later and get some more supplies. Right now, the first order of business is to work on your appearance."

Nash motioned for him to come into the bathroom, where he had already set out a variety of hair products, including dyes, perms, tints, and relaxers.

"I think the first thing we'll do is get that gray out of your head and facial hair. I thought about giving you a trim but with that picture, the less of your face exposed, the better."

187

After what seemed like a tortuously long time of standing with his head buried in the small bathroom sink, Dr. Parker was allowed to straighten up.

"Turn around. Let's have a look at you," Nash instructed him. "Yeah, that ought to do it. The trick is to get the grey out, without putting too much color into your hair. The Art of Make up 101. University of Virginia. A cop can spot a bad dye job a mile away. We won't comb or towel dry it, so you can have that 'I've been out of work forever and I'm still not looking' appearance."

"University of Virginia?" Parker said. "Is that where you went to college?"

"No," Nash answered, "but I did audit some classes there one semester."

"Where did you attend school?" asked Parker.

"Quiet," said Nash "I'm trying to get this just right."

Parker was now sitting in a chair, facing Nash, who was standing over him with a toothbrush in his right hand and a fine-toothed comb and a jar of who knows what in the other.

"The same principle applies to the mustache, beard and eyebrows," Nash said as he began to apply the liquid from the jar to Parker's facial hair before combing it through. He repeated this procedure many times, being very methodical and meticulous.

Too meticulous, thought Parker, but at least he was seated comfortably, and not draped over that hard porcelain sink.

"Voila!" Nash shouted, startling Parker, who jumped.

"Don't get up just yet," he said as he placed his hand on Parker's shoulder and stood up.

Nash stepped over to the closet and retrieved a gray shoe box with a brown top. He retrieved one of the small Bentwood chairs from the dinette set and pulled it behind him into the minuscule bathroom. Sitting directly in front of Parker, he placed the shoebox on his lap. Nash removed the top, revealing dozens of pairs of eyeglasses of many shapes and sizes.

"The correct pair of these will help to obscure your features even more," Nash said. "Never wear sunglasses or darkly shaded glasses," he continued. "They only make you look as if you have something to hide. I'm immediately suspicious of people in dark glasses. These all have lenses with no prescription."

After the fourth or fifth pair, Nash stood up and backed away.

"Look straight at me," Nash said. "Uh huh," he grunted. "Those will do, but they need a little fine tuning."

Nash removed the glasses from Parker's face and headed into the kitchen. He returned quickly, and poked his head into the bathroom.

"Come on out here, I think I'll do this in the living room. The light's a little better."

Obediently, Parker stood up, proceeded to the living area, and sat on the bed.

Nash sat in the large comfortable chair and placed a large plastic bowl between his legs. He leaned over the bowl and picked up a steel wool pad and began to scrub the plastic of the eyeglasses vigorously. He then picked up an ice pick and gouged several large pieces of plastic from the frame. Lastly he picked up a roll of white surgical tape from the bowl and applied it to several areas of the frame.

As Parker looked at Nash, gleefully performing this disfiguring task, he wondered if Nash had fine tuned any human beings.

Nash held the glasses in front of him and admired his handiwork. "They looked too new for the look we are trying to achieve," said Nash. "And as I said before, everything must fit in."

Nash got up, gently placed the glasses on Parker's face and smiled. "Take a look," he said.

Parker stood up, walked into the bathroom and gazed into the mirror on the medicine cabinet. The medicine cabinet hung above the sink, where his mutation had begun. He stared at the

189

image in the mirror, trying hard to discover any resemblance to his previous self. There was very little. Once again, Taylor Nash impressed him.

"Look," Nash said. "I'm outta here. I have to go work on some paying cases. There's enough food in the kitchen for a few days, which is probably how long I'll be gone. If I were you," and right now Nash was thankful that he was not, "I'd stay put."

Parker did just that. Busying himself by trying to become interested in the soap operas. All of which paled in comparison to his too real situation.

Chapter Eighteen

Cassie Parker's funeral was simple. A simple media circus. Her two closest female friends, Mrs. Beth Hitchcock and Mrs. Esther Wallace, who insisted on paying for the cremation and subsequent internment, had made the arrangements. Although Cassie had never discussed this type of matter with either of them, Esther and Beth thought this coincided best with what Cassie would have wanted.

Although they tried to keep the date and time of the services a secret, among a small circle of friends, the police insisted on knowing. From their knowledge, it was a small matter for the press to become informed.

The small Episcopal Church was filled to overflowing with friends, strangers, well wishers, on-lookers, reporters and of course the police. Outside were more police, reporters, photographers, cameramen, news crews, satellite crews for live coverage, throngs of curiosity seekers and Taylor Nash.

Nash stood at the fringes of what was a considerable and ultimately unruly crowd of nearly six hundred people. Everyone was hoping to get a glimpse of the remains of Cassie Parker and maybe to be the first to see Dr. Evander Parker himself.

It was a case of mistaken identity that set the crowd into a frenzy.

"There he is," someone shouted and pointed to a poor soul, who bore no resemblance to Parker at all.

The crowd surged in the direction of the man, who began to run, after realizing his protestations of innocence were being ignored. Fortunately for him, there were enough police present to reach him in time, and ultimately prevent his being pummeled into jelly by the crowd now turned into a self-righteous mob.

Nash left, deciding that nothing advantageous could be gained from hanging around.

Two days later, Nash knocked on the door and entered with a large supply of essential and nonessential, but welcome, items. He had everything from food to magazines.

"Can't stay long," Nash said. "That should be everything you need for now. Meanwhile, I have a few things for you to do. Between my other cases, I have been cruising by your condominium, to see if I could notice anything unusual. Unfortunately, I didn't come across anything, but I did cop the license plate numbers of all of the cars parked within a three-block radius of your home, for the past two days.

"I also had a friend in the department run the identification on any cars that were ticketed within a mile of your place, within the past two months. It took longer than I anticipated, but here are the names and addresses. Look over this list and see if there are any in here that you recognize. It may have some bearing on your wife's murder or your current situation."

Current situation, Parker thought. It's like he thinks I'm stranded in the airport because of bad weather.

"Pay attention," Nash snapped. "This is important."

Embarrassed at being caught daydreaming, Parker now gave Nash his full attention.

Nash continued, "Things may start to heat up concerning you and those unsolved murders. It depends on many factors. Such as what's going on in the homicide department, such as the media coverage and most of all, pressure from the Mayor's office to appease the public, should they get particularly annoyed. As you know, doctors are considered rich. And right now, rich people are not looked upon favorably in this country.

"Especially when the public sees so many wealthy people that they think are guilty walk home free. I also have a number for you to memorize. If you want to contact me, call this number and dial in 911. It's my beeper number and I'll call you back at the pay phone on the corner. It's your responsibility to be at the pay phone no longer than five minutes after you call and to make sure that no one is using it. If the phone doesn't ring ten minutes after you call me, I won't be calling. I always assume my home phone and cellular are being monitored, so I'll be calling from a pay phone myself."

Nash looked directly at Parker. He spoke very slowly. "That number is for emergencies only."

With that said, Nash walked out of the door.

Evan Parker was bored. He sat on the edge of the bed and started to read the names listed beside the license plate numbers on the papers that Nash had given to him. After the third or fourth page he became resigned to the probability that he would not receive any help from the list. That was when he saw a name that made the hair on the back of his neck bristle and contract.

JYS347   Heather Fine 436 Camloop Road

Parker's mind shifted into overdrive. What was she doing near his house and what was her part in any of this?

Parker turned back to the first page of the list and studied each name in earnest this time. He anticipated seeing several names which were familiar to him. He was wrong again. He reread the pages twice more with the same results. The only name he recognized was that of Heather Fine. He wanted to call Nash and tell him immediately. He decided to wait.

There was a phone in the apartment, but he did not even know if it worked. He walked slowly over to it and picked up the receiver. There was no dial tone. He instantly became depresssed and then became livid.

"The damn phone should work!" he shouted into the empty apartment. "Even if I can't use it, it should be in working order!" he screamed.

He felt very alone and isolated. He flopped down on the edge of the bed. He did not remember falling asleep.

Parker was just finishing his shower, when Nash knocked and came through the door. He always wondered why Nash knocked before entering. Was it because Nash did not want to startle him or was it to give him some degree of privacy and respect? He never asked.

Evan Parker was startled, when he looked into the bathroom mirror. Unconsciously, he must have thought that the shower would wash away the appearance that Nash had created for him. He would have to become accustomed to his new countenance.

"Did you recognize any of the names on that list?" Nash said, getting right to the point.

Nash was outfitted in a brilliantly white, brilliantly expensive ensemble. He had on a shirt that was cotton, but fine cotton that had the appearance of silk. He did not wear a belt and had on white cotton trousers, that were obviously tailored especially for him. Each pleat was perfect.

Parker could not tell if he had on socks because his pants draped perfectly over the whitest walking shoes he had ever seen. Parker had never seen shoes that white, that were not in a shoe box in the shoe store. Parker remembered when all shoes like that were called tennis shoes. These had soft leather tops. Not canvas like the tennis shoes of his youth.

Before he answered Nash's question, Parker looked directly at Nash and squinted. He then picked up a pair of sunglasses from the table and put them on.

Nash, who began to smile, showing perfect teeth that matched his clothing, did not miss this sophomoric humor.

"Yes," Parker finally said. "Heather Fine, 436 Camloop Road."

Parker removed the sunglasses, retrieved the list, and pointed to Heather's name, showing it to Nash as if to underscore his triumphant discovery. He was not unlike a schoolboy showing his father his name in the school paper for the first time.

"How did you come to know this Heather Fine?" Nash looked at the paper and memorized the address.

"She was a patient," Parker said. "A very tragic story really. She came from a very dysfunctional family."

"Who didn't?" Nash interrupted. "Was she very different from your other patients and what do you think she was doing in the vicinity of your residence?"

"She was extremely depressed," said Parker. "She tried to commit suicide several times. But to answer your question, I don't have any idea what she was doing there."

"In Psych 101 I remember being taught that a suicidal person is just an introverted murderer. Do you think she was capable of murder? And I mean in the real sense, not the theoretical 'any one is capable of murder' sense."

"In my professional opinion," Parker answered, speaking in his serious doctor voice, "I really don't think so."

"Uh huh," Nash said. "I guess I'll give Ms. Fine a visit. Especially since this is our only real lead so far."

"Be careful," Evan said.

"I'm always careful," Nash said, pulling on the crease of his right pants leg, revealing a gun in an ankle holster.

"I meant for you to be careful when you talk to her. She's a very fragile person."

"And here I was thinking you were worried about me," Nash laughed, shaking his head.

He turned and went out the door.

195

Nash walked out of the apartment and down the steps to his car, the one thing that did not complement his persona. It was an unmemorable, unnoticeable, faded grey 1989 Chevrolet Camaro.

Nash went directly to the trunk and opened a green plastic file box where he kept maps of the city and surrounding areas. Still standing by the trunk, he first searched a directory for Camloop Road. Next he located the map that contained that area of the city and folded it so it would be easy to read. He closed the trunk and casually threw the folded map on the passenger seat as he entered the car.

Checking his rear view mirror out of habit, Nash made a U-turn from the curb and drove off in the general direction of Camloop Road.

Nash only made one wrong turn on his way to Heather's apartment, and that was because one of the streets on his map had been converted into a one-way street. He always enjoyed these solitary road trips that began after one of his sisters told him he had no sense of direction.

Nash had no expectations when he approached the building but after a mindful assessment, he thought that it was quite a nice apartment for a suicidal ... possibly homicidal ... young girl from a dysfunctional family.

He cruised the parking lot until he spotted her car. A twenty-year old brown Volkswagen beetle, License plate JYS347.

"Guess she's home," he said to himself as he backed into a parking space. Feeling as cautiously confident as ever, Nash decided to just knock on her door and play it by ear. If she wouldn't let him in, he would say he accidentally hit a brown VW in the parking lot and the manager told him that this was where the owner of said VW, a Ms. Heather Fine, resided. Once inside, he would go into his pat undercover cop routine.

That he was investigating the death of Mrs. Cassie Parker and wanted to know how her car came to be in that neighborhood. If she had company, he would stay with the accident routine, have them come outside to inspect the car and see that no real damage was done.

Nash knocked on the door confidently. The building appeared deserted.

"Heather, are you in?" he asked in a relaxed voice, in case someone was walking down the hall or could hear from their apartment. He deliberately picked this time of day when most people were at work.

She must be away with friends, he thought. Someone must have picked her up. Nash decided to enter the apartment. He removed a small set of tools he brought with him from the car and, in less than twenty seconds, unlocked the door and pushed it open.

There was a folded towel at the base of the door. It had obviously been wedged there from the inside. It reminded him of his college days when students experimenting with marijuana would roll a towel and place it at the base of the door to hopefully prevent the aroma from wafting down the hall. The fragrance that floated into his nostrils however was not that of marijuana. It was an odor with which he was too familiar.

Odors are strong arbiters of memory and this one took him back to one of his first jobs with the old private investigator.

They had just apprehended a bail jumper who was wanted for murder and was hiding out on a small farm in Ocala. After securing him in their car, they began to search for the legal occupants of the farm. They were found in a small shack at the rear of the property. That was when Taylor Nash first encountered this stench. The farmer and his wife had been dead for more than a week.

Taylor removed a white linen handkerchief from his pocket and held it over his nose as he looked over the apartment. It was immaculately clean. This was no rush job. Whoever cleaned this place had taken their sweet time and had done a good job. There were no dirty dishes around and no food inside the spotless refrigerator, which had been turned off.

As he proceeded through the apartment, Taylor Nash was sure of two things. One was that there was at least one body decomposing in the apartment and two that whoever it was should get their cleaning deposit returned.

It is always unnerving to discover a human body, even when you are looking for one.

"Heather Fine, I presume," he said aloud, possibly to ease his own tension, as he walked into the bedroom.

She was lying on her back with her hands folded neatly across her chest. It looked as if she had anticipated death and welcomed it. Heather was wearing the ugliest mousy brown house robe that he had ever seen. An assortment of prescription bottles was neatly arranged on the nightstand. Nash was careful not to touch anything carelessly or unnecessarily and immediately wiped his prints from anything he did touch with his handkerchief.

He could tell from the stench, and now the body, that she had been dead for more than a week. With Cassie Parker dead only seventy two hours, it was going to be difficult to pin this one on Heather. He wondered if she left a note. With her obviously taking so much time, he was reasonably sure that one was around. He prayed that it wasn't typed because if he decided to take it from the apartment, typed letters can leave too much of a trail ... the ribbon, the cartridge, etc. Too much trouble.

After looking around the bedroom a third time, he saw the edge of an envelope protruding from a book on the nightstand opposite the one which held the bottles. He pulled it out carefully without disturbing the placement of the book. The envelope was addressed to Dr. Evander Parker. Nash removed the letter from the unsealed envelope.

Thankfully, it was handwritten, as was Dr. Parker's name on the envelope. He placed the letter back into the envelope and placed the envelope into his pocket. He took one last long look around the apartment. Nothing seemed out of place. He was delighted Heather had decided to make her last note very personal.

Before he left the apartment, Nash removed the shoelace from his left shoe and tied a slip knot around the towel. He then opened the door gently and peered into the hallway. His luck was still holding. There was no one in sight. He exited the apartment of the late Heather Fine, turned and kneeled to pull the shoelace across the threshold before closing the door.

Nash then gently pulled the lace toward him until he could feel the towel against the door. With that done, he gave a sharp tug on the shoe lace and the slip knot came undone. Nash wiped his prints from the door knob and walked casually to his car.

Settled in his car, Nash laced his shoe and retrieved the envelope from his pocket. He stared at it for a while and then decided to let the person to whom it was addressed have the distinction of being the first live person to read it.

Nash knocked on the apartment door and let himself in. Parker was in the bathroom again. Taylor thought to himself that Parker was too young to have bladder problems, but you never know. Nash was not aware that Evan Parker now spent inordinate amounts of time looking into the bathroom mirror trying to become accustomed to the face that stared back at him.

With Nash his only human contact, Parker was always glad to see him. He also wanted to know what had transpired at Heather's.

"Did you see Heather?" Parker asked excitedly.

"Yes," Nash answered matter-of-factly.

Parker felt his heart racing. "Did you speak to her?" he said almost breathlessly.

"Yes."

"What did she have to say?" Parker was almost shouting.

Nash wanted to say she was dead silent but knew that he had toyed with Parker enough.

"She's dead," he replied, "and has been for some time now. She certainly didn't kill your wife."

"B-B-But you said you spoke to her," Parker stammered.

"Manner of speech," Nash replied. "I did find this in her apartment." Nash handed Parker the envelope. "It's addressed to you. I opened the envelope but I didn't read it."

"Did you actually not read it or is this just another manner of speech?" Parker said, obviously annoyed.

"No, I literally did not read it," Nash said dryly. "Her death appears to have been suicide. Her body has not yet been discovered and I left everything as I found it, with the exception of that letter."

Absentmindedly, Parker took the envelope and lounged in the large living room armchair. He glanced upward at Nash sheepishly, suddenly remembering this was his favorite place to sit. Nash extended his hand to gesture that it was alright, this time. Nash then pulled one of the small dinette chairs under him and began to read a magazine in earnest.

Parker held the envelope gently in his hands. He massaged it between his thumbs and index fingers. He then put it on his lap and rubbed it as if he expected a genie to appear. He could use a genie right about now. He picked it up again and stared at it.

In fact, he studied it. His name, Dr. Evander Hollister Parker, was handwritten on the front. He was impressed. Heather had to do her homework to come up with his middle name. He never used it. The flap of the envelope was not sealed but tucked into the envelope.

He studied the flap to see if it had ever been sealed. As far as he could determine it had not. He replaced the flap into the envelope. The envelope was light brown and made of expensive paper. Thanks to Cassie, he knew expensive stationery when he saw it. He turned the envelope over several more times, even examining the seams in his nervousness. He undid the flap for a second time and finally removed the letter. It was handwritten on paper that matched the envelope.

My Dearest Evan,

It is with deepest sorrow, that I have decided to terminate our relationship. Permanently. I was as sure that you were the man worthy of my love as I was sure that you were transforming me into the woman that you wanted me to be.

During our late afternoon and evening sessions you made it clear to me that you could be the Father, Mother, lover and even the child, I so desperately wanted and needed.

Recent developments which I have discovered concerning your personal life have caused me great distress. Truly, Evan dearest, I never believed for a single minute that you were capable of committing the heinous crimes of which you are accused. It does cause me considerable concern, however, to realize that there must be a serious inadequacy within you to allow yourself to be placed in such a situation. The same inadequacy which allowed you to choose a spouse whom I initially deemed unworthy of you. It now seems possible to me that her indiscretions may have been a response to your not so perfect character.

I do not blame you and I do not want you to blame yourself for what I must now do. I can only fault myself for postponing the inevitable for so long. I am now prepared to leave this world joyously to meet the only perfect Being.

Forever,

Heather

Parker slowly folded the letter and placed it and the envelope on the table next to him. He stared straight ahead at nothing in particular. He felt very sad for Heather Fine. He felt so sad that he thought he would cry. But he did not.

Was it because he was in the presence of Taylor Nash? It should not have been, because Nash had seen him cry before. In fact, Nash had seen him display emotions that no other person had ever seen ... himself included. Was it because he was too overwhelmed? No, it would be difficult for anything to overwhelm him at this point in his life. Dr. Evander Parker did not cry, because he was too stunned to cry.

Stunned not because Heather Fine had committed suicide, not even because she had so mistaken his efforts to help her ... but most of all because she was correct about inadequacies in his personality. He must have had an almost pathological desire to succeed to the ruin of everything and everyone else to have come to this predicament.

"Pretty dramatic," Nash said, bringing Parker back to the real world.

"I thought you said you didn't read it," Parker said angrily.

"I didn't," Nash said, "but from what I saw today, I figured she had a flair for the dramatic."

"What did you see to lead you to that conclusion?" asked Parker very clinically.

Nash described the condition of the apartment and the way Heather had put herself on display to be found.

"Interesting," Parker said, retreating into his profession-alism. "She always told me how disheveled her living quarters were. Maybe this was her last act of contrition."

"I'd like for you to read this." Parker held the letter out to Nash.

"You sure?"

"Positive." Parker was firm.

Nash put his magazine aside and took the letter. There was complete silence as Nash read it.

202

"What do you think?" asked Parker when Nash finally put the letter on the table.

"About the whole letter or any part in particular?" asked Nash, being evasive.

"I'm sure you know which part I'm talking about," Parker replied. "I know that you know me well enough by now to know that I was not trying to come on to one of my patients."

Nash hesitated before he spoke. What was he supposed to say? Oh, you mean the part where Heather accused your wife of being a slut, but I don't mean that in a bad way.

"Well," Nash said, "you could interpret this letter in many ways.

"Nice try," Parker said, "but I don't think so. Cut the crap, I can take it."

"Yeah." Nash smiled. "The last time you said that you took a header off the chair."

"You're right," Parker said. "Maybe you should put seat-belts on the chairs in here."

The tension broken between them, Nash spoke. "Have you ever known your wife to be unfaithful?"

Parker shook his head.

"Have you ever been unfaithful to your wife?"

Parker shook his head again.

"I hate to compound bad news but if it turns out that your wife was having an affair it would be a clear cut motive for you to murder her."

"I thought about that," Parker said.

"Is there any one that you think she could be capable of having an affair with?"

"The only person that comes to mind immediately is her masseuse. For some reason I always thought they knew each other more intimately than they both wanted to let on."

"You know his name?" asked Nash.

"Yes," replied Parker. "It's Mark Kelly. Cassie got him from an ad in the paper. I can't remember the name of the agency but they run an ad in the Herald every weekend. It's something like triple A or AOK."

"I'll get an old paper and get right on it," Nash said. "This guy shouldn't be too hard to find if he's clean."

Nash stood up, placed the letter on top of the envelope and picked them both up from the table.

"I'll get rid of this," he said. "I don't want anyone else to know I was in that apartment today or that I removed this."

Parker nodded his head in agreement.

Nash put the letter in the envelope and walked out of the apartment door.

Nash stopped by the office building of the Miami Herald at 1 Herald Plaza near the foot of the Venetian Causeway. He knew exactly where to go.

There was only one other person in the small room. He cleared his throat loudly to get the attention of the person behind the desk who had his back turned.

"May I help you?" a smiling pimply-faced teenager said as he turned around.

He had reddish-orange hair, accompanied by a large pumpkin-shaped face. He was dressed casually in an oversized navy blue T-shirt that almost hung to his knees and a pair of faded blue denims.

"I would like copies of the paper from this past Saturday and Sunday," Nash requested.

The clerk's smile broadened, happy that this was an easy request. All he had to do was to perform an about face and retrieve the papers from the large open shelves positioned behind him.

"Will that be all, sir?" he asked.

"Yes, thank you," Nash said.

"Alrighty then. Your total comes to seven dollars and sixty cents."

Nash gave him a ten-dollar bill. The clerk who—Nash guessed was a high school student—walked into an adjacent room and returned with two dollars and forty cents in coins.

"Sorry but we don't have any bills," he said apologetically.

Nash cupped his large hand to receive the coins and, without counting them, put them into his front pants pocket. He then returned to his car.

Leaning back in the driver's seat, he started to look through the papers for the advertisement.

Since he never paid attention to massage parlor ads, Nash amused himself by trying to guess in which section of the paper the ads would be located.

Ads for golfing equipment would be in the Sports section. Additionally ads for automobiles, especially sporty or off-road model vehicles, would also be in the Sports section, since that is the area their target audience would be sure to focus their attention. Nash figured the Sports section would be a good bet but it wasn't there. After looking through most of the paper, he found the ad in a section that should have been obvious to him and left him smiling.

"Why didn't I think to look there in the first place?" he said to himself. After all, a good Private Investigator should have deduced that a massage parlor ad would be in the Entertainment section.

There it was. A 1 Massage Parlor. Specializing in all types of massages. Nash quickly wondered how any business could specialize in all types of anything. That statement was an oxymoron. The ad went on. European Oriental Turkish Swedish.

"Who wrote this ad?" he said to himself. "Last time I checked Sweden was still in Europe."

Out calls available. Masseurs and Masseuses. Men and Women.

Nash guessed that redundancy was for those who didn't get it the first time.

Low rates for first timers and repeat customers.

"I guess that covers just about everyone," Nash chuckled to himself.

Call 555-5555 or come by our facilities located at 1737 S.E. 54th Ave.

Nash decided to visit the facilities. Maybe he could talk to whoever wrote such an informative advertisement.

The A 1 Massage Parlor was little more than a storefront on 54th Ave. In close proximity to the Massage Parlor were an adult book store, a peep show and a topless bar.

One-stop shopping, thought Nash as he exited his car.

He entered the Massage Parlor though doors whose tinted, blacked-out glass matched the smoky glass that covered the windows. He walked into what must have been considered a waiting room. There were approximately a dozen cheap steel and vinyl chairs placed along the walls. Directly in front of Nash was a large wooden desk, with a single occupant sitting behind it. To the left of the desk was a narrow hallway, which Nash assumed led to the massage rooms.

The man sitting behind the desk appeared to be in his early fifties and had the pallid complexion of a person who has spent too much time indoors with too much smoke and air conditioning.

He had drooping watery brown eyes and puffy jowls, which jiggled as he munched on an unlit cigar held in a fleshy mouth. He also was wearing one of the worse looking hair pieces that Nash had ever seen. Nash wondered if the guy actually paid for that cabbage sitting on his head. It made him feel better to think that one of the customers may have forgotten it and this gentleman just decided to wear it as a joke.

It gave Nash a chill to think that there might be a salesman somewhere in the world who could convince someone to buy that. Mr. Cabbage was wearing what appeared to be a black Banlon shirt although Nash couldn't be positive without touching it, which he had no intention of doing.

"May I help you?" Mr. Cabbage asked, painfully managing a smile as he removed the cigar dangling from his mouth.

"Yes," Nash said. "I'm looking for Mark Kelly."

"So am I," came the gruff reply, "but he doesn't work here anymore."

"Do you happen to know where I might find him?" Nash asked.

"No, I'm sorry I don't, but if you're looking for a special type of massage I'm sure we can find someone to provide services just as good as Mark or better."

"Actually, I'm not here for a massage. I'm just trying to find Mark."

Hearing that, the painful smile disappeared and was replaced by a seemingly more natural scowl. "Then I'm sorry I can't help you."

"I understand your time is valuable," Nash said softly, while pulling one of the chairs to the front of the desk, "and I'm willing to pay you for your time."

Nash reached into his pocket and placed a fifty-dollar bill on the desk as he sat down.

"That is if you are willing to talk to me."

"I don't want to get nobody into trouble." The clerk eyed the money. "And I'm no snitch."

"I understand," Nash continued. "No one is going to get into trouble. I'm just trying to find Mark for a friend of mine. You did say that you were looking for him too."

"Yes," the clerk nodded.

"Well, if I find him, I'll tell him that you want to see him also."

"I certainly do want to see him because he left me with a lot of out calls and I lost money."

"Then this is an opportunity for you to recoup some of your losses," Nash encouraged.

"You know you're right. He didn't care about me when he didn't show up."

"And when was that?"

"I'll check my book and I can give you the exact date."

He reached below the desk and, after two short tugs, pulled open a sticky desk drawer. He produced a large green ledger and put it on the desk top. His search was a short one.

"Aha, here it is. He was supposed to report to me on the fifth of this month and I haven't heard from him since. I've been trying to refer his customers to other people but on short notice sometimes it don't work out."

"The fifth of the month, you say," Nash repeated, now jotting in a small notebook. He remembered that was the day after Cassie Parker had been murdered.

"Do you have an address for him? By the way, I'm Taylor Nash," he continued as he extended his hand and shook the hand of the man sitting across the desk from him. "What shall I call you?"

"Nice to meet you, Taylor. Given name's Edgar but just call me Ed. I really don't know if I should give out an employee's address. I've never given an address out. Even to a regular customer."

Nash removed another fifty from his pocket and slid it gently beside the first fifty.

"I would appreciate any help you could give me."

"Alright," Edgar said, "but don't mention where you got it."

"It's already forgotten," Nash said reassuringly.

Ed reached into another drawer and produced a small rusting grey metal file box. He opened it with a key and looked through the index cards, which were in alphabetical order.

"Mark Kelly, 4200 N E 22nd Street, Apt 3," he said.

"Did he have any contact numbers or names of relatives that he left in case of emergencies?" Nash asked.

"No, he didn't," Ed replied. "He never mentioned any relatives or close friends and he worked here exclusively for several years."

"How about customers?" Nash asked. "Did he have a regular clientele?"

"Oh, Mark was quite popular with many customers," Edgar said, "but I really don't want to get anyone else involved. I think I may have done too much already."

Looking directly into Ed's eyes, Nash pushed a hundred dollar bill across the table. "I'm very discreet."

Ed looked at the money and hesitated only a moment before he reached into his desk of endless drawers. This time he sat a large Rolodex on the desk. Listed under Kelly were approximately six cards with the names and addresses of Mark Kelly's regular customers.

Nash prepared himself to copy them down, when Edgar got up and took the cards down the hall. He returned a few minutes later with a xeroxed copy of the rolodex cards.

"You know Mark may be in trouble himself," Nash said, "and by helping me to find him you may be saving his skin."

Nash could not figure why there was a Xerox machine in a massage parlor but he was grateful as he pocketed the list. Nash produced another twenty and added it to the money that was sitting on the desk.

It's always advantageous to leave a good impression, whenever possible.

After he handed Nash the list, Ed sat patiently with his hands clasped on the desk. Nash smiled and gestured with an open hand toward the money that he had formed into a neat stack.

Edgar looked around nervously for a second before taking the money and shoving it into his pants pocket.

Ed spoke as Nash stood up to leave. "I don't mean to be too forward but whether you find Mark or not you could make good money as a masseur. I could guarantee you a steady flow of customers."

Not wanting to offend Edgar at this time in their relationship, Nash just said, "I'll keep it in mind."

He had to admit he was somewhat flattered.

Nash hadn't realized how dark it was inside the parlor until his eyes had to readjust to the sunlight. In this neighborhood he was thankful his car was still parked where he had left it and had all of its parts.

As he walked to his car Nash knew three things. One was that Dr. Parker owed him an additional two hundred twenty dollars. Two, he had some good leads to follow. And three, that Ed was wearing a Banlon shirt.

Nash drove directly to the apartment. He knocked as usual and entered. He was surprised Parker was not in the bathroom.

"You owe me two hundred twenty dollars," Nash said, getting right to business as usual.

Parker reached into his wallet and handed Nash the money.

"Aren't you going to ask what it's for?" Nash asked.

"I think I need to trust you by now."

What an offhanded compliment, Nash thought.

"Anyway," Nash replied, "it got us some good leads."

Dramatically he held his arms out at Parker's eye level with the xeroxed list in one hand and his notebook in the other.

"Here I have Mark Kelly's home address," he said, shaking his right hand. "And here I have a list of his regular customers." He shook his left hand.

"So what you're saying," Parker said, "is that you don't know where he is."

Somewhat deflated, Nash thought about that one and realized Parker was right.

"I do know, however, that Kelly dropped out of sight the day after your wife was murdered."

Parker started to ask how Nash knew that but decided that he wasn't interested enough to ask the question. Maybe he just didn't care. He assumed the information was correct.

"Let's take a look at our list, shall we?" Nash said, taking his place in his usual chair. With just a casual look at the list he had just paid for, Nash was sure this was the real thing since Cassie Parker's name was third on the list.

Another thing that Nash was sure of, was that the list was diversified. There were male and female names, Hispanic, Italian, Jewish and WASP names. The first thing Nash did was to group the names according to their addresses which would make it easier for him when he started his search. After he finished that, he handed the list to Parker.

"You recognize any of these names besides your wife's?" Nash asked.

Parker looked at the list of names and shook his head. He wondered if his wife's name on this list had any meaning other than that she got regular massages from Mark Kelly. What else was she getting from Mark?

"Keep the list," Nash said, "I have my own. I'm going to check Kelly's last-known address."

Nash made more than a few wrong turns before he arrived at the grouping of poorly maintained bungalows, graciously known as the Buena Vista apartments. Looking around as he drove his car to the apartment with the manager sign in the window, Nash could see that there was no vista and was sure there was very little Buena around here.

He parked his car and walked across a space where he imagined there once was grass and shrubs and flowers. There was not even the skeleton of a yard remaining. Nash wondered if that space was still considered a yard without any of the things yards were supposed to consist of.

Nash knocked on the wrought iron screen door, without attempting to ring the rusted bell. His knocks were soon accompanied by the barks of what was obviously a very large dog.

"Quiet, Randy," a raspy voice said from behind the door. "Just a minute, I'm coming."

The person that unlocked the industrial green-colored door could have been of either sex. Even though it was probably eighty degrees outside and ninety-five in the apartment, the manager had on a wool knit ski cap and was dressed in a very baggy grey sweat suit, no socks that were visible, and black-high top canvas tennis shoes, without laces.

The face looked as if it had been constantly exposed to the Florida sunlight, and the main facial color came from liver spots. This face appeared to have been made from a dried apple, like one of those Appalachian dolls. A cigarette dangled precariously, but at a secure angle that cannot be achieved without the benefit of smoking continuously for less than forty years.

"May I help you?" the manager asked, trying to speak over the escalating intensity of Randy's furious barking.

"Yes, my name is Taylor Nash. I'm a Private Investigator and I'm trying to find Mark Kelly."

"So am I," the manager grunted.

Not sensing any threat from Nash, she/he untied the dog from the kitchen table and led him into another room.

"That's quite a dog you have there," Nash said.

"Yea, I can't stand animals but he's good protection. Named him Randy. After my first husband. He was a dog too."

Mystery solved, Nash decided.

"Name's Ann," she said, ushering him into the apartment. "I was hoping you were here to rent one of the apartments that are vacant, but from the look's of you, the way you're dressed and all, I can tell you wouldn't be interested. Don't get me wrong. It doesn't matter to me that you're African American. You know a lot of people won't rent to African Americans, no matter how run down their places are. I'll bet you're surprised I got it right," she said.

"Got what right?" Nash was puzzled.

"You know, that you're an African American," she said, really drawing out her pronunciation-AAffeerrcan Ameerrican. "I been reading," she said proudly, "and it takes some doin' to know what to call you people these days. I mean before this you were black and before that you were Negroes and before that colored and before that, well it wouldn't be politically correct to even say. Not to mention downright foolhardy.

"And it's not only you people," she continued, not realizing, as Ross Perot hadn't, that the phrase "you people" is very offensive to African Americans. "It's lotsa groups of people. To say Orientals is wrong now." When she said "Orientals" it came out "Arentals." "They want to be called Asians. And they aren't Latinos or Chicanos any more, they are all Hispanics. That is, except the Cubans, they hate to be lumped together with the other Hispanics. They think they are better, you know."

"Is that so?" Nash queried.

"Damn right," Ann replied. "Why do you think you people keep changing labels so often?" she asked.

"I don't know," Nash said dryly. "Do you have any ideas?"

"Matter a fact I do."

"I thought you might," Nash said under his breath.

"It's because of insecurity and wanting to be accepted in the great melting pot known as America. Unfortunately for us all, they could be stirred around in that pot another four hundred years and never be melted in."

"A rose by any other name," Nash said, encouraging her to continue.

"Exactly right," Ann said animatedly. "Billy Shakespeare said that, didn't he?"

"Correct." Nash had never heard Shakespeare referred to as Billy.

"Bet you didn't think I knew that." Ann beamed proudly. "Italians have a saying close to that. They say a monkey dressed up in a silk suit still a monkey." Pausing a bit and thinking about what she just said, she looked shyly at Nash. "No offense meant by that monkey thing."

"None taken."

"That's what I mean," Ann said, slapping her knee and smiling broadly. "You probably don't care if you melt in the pot and could give a hoot what label they give your ethnic group."

Nash had to admit to himself that she was right about that.

"If my group weren't already melted into the mainstream, we would have to come up with some new names every few years ourselves," she said.

"And what group might that be?" Nash asked curiously.

"Po' white trash," she said. "We might have to call ourselves financially and socially challenged Caucasians."

This last statement so amused her that she held her head back and opened her mouth widely to expose a perfect set of teeth. A perfect set of false teeth that were at least two sizes too large for her mouth. When she began to laugh a sound came from her that would have chilled the heart of a vampire. It frightened Nash so much that he instinctively reached for his weapon in his ankle holster before he regained a small amount of his composure. There was not much in this world that totally unnerved Taylor Nash to the point of distraction, but this sound was shrouded in evil that was primordial. It affected Raymond too, who had been quiet until this point. The dog, who was formidable to begin with, now howled with the intensity of a hound from hell.

Just as suddenly as she started, Ann stopped laughing. Raymond then stopped howling and Nash stopped shivering.

"Wheeooee. That was a good one," she shrieked, wiping tears from her eyes. "You should have seen the look on your face, when I said po' white trash. Anyway, thanks for listening to an old lady. Now, how can I help you find Mark Kelly?"

214

Nash could tell she was genuinely going to try and help him and he felt some remorse for looking down at her. He had only admiration for anyone that tried to better themselves but he made up his mind that if she started to laugh again he was going to shoot her.

"If I may, I'd like to look at his apartment, unless it's been rented," Nash said.

"I wish." Ann replied. "You can look, but it ain't, I mean isn't, going to do you any good."

"Why is that?"

"Cause, I cleaned it up two days after he moved out. I been in this business a long time and I knew he wasn't coming back."

"What about any personal belongings?"

"I sold everything I could and the few things I couldn't I put in the storage shed out back. It's all labeled and boxed up."

"May I see it?" Nash kept his voice to a conversational tone.

"Well I don't know if I ought to let you look at some-one's personal possessions," she said. "After all I ain't ... haven't, seen no badge."

Here it comes, thought Nash. *The subtle shakedown.*

"You mean I didn't show you my badge?" Nash said in mock astonishment. "Here it is right here."

He reached into his front pants pocket and pulled out a twenty-dollar bill.

"And as a matter of fact," he continued, "if you are really cooperative in this investigation there is the distinct possibility that I may leave a few badges here with you."

When she smiled her chock-a-block toothy smile, Nash knew they had an understanding.

"Make yourself comfortable." She beckoned for him to follow and waved her hand towards the room. "I'll be right back."

"Do you need any help?"

215

"No, thanks. I can handle it."

As the screen door banged shut behind her, Nash got up to look around the small apartment. First he made sure that the door separating him and Randy was secured. He then began to peruse her collection of books that were scattered throughout the apartment. There were books stacked everywhere. In the living room there was also a china cabinet which had the glass doors removed and was thus converted into a book cabinet.

This cabinet contained pre-owned Readers' Digest condensed books. Nash could not ever remember seeing that many in one place. Lying in a pile in one corner was a 1962 edition of the World Book Encyclopedia, with the D volume missing. There were also innumerable copies of novels, books on philosophy, music, art, economics, and every subject imaginable.

All of those that he closely inspected were stamped "Sold by the Dade County Library." It was his guess that she bought any and all books that were cheap enough. There were also discarded textbooks on grammar, spelling, math and history. Almost the whole high school curriculum.

What impressed him most of all was the large collection of Cliff notes under the coffee table. The imprint showed that they had been bought used from the Dade County Junior College Bookstore. Cliff notes meant that she was not only reading books, but making a concerted effort to understand what she read.

With such an eclectic selection of books, Nash thought she would be a good candidate for Jeopardy as long as they didn't ask any questions about anything that happened after 1962. She also shouldn't pick the category of "Things that start with D."

Cliff notes made Nash reminisce about his college days that had ended too abruptly. He wondered what he would be doing now if fate had allowed him to graduate. He also wondered if anyone graduated without the help of Cliff notes and who the hell was Cliff.

Randy alerted him that someone was approaching the apartment. He knew it should be the manager but you could get hurt in this business if your assumptions were wrong and you were not prepared. He therefore prepared himself for whoever might come into the apartment.

"I'm back," Ann said, kicking the door open with her foot. Behind her trailed a rusting red Radio Flyer wagon with a medium-sized box in it. She turned around, picked up the box and put it on the crowded coffee table.

Nash wondered if saying red Radio Flyer wagon was redundant, since he had never seen one in any other color.

Ann retreated to the kitchen and reappeared shortly with a small kitchen knife, which she used to open the box she had sealed herself with packing tape.

Nash was anxious to get a look inside.

Once the box was opened she slid it gently in his direction. "Help yourself."

The first objects that Nash retrieved from the box were some girlie magazines. The titles were vaguely familiar, the type of girls who filled the pages was very familiar. He turned the books with the cut pages toward the floor and riffled the pages to see if anything fell out. The only thing that fell from each of the magazines was the centerfold. He carefully refolded them and put them aside.

The next set of magazines were gay men's magazines, the titles with which he was totally unfamiliar and the pages filled with pictures of people doing things he had only heard of. He riffled through these with the same results except that he was much less attracted to the centerfolds.

There was an ashtray with the A 1 Massage Parlor logo imprinted on it. There was also a memo pad that at first held great hopes but upon closer inspection was completely unused. There was a pair of very worn cowboy boots, size ten, and a Polaroid of a bare-chested man sitting in a chair. He appeared to be between thirty and thirty-five years of age, with a medium muscular build and a George Hamilton quality tan. He had

217

shoulder length brown highlighted hair and brown eyes which seemed to protrude from his head.

"This Kelly?" Nash asked, holding the picture so that Ann could see.

"Yea, that's him alright. I can tell from the background that it was taken in his apartment here. Looks like a relatively recent photo too. Like ... I mean ... as I told you, there wouldn't be much in that box. Only the stuff I couldn't sell."

"You're telling me you couldn't sell those magazines?" Nash asked jokingly.

"Oh I'm sure I could have," Ann answered, "but I was too embarrassed to put them out."

"And what have we here?" Nash pulled out an object sealed in a freezer bag.

"I'm not sure." Ann twisted her mouth to the side. "I found that beneath a loose floor board. I'm a very thorough house-maid, as I told you."

Nash peered at the object still in the plastic bag. It had a strange, but somehow familiar, shape. He carefully turned it over and over, looking at it from every angle. It consisted of a large blackened glass bowl at one end, with a long stem wrapped in surgical tape, and a brass coin-shaped object tethered to the middle.

Nash suddenly smiled to himself. *I'm learning quite a bit about you today, Mark Kelly*, he thought.

"Do you know what it is?" Ann asked.

"Yes, I'm pretty sure I do," Nash answered.

"Well. What is it?" she asked impatiently.

"In a minute." Nash held his hand up. "First tell me what you do when you clean the vacant apartments?"

"First," she said, "I get all of my cleaning materials, put them in my wagon and go to the apartment. I put on a pair of plastic gloves and sort all of the objects that were left behind, if any. I wear gloves because of the AIDS thing and all."

"Of course, you'd be foolish not to."

"Then I take all the things that don't belong in the apartment to my storage shed. Then I clean the apartment, starting with the bathroom and move to the front room and out the door. I usually use a diluted solution of detergent and bleach. I read where bleach is supposed to kill the AIDS virus. I tried bleach and ammonia together once and ended up in the emergency room. They cause toxic fumes you know."

"Do you wear gloves the entire time you're cleaning?"

"I sure do."

"When did you find this object?" Nash held up the bag very carefully.

"It was the next day when I do the floors. I always do the floors last. It was hidden under a floor board in the bedroom closet. I noticed the loose board and reached my hand in there. I think I was hoping it was hidden treasure.

"I pulled that grimy lookin' thing out and went and got a plastic bag and sealed it up. It was so disgustin' lookin' I didn't even want it next to the other things in storage. I started to throw it out but I figured it might be important to whoever left it there. It was probably Mark's since I cleaned that same apartment before he moved in. I've found some strange things in these apartments that I thought wouldn't have no value to nobody and have folks come back and act like they had the Shroud of Turin. I remember finding some old bones in an apartment once, a tenant left behind.

"He owed me a month's rent 'cause he hadn't given me thirty days' notice. I thought that was the end of that until he reappeared and wanted those bones back. Told him he had to pay me the month's rent plus interest and he did. Said those two little chicken bones were his mojo or good luck which I thought was pretty funny since all he had was bad luck for the whole two years he lived here."

Nash thought that for someone who probably smoked for over forty years that Ann was extremely longwinded.

"Did you have gloves on when you picked this up?"

"Heavens, yes!"

"Great."

"Why's that so great?"

"Because this is a crack pipe and if Mark Kelly was the user then I might be able to get a decent set of prints from it."

"You have his picture and name." Ann had a quizzical look on her face. "What do you want with fingerprints?"

"True, we have a picture, but that might not be his real name. If I'm lucky enough to get a good print I'll be able to learn quite a bit more about him in a relatively short period of time."

"Well, I hope you get the bastard. Whatever his name might be."

"You have certainly been helpful," Nash counted out one hundred dollars in twenties and placed them on the coffee table.

"Why are you so anxious for me to catch him?"

"Like I told you, if they don't give thirty days' notice they owe me a months' rent. It's right there in the lease. If you catch him I have some chance of getting my money. I run these apartments for a cheap bastard that lives up north in Connecticut. He lets me live free and manage the place if I continue to turn a profit, which isn't easy. So every little bit helps. You see, I'm only a vacant apartment away from being homeless myself.

"With the condition and location of these places I can't even rent to illegals. It's too far from the freeway system or the bus routes. The only people I get are basically those that don't want to be found easily ... or at all."

Nash knew that he had to leave without giving her another chance to wear out his ear.

He stood and spoke casually. "May I have that picture and that pipe? I'll return them if you like."

"Keep 'em." She held the door for him to exit into the dusty front yard.

As the door closed behind him, he could hear her letting Randy back into the front room.

Maurice Webber's name was the third one on Mark Kelly's list, excluding Cassie Parker. The two names that preceded his were dead ends. One literally. Eduardo Fernandez had managed to get himself stabbed to death outside a topless bar in Coral City two months ago.

Milo Foreman was an eighty-year old widower who had suffered a stroke more than two years previously, resulting in a right-sided paralysis. Mark Kelly had assisted Mr. Foreman's physical therapist three times a week. When questioned about Mark Kelly's absence, Mr. Foreman expressed some concern, but told Nash that Kelly was the fourth assistant he had hired in fourteen months and had already replaced him.

Maurice Webber owned and managed a small art gallery and frame shop. Nash drove to the address and surveyed the surroundings. *Very nice*, he thought, *verrry nice.*

Nash always tried to "interview" people at their place of work if at all possible. He believed people would feel more comfortable there than having a stranger in their home. There was also less chance of any surprises or grave misunderstandings.

Although Maurice's Art Nouveau was upscale and trendy, when Nash entered the shop, it was empty. Nash noticed that the single occupant seemed extremely nervous. As Nash moved toward him, the asthenic proprietor looked past Nash to the door, and also around the store, to see if they were truly alone.

Nash had encountered this reaction innumerable times in the past. He knew many whites were uncomfortable in the presence of blacks. Nash always felt somewhat disgusted with this scenario, but knew that he could often use it to his advantage.

"Mr. Webber?" Nash asked politely.

"Yes," the man replied, obviously relieved. He figured a robber would hardly know his name.

"My name is Taylor Nash and I'm a Private Investigator. I'm here to ask you some questions about Mark Kelly in regards to a murder investigation."

"I don't have to answer any questions from you about Mark Kelly or anyone else." Maurice caught a breath of confidence. "Besides, I don't believe Mark is capable of murdering anyone."

Didn't say Mark Kelly killed anyone, thought Nash. And with Mark missing, Nash thought it was strange that Maurice Webber didn't ask if Mark Kelly were the victim.

"Of course you don't have to answer any questions," Nash said, putting his face as close to Maurice's as possible without touching him. "But I think it would be in your best interest if you do."

That should be sufficient, thought Nash. Not an overt threat, just a subtle push. He would play the good cop and the bad cop if necessary. In any case he was going to make certain that Maurice wanted him to be happy.

Once again Maurice glanced towards the door. *Never a customer when you really need one,* he thought. Even a browser, which he usually hated, would help. Maurice quickly assessed his position before he spoke. "I guess it wouldn't hurt to talk."

"Totally painless," said Nash, smiling and being the good cop again.

Nash was not a man to make instantaneous judgments, but Maurice Webber was an uncompromisingly, unabashedly, decidedly effeminate man.

Nash remembered a conversation he had once with an admittedly gay cop who told Nash that he disliked extremely effeminate behavior in gay men. Nash remembered that he called them raging queens or Nellies. When Nash looked somewhat confused about the whole issue, the cop said that surely Nash was offended by the stereotypical behavior of some blacks.

Nash replied that he was only offended by people who did not try to live up to their personal potential and thus became parasites.

The cop then asked Nash about the scenario in the movie, "Soldier's Story," where the sergeant was embarrassed by the foot shuffling, Uncle Tom character of Junior.

Nash said that he indeed saw the movie and remembered the scenes quite vividly, but that Junior was being the only person that he knew how to be and if people had difficulties with that, it was their problem and not anyone else's.

The cop gave Nash quite a long stare, told him that he was being grand and never spoke to him again.

Maurice Webber was approximately five-feet nine inches tall and on a good day weighed maybe one hundred twenty pounds. His angular, colorless face contained pale blue eyes, a Grecian nose and lips that were barely visible. There was no muscularity to be seen in his physique.

It was if he had never exerted himself physically during his thirty-four years on earth. His thinning hair was bleached blond, but only on the top. The remainder was dyed an extreme black. He had two diamond stud earrings in his right ear and a large gold hoop in his left. He was wearing a loose-fitting lavender shirt with frilly sleeves that could only be described as a blouse. To complete the outfit, he wore tight white pants made of some kind of stretch material that brought the word

Lycra immediately to Nash's mind, and black leather boots that extended above his knees.

Studying Maurice in all of his splendor made Nash wonder if there had been gay pirates. Thinking about it a little more he was sure there must have been. The percentage of homosexuals in the human gene pool has probably remained constant from time immemorial. Genetics 101. Maybe they had a ship called the Flaming Queen.

Feeling more at ease and not wanting anyone to interrupt or overhear his conversation with Taylor Nash, Maurice Webber walked gracefully to the front door and locked it after turning over the open sign to indicate that his place of business was now closed. He then led Nash into a back room that was full of completed frames, nearly completed frames and frame parts of all descriptions. Watercolors, oil paintings, lithographs and artwork of all sizes and diversity were heaped upon one another in a conglomeration of clutter.

Maurice motioned for Nash to sit at a small round Lucite table with two matching chairs and joined him.

"Would you like a soft drink or some Perrier?" Maurice asked.

"No, thank you," Nash was cordial.

"How did you first meet Mark Kelly?"

"He was introduced to me by a mutual friend." Maurice studied his fingernails.

"Can you tell me the name of this friend?" queried Nash.

"I could," Maurice spoke quietly, "but it wouldn't be of much help to you. You see he died over a year ago from ... from ... you know."

"No, I'm afraid I don't know."

"You know," Maurice spoke again in hushed tones, blinking his baby blues and fighting back tears, "that wretched disease."

"You mean AIDS?"

Maurice clutched the front of his shirt with both hands, leaned backwards in the chair as he raised his closed eyes to the ceiling, and nodded his head emphatically.

Nash hoped Maurice would not faint.

With his interviewee in a weakened state, Nash decided to listen to his intuition and go for broke.

"I want you to tell me where Mark Kelly is," he said with a deadpan expression.

His forceful request had the desired effect.

"Why should I? I mean, I don't know where he is," answered Maurice nervously. "Even if I did know. Why should I tell you?"

"As I told you previously, I'm investigating a murder. I think your acquaintance was involved. Do you know what an accessory after the fact is?" Nash was careful not to use the word, "friend."

Maurice managed somehow to become even paler and shook his head slowly.

"That means if you give assistance to someone after you know they may be guilty of a crime, you may share in the punishment. And I'm going on record right now and will inform the police department that I made it known to you that Mark Kelly is a fugitive in an ongoing investigation for murder in the first degree. Personally, I don't think you would do well in a penal institution," said Nash, putting extra emphasis on the word penal.

"I kinda know where he is," Maurice said timidly.

"How the hell do you kind of know where someone is?" Nash shouted, jumping to his feet and becoming the bad cop again.

Maurice looked as if he thought Nash would strike him. Nash almost felt a twinge of guilt.

Maurice continued as Nash sat back down in his seat. "About three weeks ago, I got a call here at the shop from Mark. He told me he was in a bit of a jam and had to leave town in a hurry. He's been in one scrape after another since

225

I've known him," said Maurice, trying to dispel some of the tension.

"Get to the point, " Nash said sourly.

"He asked me to send him some money. Which I did. He only gave me a post office box number."

"Which you'll be more than happy to give to me."

Maurice stood up and gave Nash the meanest look that he could muster under the circumstances. It wasn't much. It reminded Nash of a pouting child.

Maurice turned to walk away when Nash yelled, "And where do you think you're going?"

"You said you wanted the address," said Maurice with his mean and angry voice. It wasn't much better than his mean look.

Maurice stomped over to a large metal file cabinet and pulled out a stack of papers. After looking through them, he handed an index card to Nash. He then stepped back, crossed his arms and put on his mean face again.

Looking at Maurice standing there, pouting, Nash first thought that all he needed was a good spanking. But then he thought that Maurice might enjoy that too much.

"Thank you for your cooperation." Nash turned to leave.

"Tell Mark I tried to resist. Better yet, tell him you beat it out of me." Maurice batted his eyes and smiled playfully.

Mark Kelly had not traveled far, and with the post office box address that Maurice had given him, it didn't take long for Nash to locate Kelly's new address. Nash simply waited for him to come home and followed him into his rented trailer home.

"Who are you, and what do you want?" asked a frightened Kelly as Nash literally pushed him into his own residence.

"You Mark Kelly?" Taylor asked.

"Who wants to know?" Mark replied.

"Someone who's going to tell the police where to find you unless you answer a few questions."

"So what do you want to know?" Mark took a seat in a tattered green velveteen loveseat which had come with the furnished trailer.

"Do you know Cassie Smith?" Nash asked as he looked for a clean place to sit.

"Yeah, I knew her."

Past tense, Taylor thought, he knows she's dead. "How well did you know her?" Taylor, not finding a clean spot, placed a folded newspaper on a terminally soiled ottoman before sitting on it.

"What do you mean by that?" Kelly asked.

"What part of the question lost you? How well did you know her?" Nash's voice sounded harsh.

"I was just her masseur."

"Just her masseur who happened to leave town right after she was murdered."

"I didn't kill her." Mark had a pleading sound in his voice.

"I know you didn't," Taylor answered sympathetically. He always said that, even if he thought or even knew he was talking to the perpetrator. It was a ploy that said to them that you were on their side.

"Maybe you had better tell me the whole story." Nash crossed his legs.

"Cassie and I go way back. Bridgeton, Iowa. We were in high school together. Even in the same class. In fact, we both decided to drop out at the same time. We were real close. Not sexually or anything but we kinda thought alike. We bummed around town doing nothin' 'cause there was nothin' to do. Coupla dead end jobs here and there and after we saved a little money we left. We decided there had to be something better somewhere and we were gonna get our share."

"Go on," Nash pressed.

"We had a few run-ins with the local authorities before we left but nothing big. You can only have big things in big places is what she always used to say. So we set out for a big place."

"And that was?" Nash was getting impatient.

"The same place all Midwestern trouble makers go, of course. Los Angeles. We hung around a while, found people with similar attitudes and naturally got into more trouble."

"People always thought Cassie and me were lovers but we were just accomplices. I really don't think she even had sex until we got to L.A.

"Unless it was with her stepfather like people said at home. Anyway, she is ... or was nice-looking. If you ever saw her you know what I mean, and a coupla times when things were real hard up she turned a few tricks to keep us from getting thrown out on the street. That was the way we survived. You know what I'm sayin'. Just small time hustling and petty thievery until I got introduced to drugs. Cassie never had a weakness for stuff like that. I mean she would smoke a joint or take a drink every now and then just to be sociable but that was all. She liked money, money, and mo' money.

"Then one day those drugs told me I had to have more money than our little games could supply. So, I wake up one morning and decide to stick up a drug store. Just like that. No ifs ands or buts about it. I figured I would walk out of there with either some money or some good pharmaceuticals, if you know what I mean, brother."

Nash responded with a silent nod.

"I had a loaded gun some guy had traded me for some dope so I had the right tools for the job at hand. I never even got out the store. I was booked into County and that was the last I saw of her. I pulled a double nickel for armed robbery, but got out in three because of overcrowding. Thank heaven for all the dope pushers, gang bangers, driveby shooters and assorted antisocial psychopaths in this country. Shit, without them I might a still been up there. You know what I'm sayin'?"

Nash again nodded knowingly.

"When I got out I was wondering where I could go. I heard that down in Texas if you get caught you only serve about a month for every year they give you but who the hell wants to live in Texas. I thought about what Cassie had said about needing a big place to make a big deal so I headed for the biggest ballbreakin', dealmakin' place of all. Miami."

"I just sorta drifted into this massage stuff. I really wanted to be an escort for high society ladies. So I go and join this escort service and what happens? All the calls I get are from guys. I been in the joint and all, but men really ain't my cup of tea."

"Um hmmm," Nash thought to himself.

"So I ask the guy runnin' this service if he can help me out. He says sure and introduces me to a guy runnin' a massage parlor thing. I do this for a while which is only a front for prostitution but I ain't makin' any money. All of a sudden it hits me. I put ads in the paper and upscale magazines and say that I have this credential and that credential and all kinds of bullshit and that I'll come to your home. Make it real convenient like. And damn if people didn't start calling.

"I pumped a lot of iron in the joint, and while I was working the massage parlor, I stayed in the tanning booth so I look like a real healthy guy. I even gave up drinking and smoking cigarettes and marijuana so people wouldn't smell it on my breath.

"Tell the truth I never liked booze that much and I could get by with smokin' dope on my days off. People really liked me comin' over to their house and givin' them a good massage which I had learned how to do at the parlor. But while I'm in the house I'm casing the place real good. Soon I know the whole layout. Usually I would work there a minimum of three

229

months before I would go back and take everything they got."
Mark took a deep breath.

"You'd be surprised at how many people treated me just like a member of the family. If we went out the door together, sometimes they would turn off the alarm right in front of me. The dog loves me, the neighbors know me. What a deal. If the cops investigate after a break-in, my prints are expected to be all over the house, anyway."

Nash didn't have to prompt Mark to continue. He was definitely long-winded.

"And let me tell you nobody was sorrier than me when the vics told me about all the stuff somebody had stole. I swear I even cried a time or two. Sometimes after the home-owners and I bitched about what a shame it was and how the city was goin' straight to hell nonstop, they would end up showing me how their amazing new system was gonna keep the burglars from coming back. The best part of all was that they would refer me to their other rich friends. I'm startin' to think some-one up there likes me. 'Course I don't rob 'em all in case the cops start gettin' too smart."

"Just what does this autobiography of a small-time crook have to do with what I asked you?" growled Nash, growing impatient.

"I'm gettin' to it," replied Mark, grinding his cigarette butt into the grimy carpet with the toe of his shoe. "You got another one a them smokes?"

Nash reached into his jacket pocket and tossed Mark the remainder of the pack.

"Thanks, bro'." Mark lit up, inhaled deeply and gushed a stream of smoke from the corner of his mouth. Satisfied, he resumed his story.

"Now where was I? Oh, yeah. Just when I think things couldn't get any better, I get a call from one of the plushest addresses in the city. I make my usual appointment and act very casual about the whole thing on the phone but I'm settin' this one up in my mind even before the first visit. I go to the address and when I walk in who do I see but Cassie.

"She and I recognize each other right away but there's an older man in the room who I take to be her husband or boyfriend or somethin'. She gives me the look to be real cool. So cool is how I play it. And very professionally, if I do say so myself. The guy introduces himself as her husband, Dr. Parker, and leaves. I think he just wanted to see who was gonna be rubbing on his wife." He paused and took a drag on his cigarette.

"After he introduced himself I knew immediately he wasn't getting no massage, 'cause doctors are the worst when it comes to their own health. I was on this scam over three years and never had a doctor. Had a lot of their wives, though, if you catch my drift," said Kelly, winking at Nash through exhaled cigarette smoke. "They sure are a bunch of pampered bitches. I always say that when I die I want to come back as a doctor's wife. Or maybe Liz Taylor's poodle."

"So he leaves the room," Taylor interjected dryly.

"No, he leaves the house. And we kinda stare at each other for a while. Then we start to do this strange kinda dance where we start circling each other and lookin' at each other from every possible angle. After about a minute when we're sure that it is, who we're lookin' at, we sit down facing each other. We still didn't say nothin' for quite a while. Finally she looks at me and says, 'How long you been working this number?' Then I look at her and say, How long you been working yours? We both started laughin' and huggin' and it was like no time had passed between us at all. Just like we could take up right before I got sent to the joint.

"Right off she tells me she left L.A. the day I got picked up and decided to try to be a nine-to-fiver. She moved to San Diego and enrolled in a business school. Learned some elementary skills. Typing, answering phones and shit and hired out as a temp. Thing was with her good looks, the bosses were always hitting on her. She told me she found some guy in San Diego who had a little change in his pocket and was doing pretty good until his wife wised up. The wife not only got her fired but ruined her rep so bad she had to leave town.

"She leaves San Diego for Miami and winds up working in a hospital as a Unit Secretary. You know those are the broads on the floor that answer the phones and ain't a nurse. Well, it wasn't long before the doctors started taking notice. Prob'ly wan't much of a contest really since she told me she could sit at the desk with her make up perfect, wearing street clothes and look stunning, while the nurses had on baggy uniforms and were emptying bedpans and shit. She goes on to tell me that this Dr. Evander Parker seemed to be the most agreeable, affluent, and available. Her triple A club. She set her sights on him and he was a dead fish. She told him she was from a small town in the Midwest and that her parents were dead. They get married and live happily ever after."

"Until you showed up," Nash said bitterly.

"Uh uh, you got it wrong. I never wanted anything from her, but things started going sour for me. The state of Florida in its wisdom decide that they want to outlaw all of these massage parlors that are fronts for prostitution. So instead of closin' 'em what do they do? They decide to make all the people that work in the places get licenses from the state.

"You have to fill out forms and get investigated. Finger-printed and stuff. Well, that kinda left me out in the cold. They mighta put two and two together and figured that a felon who spent time in some of the houses what got robbed, might just know somethin' about some a those burglaries."

"So you start to blackmail your old friend?"

"Wasn't like that at all. I just told her that I needed to borrow some money and when things got better I would pay her back."

"And things just never got better."

"How'd you guess, Sherlock? That easy gig I had been workin' left my brain numb. I couldn't think of shit to do. I couldn't even go back to the massage parlors. I swear I almost called some of those queer guys from before."

"So what did you do?"

"What does any red-blooded American, who's down on his luck, do? I went on welfare and started sellin' drugs."

"And was that enough for you to get by?"

"Not with the kind of money I was used to. Cassie would still have to lend me money .... And she never said a mean word to me." He pointed at Nash with the cigarette held between his middle and index fingers.

"Maybe she knew better," Nash snorted.

"Maybe so." Mark laughed.

"So there was an implied threat?"

"Look, I never said I would tell anybody, anything ... and if a woman wanted to give me some money whose business is it?"

"So now it's give you money," Nash said through tightened lips.

"Loan, give, whatever, it was nobody's business but hers and mine. She would even bring it over if I was too busy."

"When did you start using again?"

"I swear I didn't want to but since I went to the joint they came out with this crack thing. So I tried it. Biiig mistake."

He slapped his forehead in regret. "I started smoking up all my profits, then I started smoking up what I was supposed to sell. If it hadn't a been for Cassie my suppliers woulda boxed me a long time ago."

"So when did you decide to kill her?" Nash asked nonchalantly.

"Kill her. Man, she was the goose with the golden eggs. I wouldn't never a killed her. That wouldn't a made no damn sense."

"People on drugs do a lot of things that don't make sense."

"That high I ain't never been. Besides, I thought you said you knew that I didn't kill her. Get outta here, you fuck. I thought you were going to say it was the other guy. You don't know jack."

"Don't get too excited, my friend." Nash calmly tugged his pants leg slightly to reveal the gun in his ankle holster. "What other guy?"

His composure instantly restored, Mark Kelly continued. "The night before she gets killed a guy comes to my apartment."

"Had you ever seen him before?" asked Nash.

"No ... and I hope to hell that I never see him again. It's late at night when I get a knock at the door but I don't think nothin' of it. I'm figurin' it's a customer so I let him in. This guy sits down nice as you please and then starts to ask me a lot a questions about Cassie. He says it ain't no use lying, cause he knows that I know her since he followed her to my place a coupla times.

"Immediately I take this guy for a real flake. He's got on a fake mustache and dark glasses with a hat pulled down almost to the top of the sunglasses.

Right away I make up my mind not to tell this guy nothin.' I ask him in a not too nice way to leave and when he doesn't budge, I get up to escort him to the door. I been on the pipe but I figure I can still handle this guy 'cause we're about the same size.

"That's when this fake guy pulls out a very real gun. I still got my mind made up not to tell him shit. I look over at him and give him my best, 'I'll kill you, you dumb prick' look. That's one of the few useful skills you acquire in the joint. A look to let people know that you mean life or death business. I never expected what happened next. This Halloween prick pulls off his hat, glasses and mustache and lets me look deep into his eyes. And his eyes are tellin' me that if I don't spill my guts, he's gonna spill 'em for me.

234

"He was talking to me with his eyes in no uncertain terms and brother I wanna tell you I got the message loud and clear. So I sit down and tell him the whole story just like I just told you. Then as polite as you please this Trick or Treat fool gets up and walks toward the door. As he's leaving he actually thanks me. He finally closes the door behind him, hopefully never to be seen by me ever again. The next day I see on the TV that Cassie's been murdered and I hit the road. I wasn't waiting for that maniac to show himself to me again, 'cause I didn't get his motivation the first time. I been keeping a low profile here 'til you showed up. "How did you find me anyway?"

"Maurice," Nash replied flatly.

"Maurice. That bitch. I shoulda known it was him."

"Yeah, it wasn't too hard actually. I just went to your last place of gainful employment. The massage parlor. Told them I knew that you were out of town and I would pay them for your special client list. Maurice was near the top of the list. When I went to see him he told me about the P.O. box number you gave him to send you a little help now and again. I waited by the P.O. box for you to show up and here we are."

"If you went to his place, I can imagine he told you everything right away," said Kelly. "He's scared to death of black people. No particular reason. I guess it was his small town southern upbringing. He's Jewish, you know. He'd tell Adolph Hitler where his mother was hiding if they sent a black person to ask where she was.

"I always kidded him about being the only Jewish Redneck I ever met. He had a tough time growing up in the south. Being Jewish and .... sensitive. His family has a little dough and I think his father sends him money never to come home. His father being a Jewish good old boy."

"Don't you mean one of the good-old Goys?"

"What?"

"Forget it. By the way, where were you at one o'clock on the morning of Cassie's death?"

235

"Oh, so now here comes the rubber hose. I was pawning everything I owned, borrowed, traded dope for, or stole, to make my getaway. You can check with Reuben, who works at the TV repair shop on the corner of Southwest 14th and third. He must a read the panic on my face 'cause he practically stole those stolen things from me. He only gave me about one third of what I could have gotten from a pawn shop, if I coulda gone to a pawn shop. You check with him, 'cause he had me help him put the things in his truck which took a minute less than forever."

Back in Miami, it wasn't so easy for Nash to get Reuben to talk. He wasn't afraid of black people. In fact, he tried to intimidate just about everyone. A useful trait in the fencing business. It takes a lot of courage to tell a guy who may have just killed someone for a diamond ring that you are only going to give him half of what he thought he could get for it. Add to the fact that the guy is a killer or potential killer who may still have his weapon with him and may be high on drugs. No, it wasn't easy to get Reuben to talk.

As a matter of record, Reuben actually looked twice at the videotape Nash made in its entirety, including the part which showed him loading stolen merchandise into his truck. The tape showed the comings and goings of perhaps two dozen people over a period of three days, bringing in quite an assortment of goods, most of which were not televisions.

Furthermore, no one ever left with a television. Nash told him he would have a hard time explaining to the police how he was going to repair the myriad of items he was receiving, such as a rack of men's suits. Despite the video-taped evidence, he still looked at the video twice before he would talk. Unhappily Reuben finally confirmed the times that Mark Kelly had told Nash.

One thing though. Nash gave Reuben credit for having balls, but having a good set of cahones is never enough in the fencing business. Sometimes you had to think quickly or die, because a guy wired on drugs is not threatened very easily.

There was quite a story about Reuben in the neighborhood and how a guy came into the store with his latest acquisition, for which of course Reuben offered him pennies on the dollar. The guy pulls out his gun stating that Reuben was the biggest thief in the neighborhood but there would soon be a vacancy in that esteemed position. However, before things got out of hand, Reuben offered him a good price for the gun and everyone was happy.

Chapter Nineteen

D r. Evan Parker smiled to himself. He thought that life on the streets would be difficult for him. He was wrong. It was impossible. There were no disillusioned philosophers, there were no eccentric literati suffering willingly for their art.

However, there were people who were more than willing to separate your head from your shoulders for such a faux pas as standing too close to their shopping cart, for sleeping in their space under the freeway, for having a pair of shoes that were better than their own, for having a dollar that they needed, or for the most frequent reason of all ... no reason.

Dr. Evander Parker did not think of getting a paper out of this experience. He just wanted to get out of this experience with his ass intact.

Forty-eight hours earlier, at approximately four in the morning, Evan Parker heard a familiar sound at an unfamiliar time. Nash knocked lightly on the apartment door once and then let himself in without waiting for a reply.

"What's going on?" a sleepy Evan Parker asked.

"Heat's been turned up," Nash said.

"What do you mean?" Parker sat up but was still groggy.

"What I mean is, that since the near riot at the funeral, the Mayor, the City Council and most of all, the police, have been whipped into a frenzy by the media and various influential citizen groups. Especially the ones to which your wife belonged. They are wondering why a man suspected of triple homicide, one of which was his beloved wife's, cannot be located and brought to justice. A man who seems to have no fear of killing, an intelligent man whose sense of reason seems to have abandoned him ... thus putting the entire populace of South Florida and possibly the world at risk."

"You know that I had nothing to do with all of that. So why are you waking me up at this hour?"

"I'm waking you up to tell you that you have to hit the streets. Now!!! One of my friends at the police station has told me that they are under a tremendous amount of pressure and I'm thinking Rolle might have second thoughts about having me help you. He may not be as convinced as I am that you are totally innocent."

"So what? You told me yourself, that no one knows about this apartment."

"And that's true, but Rolle is a very good detective and it wouldn't be long before he could turn this or any address. So, doctor, put on your clothes, grab what things you may need and get out ... please ... while I eliminate all traces of your being here.

"Oh, yeah," Nash continued, "I got a new number for you to remember."

On the streets Dr. Parker kept to himself, which was not hard to do, since he did not seem to fit in with any of the general cliques of people around him. There were people who obviously needed to be committed to a psychiatric facility. These were the ones with the vacant stares, who often talked back to the voices they heard emanating from their own psyches. There were the addicts of one substance or another.

The prime drug of choice to abuse was alcohol. This was consumed in the form of cheap wine in which certain winemakers had increased the percentage of alcohol for just such a market. The last group consisted of those who had fallen through the safety net of society and had given up on returning to their former status. There was no self-esteem and hence no effort for any positive accomplishment.

Their main aspiration was to seek revenge on the society that had forsaken them. This anger took many forms, ranging from violent behavior and promiscuity, to almost any antisocial behavior that Parker had ever encountered or read about. These groupings were not mutually exclusive, with some individuals claiming membership in each club, thus blurring any boundaries that may have otherwise been established.

The alienation that Parker felt reminded him of his early life. He didn't seem to fit in with any group at that time either. And back then he was trying.

Parker's father was a self-made man. A hard worker from humble beginnings, who eventually escalated from plumber's apprentice to owning his own plumbing company, complete with a fleet of vans and sixteen employees. A late-blooming gambling addiction would eventually erode all of the family's assets except the trust fund he and his wife established for their only son.

Parker's father had lofty aspirations for his son, none of which included being involved in the plumbing business. He felt that his son should have the best education available and therefore sent him off to a private military school at the age of ten. Although his father's intentions were good, he didn't adequately research the schools before making a selection. The school that Parker eventually attended was more of a reformatory than a bastion of higher learning. It was a school where parents sent children who had been kicked out of other schools or who had other disciplinary problems. The student body of his pre-college days was not too dissimilar from the people with whom he was now affiliated.

His father was always proud of his grades, which truthfully would have been a full point lower at a good public school.

Often times, he was the only student in class who was paying any attention at all. His grade point average, however, was good enough to get him admitted to the state university, where he had to work very hard. Fortunately he had developed extremely good study habits in his preparatory school where almost every other student was a distraction.

Evander Parker thought that the Greeks were correct when they decided that a circle was the perfect figure. Here, near what he was sure to be the end of his life, he felt that he was again surrounded by people that he did not care for and who could care even less for him. He became very morose when he thought of what his parents had sacrificed for him and how disappointed they both would be. He was thankful they were both dead so that they would not share his shame.

Parker's daily routine was simple, regimented and un-changing. He was usually the first one of his loosely-knit group, that shared sleeping quarters under the Twenty-Second Avenue overpass, to awaken. To awaken being the key phrase as some of them seemed never to sleep. He then checked his grocery cart for his meager possessions and went to the corner service station to wash, using the hose intended for filling radiators.

He would then dry himself with the army surplus blanket in his cart that he also used on infrequently cool nights. Finally he was ready to make his rounds of the trash bins in search of aluminum cans. Although he still had over eight hundred dollars left from the money Salvatore had given him, he knew it would be safer not to let that fact be known.

After collecting cans all morning and afternoon, it was off to the redemption center for three or four dollars, depending on his cache of cans. His trek then continued to one of two regional soup kitchens.

One was supported by the government and the other was sponsored by the church. He never trusted the government much and was rapidly losing any faith he had in the church. But he had to eat. The food was equally bad at both centers. How they managed to imbue all of the food—irrespective of it

241

being meat, vegetables, poultry, soup, fish or casseroles—with the same brownish hue would remain a mystery, as did some of the entrees. However, at the church kitchen, you had to listen to a sermon before you could be served. He then would walk the eight miles back to the overpass, take a ten or fifteen minute nap and start his route over again, searching the bins for their late afternoon and evening deposits.

On his afternoon journey home, he would pass several dozen pay phones and sigh mournfully at each one. It had been a long time since he had talked to Taylor Nash. After his evening meal, he would stop by the service station on his way back to the overpass and try unsuccessfully to wash the day's grime from his body. Even with the ever-present danger, he slept better than he had in years. And with the exception of occasional head lice, he was probably in the best physical condition of his life.

He thought it was ironic that the privileged of our society had to struggle to attain good physical condition in order to survive, wherein the underprivileged kept in good physical condition by struggling to survive.

The lack of excess fat and calories in his diet, coupled with daily exercise, may have been good for his body, but the stress of living on the streets was beginning to take its toll. The last time Parker had looked in the mirror in the men's restroom at the soup kitchen, he saw his father's face reflected in the glass. It was the face his father wore from the time he was informed of his financial ruin to the day of his death, six month later. Dr. Parker vowed to never look into a mirror again.

He knew the signs and symptoms of clinical depression and he had every one of them, especially morning fatigue. He started getting up later and later and neglected to eat. He was starting to lose weight and the others of the group stayed farther and farther away from him, thinking that he must have the AIDS virus.

"Hello."

"It's me."

At poolside, Midge was resplendent in a turquoise ensemble, which included a turquoise Izod LaCoste shirt, turquoise poplin slacks, socks, deck shoes and a turquoise Charlotte Hornets' baseball cap, with the visor turned to the back.

"Nice outfit," Sal said sarcastically. He thought Midge looked like a popsicle he had seen a little black kid eating yesterday. And just about the same size.

"What's the problem?" Midge asked, knowing that Sal never invited him over socially, which was okay with him.

"The problem is Dr. Parker."

"How can he be a problem? Nobody's seen him for weeks."

"That's the problem," Sal continued. "I thought the police would have picked him up way before now. I don't know what this city's coming to. Here's a guy wanted for multiple murder and arson and the police can't find him. I have a good mind to call the police department myself and complain."

Sal smiled, because he thought what he just said was clever.

Midge smiled because Sal did.

"It's possible for too many things to go wrong with a guy running around loose," Sal said. "I think we better have the good doctor taken care of."

"How we gonna do that, if nobody's seen him?"

"We just have to find him. It's a good bet he's not staying at the Fountainbleau, so get some people to scour around and look for him. Get some copies of the picture that was in the papers and use some independent people so no one knows it's us that's looking for him."

"So you think you saw him."

"Uh-uh. I know I saw him. I been following him for two days."

"So where is he?"

"So where's the money? If I tell you where he is, you might take him out, and cut me out of the action all together."

"You're hurting my feelings. After all the jobs we done together, you think I'd do that to you?"

They looked at each other and laughed. No honor among thieves here.

One was a skinny, black, hard knot of a man named Freeman Alexander, better known as Slick. Not because he was smooth, but because he was oily. He wore a black leather vest without a shirt, and knee length camouflage-patterned cargo pants. The other was Franco Mangelli, an Italian with an inflated Bocci-ball build, better known as Mango Mangelli, because of his penchant for doing business in the city's black sections.

"I'll tell you the deal," Franco said," you tell me where the doctor is and after the job is done, I'll come back and pay you."

"No way," Slick said. "You give me the money and then I'll tell you where the doctor is hiding out."

Again they stared at each other and began to laugh vigorously.

"Enough of this bullshit," Franco said, wiping a tear from his eye. "We'll do it as always. I'll bring the money, you do the job and after I can see that everything's been taken care of, you'll get your share."

"Solid," Slick agreed.

"Who's puttin' up the dough"? Slick asked, offhandedly.

"Does it matter to you?" Mango sounded belligerant.

"No."

"Keep it that way."

"How much is it?" asked Slick, getting basic.

"We'll split five thousand. Sixty-forty, with me getting the sixty."

"Come again," said Slick, his voice now an octave higher. "How you figure that?"

"Cause I got the money."

"Which you gonna have to give back. Besides I found the mark and I'm gonna have to do all the dirty work."

"Which you like."

"Don't like it enough to give you sixty percent. Way I figure it, you pro'ly already got the five thousand, just on word I saw the doc. Might even have it on you now, which don't matter to me. Man, like you would hate to give all that money back. But on the other hand, I ain't seen no money, so I can walk away from this whole deal feeling no worse than I started out."

"Okay, fifty-fifty."

"Mo' better," Slick said, enthusiastically.

"You get paid after I see the body, naturally."

"Naturally."

"How did you find him anyway?"

"Wasn't hard actually. Heard a rumor that some new white dude was hanging 'round under the overpass on Twenty Second Avenue. Showed his picture to a coupla of winos and they weren't too sure, but said he talked real proper. I went over and took a look myself. He's real bummed out, but it's him. Took some binoculars second time, to get a closer look and it's definitely him. Like I told you I followed him for two days. Shouldn't be too hard to get rid of."

Slick wasn't worried about revealing the location of the doctor now, because he had struck a deal, and even a man with connections like Mango would think twice about crossing this vicious weasel.

"You sure you can find him again?" asked Mangelli, wanting to be assured once more.

"I told you, I been followin' him for two days."

"You sure he didn't see you? You didn't scare him off?"

"Don't worry. I'ma profess'nal."

* * *

245

"Somebody's been following me!" he shrieked into the phone. "I mean, Hello. This is me, Evan Parker, is that you Nash? I mean who is it?"

The pay phone had not completed a full ring, before Parker picked it up and started his rambling tirade.

He felt himself beginning to panic. So could Taylor Nash on the other end of the line, who had placed the call from another pay phone.

"Calm down, my friend," said Taylor as serenely as possible. "Take a deep breath and tell me what's going on. I got to a pay phone as quickly as I could, after I got your beep."

"Someone's been following me. I did like you told me and walked past big display windows, looking for reflections of anyone trailing me. At first, I wasn't sure, but I saw the same guy for two days in a row. I'm getting out of here."

"Don't do that just yet," Nash said. "Have you seen him recently?"

"No. But if he's a policeman then ...."

"I don't think you have to worry about his being a policeman, because they would have picked you up immediately."

"Yes, yes of course. You're right," Parker said nervously.

"What did he look like?" Nash asked.

"You have to remember, I never looked right at him like you told me and all I saw of him were reflections in the windows, but I'm sure it was the same person both times and he was right behind me. Not too close, but close enough and ...."

"Parker."

"Yes."

"What did he look like?" Nash said slowly and deliberately.

"Oh yes," he replied, mildly embarrassed. "He was about six feet tall, very dark, and thin. He looked like he didn't have an ounce of body fat on him."

"Uh-huh."

"Is that all you have to say is Uh-huh? What am I supposed to do?"

"You just continue your regular routine. I'll be close by if there's any trouble. You may not see me, but I'll be watching you. And him too, if he shows up again. Call my pager number from a different pay phone at six tomorrow evening."

"Okay," Parker said. "But what if ...."

Nash had already hung up.

On his cement bed under the overpass, Parker did not think he would be able to sleep. But sleep came to him, as a means to flee his reality. He did not dream of the bony black man, as he thought he would, and he was thankful.

Parker awakened to an unnatural flicker of light in his eyes. It seemed to follow him, no matter how he positioned himself. Finally he stood up, determined to locate its source.

Momentarily, he spotted the unmistakable silhouette of Taylor Nash standing on the roof of a dilapidated apartment building, across the street. He had been shining a laser pen light in Parker's face.

Parker was grateful that Nash let him know of his presence. Smiling to himself, Parker began his daily routine.

After shadowing Parker for three hours, Nash saw the man Parker had described.

"Slick Alexander," Nash muttered to himself. "I was hoping it was you."

Satisfied with his morning surveillance, Slick, now being followed by Nash, walked back to his car, and sat behind the steering wheel. He never started the engine, but turned the key in the ignition, so that he could listen to the radio. Soon, a squat figure in a suit that may have been large enough for him thirty pounds ago, toiled up the street. He took a seat beside

Slick and began an animated conversation, gesticulating wildly with his hands.

"Franco Mangelli. The Mango Man himself," Nash thought.

He studied them until Franco had exited the car and Slick had pulled off.

Nash's beeper went off at exactly six o'clock p.m. He had anticipated Parker being prompt and was standing by a pay phone with the exact change in hand.

"Hello," said Parker nervously. "Did you see him today? I didn't try to see if anyone was following me. I didn't want to scare him off if he was."

"Yea, I saw him," said Nash. "His name is Freeman Alexander, but everybody calls him Slick."

"You, you know him?" Parker stuttered.

"Yes, I do. He's a sadistic, ethnophobic insect, whose death would only be good."

Parker did not reply, but was disappointed that Nash would think that anyone's premature demise could be something good.

"You there, Evan?" Nash inquired.

"Yes, what am I ... we going to do?"

"I want you to continue doing exactly what you have been doing with one small exception. I want you to start sleeping in the Regal beer brewery."

"The what?" Parker asked.

"The Regal brewery. It's an abandoned building on Eighth Avenue. You can't miss it. It's a six story building with a chain link fence, topped with razor wire surrounding it."

"And I guess I can just ask the security guard to let me in," Parker said, curling his lips sarcastically.

"That building has been deserted over thirty years. There are no security guards."

"Then I guess there's a hole in the fence for me to enter the grounds."

"There will be," said Nash smugly. "On the east side of the property. The delivery entrance door will also be unlocked. There are some offices on the third floor. You take up nightly residence in the one closest to the stairwell."

"How do you know so much about this building?" Parker tilted his head to one side.

"My uncle, on my father's side, was employed there, and I worked a few summers there, as a kid."

"When do you want me to start sleeping there?"

"Start tomorrow. That will give me a chance to get some things organized."

The next evening Parker frowned as he approached the dilapidated building. It looked as tormented and empty as he felt. The chain link fence with its razor wire crown was breached—as Nash had promised. Parker approached the entrance as if he owned the building and used a small penlight once inside, to guide him up the stairwell. It reminded him of the thousands of throats he illuminated with just such a light when he practiced Internal Medicine.

The office, nearest the stairwell, was to the right. It had a solid wood door, with the name of some long forgotten company executive stenciled on it. As he opened the door, and shined the light around the room, there was a pile of debris in one corner and Taylor Nash sitting comfortably in a rickety wooden chair in another. Nash had placed a large oak desk in the middle of the floor. On it were two sleeping bags, four paperback books, a large duffel bag, two cases of mineral water, a cheap garment bag, and a box of assorted dehydrated foods.

"Hope you don't mind a little company," Nash said with a broad smile.

Evan Parker felt a small lump of gratitude in his throat.

Nash continued, "I saw Slick with a man named Franco Mangelli. Mangelli is an enforcer in this and other black sections of the city. The way I see it, is that whoever framed you, has hired these two to close the loop."

"Close the loop?" Parker raised his eyebrow.

"Get rid of you," Nash said calmly as he stood up. "Being the cowardly creature that he is, I figure Slick to try when all the odds are in his favor. Like when you're sleeping. Too many people at the overpass, so we give him a better place. This place."

"You think he'll try to kill me in here?" The lump in Parker's throat was now the size of a grapefruit.

"If we have any luck," Nash replied. "Hopefully he'll eventually follow you here. This will seem like an ideal spot for him."

"What about the other person you mentioned?" Parker's mind drawing a blank on his name.

"Mangelli? He never gets his hands dirty. Just acts as overseer. Tomorrow, you go out and get a hurricane lamp for this room. I didn't get one tonight, so anyone looking wouldn't wonder where the light was coming from."

Nash walked over to the table and grabbed one of the sleeping bags. As he spread it on the floor, Parker voiced some concerns.

"What if they come tonight? Do you want me to take the first shift? How are we going to defend ourselves?"

"Everything will be alright," Nash said as he made himself cozy.

Surrendering to Nash's judgment, Parker was soon immersed in the most comfortable bedding he had experienced in quite awhile.

When Parker awoke, he found Nash staring out of one of the three large windows in the small office. The windows were almost floor to ceiling, reminiscent of days in Miami prior to air-conditioning. All of the windows in the building had long since been nailed shut, and steel mesh, now rusted, had been installed on the outside of each one. Obviously it was someone's hope at one time that the building would again be occupied.

"Good morning," Parker said.

"Could be," Nash said, apparently lost in thought. "Time to start your daily activities. Remember, everything just as before, except you come here nights. Don't forget the lamp and fuel for it."

Parker left without speaking.

Nash returned briefly, to his thoughts of summers spent here as a youth. He had known this building better than anybody then. He hoped he still remembered. He left the small office and began to walk through the building, refreshing his memory.

As he did this, he picked up bottles and bits of broken glass and placed them into the cardboard box that once held the dehydrated foods. He then broke the bottles and scattered the glass on the flight of main stairs, leading to the third floor offices. He also scattered some glass on the delivery stairs, even though he doubted that anyone looking for Parker would know of their existence. This way anyone walking up the stairs, would give him an auditory warning.

Satisfied with his reacquaintance with the building, Nash positioned himself by a window so he could observe the street below. The Regal Brewery was located in a defunct industrial area, with one narrow street that ran in the front of the building. No vehicles would pass this way accidentally.

At approximately two in the afternoon, Nash's reading of John Steinbeck's *The Pearl* was interrupted by the sound of a slow-moving car.

"Excellent," he said as he stood to peer out of the window.

He could see Slick Alexander behind the wheel, and Franco Mangelli, riding shotgun, squeezed uncomfortably next to him.

251

"Excellent," he said as he stood to peer out of the window.

He could see Slick Alexander behind the wheel, and Franco Mangelli, riding shotgun, squeezed uncomfortably next to him.

"Showtime !!!" Taylor shouted to himself.

When Evander Parker returned at approximately seven p.m., the first thing he noticed, other than the fact that he was alone, was that Nash had done an incredible housekeeping job. The large oak desk was placed in a corner of the room and not only had all the debris been removed, but the floor looked as if it had been swept. The top of the table was bare and Evan speculated, correctly, that Nash had moved the articles to another room. He placed the kerosene lamp that he was carrying on the top of the table and sat in the room's only chair.

Shortly, the door to the small office opened. Evan stared in shock and disbelief. Before him stood Nash, smiling. Immaculately dressed in the most up-to-date fashion. If the date you were up to was nineteen sixty-nine.

He had combed his hair out into a small Afro. He had on love beads and a long-sleeved, paisley polyester shirt, with a collar that extended to his shoulders. His pants were tight-fitting bell bottoms, whose cuffs almost entirely covered his platform shoes, which sported six-inch heels. These pants were held snugly in place by a three-inch wide leather belt, with a gold belt buckle, whose resplendence was eclipsed only by the gold cap that Nash had placed on his left front tooth. A gold cap which had the design of a quarter moon etched into it.

Evan continued to gawk, with his mouth open.

Nash struck a pose. Crossing his arms and lifting his chin toward the decaying ceiling.

Still no response from Parker, who remained dumbstruck. Unfolding his arms and brushing past Parker, Nash spoke.

"I have my reasons," said Nash, sitting on the desk and crossing his legs, which revealed his highly polished, black leather platform shoes. "Suffice it to say, I've gone retro."

"*Gone crazy*," Parker thought as he began to feel somewhat lightheaded. Had he trusted his fate to a madman? One and possibly two men were going to attempt to kill him. Probably tonight, if his bad luck remained true to form. He had no weapon to defend himself and was stuck in a room with the black Denny Terrio. Nash had to have a plan, Parker thought. He always had a plan.

"What's your plan?" Parker asked timidly.

"Don't have one," Nash said, fingering a toothpick in his gold-capped tooth. He spit the toothpick onto the floor.

"What about a weapon?" Parker asked. He hoped Nash had something in the duffel bag, wherever that might be now. It was quite obvious that he couldn't conceal a gun within the outfit he was wearing.

"Got it right here," Nash said, standing and smiling widely, flashing Parker the gold tooth anew.

Nash, with a modest amount of difficulty, reached into the constricted right front pocket of his bell-bottomed trousers and retrieved a folded straight razor. As he carefully opened the razor, Parker began to look frantically about the room. There had to be something else that could be employed as a weapon. A table leg, a metal spike. He was stuck. He was in a moral and physical quandary. There was nothing in the room, and he was afraid to leave.

"What makes you think they'll come tonight?" Parker asked, hoping for more time.

"I don't think it, I know it," Nash said assuredly. "It's getting dark outside." He struck a match. "Time to light the lamp, so they'll know where you are."

Parker felt as if he might faint, so he sat in the old desk chair.

Nash moved to the center of the room and began to speak to no one in particular.

"You know a razor can be quite deadly in the right hands, but it requires some skill to wield one properly. I was quite adroit, with one of these, back in the day. I developed a series of exercises that helped me become quite proficient." Nash paused. "What you do is hold the razor firmly, but comfortably, and you draw the letters of the alphabet into the air in an exaggerated fashion. Capital letters first."

Nash then began to draw a phantom A into the air, as he stood in the center of the room. As he would draw a letter, he would pronounce the letter in a very prolonged manner. "AAAAAAA Beeeee, Ceeeee ...."

Parker's brain could not affirm what his eyes and ears were conveying to him. He closed his eyes and began to massage his temples. How could he, a Harvard educated doctor with a specialty in Psychiatry, failed to have seen that Nash was completely insane? If he had turned himself in to the police, at least he would be alive tomorrow, which at this time seemed a remote possibility.

"... Eckssss, Whyyyyy, Zeeeee. Now for the small letters. aaaaaaa, beeee, ceeeee ..." Nash continued.

If he wasn't going to be murdered tonight, Parker would have killed himself. What could he do to help himself? What were his options?

Suddenly, in the middle of W, Nash stopped moving and put his finger to his lips. Parker didn't hear anything at first, but then there was the unmistakable sound of breaking glass. Someone was walking up the main stairs. Nash motioned for Parker to stand in the corner of the room farthest from the door.

Parker tiptoed over to the corner and hid obligingly and silently. Nash positioned himself behind the door and waited for it to open. He had placed the razor in his left hand and held it high above his head.

Someone on the other side of the door had begun to gently turn the doorknob with the greatest of care. As he watched the door crack, almost imperceptibly at first, Parker could feel his heart beating so loud, he was afraid it would burst. Instinctively, he held his breath with anxiety. Then he saw him. The man who had been following him. He was holding a pistol of some sort in his right hand. He wore a black T-shirt, black jeans and black high-top tennis shoes. When he saw Parker cowering in the corner, he wore a black smile.

"This might be the easiest twenty-five hundred I ever made," Slick thought.

As he passed through the door, quick as a thought, Nash grabbed the hand which held the gun, positioned himself behind Slick and placed the razor to his throat with just enough pressure to assure him that he meant business.

"Don't move ... don't breathe ... don't even blink," Nash said, slowly and softly.

"Now drop the gun."

This was an easy request to follow as Slick Alexander felt his wrist being crushed. The gun fell to the hardwood floor with a dull thud.

"Now kick it away from you," Nash said firmly.

Being careful not to put anymore pressure on the razor with his neck, Slick kicked the gun in Parker's direction, who promptly picked it up. Carefully releasing his grip on Slick and putting the razor in his right hand, Nash told him to turn around.

"Out of sight," Slick grinned broadly and began to chew some gum he had stowed in his cheek.

If they hadn't been mortal enemies, they would have slapped each other five.

"What this got to do with you, Taylor?" Slick asked earnestly.

"You'll find out soon enough," Nash replied as he made small circles with the razor, directing Slick to turn around again.

255

"If he moves," Nash yelled at Parker, "just point the gun at him and pull the trigger as fast as you can."

Nash patted him down from the rear, starting at his neck and ending at the soles of his high-top tennis shoes, which he had him lift one at a time. He then reached around to check his chest, waist and his groin.

"Gettin' kinda pers'nal, ain't you, big man," Slick said.

"Have a seat, Slick," Nash said, pushing him in the general direction of the chair.

Seated, Slick looked up coolly and said, "What you dressed up in that costume for?"

"I wore this the first time I met Joi Hughes. You were at that party, at her house. Don't you remember?"

"Can't say I do," Slick replied, leaning back in the chair and smiling. "What century was that?"

Ignoring Slick's remark, Nash continued. "That was the first time I fell in love. I was home on semester break. You and Wesley Powell tried to start some trouble, but her daddy threw you both out."

"I been thrown outta lotsa parties," Slick said proudly, his chest beginning to noticeably swell.

Still ignoring him, Nash went on. "Joi and I went out a couple of times and we were really tight, but I had to go back to school and the distance came between us. We're still very good friends. She married Raymond Jefferson. You happen to know him, Slick? They used to call him Ray-Ray."

"Can't say I do."

"He got killed about eight months ago."

"Damn shame," said Slick, now chewing with his mouth open, "Real sorry to hear that."

Not half as sorry as you're going to be, Nash thought.

"You know, I'm the godfather to both of their kids—Little Ray and Shaunice."

"Congratulations all around," Slick said, looking nonchalantly at the ceiling, and trying futilely to blow bubbles with his chewing gum.

"He was stabbed to death, in an alley, on Second Avenue, not too far from here. Story was that he borrowed money from some loan sharks and was killed when he couldn't repay it. Only fatal wound was the last one, although he was stabbed over six times. Whoever did that, knew what they were doing. He suffered a lot before he died."

"Like I said. Damn shame. But shit happens when you mess 'round with loan sharks. Especially when you don't have they money. Did he have a gamblin' problem?" Slick asked as sincerely as possible.

"No, he didn't. As a matter of fact, he borrowed the money because he and Joi were having another baby and he wanted to build an addition to the house. He was temporarily out of work, so he foolishly went to a loan shark. He only borrowed twelve hundred dollars, but with their exorbitant interest rates, within two months he owed over three thousand .... You sure you don't know Joi? She has kind of Asian-looking eyes. Sometimes they call her Almond Joi."

"Still don't remember her. Him neither. But I heard them loan sharks can be nasty people about their dough."

"That's the curious part," Nash said. "He had the money to repay the loan."

"How would you know that?" Slick asked, now sitting up straight.

"Because I gave him the money that same evening," Nash replied, walking toward Slick. "And I know something else." Nash's voice was low, deadly. He now stood directly over Slick, brandishing the razor, which glimmered in the light from the kerosene lantern. "I know he was going to meet you, because he told me so. Only, I never figured you would kill him, if he had the money."

"Why would I ... anybody kill him if he had the dough?" Slick stammered, voice wavering, eyes now wide open.

257

"You killed him for the money and then you told fat Franco he didn't have it. You tortured him to make it look like you tried to get the money out of him and accidentally killed him, or to make an example of what happens to people who don't pay. Which is the story you spread around."

Slick opened his mouth to speak. "I didn't do it, I swear."

"Don't bother to lie about it." Nash pushed the razor firmly under Slick's jawbone. "I don't think Raymond got you confused with any other bony lowlife named Freeman Alexander. I feel guilty because I should have gone with him that night, but I never figured you would kill him if he had the money. I didn't think that even you would stoop that low. That's a good one for me, huh, Doc? I overestimated the character of someone I knew to be a venomous rodent."

As Parker looked into Nash's eyes, he could see that they were cloudy with tears.

"Now, dog," he said to Slick. "Call your master."

Seeing the tears in Nash's eyes gave Slick a little confidence.

"And what if I don't call him?"

"Oh, you will call him," Nash said, taking a deep breath, and putting a little more pressure behind the razor. "You only have to decide if you will call him now, or after I carve my initials into your forehead. And just for the record, I have two middle names. And once I start carving, even if you call him immediately, I won't stop until I'm done. I don't like to leave things unfinished."

"Okay, man, okay," Slick said.

Nash elevated Slick from his seated position by delicately raising the razor, which was still placed at the angle of his jaw. He kept it there as he walked him to the door and cracked it open.

"Come on up, Frank. Everything's cool," Slick yelled into the dark corridor.

Nash hurriedly returned Slick to the chair, and wheeled it next to the edge of the desk, with Slick facing him. He then instructed Parker to sit on the edge of the desk, facing Slick's right side. Next he took the gun from Parker and pulled the hammer back. Carefully, he gave the gun back to Parker and positioned the gun in his hands, so it rested against Slick's right temple.

"Careful there," said Slick, now sweating profusely and afraid to chew his gum, "that gun got a hair trigger."

"Good. Then you know not to move," Nash said as he tiptoed back toward the closed door.

The sound of glass shattering on the stairwell preceded Frank, the Mango Man's, casual stroll into the room.

"What the hell is going on here?" he bellowed as he looked around.

"This is what is commonly known as a screw-up," Nash said, coming up from behind the Mango Man, his gold-capped tooth beaming. He twisted the razor in Franco's face. "Put your hands up."

Quickly appraising the situation, Franco saw a trembling doctor, who obviously had never used a weapon, holding a gun to Slick's temple, and a fool dressed like Superfly, standing in front of him with a razor. With a .38 caliber revolver in his outside coat pocket, that he had used many times, Franco felt he had the superior position.

"Put your hands up now," Nash ordered more firmly, "or my friend will blow Slick's brains across the room."

Franco stepped back and smiled.

"I doubt the good doctor can do it. And if he does, there are plenty more where Slick came from."

He was right of course, and Nash knew it. There was no shortage of individuals willing to destroy their own people, for profit.

Franco, the Mango Man, Mangelli then jammed his stubby fingers into his coat pocket.

As Franco did this, Nash took two long strides forward and with a backhanded arc sliced through Franco's right carotid artery. At the apex of the arc, without interruption of his fluid movement, Nash looped the razor through Franco's left carotid artery and trachea. The entire feat was accomplished in the blink of an eye. But no one blinked. Not even Franco.

Dr. Evander Parker, who had often seen the results of violence, but who had never seen it perpetrated first hand, flinched when the razor struck Franco the first time. Parker's jerking motion caused the barrel of the gun to tap Slick on the temple, who, thinking the gun would go off, promptly swallowed his gum.

"Perfect lower case p," Nash said as he stepped back from the mortally-wounded man.

Instinctively Franco reached for his throat with both hands, leaving the gun in his coat pocket. His plump fingers could not retard the flow of blood, which became heavier with each heartbeat, as the thin lacerations evolved into gaping wounds. Fat Franco, his eyes bulging in horror, began to run aimlessly around the room, still holding his throat, and spraying the ceiling and walls with the first fresh pigment they'd seen in over thirty years. He reminded Parker of the way a chicken's body could still run around after it was beheaded.

Parker thought he heard Nash whisper, "Thar she blows," just before Franco fell to his knees and crashed, face first, onto the floor, his fingers now deeply embedded in the macerated neck wounds.

Nash went over to the lifeless body and removed the revolver from Franco's coat pocket. He then searched the body for any other weapons. There were none.

Parker was still perched on the edge of the desk, holding the cocked gun with two hands, to Slick's temple. However, he had turned his head ninety degrees, to see the action. He could not move, because he was in shock, and Slick would not move, for fear of startling the doctor holding the gun with the hair trigger.

As Nash turned toward them both, they appeared to be posing for some sort of macabre portrait. He walked slowly over to where they were both seated and pried the gun gently from the silent Parker's paralyzed fingers. As Nash released the hammer on the gun and walked back to the center of the room, Slick took his first full breath in over ten minutes.

Nash seemed to be thinking absentmindedly for a few minutes, and then waved Slick into a far corner of the room and told him to sit on the floor. He then walked over to Parker and gave him both guns.

"I want you to leave now." Nash turned to the visibly shaken Parker. "Take these with you and be prepared to use them. I can't guarantee that they didn't bring someone else along. If you see someone, shoot first and ask questions later. Go back to the apartment. I'll join you as soon as I can. You understand?"

More than willing to leave, Parker nodded animatedly.

"You saved me again," Parker said, not far from hysteria. "I didn't think you could do it but you did. I didn't think you could do it with just a razor, but you did. I thought you were crazy.

I ... "

"Out," Nash said, who guided him to the door and literally flung him through it. Nash gazed down the dark corridor and strained his eyes to confirm that it was empty.

What was just said did not escape Slick's notice. He assumed that Nash had another weapon secreted somewhere in the room. When Nash again turned his attention to Slick, he was holding an eight-inch stiletto and wearing a silly grin.

"For me?" Nash rhetorically asked, sounding as if Slick were giving him a present.

"You shouldn't have .... You reallllly shouldn't have." As he spoke Nash removed the razor deftly from his pocket and opened it, without taking his eyes off Slick.

"I was wondering what I was going to do with you," Nash said coldly, "and now I know. I thought that was a knife on your ankle when I frisked you."

"Now you know, pretty boy," cackled Slick, "and you'll get to see it close up soon enough. You may slice me a time or two but I just have to protect my neck."

"You sure you don't remember that party?" Nash asked as he and Slick began to circle each other.

"I told you, I don't remember no damn party, fool. But I do remember your friend Ray-Ray. Matter fact, this here is the same knife I used to carve him up. I guess I have you to thank for the three grand."

If he could just injure Nash enough to disable him. Slick knew how to stab a person twenty times without killing them. The thought of stabbing a helpless Nash, repeatedly, actually made his mouth water. Slick wiped the corners of his mouth with the back of his free hand.

"After I kill you," Slick bragged, "I'm gonna find that doctor again and blow his brains out. Oh yeah, I didn't know Ray-Ray had a pretty wife. I think I'll look her up. Maybe I can be the kids' step daddy, 'til I get tired of her."

Suddenly, Nash stopped moving.

"Man you have to remember that party. Everybody was doing 'The Hustle.' You know, da-da da-da, da-da-da da da." As he began to chant, Nash started to dance.

Although he watched this fool with fascination, Slick never let his guard down. Maybe the Doc was right. Maybe he is crazy. He might be crazy, but he sure could dance, thought Slick.

Amazingly, as part of his dance routine, Nash spun around three-hundred sixty degrees. Slick could not believe his eyes.

Nash had actually turned his back to him, if only for a second. If he would be stupid enough to do this again, the game would be over.

"Get with it," Nash cajoled. "The best part is the spin."

Slick readied himself. As Nash began to turn, Slick lunged forward, his knife positioned. With perfect timing, Nash performed a full spin kick which smashed a six inch heel, from a size twelve shoe, into Slick's right temple. The subsequent decorticate activity in Slick's brain, caused by the blow, resulted in Slick's grip tightening on the knife.

As quick as a cat, Nash reversed himself and spun kicked his other heel into Slick's jaw, breaking it just below his left ear. Still standing, but senseless, Slick dropped the knife and staggered backward toward the windows. Nash and Slick were again a few feet apart, facing each other, but this time Slick was not aware of it, or anything else.

Nash now took a running start, directly at Slick. And with a slight leap, kicked his right leg straight forward, resulting in the full force of his stacked heel striking Slick squarely between the eyes. The impact launched Slick through the plate glass window and the rusting metal mesh, whose prehistoric screws gave way with little resistance, head first into space. He landed face down on the razor wire below, which retained most of the left side of his face and his right arm, before releasing what was left, to the narrow asphalt driveway below.

Dr. Evander Parker had managed to wind his way down the four flights of darkened stairways and emerge from the building unscathed, just in time for Freeman 'Slick' Alexander to land at his feet. It would take five minutes of retching in the alley way, before he could shamble shakily to the apartment.

Meanwhile, Taylor Nash, who had watched Slick's descent into hell, was sitting in the creaky wooden chair.

263

"I hope he didn't die," he said, with his face buried in his hands. "I hope he didn't die, before he hit that razor wire. Son-of-a-bitch."

Nash then got up and began to carefully go through the clothing and belongings of the late Franco Mangelli.

"Let's see what you got here, Mr. Mango Man," Nash said. "One wallet containing eight hundred dollars in cash and some credit cards, probably stolen or forged. A money clip with five thousand dollars. Twelve small plastic bags, with what appears to be rock cocaine. One key ring with keys to who knows what. A gold Presidential Rolex watch. A pinky ring, with a diamond of approximately one-carat weight. Not much for such an important man," Nash sighed as he strained to turn Franco over. He then grabbed Franco's shirt collar and ripped his shirt open.

"That's more like it," Nash said as he eyed the money belt encircling Franco's considerable girth. "Big loan shark like you has to be a walking bank."

The money belt contained forty-two thousand dollars in bills of various denominations.

Nash took the contents of the plastic bags and scattered them onto the floor before stepping on them. The other things he took into the next room and packed them into his duffel bag. He changed into his street clothes and left.

Driving back to his apartment, Nash spotted some vagrants drinking around a fire they had set in an oil drum. He pulled over, retrieved a bottle of Chivas Regal from his trunk and joined them. They happily admitted him to their circle. He used the Superfly outfit and the garment bag that contained it as fuel. He stayed until the fire had consumed the evidence. He poured some of the Chivas into the fire, doing a libation as the gangbangers did when a "homie" got killed.

"This is for you, Ray-Ray." He left the bottle, with his new found best friends, and drove off.

Two weeks later an anonymous donor would set up a trust fund in the amount of fifty-four thousand dollars for the education of Shaunice and Raymond Jefferson Jr., and their unborn sibling.

Having had too much to drink, Nash did not remember the drive back to the apartment. Instinctively, he knocked on the door before putting his key in the lock and letting himself in. Parker was sitting on the edge of the bed, dressed in a fresh white T-shirt and blue striped boxer shorts, after having taken a marathon shower.

Parker spoke first. "You killed them both."

"Yes, I did," Nash replied, slumping into the recliner.

"You're drunk."

"Right again, Sherlock, or should I say Dr. Holmes." Nash chuckled and slurred his words.

"You've been celebrating," Parker said incredulously.

"You Ivy League men are brilliant," Nash said, as he flopped onto the bed and began to nod off.

"How can you celebrate the deaths of two human beings, even if they meant to kill us?"

"Easy," Nash said, unaware he was smacking his lips.

"That's not normal," Parker said indignantly.

"Normal. How do you expect me to be normal?" Nash muttered, now talking in his sleep. "Didn't grow up normal. Was only allowed to go certain places in the city. Couldn't sit down and eat in the restaurants. Riding the back of the bus. Despised just for being black. And I'm supposed to be normal. Harvard educated fool, you don't know anything about me."

Nash turned on his side and began to snore loudly.

* * *

Parker got up early, showered and put on some fresh clothes. He eased quietly out of the apartment, leaving a still sleeping Nash behind. He did not know where he was going, as he began a brisk walk.

Still walking, five hours later, Dr. Evander Parker decided that the only way to save his life was to turn himself in.

He was tired. Very tired. He was tired every way you could be tired. He was physically tired, he was mentally tired, he was spiritually tired. He was tired in a figurative sense, he was tired in a literal sense, he was tired in a metaphysical sense, he was tired in an L. Ron Hubbard Scientology sense. He was tired from the top of his head to the soles of his feet. He was tired to his very marrow. His hair and his teeth were tired. And he was hungry.

As he stood in front of the 25th precinct, he slowly took in his immediate surroundings. He was innocent of all charges, but he was soooo tired. He knew that there was overwhelming evidence against him and he knew that innocent people had been sent to prison before and even executed. He doubted that there would be any bail set for him so this might realistically be his last taste of freedom. Gazing at the dilapidated neighborhood, Evan Parker could only wish that his last look at the outside world were more idyllic. Would this be his last recollection of freedom?

His field of vision revealed a vacant lot filled with discarded tires, a mountain of broken glass and two abandoned automobiles. Ramshackle apartment houses, that had been deserted so long ago, even the homeless considered them unsuitable. Graffiti covered walls were spray painted with symbols that he could not understand. To think, that people lived like this all their lives.

A lot was happening that he did not understand. As impossible as it seemed, this made him feel even more tired. Although his stomach grumbled, his hunger was fading. He was becoming nauseated.

He smiled as he entered the precinct, because he knew that the last laugh would be on him, when in time, he would wish with all his heart that he could be back in this impoverished area surveying this glorious panorama. But not now. He was too tired.

As he walked up to the desk, Sgt. Buntz looked up from the newspaper for a second, and then down again, without uttering a word.

"I have come to report a crime," the doctor said weakly.

The Sergeant still did not answer.

Summoning up more strength Evan said in a louder voice, "I have come to report a crime."

This time the obviously annoyed sergeant yawned, reached absentmindedly into a desk drawer and gave Parker a handful of papers.

"Sit over there and fill these out. Press hard 'cause you're making four copies."

"But, sir," Evan started to protest, "I have come ...."

Before he could say to turn himself in, the sergeant yelled, "I said sit over there. Now. And don't say anything until you have completely filled out those papers."

Normally he would have stood up to this type of bureaucratic authoritarianism, but he was too tired. He took the papers and a ball point pen and sat on a most uncomfortable bench.

"Dumb bastard," Buntz thought. "What do guys like that expect, walking around in a neighborhood like this?"

White males were always coming into the precinct reporting crimes. If they're dumb enough to be here, whatever they get is what they deserve is how Buntz looked at it.

And when a white female came through the doors she was one hundred percent guaranteed to be a hooker. But that's another story, he thought.

"I wouldn't walk around this neighborhood by myself. Even with my gun drawn," he mumbled to himself. "Yeah, they always come in to report a crime but they can never explain what they were doin' here in the first place. They never tell you they were buying drugs, looking for prostitutes or buying and selling stolen property. It's always, 'I took a wrong turn and got lost'." If all white people had that poor a sense of direction, he thought, we'd a all still been in Europe. Which right now didn't seem like such a bad idea.

Evander Parker looked at the paper the sergeant had given him. It was a standard form for people to fill out who were making a complaint. He was somewhat astonished at first that no one recognized him, although he had been on the television and in the newspaper. But after a few moments in the confused melee of the 25th, he was not surprised at all. He wondered if he should just describe himself as the assailant in the space provided and give it back to the sergeant. As he was contemplating his alternatives, his thought processes were interrupted by the Sergeant taunting someone at the front desk.

"You two can't be back again?" the Sergeant yelled in a condescending tone.

"Yes, we're back again and we're going to come back as often as necessary to find the person that robbed us," Noel said.

"The white guy?" the Sergeant asked, smiling.

"The white guy," Noel said, frowning.

"Hey, we just got a white guy in here over on that bench," said the sergeant, smirking. "See if that's him."

Noel and Chandler walked excitedly over to where Dr. Parker was sitting. Standing directly in front of him, they studied him intently. There was something familiar about him, but this definitely was not their man.

"Yes?" Dr. Parker asked quizzically as they continued staring at him.

"Do we know you?" Chandler asked.

"I don't think so," Dr. Parker said.

"That's not him," Noel said angrily as he stormed back to Buntz's desk. "He doesn't look anything like the description we gave to you."

"My mistake," said Sergeant Buntz, laughing, "all white people look alike to me."

"C'mon," Noel said to Chandler, tugging on his sleeve, "let's find Lt. Rolle."

"Good luck to you now," Buntz said.

"Idiot," Chandler said under his breath as they walked away.

Buntz heard the remark and shouted angrily, "You two better have more respect for the law." Unmindful of the fact that policemen of his ilk were the reason many people did not.

"Where is Lt. Rolle?" Noel asked Detective Guttierrez, who was walking out past them.

"He's in the back. You can wait for him over there," he said, pointing to the bench where Dr. Parker was sitting.

They both joined Dr. Parker on the bench and waited.

Lt. Rolle was having a heated discussion in the office of Lt. Frank Stevenson, Chief of Narcotics.

"Frank, it's your case and you know it," Rolle said.

"I don't know any such thing," Stevenson said. "You bring these facts or rather allegations to me and I think it's up to you to follow up on it."

"Look, Stevenson," Rolle said, becoming more formal, "this case involves a substantial amount of narcotics, so by default it's yours."

"But you said that a robbery took place, so in my estimation that makes it your case, Lt. Rolle," Stevenson said, becoming even more formal.

"If the Captain weren't out on leave you know he'd agree with me," Rolle said.

"As I said before," Stevenson replied, "I don't know any such thing."

This discussion was taking place because two youths had robbed a mid-level dope courier of his money and his drug

269

supply. Either they didn't know who he was, or they were just plain stupid. Rolle heard of the incident from one of his informants and told Stevenson about it because the robbers were now involved with narcotics and were both supposed to be in their early teens.

Of course, no crime was reported but they wanted to get to the teenagers before the drug dealers could make an example of them. They both knew they would get no cooperation on the streets from anyone. Rolle even heard that the youths were selling the drugs that they stole. Even the parents of these hardened adolescents were usually not helpful. Sometimes because they were benefiting from the kid's life of crime and sometimes because they were afraid of their own children. What a world, thought Rolle. Parents were now afraid of being punished by their children.

No one wanted the emotional and physical difficulty associated with a case like this. After you found out who the youths were, you had to try and apprehend them. Any grown man in police shoes who had ever tried to catch a sixteen year old in tennis shoes knew the feeling. And if you didn't get to the kids before the dope dealers, then you had that whole guilt trip. You really didn't know if you could even protect them if you got them off the streets. It was just a no-win situation but someone had to try. Rolle and Stevenson each hoped that they could lay it off on the other person. Their argument was turning into an endless debate, when they were abruptly interrupted by an impatient Noel and Chandler Christian.

"Excuse us, Lt. Rolle," Noel said apologetically as he stuck his head into the room, "but do you have anything new on our case?"

Lt. Rolle did not usually like to be interrupted, but this lengthy discussion was starting to get on his last nerve.

"No," he said tersely.

"Can we look at some more pictures? I mean, mug shots," Chandler said, following his brother into the small room.

"I guess so," Rolle said, calming down. There certainly was no shortage of mug shots. It would take anyone a year to go over them all.

"We're very sorry for barging in, but this is the only afternoon that both off us are off and we have to be at work at six this evening."

"It's okay." Rolle nodded in understanding. "I'll be with you soon."

As they turned to leave, Noel glanced around the room and felt his heart skip a beat. Maybe two.

"That's him, that's him," Noel cried, pointing to an old poster tacked to the dingy chestnut-colored wall of Lt. Stevenson's office.

"That's who, where?" Lt. Rolle demanded, somewhat startled.

"What are they talking about?" Stevenson queried.

Noel took two steps across Stevenson's tiny office and snatched the photo of Salvatore Rosellini from the wall and slammed it on the desk.

"That's the man what robbed us," he said, pounding his finger into the picture.

"That's him, alright," Chandler said, now as excited as his older brother. He was jumping up and down, he was so ecstatic that their robber hadn't been a figment of their imagination.

Rolle and Stevenson looked at each other silently.

"That's him," Noel repeated, chin jutted out.

"Are you sure?" Rolle said firmly, looking directly at Noel.

"Positive," Noel said.

"How about you, Chandler?" Rolle asked.

"That's him," he said, backing up his brother.

"What's this all about?" Stevenson asked.

"Briefly," Rolle said, "these two gentlemen came to the precinct about eight months ago ... "

271

"Nine," Chandler corrected him.

"Nine months ago, I stand corrected, to report that they had been robbed at gunpoint of a substantial amount of their native Jamaican currency ...."

"Which we were sending home to our mother," Chandler chimed in once more.

"Which they were sending home to their mother," Rolle continued, "by a well-dressed white male near Bucky's Restaurant."

"And now," Stevenson said skeptically, "you are both saying that your previously unidentified male happens to be the man depicted in that F.B.I. poster. A man who is one of the most notorious underworld figures and largest dope peddlers in south Florida, and therefore, the known world."

"That's him," Noel said confidently.

"Would you please excuse us for a few minutes?" Stevenson asked.

"No problem," Noel replied. "Can we have the picture?"

"Sure, sure," Stevenson said, a smirk on his face. "I can get another from the F.B.I."

After Noel and Chandler left, Stevenson turned to Rolle. "Are those two for real?"

"Apparently so," Rolle said.

"What do you make of it all? You don't believe it, do you?"

"They apparently do."

"But do you believe it? It's absolutely absurd. They have to be mistaken," said Stevenson.

"People do make mistakes," Rolle said. "A major player in the drug market, strong arming two illegals in the ghetto. Pretty unlikely."

Without parting his lips, Rolle smiled widely at Stevenson, showing his back teeth. Immediately, Stevenson knew what he was thinking of.

"Don't even think about it," said Frank. "Just because two guys think a drug dealer robbed them, I am not going to be dragged into that fiasco waiting to happen. I can hear the people at F.B.I. and D.E.A. now. 'Frank called in with a hot lead. Sal Rosellini is strong-arming illegals in his precinct.' I'll be the laughing stock of the entire southeast corridor. I tell you what," he continued, "if you don't force me into this, I'll take that other case we were discussing. Deal?"

"Deal," Rolle said.

From the downward push of his head about sixteen inches from the focal point and the downward pull of gravity about four thousand miles from the focal point, Evander Parker was startled into consciousness when the focal point, his elbow, was dislodged from the armrest of the bench.

I wonder how long I've been asleep, he thought. He wasn't surprised, however, by his unanticipated nap. He looked down at the form that the desk sergeant had given to him. It was still blank. In the next few minutes of cognitive thinking, Dr. Parker decided what he must do.

"First," he mumbled to himself, "I must find out who is in charge of this madhouse. Then, whenever I discover which officer, politician, community advocate or inmate is in charge, I will say to them "I am Dr. Evander H. Parker, a wanted fugitive, whose image has been committed to memory by every respectable law enforcement officer in South Florida, especially Dade, Broward and Monroe Counties. I am here to surrender myself to you on three charges of murder and one of arson, neither of which I committed, by the way. Your help in getting me out of this sanitarium you fondly refer to as a precinct as soon as possible would be greatly appreciated ..."

Dr. Parker struggled with difficulty to pull himself up from the bench, leaving his paperwork on the seat, and had taken about two steps in the direction opposite from where Sergeant Buntz was sitting, intent on finding someone with a modicum of intelligence and competence. As he faced the rear of the precinct, he noticed two recently familiar black faces approaching him in a hurried state, their gaze focused only on a sheet of paper that they were both holding.

He thought to himself that these were the same two African-American ... no they had accents ... West Indian Americans ... no, Caribbean Americans ... blacks, no ... men, that had given him the once over previously at Buntz's suggestion. He also thought that if they didn't look where they were going that they were going to run right into him ....

A theory which proved to be factual when the two brothers sent him sprawling backwards onto the uncomfortable bench, arms and legs flying, which caused both of them to fall forward on top of him.

Under normal circumstances, the bench would have toppled over too had it not been secured to the floor with three six-inch cement bolts on each side. Each personally screwed in by one Sergeant Gerald Buntz.

Two years previously Buntz had decided that this action was necessary when, during a particularly busy day, two prisoners who were handcuffed to the bench picked it up and tried to use it as a battering ram against four patrol officers. The joke around the precinct then and now was that the wooden bench was the only thing Buntz had screwed in the past ten years.

The unyielding bench proved to be even more uncomfortable than formerly, as the doctor's head grazed the bench's seat before they all toppled to the floor. Evan Parker, in his somewhat debilitated state, felt the room spin ever so slightly.

As they picked themselves off their helpless victim, Noel said courteously, but not deferentially, "Excuse, us sir. Are you alright?"

"Yes, I think so," said Evan Parker, as he stood shakily, brushing himself off. He reassumed his seat on the bench and watched as Noel picked the picture from the floor.

They were all seated on the bench again when Evan Parker caught a glimpse of the picture and thought that he must surely have injured himself significantly.

"May I see that picture, please?" Evan asked, rubbing the back of his head.

"Sure," Noel said, eyeing him suspiciously now.

Evan couldn't believe what he was seeing. *Who was this Salvatore Rosselini?* he thought. "This is John McIlvance," he said aloud. He turned to the two brothers. "Where did you get this picture?" he asked.

"We got it from Lt. Stevenson's office," Chandler said as he willfully retrieved the poster from the now wide-eyed man. "That is the man what robbed us," he said. "But the police, I don't think them believe us." Hoping for additional corroboration, he asked, "Did this man rob you, too?"

"Yes," Dr. Parker said somberly.

"He took a lot of money from us that we were sending back home to our mother," Noel excitedly piped in. "What did he take from you?" he asked.

"My life," Dr. Parker replied softly. "He took my life."

When Nash entered Noel and Chandler's small apartment and looked at the three of them sitting in the crowded room, he had to bite the inside of his cheek to stop himself from laughing out loud. What an unlikely trio. Two undocumented Jamaicans and a once prominent physician.

Nash had been contacted by Parker, who filled him in on all of the details and told him where he could meet them. Parker did not hesitate to call Nash this time. This was a true emergency.

275

Immediately, Nash thought of the three stooges, Curly, Moe and Larry. Then he wondered if that made him the fourth stooge. Was he to be Shemp or Joe? He always liked Shemp better.

"How may I help you gentlemen?" Nash asked.

Straight to business, thought Parker.

"I know the identity of the man who has ruined my life and coincidentally has caused grievous harm to these two men also."

"Grievous harm?" Nash said. "You going to law school next?"

"What happened to you two?" he said, turning to Noel and Chandler.

After reciting their story for Nash, Chandler got up and gave Nash the poster with Sal's picture on it.

Seated now, Nash studied the picture and the sparse information underneath. Holding the picture perfectly still, he peered over the top of the poster and looked into the eyes of each of the men in the room. How had they all managed to go mad simultaneously? he thought.

"Do you know him?" Chandler asked.

The room fell silent.

"I mean, aside from the picture," Chandler said.

"Do you know who he is?" he asked again, anxiously.

Slowly, Nash put the poster on a small table nearby.

"Do you have any idea who this man is?" Nash asked the trio.

"Yes, Lt. Rolle said that he's a big drug dealer," said Noel.

"Probably the biggest in the Southeast United States, since the arrest of Roberto Mendez," Nash said, looking straight ahead.

"Who is Roberto Mendez?" Chandler asked, becoming more confused.

"Someone you hope never to meet," Nash replied blandly. "You two say that he robbed you at gunpoint. And you," he said, looking at Parker, "think he is the man who came to your office, framed you for three murders and burned your office building."

"That's him," Evan said.

"You can see how this might be hard to believe," Nash said.

"We understand," Parker said, "we have been talking about this from the time we met in the police precinct until now. It makes no sense, but it's true."

"Bullshit," Nash said emphatically.

"You don't believe us?" Parker asked incredulously.

"I'm talking about my life," Nash said. "It's all bullshit. How did I get involved in such a mess? Rolle really owes me big time."

"You think you can find this Salvatore Rosellini for us?" Chandler asked hopefully.

Nash replied. "Finding Sal Rosellini. No problem. What to do after you find him? Big problem."

"We could confront him and tell him that we know all about him. Maybe that would shake him up and he would do something foolish," Chandler said.

"That is very good thinking and what you are saying is true, but I'm afraid that the foolish thing that he would do would be to kill us all."

"During one of our sessions, he did mention that he kept a diary," Parker said.

"Even if that's true," Nash said, "I hardly expect him to let us leaf through it."

"If he's the egomaniac that I think he is," Parker said, "I'm pretty sure he would keep it in his house, so that he could revel in its contents from time to time. And that's not wishful thinking, that is my professional opinion."

"Bullshit." Nash spat out the word again.

"Are you questioning my opinion or my motives?" Parker asked.

"Neither." Nash examined his fingernails. "I'm just reflecting on my life again."

"Why, this time?"

"Because," he said, "to break into the house of the most dangerous man in South Florida, to look for a diary that just might not exist, and live to tell about it, really has a certain appeal."

"Sooo," Parker said, his eyes smiling, "Sal Rosellini isn't the only egomaniac in South Florida."

"I just like a challenge," Nash said, now smiling faintly and wide-eyed with excitement.

"Then you'll do it," Noel said gleefully. "We're all with you."

"Right on both counts," Nash said "I'm going to do it, and all of you will be with me."

Suddenly the room became very silent, as each man in his own way contemplated what the consequences of their future actions might be.

Nash parked across the street from Sal Roselli's home in a borrowed blue and white volkswagen minivan with his cargo of a wanted physician and two illegal aliens.

"Well, gentlemen, there it is," Nash said, peering through the van's window, pointing his index finger.

"There is what?" Chandler queried.

"The residence of one Salvatore Roselli," Nash said.

"I don't see anything but a gate in the middle of some trees," Chandler said.

"What about the back?" Noel asked.

"The rear, gentlemen, is accessible only by boat."

"After all we've been through to get to America," Noel said, "the last thing I want to see is a boat."

Everyone laughed nervously except Nash, who seemed lost in thought.

"Of course, you have a plan," Parker said.

"Of course," Nash said. "But the success of the plan depends on two things. First and foremost will be luck. Second, and also foremost, will be the amount of money you have left to finance this foolhardy scheme."

"Still playing it close to the vest, huh, Nash?" Parker teased.

"Always," Nash replied, "I don't know any other way."

"You gentlemen have seen enough. This ends our scenic tour. Let's get back to the flat."

"Still haven't seen no house," Chandler exclaimed. "I don't see how we're going to get into a house we haven't laid eyes on."

Chapter _____
Twenty _____

Four black men with beards, and the whitest robes he had ever seen, were escorted into his office by his secretary, Ms. Jansen. Attorney Robert, "call me Bob," Wellsing had dealt with many black clients in the past and some of them were unusual to say the least, but this group made him a little un-easy. They just looked too serious.

His legal aid had screened this case previously, as he did all cases before Wellsing interviewed the client, to see if it had any merit.

Bob Wellsing, however, had never seen a case that didn't have some merit. The mere fact that someone came to his office or called was usually good enough. He did know that the principal was a man named Ahmed Farouk. Good American name, he thought.

"Have a seat, please." Wellsing gestured toward his two brown vinyl office chairs and the two metal folding chairs Ms. Jansen had brought in just minutes before.

After they were seated, he asked, "Which of you is Mr. Farouk?"

"I am," said the youngest-looking member of the group. "And these are my advisors."

"Very well," said Wellsing, "how may I help you?"

"My daughter and newly born granddaughter died," Ahmed said.

"Were killed," interjected one of the men.

"Yes," he continued, "were killed by the doctors and staff at Memorial Hospital."

"And when did this occur?" Wellsing asked.

"Over a year ago." Farouk's eyes moistened as he spoke.

"And why are you just now coming forward if you thought that your daughter and granddaughter were harmed secondary to malpractice?"

"Not harmed," chimed in the same gentleman. " Killed."

"Yes, of course," Wellsing gave a professional nod.

"Well, to tell you the truth," Ahmed said, "until I saw your commercials on television and your billboard on Seventh Avenue, I didn't know that I might have anything coming to me. The nurses and doctors said they did all they could."

"I see," Wellsing said, thinking cheerfully about how many clients those ads had generated. He ran his television ads during the daytime soaps and had billboards plastered over the worse sections of the city.

IF YOU HAVE BEEN IN A CAR ACCIDENT, WHETHER OR NOT YOU WERE AT FAULT. IF YOU HAVE BEEN TERMINATED FROM YOUR JOB AND NOW HAVE MENTAL ANGUISH. IF YOU HAVE BEEN A VICTIM OF MEDICAL MALPRACTICE. PLEASE CALL THE LAW OFFICE OF ROBERT WELLSING, ATTORNEY AT LAW, FOR A FREE CONSULTATION. THERE WILL BE NO CHARGES OR FEES UNTIL WE WIN YOUR SUIT AND COLLECT FOR YOU.

He never mentioned that his percentage was usually sixty percent, plus expenses. But never mind that, people still came in.

"What else would they say under such ... such tragic circumstances?" Wellsing faltered.

He always thought that speaking haltingly made him seem more thoughtful and concerned.

"I told you," recited another of the men, looking directly at Farouk.

"Please give me the details of what happened," said Wellsing.

"Well, there isn't too much to tell," Farouk said. "My daughter, who was sixteen at the time, went to the hospital to deliver her baby. We, meaning my wife and I, waited in the waiting room and then the doctor came out and told us they were both dead. I got really upset and I think I might have pushed the doctor a little. You don't think that would hurt my case, do you?"

"In your agitated state," Wellsing responded, "anyone would have done the same thing. What about your daughter's husband?"

"She wasn't married," said Farouk, now staring at the floor. "She never told us who the baby's father was."

"And where is your wife?" Wellsing asked.

"She's home," Farouk replied, "only our men conduct business. That is why I brought along my brothers."

"I'm certainly distressed to hear of the loss of your ... your precious daughter and grandchild, Mr. Farouk, and to you gentlemen in the loss of your niece and great niece."

"No, no," one of them said, "we are brothers in our religion, not by blood."

"Ahhh, I understand now," Wellsing said. "But you do understand for the good of this case," and he thought for the sympathy of the jury, "we may have to involve your wife in the proceedings."

"We will talk it over with our leader," one of the men said.

"I'll need the names of all of the doctors who attended your daughter and grandchild, and the exact date she was in the hospital. I do think you have reason to be optimistic about the outcome of the case," Welsing added. "Leave your address and a number where I can get in touch with you with my secretary, Ms. Jensen. Do you have any questions?"

The four men shook their heads in unison.

"Thank you very much for coming in," Wellsing said as he stood to escort them to his office door.

THANK YOU VEEERRY MUCH FOR COMING IN, he thought as they left.

A malpractice case with two deaths. One, a sixteen-year old and the other, her stillborn child. He began to salivate. If he was lucky he wouldn't have to go to court at all. He could just settle with the malpractice carrier. This might be his ticket to the big time. He had never been able to grasp the brass ring, but this time it seemed within his reach.

Thank you, Mr. Farouk. Thank you. Thank you. Thank you. His thoughts echoed over and over.

Chapter
Twenty-One

Marybeth and Emerson Hitchcock were the Parkers' best friends and their lives had a lot of similarities. Both couples were married in the same month, August, of the same year, 1987. They had all worked in the same hospital, although Marybeth, more commonly called Beth, and Cassie did not meet until Evan and Cassie, his new girlfriend at the time, invited them to dinner.

Evan and Emerson had known each other since they both interned at Jackson Memorial Hospital. Emerson in obstetrics and gynecology and Evan in Internal Medicine, before he decided to change to Psychiatry.

This was the first marriage for Beth, Cassie and Parker, but Emerson had been married previously. His first wife, Maureen, died in a tragic accident several months before he met Beth. He had, in fact, encountered Beth on several occasions before his wife's death, because she was a nurse on the obstetrics and gynecology floor. He just never noticed her before.

After his first wife's sudden death, Emerson did not return to work for several months. Everyone said that he and Maureen were the perfect couple. He was the handsome doctor from a wealthy New England family, and she was the beautiful socialite, whose fundraising parties were legendary.

Emerson's only regret concerning their marriage was that they were childless. It certainly wasn't like they didn't try.

Theirs was a very passionate, but fruitless, marriage. Neither of them was ever evaluated to see why this was so. They were both happy with the way things were and just never seemed to get around to even bringing up the subject of children. They were just too busy enjoying their lives.

When Emerson Hitchcock finally returned to work, he seemed distracted, because this is how a person seemed who was imbibing almost a fifth of scotch daily.

During his second week back in the hospital, Beth and Emerson engaged in a conversation that was a turning point in both of their lives.

"May I speak to you a moment, Dr. Hitchcock?" Beth said.

"Of course, nurse," he replied wearily, "how may I help you?"

Taking him gently by the arm and leading him to an unoccupied room, Beth showed Dr. Hitchcock the chart on one of his patients that he had seen earlier that morning.

"I just wanted to review the orders that you wrote on Mrs. Thompson this morning."

"No problem," he replied confidently. "I know my handwriting is hard to interpret at times and lately it's been getting worse." He flashed his brilliant smile that Beth had admired for years.

"As you are well aware, doctor," she proceeded, "Mrs. Thompson is a forty-five year old female on whom you performed an emergency hysterectomy early this morning for dysfunctional uterine bleeding. She has a history of congestive heart failure and diabetes."

"Yes, I know all of this," he said somewhat impatiently, waving his hand languidly. He was still a bit hung over.

"The fluid order you wrote was for dextrose and normal saline at a rate of two-hundred fifty cc's per hour," she said unassertively.

"Impossible," he said, "I would never give a diabetic that much dextrose or a patient with a history of congestive failure that much fluid."

Beth calmly showed him the order in his own hand-writing.

"That's inexcusable," he said to no one in particular. "I'll change that immediately."

"I took the liberty of changing it already," she said. "I hope you approve."

"Certainly," he said. "I approve of anything done in the best interest of my patients."

She had hoped he would say something to that effect and she was greatly relieved. She then proceeded to review all of the patient charts with him and together they corrected any and all errors. Of which there were a significant number.

At the end of their session, he thanked her for her help and genuinely expressed his embarrassment.

"No need to be embarrassed, Dr. Hitchcock. Everything is taken care of. I hope you didn't mind my bringing in those other charts. By the way," she said off-handedly, "I took care of all of these patients personally and have not spoken to anyone about the orders but you."

Emerson Hitchcock breathed a deep sign of relief.

"Thank you," he said sincerely. "I'll be signing out my patients to Dr. Zeffrin for the rest of the week."

When Emerson returned the following week he seemed to be his old self. At least professionally. Previous to that, many of the hospital staff had begun to worry. He was disheveled, inattentive and withdrawn. Several colleagues even thought that they smelled alcohol on his breath. His colleagues were concerned for his well being, but he was not open to anyone, not even Evander Parker, whom he accused of trying to psychoanalyze him now that he had given up internal medicine for psychiatry.

Dr. Emerson Hitchcock no longer seemed distracted because he no longer was. He gave up the alcohol as quickly as he had begun, which he found to be surprisingly easy. He realized that there was nothing he could do to bring back his beautiful wife, and as the kids say today, "Shit happens."

Dr. Hitchcock gradually discovered that he was visiting East 300, which was the floor on which Beth worked, even when he did not have any patients there. Slowly he began to notice her as a complete human person, as opposed to a nurse. He admired her soft-spoken easy manner, and her dry sense of humor. Her superior intellect and knowledge of a broad range of subjects were very appealing. Not to mention that you could tell a sensuous body lurked just below her less than attractive uniform.

Their first date was almost a year after his wife's accident and, when they started dating regularly, Beth's friends, Emerson's colleagues and even Maureen's friends were happy, because they seemed so right for each other. When they eventually married, many people publicly credited Beth with saving Emerson's career and possibly his life. Privately, Beth credited him for doing much more for her.

Beth Hitchcock was born Marybeth Anderson in a rural area of southern Georgia. Her father, Sims, was a tall, gangly man with thin roan-colored hair, lifeless brown eyes, and acne-scarred skin which tautly stretched over a bony face. He managed a small hardware store. Her mother managed everything else.

Beth's mother, Irene, was a petite, wiry framed, tight-lipped woman, whose main goal in life had once been to be invited to join the Junior League in Atlanta. Her small, narrowly spaced, permanently squinted eyes were constant reminders of the unwavering determination and effort she put into any task she set her mind to.

Upon learning that poor women, who were the wives of rural hardware store managers, were not inclined to get such invitations, she poured all of her energy and will into their only child Marybeth, who was never referred to as Beth at home.

Sims desperately wanted them to try to have a son, but Irene knew that it would take all of the resources that they had available and some luck also, if they were to help Marybeth escape the baggage that they had unfortunately burdened her with. Besides, she told Sims on several occasions that he could go out and have a dozen sons if he wanted to, but to be sure not to spend one dime of the money that rightfully belonged to Marybeth, because if he did, "those bastards" would have the opportunity to carry on his name sooner than he expected.

The only school in the vicinity was the same public school that Sim's and Irene's parents had attended. There were usually about thirty or forty students dispersed from grades one through twelve. The exception being the harvest season when the school's population would double or triple, depending on how many of the sharecropper's children would attend. All instruction was done in the same building which consisted of two classrooms. One for grades one through six, the other, grades seven through twelve.

Sims was one of the smartest people Irene had ever met. She often heard the teachers remark on how bright he was. He was a grade ahead of her in school and always had an eye for her. She thought that marrying him would be her passport to a better life. Sims had planned to go to college and Irene was prepared to drop out of school to help support him.

Unfortunately, these aspirations were not realized when the college aptitude tests showed that Sims had the equivalent of an eighth grade education. Irene and Sims got married anyway, and she dropped out of school right after his graduation. Marybeth was born almost nine months later.

Irene had no feelings of inadequacy or desperation until it was almost time for Marybeth to enter first grade. Irene figured that since she had gone as far as the eleventh grade, she should have the ability to give Marybeth at least a good preschool education. Beyond that she was not sure.

The closest private school was in Atlanta, and the brochures that she sent for made it absolutely clear that she could in no way afford to send her child there. She did not even have kin folk in Atlanta that she could send Marybeth to live with, so she could attend a decent public school.

Irene decided to talk to the only person in town that had actually attended a college. She automatically excluded the two old bats that taught in the school. What help would they be, since they had both gone to state teachers' college over forty years ago, and only managed to give Sims an eighth grade education in twelve years?

She knew that Ella Pearson had become a nurse in Atlanta, after she left town. She also heard that she was a real fine nurse and had even seen some clippings of her outstanding achievements that Ella's mother had shown her before she died. If it wasn't for that abortion thing, Ella would still be in Atlanta, instead of trying to take care of her useless, alcoholic father.

Irene heard the story that Ella was trying to help some young girl out, who had become pregnant and, well, the girl died. End of story.

As Irene and six-year old Marybeth walked down the only paved street in town, to Nurse Ella's, as she was affectionately known, Irene's heart was full of hope and expectations for her daughter but also of fear and anxiety. She knew all too well that good things in this life are never certain.

"Now you be good like I told you," Irene instructed her daughter. "You remember to say 'Yes, Ma'am' to Nurse Ella and 'Yes, Sir,' to her Daddy ... even if he is a no good drunk. And always sit up straight, and keep your legs together, like I showed you. You're gonna be a real lady one day."

"Yes, Mama," Marybeth muttered as she held her mother's hand and tried to keep up.

289

Marybeth was dressed in her "good clothes," which weren't too good, but had been starched and ironed to perfection by her mother. In her other hand, Marybeth carried her white shoes so as not to get them dirty on the walk over to Nurse Ella's. Their car was broken down as usual and Irene did not speak to Sims, as they passed him working under the hood in the front yard.

Down a gravel road, about a hundred yards from the paved main street—which was named Main Street—was Nurse Ella's house. It was a three-bedroom shotgun house in need of repair and paint. On the east side of the house, there was no paint at all and the bare wood was heated and warped by the morning sun. This style of house was called a shotgun house, because the front and back doors were perfectly aligned and the rooms were off to the sides. It was said that you could shoot a shotgun blast into the front door and out the back door without damaging the house.

Before they turned into Nurse Ella's yard, which was bordered by a flaking, disjointed, two foot high wooden picket fence, Irene pulled a damp rag, which she had wrapped in waxed paper, from her pocketbook. She used this to freshen up Marybeth's face and then to wipe off her feet, before putting on her white socks and shoes.

"You look so pretty today," she said wistfully to her daughter as she tossed the ragged cloth into a vacant lot. "Mama wishes she could dress you up every day."

Marybeth smiled, because she knew her Mama really meant that, but she didn't know why her Mama looked like she was going to cry. It would be many years before she understood.

Standing on the uneven porch, which looked as if it just might support both their weights, Irene knocked twice on the warped screen door, which was hanging at a jaunty angle. The aluminum screen door clattered loudly with each knock, as it banged against the wooden front door.

There was no sound from the house. It was now a little past one o'clock and she had phoned Nurse Ella to tell her they would be a little late, since they had to walk. It seemed as if an eternity had passed before Irene finally heard footsteps on the wooden floor. The front door opened slowly.

"Sorry to keep you ladies waiting," Ella said, smiling through the rusting screen door, "but I was busy in the back."

Irene interpreted that to mean she had to do something for her drunken father.

Ella Pearson had to tug on the screen door, a few times, before it would swing open.

"What a little princess," she said as she looked at Marybeth who was trying to smile, despite the fact that the shoes were hurting her feet, swollen from the long walk.

"Come on in and follow me," she said to them both as she led them into a room just to the right of the doorway. The room had originally been a bedroom which Ella had converted into a combination sitting room and study. As Irene entered the room, with Marybeth clinging to her dress and literally walking on her heels, she was awestruck. She had never seen so many books in one place in her life. Not even at school.

Ella was the kind of person who kept every book she ever owned. Other than homemade bookshelves crammed with books, the room was sparsely furnished with three overstuffed chairs, upon which doilies were strategically placed, covering the many well-worn areas. There were threadbare curtains covering the only window in the room, which had been nailed shut, long before Marybeth was born.

The only other item of furniture in the room was a large dark oak coffee table, which looked as if it had been salvaged from a rummage sale, which it had. It too, was covered with books. All neatly arranged, as was the entire house.

After they were all seated, Nurse Ella spoke. "We talked briefly on the phone and you indicated that I might be of some help to you and your daughter."

291

Normally, straightforward and in-your-face, Irene was staring at her interlaced fingers, which were placed in her lap. She was nervous and unsure as she was about to plead her case. After all, this was her daughter's life. She was as tense and humble as a mother pleading before a judge to spare the life of her convicted child. The circumstances were not so dissimilar.

"I would like ... I want you ... I would be grateful to you ...."

She started several times and was embarrassed that she had not rehearsed her request.

Ella Pearson took the opportunity to give Irene a little time to compose herself.

"Would you ladies like some lemonade? I have some fresh made, in the ice box."

Marybeth looked wide-eyed at her mother, who nodded her approval.

"Yes, Ma'am," she said enthusiastically. She was proud of herself for being able to speak right up, but she was puzzled by her mother's hesitation. This was a side of her mother she had never seen before and Marybeth tried not to let it make her uneasy.

Nurse Ella got right up and returned momentarily, with three large glasses and a pitcher of lemonade, with the squeezed lemons floating on the top, just like Marybeth liked. She poured the lemonade, giving a glass to Irene first, Marybeth second and serving herself last. After they all had a few sips in silence, Irene began again.

This time she looked directly at Ella Pearson. "I would be much obliged if you was to help educate my daughter. I have done all I know how to, up to now, but she's gonna need more help than her father or I can give her and I don't have much faith in the school teachers, in these parts. We don't have much money but I can clean and wash and iron real good. I did Marybeth's clothes all myself." Irene let out an audible sigh and took a big swallow of lemonade, relieved that she had said her piece without stammering again.

Ella knew too well the predicament that Irene was in. If her own mother had not sent her to live with relatives in Atlanta to get away from her dysfunctional father, her education too would have been stunted. Without hesitation, Ella smiled. "Of course," she said.

Upon later reflection, Ella wondered if she saw her gesture as an opportunity to help make up for the Atlanta incident. She certainly only took care of her father as a kind of penance, never having had any good feelings about the man.

Nurse Ella initially offered to tutor Marybeth twice a week, after school. Soon she was tutoring her four times a week, and after the end of the first school year, she was responsible for Marybeth's entire education.

Marybeth not only absorbed her school lessons like a sponge, but was very receptive to the guidance Nurse Ella gave her regarding becoming a proper southern lady.

The lessons she received at home were much more mundane. Her mother was a professor emeritus of life and dispensed such charming advice as how not to marry a no-good man, and how not to let nothing get in your way.

At the age of seventeen Marybeth took the Scholastic Aptitude Tests and found it to be almost familiar. She scored very well and received a scholarship to Emory University in Atlanta.

The four years of undergraduate school passed very quickly, and Marybeth graduated with honors. Her mother, father, and Nurse Ella took the bus up to her graduation, not wanting to be at the mercy of another one of Sims' old cars.

Marybeth, now known as Beth, would always remember that day, as one of her finest moments. She had made her parents, as well as Nurse Ella, proud. She made Nurse Ella even prouder, when she announced that she would be getting a graduate degree in Nursing.

Graduation Day was also the last time she spoke to Nurse Ella, because soon afterwards, Ella suffered a fatal brain hemorrhage while trying to lift her inebriated father into the house from the front yard.

Nursing school presented a challenge that she relished. The physical exertion was much more taxing than the mental, because many of the texts she was assigned to read were just new editions of books she had studied with Nurse Ella.

Nursing school was also where she had her first love affair. He was a young doctor from Cincinnati, who was just having a fling, while she was having a romance. She was never bitter about the experience, but tried to learn from it. She continued to focus most of her energy on her studies and dated only rarely. She never fell in love again. That is, until she first saw Emerson Hitchcock.

Chapter
Twenty-Two

Tonight was the night. Nash was driving a white Florida Power and Light van. At least it was a vehicle that looked like a Florida Power and Light van. He was on his way to pick up Noel and Evan. Chandler was at Paisano's, Sal Roselli's night club, as he had been for the past four Friday nights.

Chandler had a cellular phone with him to let them know when Sal arrived and if he left the club early. Chandler had watched Sal for the last month of Fridays and knew that he usually arrived at the club at nine p.m. and stayed until two or three in the morning. Most of the time in the company of a beautiful young woman.

Nash picked Noel and Evan Parker up at eight thirty and drove in the direction of Sal's home. Nash already had on a Florida Power and Light company uniform and Noel and Evan changed into theirs in the van.

"This van looks like the real McCoy," Parker said. "I'm really impressed."

"Thank you," Nash said, "but our task has just begun."

At ten minutes after nine, Chandler called to tell them that Sal had just entered the club.

"Well, gentlemen, this is it," Nash said. "Let's roll."

They stopped first at the house next to Roselli's. It was of the same general splendor and, according to the city clerk's office, belonged to a retired record producer. They thought that they would try their routine on the house next door for two reasons. One, to iron out any details, and two, so that if the people at Roselli's were observing, it would not seem that their house was the only one being checked.

Nash drove the van to the gate and rang the bell.

"May I help you?" a soft, elderly female voice said, emanating from the loudspeaker located next to the buzzer.

"Flordia Power and Light Company," Nash shouted at the speaker, "there's a leak in the area and we need to shut off your meter and check your house for gas leaks."

"Piss off, you morons, this is an all-electric house," came the reply.

So much for their practice run.

Nash then proceeded to Sal's home. He drove up to the gate and pressed the buzzer.

"Can I help you?" a decidedly gruff male voice barked.

"Flordia Light and Power Company. There's a leak in the area and we need to shut off your meter and check your house for gas leaks."

"I don't smell no gas," came the reply.

"Well, sir, the gas may not be leaking exactly where you are and could be accumulating somewhere else. Also the breezes off the bay may be diluting the fumes."

"What should we do?" Lennie asked, turning to Jimmy the Swan.

"I dunno," Swan said, "but I do know Mr. Roselli would be real upset, if he came back to find his house blown up."

"Get your Mac 10 out of the office. If this ain't on the up and up, we'll be ready."

Nash pressed the buzzer again. "Please, sir, if you don't want us to inspect the property, you'll have to sign a form releasing the company from any liability."

After a brief moment, the gate opened.

Lenny and Swan were two of the same mold. Intense hulks with permanently bad attitudes. Nash wondered if they were related. Probably the same mother, he thought. The streets.

Nash had previously outfitted himself, Noel, and Dr. Parker with two-way radios, so they could alert one another if anything went wrong or just so they could communicate while searching the house. Nash was the only one with a weapon. He had it hidden in a door panel of the van, just in case Sal's men insisted on frisking them. He knew that he could always make up some excuse to return to the van and then secret it on his person.

The plan was for Nash to stay outside with the body-guards, if possible, and for Parker and Noel to search the house.

"The company extends its apologies for any incon-venience," Nash said, "but better to be safe than sorry, right?"

Neither Lenny nor Swan replied. They looked the trio over. The one doing all the talking might be the only one to be concerned about.

"Anyone in the house?" Dr. Parker asked.

Lenny had seen Patrice walk to the boat house earlier and had not seen her return. He shook his head.

"Let's go to work," Parker said.

Parker and Noel put on gas masks and started to enter the house, when Jimmy spoke.

"And where do you think you're going?"

This time it was Parker who answered. "We're going to check for any leaks in the house and he," nodding towards Nash, "is going to turn the gas off out here. If you insist on going back into the house, you will have to sign a form releasing the company from any and all liability from lung, brain or liver damage up to and including death, because we only have two masks. He's not even going in," Parker con-tinued, again looking in Nash's general direction.

Lenny seemed to be satisfied with that explanation. As long as he could keep his eye on this one. The other two didn't seem so, so .... He didn't know what it was, but his instincts told him to stay close to the big guy. Besides he didn't want to get liver disease or any of those other things that were mentioned.

As Noel and Dr. Parker went into the house, Nash went back to the van and got his 9 mm and the tools to turn off the gas meter. A maneuver he had practiced dozens of times in the past two weeks.

Natural gas has no odor, so to make it noticeable when there is a leak, highly odorous sulfur-containing hydrocarbons are added. Nash had Parker and Noel release some of this chemical from a canister they carried into the house as soon as they entered. Before he turned the main line off to the house, Nash motioned to Lenny and Jimmy to come near the rear entrance. Jimmy felt for his pocket revolver.

"Do you smell anything?" Nash asked.

"Gas," Lenny said.

Jimmy nodded in agreement.

"I'd better turn that main line off, pronto," Nash said excitedly. "And leave that door open. Let some fresh air into the house. Needless to say, no smoking."

Inside the house, Noel and Dr. Parker proceeded with their strategy. They had obtained a floor plan of the house from the city building department. The plan was for Noel to start in the downstairs library, while Parker would begin in the master bedroom upstairs. If either of them found anything or encountered any problems, they were to use the two-way radios immediately. They were both happy that the house was in Miami and, therefore, had no basement to explore. The house was too large as it was.

As Dr. Parker ascended the stairs to the master bedroom, he could not help but admire some of the workmanship of the house. He also could not ignore the fact that his heart was racing. How some people transferred this feeling of anxiety into pleasurable excitement was always beyond his comprehension.

The master bedroom was half as large as the condo he and Cassie had shared. Thinking of her made him sad, but determined.

He had never seen a bed that large in his life. It must have been a double king-size. It was as large as a trampoline. There was a sitting area with a small fireplace, and there was a large fireplace directly opposite the bed. He could not remember ever seeing a bedroom with two fireplaces. I'm sure he got a lot of use from those here in Miami, he thought.

A large table draped with a paisley cloth sat near the French doors that opened to the balcony. On the table were some objects d'art and a burl wood picture frame, with no picture in it.

The walk-in closet was completely self-contained with built-in cabinets, drawers, and his and hers dressing areas. The bathroom was straight Tony Montoya, the gangster played by Al Pacino in *Scarface*. Pink marble was everywhere, as were ornate fixtures. The center piece of this designer madness was a huge heart-shaped Jacuzzi tub with gold plated fixtures in the shape of mythological creatures. Parker had never seen such a garishly decorated mansion.

Parker started by looking in the closets for secret wall panels or a floor safe. Satisfied that there were none, he reentered the sleeping area. He looked behind the two large wall paintings and discovered only stucco.

He looked in an ornate, Italian style desk and saw only old magazines and mail order catalogues. He decided to look under the bed. As he searched under the bed for the missing diary or whatever he could find that would be of help to him, Dr. Parker heard someone enter the room. He fully expected to see Noel, but as he popped his head into view, over the mattress, he startled himself and the woman that had entered the bedroom.

"Please don't kill me," she pleaded. "Sal isn't even here. He goes to his club every Friday. I don't know anything, honest. I'm just his girlfriend. He doesn't even confide in me. I know I should have gone to college to try to make something of myself, but lately I've been reading and I haven't had a drink or anything to smoke for months." Tears sluiced down her face, causing her mascara to run into muddy streams.

"Sure, I did some drugs before, but I was never hooked and I haven't touched any of that stuff for over a year. My mother told me this life would be my ruin and I should have listened to her instead of taking the easy way out which I know now to be the hard way. Please, Mister, don't kill me for being lazy."

He could tell she was having a panic attack. She was hyperventilating and very close to passing out. He could also tell she was beautiful.

"I'm not here to harm you," he said. "I'm from the gas company."

"Yes, of course," she said. "You're checking the gas lines that run under the bed."

She was nearly hysterical at this point. She wanted to run back through the door but she couldn't move her legs. In fact, she had no feeling in her legs at all.

Parker could tell that a syncopated episode was imminent. He moved quickly from where he was standing and caught her just as she fainted. He placed her on the bed, wondering what to do next. He thought about calling for Noel, but then smiled when he remembered that he was the physician. He elevated her legs with two pillows and continued to look around the room.

After a few brief moments, Patrice began to stir. At first, she was confused, but she quickly regained her senses and realized the situation that she was still in.

"How are you doing?" He said, trying to comfort her.

"Not well at the moment, thank you," she replied.

"You fainted."

"I gathered as much."

"I told you I wasn't here to harm you. I'm from the gas company," he said, keeping his story line intact.

Patrice decided that he was not there to kill her. Specifically, she knew hit men didn't waste time talking. At least that's what she had heard Sal say once. She was still cautious. Just because he wasn't there to kill her specifically, didn't mean that he *wouldn't* kill her.

He had obviously been looking for something when she came in. She couldn't imagine what it might be. Maybe he wanted to wait until Sal returned to question him about it. But what would happen then?

She decided that she better come up with something fast. "Look, Mr .... I didn't get your name?"

"Jerry, just like it says on the shirt," he replied, pointing to a name label sewn above his shirt pocket.

"Un huh," she replied, not even slightly convinced. "Look, Jerry, I'll make a deal with you. I don't care if you're from the gas company, the electric company or the dry cleaners. I've been a virtual prisoner in this place for almost two years now. If you promise to take me out of here with you, I'll help you find the gas meter or whatever it is you're looking for."

Parker decided he had to take a chance. He needed some help if they were ever to make any progress. The house was huge and a diary could be anywhere, especially if it were hidden.

"Okay," he said, "we'll take you with us, if you help me find Sal's diary."

The "we" part didn't surprise her, as she figured there must have been more than one person to get by Lennie and Swan. They were looking for Sal's diary, now she knew she was dead.

"If I show you the diary, you won't kill me, will you?"

"No," he answered.

"No matter what?"

301

"No matter what," he replied.

She walked to a night stand beside the bed, reached under some magazines and produced a very ornate book with leather bindings and the initials S.R. in gold leaf.

The night stand, he thought. How could he have been so careless? He was looking in secretive places and had missed the obvious. But nevertheless he had it. She handed the book to him very gingerly and reminded him of his promise. She hoped she could trust him.

Parker sat in a chair nearby and opened the book. He leafed through about a dozen or so pages carefully at first then very hurriedly, and finally, he rifled through the entire book.

"What are you trying to pull on me?" he shouted.

"You said you wouldn't get angry."

"No, I said I wouldn't kill you, but I'm having second thoughts."

For some reason his threats didn't frighten her. She had been threatened by the best.

"That's his diary. He always meant to keep one. He read somewhere that all great men had diaries and he wanted one, too. He just never got around to writing anything in it."

This is too great, Parker thought. We risk our lives getting into this place for a book of blank pages.

"Now you have to take me out of here," she said playfully. "A promise is a promise."

As he nodded his head in agreement, he felt sick to his stomach.

"You don't have time to pack anything," he said.

"I don't need to," she said, "I'm going to buy all new stuff."

She walked to a corner of the room and removed an empty pink art deco vase and a small bronze statue of a lion, from what Parker thought was a table draped with a paisley cloth. When she removed the cloth he saw that it was a safe.

"Sal keeps things in here, but he never locks it. Some kinda macho thing. I'm going to take enough money to get me started again, but not enough to make him come looking for me."

Parker rushed over to the open safe and looked over her shoulder as she was removing what appeared to be twenty or thirty thousand dollars. There must have been ten times that much in the safe. He also saw plastic bags of what he assumed to be cocaine and the coffee-stained money the Christians said had been taken from them.

Next to that was a folder from his office with the name McIlvane on it. He deduced that this was Sal's shrine of artifacts from some of his criminal activities. He and Chandler had hoped to find some of these things, but finding them all was really a stroke of luck. He knew if he removed them, that they could not be used as evidence against Roselli. Parker reached in his pocket, removed a small camera, and took several pictures of the contents of the safe and of the room.

Patrice did not even question him about what he was doing. She counted out approximately twenty-five thousand dollars and indicated that she was ready to leave. Parker signaled Noel on the two-way that he had what they were looking for and to meet him at the truck. He then motioned to Nash that they were coming and to make everything ready. He also told Nash they had acquired another passenger.

Nash took everything in stride as usual. He told Lennie and Swan that a large leak had indeed been found and told them to wait at a point very distant from the house. They positioned themselves between the house and the main gate, still wary of the gas company crew. Nash then took the truck to the service entrance of the house, ostensibly to repair the leak. Using the van to obstruct their view, they smuggled Patrice into the truck.

"Who is she?" Nash asked.

"No time to explain now," Parker said, "Suffice it to say she helped us and now we are helping her."

She smiled at him and then blew a big kiss in the direction of the house.

After fumbling around the gas meter for another five minutes or so and making a big production of carrying equipment into and out of the house, Nash gave an exaggerated hand wave to Lenny and Swan and told them it was all clear. Lenny and Swan were walking toward the house, wondering where Patrice had been all of this time. They knew she would eventually show up. Besides, lately she was always off by herself, reading.

Once they were safely through the gate and on the main highway, they phoned Chandler that he could leave the club and meet them at the appointed rendezvous, which was the 25th Precinct.

Inside the precinct, they met with Lt. Rolle and showed him the Polaroid pictures that Parker had taken. Rolle said he could not use these pictures to get an arrest warrant since he guessed they were obtained illegally. That is, by entering the premises unlawfully under false pretenses, or breaking and entering, as he was quite sure they were not invited to the home of Sal Roselli.

That is when Patrice, matter-of-factly, stated that the pictures were hers and that she had taken them and given them to Dr. Parker of her own free will. And that she, herself, had indeed been invited into Sal Roselli's home by Roselli himself.

Rolle did not ask how she met Parker or Nash or the Christians, he did not care to know. What he did know, was that he had enough for an arrest warrant.

The judge on call for this weekend was Judge Andrew Volmer. A tall athletically inclined justice, who once had a tryout for the Olympic swimming team. His receding brown hair was now tinged with grey, but he had the body and stamina of a man half his age. Due in no small part to his morning exercise regimen, which included a one mile swim before breakfast. His only vice was smoking cigars. A habit he had acquired during law school, but which he had managed to cut to two a day. One after lunch and one after dinner.

He was widowed now over ten years and his children, both girls, were married and had families of their own. One in California, the other in Massachusetts. Rumor was that his wife had been a beauty and he still had a keen eye for the females.

Judge Volmer was reading some briefs for the following week in court when he received the call.

"A warrant to be served on Sal Roselli? Wonderful," he exclaimed. "Bring over the evidence to show due cause. I'll stay up all night on this one, if I have to."

Rolle took the pictures and Patrice's statement to the judge's home. He had worked with Judge Volmer many times over the years and they had a mutual admiration society, as well as a common dislike for criminals and the criminal justice system. Neither man thought that the justice system worked very well, but always worked within it.

When Rolle arrived, the judge opened the door and invited him in. He was dressed in a robe that looked as old as Rolle, but extremely comfortable. Reading glasses hung on a gold chain around his neck. His slippers were new, probably around the time of the big one, WWII.

"Everything seems to be appropriate," Volmer said. "I'm going to do my small part by signing the warrant. You do yours, by bringing this criminal to his just and well-deserved reward."

"I'll do my best," said Rolle.

"Be careful," Volmer said as Rolle walked out of the door. "This is not a nice man."

An understatement, Rolle thought.

Back in his car and on his way to the precinct, Rolle called the watch commander.

"Jason, this is Lt. Rolle."

"Yes, Lieutenant?"

"I want you to get the E squad together and have them assemble at the precinct within the hour."

"Yes, sir."

The "E Squad," or Elite Squad, was a task force comprised of officers from different divisions of Dade County. They were on call twenty-four hours a day, and its members included former patrolmen, former SWAT team members, and detectives. Their job now consisted of serving search warrants and apprehending those named on the warrants. Their work had been outstanding since its inception and the group had received many commendations. The squad was formed to serve warrants on especially high profile, high-risk cases. They had received special training in house searches and how to handle evidence properly. The group was formed with the blessing of judicial and enforcement agencies, because too many criminals were walking away because of technical mistakes.

The squad was already assembled in the briefing room, when Rolle arrived. Robert Wilson was the chief of the E Force and had an exemplary record. Two hundred and three warrants served. One hundred and seventy-two convictions. Four officers wounded. None fatally.

There were approximately 15 men sitting very uncomfortably at desks, which appeared to have been scavenged from elementary schools.

Wilson himself sat in a wooden chair behind a large metal table that was painted county green. Rolle entered the room with a large smile on his face, waving the warrant vigorously above his head. He walked to the front of the room and took a seat next to Wilson. Rolle had not released the name on the warrant, for fear of leaks. He dared not call it in over his police radio, because those frequencies were no longer secure.

"Attention, people, we have a very large fish here," he proclaimed. "I have, in my hands, a warrant for the arrest of one Salvatore Roselli, along with a search and seizure warrant for his home."

The room, which had been subdued, was now abuzz with excitement. They had wanted Roselli for a long time and many thought that he would not go down in their lifetime. There were whoops, barks, and high-fives all around.

"Congratulations," Wilson said, smiling. "How did you do it?"

"You wouldn't understand, if I told you," said Rolle, jokingly.

A beefy squad member, named Gino Carpagian, whose shirts always looked two sizes too small, stood up and yelled, "I go in first."

No one knew why, but Gino always wanted to be the first on the premises or through the door, even though that was the most dangerous part of the job. He had been shot at and attacked more times than anyone could remember, but no one could remember his losing a fight.

"I think we better get some more backup on this," said Wilson, quietly to Rolle. "That guy's house is a fortress and we don't know how many people may be in there, or what kind of weapons they might have."

No one had to be reminded of the DEA raid approximately a year ago when two agents were killed and three seriously wounded.

"I'll call SWAT for the backup," Wilson continued, "and a chopper if one's available. This Roselli is not a nice man."

"So I've heard," Rolle snorted.

"Listen up," Wilson said. "You are all familiar with Sal Roselli and his organization. I'm going to call in the SWAT boys for backup. Until they arrive, try to stay loose and review your procedures if you need to."

"How about some food?" Gino called out.

307

"Okay," Rolle said, "but you all better be back in fifteen minutes."

"That's enough time for Gino to eat a thirty-six piece bucket of chicken," came a voice from the back of the room.

Sal was sitting at his private booth in his club, trying to put the moves on a curvaceous redhead, when he was interrupted by the club manager, Tony. "Sorry to bother you, boss, but you got a call."

"So take a message," Sal said, "I'm busy here."

"It's your private line."

"Don't move, darling," he said, "order anything you want. It's on me."

Sal walked into his small but very high-tech office, and closed the door behind him. On the walls were video monitors from which he could see every spot in the club. He saw the redhead at his table. A tall, very good looking Hispanic guy approached her and Tony shooed him away.

"Good boy, Tony," said Sal to the monitor, as he pressed the blinking red light and then picked up the receiver.

"Yeah. Uh-huh. What? Damn. Okay. Thanks."

Sal had to move quickly. His informant told him of the warrant and said that he would try to delay the task force as long as he could, but that was about all he could do.

The only incriminating evidence in the house that Sal could think of was his ledger, where he kept track of his pay-offs to everyone from cops to clerks to government officials, and the safe where he had that money from the Little Jamaica incident, the folder from Dr. Parker's office and some cocaine which he used to get his way with the women he met in the club when all else failed.

Of course, there was also two hundred grand in there. It was clean money, but he better have it removed with the other stuff just in case. They might try to make a tax case or some-thing out of it. It would just be easier if all of that stuff disappeared.

He called Midge, but he wasn't at home. Then Sal remembered that Midge told him he was taking his family to Disney World for a few days.

This has to be handled just right, he thought. You couldn't trust just anyone with this job and all of that money. It would also be better if it were someone the cops didn't associate with him. For all he knew Midge's name might be on that warrant, too. Reluctantly, he decided to call Vinny. After all, he was family.

Vinny answered the phone on the fourth ring.

"Hello?" He sounded dazed.

"Vinny, this is Sal. Wake up."

"Who?"

"Your Uncle Sal. What are you doing?"

"I fell asleep watching the TV. I didn't even know you had my number. Long time, no hear."

He's awake now, thought Sal. Smart mouth and all.

"I need your help with something right away," said Sal.

Another glamorous project, Vinny thought.

"What is it?" he asked.

"I want you to go to my house right now and remove some things for me."

"Like what?"

"First, I want you to go into my library and look behind the picture of me and Patrice and you'll find a safe. The only thing in there is a book. Take it out and keep it in a safe place until you hear from me."

"I'm sleepy," Vinny whined. "Why can't Midge do it? Or Patrice."

"This is very important and sometimes there are things that you can only trust your family to do." Besides, he thought, I can't reach Midge or Patrice.

They both must be outta town, Vinny thought. "What's the combination to the safe?"

"It's 7 right, 4 left, and 7 right. 747 like the plane. You should be able to remember that, but write it down if you have to."

"Gee, I think I better write it down," said Vinny sarcastically. "Is that all?"

"No. After you've got the book, go up to my bedroom. There's a large safe near the balcony. Patrice has a vase and a swirled patterned cloth over it. Take everything out of there and keep it with the book."

"What's the combination?" Vinny asked dryly.

"It's open," Sal said.

"Suppose Lenny and Swan won't let me in, with you not being there?"

"I already called them. And if nobody's around, you can break into the house, like the little thief I know you are," said Sal, losing his patience.

"Thanks for the confidence, Uncle Sal, but what if breakin' into the house sets off the alarm?"

"That alarm hasn't been on for five years. Also time is of the essence."

"What?"

"Move your ass."

"You're in an awful hurry for me to do this for you, Unc. How come you don't just do it yourself? If you don't have time tonight, then you can get it done, oh, say, tomorrow."

He's not as dumb as he looks, Sal thought. "Look, I don't have time to explain all of the details, but I need this done, now. It's just impossible for me to do it myself."

"What if I'm in the house and then someone comes around? Like say the police? What should I do then? You know there's only one road in and out."

"If, on the slight chance that the road is cut off," Sal replied, "then take the boat in the back. The keys are in the ignition. Just drive across the bay and get a cab."

"You mean I get to drive the boat, too. Why, I never even been on your boat, Uncle Sal. Gee, I don't know if I can operate such a fancy piece of equipment."

"Cut the crap, Vinny. You drive it just like a car."

"But then my car would be left in your driveway. And the bad, bad people might come after me."

"That car is leased in my name. It has no connection to you at all."

Cheap bastard didn't even put the car he gave me in my name, Vinny thought. He's probably been writing it off his damn taxes.

"Okay, Uncle Sal, I'm on my way."

Lennie and Swan were still at the house when Vinny arrived. They told him that Sal had informed them of the imminent arrival of the police and that he should hurry with whatever task Sal had given to him.

Vinny went directly to the library and retrieved the ledger as Sal had requested. He then proceeded to the master bedroom.

"Well, well, so this is where Sal and Patrice get it on," Vinny said to himself. He took a moment to fantasize about himself and Patrice and then walked over to the safe which had neither a vase on it, nor a cloth.

There were, however, a vase, a bronze statue and a paisley cloth lying on the bed.

Vinny couldn't believe his eyes. "There must be a million bucks in there," he yelped. Cheap bastard, he thought, now I can see why he didn't give this job to Lenny or Swan.

Vinny had not brought anything in which to carry away the safe's contents, so he took a pillowcase from the bed and looked into the safe, as a child would look into an FAO Scwartz window. Open mouth, and all.

"Let me take a coupla minutes to figure this out," he said to himself, as he sat on the floor, still staring into the safe. "The ledger must be the most important, since he told me to get that first. I'll look at it later to see what it's all about."

The first thing he removed from the safe was the manila folder marked "John McIlvane." Vinny perused it casually and put it into the pillowcase. "I don't know what it is, but I'll look at that later, too."

Vinny then looked at the two plastic bags of coke. The first bag was full, wrapped and sealed at the top with tape. The second bag was more than half-empty and, while closed, it was not sealed. Vinny took only the sealed bag. He then looked at the currency. He removed it all, except for about an inch of hundred dollar bills. He was very careful not to touch anything that he did not remove. Lastly, he looked at the Jamaican money with the coffee stains on it. He didn't see how this could be of any use to him at all. He had seen plenty of that monkey money on the first job that Sal had given him, and he never wanted to see it again.

Vinny tied the pillowcase into a knot and slung it carefully over his shoulder. He then stepped out onto the balcony. From there he could see the road leading to the house. Still no signs of the police. He decided to hurry, as he didn't want to be stopped and questioned about the contents of his knapsack. He was sure they wouldn't believe he was jolly old Saint Nick.

As he got into his car, Vinny gave Lennie and Swan a wave. He started his car and, when they turned their backs, he enthusiastically gave them and the house the finger.

Thank you very much, Uncle Sal, he thought, as he drove away. This ought to get me on my way and in style. And what I left behind should keep you out of my hair.

* * *

Sal returned to his table. The redhead was still there, but he had been gone too long. She had imbibed one too many Long Island Iced Teas, and could not be revived. Tony searched through her purse until he found an address. Then he and Victor, the club doorman, put her into a cab. Sal sat at the table, feeling very smug and secure. He had just gotten off the phone with Lennie, who informed him that Vinny had already left with a large bag.

Sal saw no reason to leave the club. The music was hot, the girls were even hotter and he was clean. Besides, if there were someone watching him, he did not want to give the impression that he knew anything at all. Let them search the house. Let them pick him up at the club. They couldn't prove nothing.

Chapter
Twenty-Three

The interrogation room was small—yet uncomfortable. There were five wooden chairs in the room, all of which were too small for any grown American male. There were two bare bulbs overhead, each of which felt like the night lights at the Orange Bowl, but emitting twice the heat, and insufficient illumination. On one wall of the room, there was an oversized one-way mirror, the other walls were painted county green, a color somewhere between bile and split pea soup.

Sal sat next to his lawyer, both of them facing Lt. Rolle, who was also seated. The other two chairs were in a distant corner of the room, some four feet away.

Rolle straddled his chair, which was turned backwards, with his forearms resting on the chair's back. Rolle looked directly at Salvatore Roselli. "Long time, no see," he said.

"I've never seen you before in my life," Sal said smugly.

"Exactly," Rolle replied.

"Before we start, Lt. Rolle," said the man seated next to Sal, "I'd like you to know that I am Mr. Roselli's attorney and have served in that capacity for quite some time. Here is my card."

Rolle looked at the card. *Expensive,* he thought. Not like the kind the county gave him to pass out. Kelly O'Brian, Attorney at Law. It listed his address and phone number, which from the exchange, Rolle knew was in a very upscale part of the city.

An Italian gangster with an Irish lawyer. Rolle thought to himself that Sal had seen *The Godfather* one too many times.

After giving Rolle an adequate amount of time to admire his card, O'Brian continued. "Mr. Roselli, my client, has told me that you have advised him of his rights, but wants to know why he is being detained."

"Well, sir," said Rolle, "at nine p.m. tonight, a properly executed search warrant was issued on your client's home. We had substantial reason to believe that your client, Mr. Roselli, had in his possession certain articles, that could be linked to crimes committed in this and other jurisdictions."

"And did you find anything?" asked Sal, with a big grin on his face.

"Well, to be honest, Mr. Roselli. May I call you Sal?"

Sal nodded.

"Thank you, you may call me Lt. Rolle."

Sal turned his head slightly toward O'Brian, and gave him a slow eye roll, before returning his full attention to Rolle.

"Well, to be honest, Sal," said Rolle, "we didn't find everything that we had hoped for."

Sal grinned from ear to ear. Rolle was being so smart-ass with him because he didn't have anything. He just wanted to yank his chain a bit.

"We did, however, find a few things that we would like to question you about," said Rolle.

"Certainly," said Sal almost cheerfully.

"Would you both excuse me for a moment?" said Rolle, getting up from his chair.

He took three steps to the door and an unseen person gave him two large clasp envelopes. He returned to his chair, turned it around and sat down in the conventional manner. He placed both of the fastened folders on his lap. He opened the first one very slowly and dramatically. Inside was a clear plastic bag sealed with yellow tape. Exhibit One had been written on the tape with a black grease pen. Lt. Rolle removed the plastic bag from the large envelope, grasping each end with a thumb and index finger. He held it up closely to Sal's face so that he could see the contents clearly.

Sal's smile quickly disappeared. "Bastard," he growled.

"I hope you are referring to the person who was supposed to remove this from your house, and not to me," said Rolle, smiling pleasantly.

"And just what is that supposed to be?" asked O'Brian.

"This, sir, is Jamaican currency that has been stained with coffee. It was taken from two gentlemen at gunpoint earlier this year. The crime was reported at this very precinct. We already have a match with Sal's fingerprints and we are now checking to see if we can match the victim's prints and the type of coffee that was spilled on it."

"I'm sure Mr. Roselli has no knowledge of that crime or how that money happened to be in his home. It could have been planted there."

"That's always a possibility, sir," said Rolle, "but, nevertheless, his prints are on the currency."

Rolle continued to hold the bag in the same manner as he talked. He was hoping to let the full impact of this discovery sink in on Sal. When Rolle did return the plastic bag and its contents to the envelope, he did it as gingerly as humanly possible. It was if he were holding a bag of nitroglycerin. He now placed that envelope under the other and began to open the second envelope. Now he removed a plastic bag which was similarly taped and marked Exhibit Two. This plastic bag contained another plastic bag which held a white powdery substance. Rolle held this up to Sal's face in the same manner as he had done previously.

"This, gentlemen," said Rolle, "is approximately a half kilogram of ninety-two-percent pure cocaine. The bag containing the cocaine also has the fingerprints of one Salvatore Roselli."

Rolle placed this bag back into the envelope, secured the clasp and without excusing himself this time, walked to the door and passed both envelopes to someone beyond it. Lt. Rolle then returned to his chair and stared nonchalantly at Sal Roselli.

The room was deadly silent.

Finally, O'Brian spoke. "Could we have some privacy, please?"

"Of course," said Rolle, who got up immediately and headed for the door.

"I need not remind you, Lt. Rolle, that everything said between a lawyer and his client is confidential, no matter if it is overheard," said O'Brian, glancing toward the mirrored wall.

After approximately forty minutes, O'Brian summoned Rolle to the room. Rolle sat in his seat facing them both and waited for one of them to speak. He guessed it would be O'Brian and he was right.

"Lt. Rolle, neither my client nor I think you have a good case based on the so-called evidence that you have shown us. The two men who claim to have had their money taken at gunpoint by someone who may resemble my client are probably illegal immigrants to this country with suspect credentials and reputations. And as we all know, the citizenry of Dade County, of which the jury would be comprised, are not at all sympathetic toward illegal aliens at this time, with the economy, crime rate and all. And with respect to the cocaine that you say you discovered at Mr. Roselli's residence, that was for personal consumption. As you know, precedence has already been set in rulings regarding small amounts of drugs. If he is sentenced, the fine and time served, if any, would be minimal."

The smile was beginning to return to Sal's face. It ended in what now was a smirk.

"Everything you have said may be true, counselor," said Rolle, "but I can assure you that if the two men who were robbed by your client in broad daylight ...."

"Allegedly robbed," O'Brian said.

Sal's smirk broadened.

"I stand corrected," Rolle replied, "allegedly were robbed are indeed illegal aliens, I can assure you that by the time the trial comes to fruition, they will be full-fledged citizens of the good old U.S. of A., with backgrounds to show them to be the most righteous people to set foot in America since the Pope's last visit.

"And as for your personal consumption defense, I happen to know that no one has ever seen or heard of Mr. Roselli using drugs. In fact, his reputation is quite the opposite. I don't believe he even partakes of alcoholic beverages. Hair samples will tell us if he has been a long time user or not, and you will have to submit hair samples, if you intend to use personal consumption as a defense."

Sal was back to a smirk.

"Furthermore, we have reason to believe that there was a critical piece of evidence that was removed from Sal's home before we entered."

"And what might that be?" O'Brian asked.

"A medical file belonging to a Dr. Evander Parker on a patient who called himself McIlvane who we think was also Sal Roselli. As you may remember, counselor, Dr. Parker has been charged with several crimes, including murder and arson. He has turned himself in to us and is now under protective custody."

"What does this have to do with Mr. Roselli?"

"Well, it seems as if Dr. Parker thinks Mr. Roselli is responsible for the arson of his office as well as the murders."

"And what was Mr. Roselli's motive?"

"I don't know," Rolle said, "Would you like for me to step out of the room so that you can ask him?"

"I'm sure that won't be necessary."

"We're still looking for that file," Rolle continued, "and we think that Sal had someone remove it from his safe before we got there. Maybe it'll turn up, who knows.

"You know," Rolle looked at the ceiling, "my father was an Episcopalian priest, and he taught his children to pray for many different reasons. He taught us to pray for forgiveness, guidance, strength and help for ourselves and others."

Still looking upward, Rolle closed his eyes and clasped his hands to his chest.

"Dear Heavenly Father, I ask you to please help us to find the file that was taken from Mr. Roselli's residence. I ask you to please not let it have been destroyed. I also ask that whomever Sal Roselli sent to eliminate the evidence against him, prove to be a bigger disappointment to him, than he or she has already been. Amen."

When Rolle opened his eyes and looked straight ahead, he saw that Sal's countenance had changed considerably. He was visibly upset and angry.

"I don't have to sit here and take this!" Sal yelled.

"Until I'm through questioning you," Rolle said, "I'm afraid you do. Actually, what we're hoping to find is that folder with just one of your prints on it. That is, unless you want to tell me if you have ever been to Dr. Parker's office in Doctors' Medical Plaza."

"I tell you, I don't know no Dr. Parker and I never been in that building. Besides, I don't need any head shrinking. There's nothing wrong with me."

Rolle stepped away, both hands clasped behind his back. He spoke as if he were talking to the wall. "There are a lot of people who would disagree with that statement." Rolle pivoted around on one foot. "And by the way, how did you know that Dr. Parker was a psychiatrist?"

Hesitating briefly, Sal replied, "Contrary to what you may think, I can read. I read it in the paper."

"You know," Rolle said, "fire is a curious thing. It be- haves like a tornado. Sometimes it will destroy everything in its path and sometimes it will leave things untouched. All we have to find is one print. Maybe on the inside of a metal file

319

cabinet, maybe on a door knob. Even if we can manage to find one in the lobby of the building it would prove that you had the opportunity or, at least, that you were in the building once. But if we could just find one in Dr. Parker's office," said Rolle, shaking his clasped hands in Sal's face.

"Yeah," Sal said confidently, "If I remember correctly ... from the papers, that is, that fire was over a year ago."

"I know," Rolle said, "but can you believe the landlord never repaired the suite or even pressured us to clean it up? It still has the police barrier tape and padlock on the door. Landlord said the insurance company would pay the rent as long as there was an ongoing investigation. He said that if he fixed it up it would be hard to find another tenant in this economy. Told me he hoped we never caught Parker."

"That's really grasping at straws, isn't it, Lieutenant?" O'Brian said.

"Maybe," Rolle said, "but I'd like you both, to meet someone very special to me."

"Is this relevant to what we're discussing?" O'Brian sounded doubtful.

"Oh, very," Rolle said as he walked out of the door.

Momentarily, he returned with a short, thin man with horn-rimmed glasses, dressed in a white lab coat, that almost touched his ankles. His full head of mixed grey hair was parted in the middle, and he had a gap-toothed smile that made him look a bit like Alfred E. Newman, the guy in *Mad Magazine*.

"This, gentlemen, is Pauli Bono, no relation to Sonny, our fingerprint expert. Before you came in, I was talking to Pauli about the possibility of turning up a good set of prints in Dr. Parker's office or in the building itself. Tell them what you told me, Pauli."

Pauli's voice was exactly what you would expect. High pitched and full of tension.

"I told you that it was very possible, but that it might require an extraordinary amount of work."

"And what is your current workload like right now?" Rolle asked.

"Oh, I'm busy from seven in the morning until past quitting time. There's enough work for an additional two print technicians, but as you know, Lieutenant, the city has a freeze on hiring right now that's been in effect for the past fourteen months."

"So, you're saying that you could not possibly get this work done during your regular hours?"

"Oh, heavens, no, Lieutenant. No way."

"So, you would have to do it after hours?"

"Yes, Lieutenant."

"Do you suppose I can get the authorization for the city to pay for it?"

"I already know they'll never approve it, Lieutenant. They stopped paying me overtime eight months ago."

"Would you still do it?"

"Of course," Bono said. "I'd be happy to. First, I'll recheck the prints we already have from the initial invest-igation. Then, if necessary, I'll redo the whole suite myself and if we still come up empty, I'll start on Dr. Parker's floor and work my way to the lobby, including all elevators and stairwells."

"Thank you, Pauli. I'll talk to you later."

"No. Thank you, Lieutenant," Pauli said as he exited the room.

Rolle now fixed his gaze on Sal. "And he'll do it, too. You know why?"

Sal did not answer.

"Because, he says it's guys like you, that give Italians a bad name."

Sal bolted from his chair and began to erupt. "I don't give a damn if you get an army of paisanos and dust the outside of the building, too. I tell you, I've never been there."

"We'll see," said Rolle calmly, almost whispering.

321

"With all respect, Lt. Rolle," O'Brian said, "if you're through playing mind games here, Mr. Roselli and I would both like to leave unless you are ready to make a formal charge."

"So, you think I've been playing games with you? I can assure you, that certainly is not the case, but you have given me an idea. Sal, since your freedom and possibly your life is at stake here, let's play a little *Jeopardy*. Are you familiar with that game show?"

"Please," Lt. O'Brian spoke, "I must insist that .... "

Sal, who was now seated, and embarrassed over losing his temper, held his hand out to motion O'Brian to stop talking.

"It's okay," Sal said, his composure regained. "Sure, I watch *Jeopardy*. It's good mental exercise."

With his eyes half closed, Rolle gave O'Brian a quick glance that conveyed his total disgust with Sal.

"If it's alright with you, counselor, I'd like to borrow Sal for just a moment..."

"And just where do you think you are going to take him?"

"We're just going to visit the Booking Room."

This time, it was O'Brian who stood up. "And what are you booking him for?"

"I didn't say I was booking him. I said we were going to the Booking Room."

Sal waved his hand dismissing O'Brian's concern, and he and Rolle disappeared out the door. O'Brian sat in the Interrogation Room alone trying to figure out what Rolle was up to. He didn't have long to contemplate, because they were back within five minutes. Sal returned to his chair. Rolle turned his chair around and again sat with his forearms resting on the back of the chair.

"Alright, Sal," Rolle began. "You said you know the rules of *Jeopardy*, so I don't have to explain them to you. What about you, counselor?"

"I've seen it a few times," O'Brian replied, "but I've never been fascinated by trivia or game shows."

"Well, in a nut shell," Rolle said, "there are different categories from which you pick a dollar amount. The higher the dollar amount, the harder the question. Except that it isn't a question, it's an answer to which you have to phrase the correct question.

"For example, if the category is PRESIDENTS and the answer was 'The first president of the United States', the correct response given in the form of a question would be 'Who is George Washington?' There is a segment of the show called Double Jeopardy, but we won't be able to get into that, since we all know to put your client in double jeopardy is forbidden by the Constitution."

Rolle felt very smug and thought that line would elicit a smile from O'Brian. It did not.

"All right, Sal," Rolle continued, now in a businesslike manner. "The first answer is, it's the most frequent reason that we book suspects into this precinct every day."

Feeling very confident, Sal replied, "Drugs," and nodded his head, smiling.

"Correct," Rolle said, "but remember that your response must be in the form of a question."

"Oh, yeah," Sal piped up. "What is drugs?"

"Next answer," Rolle continued. "The country of origin of most of our drug felons."

"What is South America?" Sal smiled broadly, getting into the spirit of the game.

This time Rolle tried to mask his disgust and wanted to tell Sal that South America was not a country, but instead he just asked him to be more specific.

"What is Columbia?"

"Correct again," said Rolle. "Now staying in the same category. The fellow countryman that the Colombians would like to impress most."

"You got me on that one." Sal thought it over for a while. "I don't know. Who is the President of Columbia?"

"Wrong answer," Rolle said, trying to contemplate why Sal thought that drug felons would try to impress the President of Columbia. "The correct response is 'Who is Roberto Mendez?'"

"Roberto who?" Sal put on his most puzzled face.

"Never heard of him, huh?" Rolle sneered.

"No." Sal shook his head. "You got me on that one too."

"Now we're ready for Final Jeopardy," Rolle had a twisted smile on his face, "which in your case is final as in terminal, but this answer has a visual clue, as well. The answer is, 'What these felons would do to gain the slightest favorable attention from Roberto Mendez'."

Having said that, Rolle produced a folded picture from his jacket pocket of a mutilated body. He held the picture up for Sal and his attorney to see.

"No response?" said Rolle. "Well, I'm afraid time has run out," he remarked as he finished humming a few bars of the Final Jeopardy theme. The correct response is 'What is Murder?'"

"Just a minute. Now I think you've gone too far," O'Brian said.

"Oh, you do, do you? Just let me tell you what happened in this picture. I can assure you that this is of the utmost importance to your client. This is maybe the most important thing he will ever hear in his life. The man you see lying on the prison latrine floor is ... or shall I say was ... one Alberto Santiago.

"The coroner told me that most of the urine that you see on the body and the floor are not from the decedent, but he certified that all of the blood belonged to him. Mr. Santiago was suspected of stealing from his fellow Colombians. They held his head in the toilet while they stabbed him. The coroner couldn't tell if he died of drowning or massive hemorrhaging, so he listed them both on the death certificate.

"Presumably, after he was dead, they urinated on his body and, if you look closely, you can see that his eyes have been gouged out. I think that means he was too greedy or something, but you are more familiar with that macho symbolism than I am. If they did that to one of their own for stealing, what do you think they would do to you, Sal?"

"What do you mean, do to me? These punks couldn't get near me. And you keep mentioning a Roberto Mendez. I don't even know no Roberto Mendez."

"Oh, I think you do, Sal. And word on the street is that he blames you for being in jail. I don't know exactly why, but the fact is that he does. Some people say that you are the one who benefited directly from him going to the slammer and he wants revenge."

"Guy must be some kinda lunatic." Sal's eyes widened though.

"Might be, but I also got it from a reliable source that he has been trying to put a contract out on you for months now. The only reason he hasn't been able to do it, is that the cartel to which you both belong has denied him this privilege. They think it would disrupt their business. But if you were in jail, Sal, all bets would be off. And how long do you think it would take for Mendez to find out that you're behind bars? He probably has as many dirty cops on his payroll as you have. A subject I'll come back to in just a few minutes."

Putting on his most sincere face, Rolle continued. "I know you don't mind dying, Sal. People in your line of work almost expect an untimely death. But dying like this," said Rolle, again holding up the picture, "has no honor. Dying in a city jail latrine with punk kids urinating on you."

"This has all been very interesting," O'Brian said, "but it's all academic since Mr. Rosellini is not going to jail."

"I beg to differ with you, counselor," Rolle said. "We have enough evidence to book him and it's already after four p.m. on a Saturday afternoon. Which means he won't even get a bail hearing until Monday or Tuesday. I'm betting that with Sal's reputation, the judge may consider him a flight risk. And if we can locate that folder, then the charges will be premeditated murder in addition to armed robbery. As you know, counselor, there is no bail for premeditated murder."

"So what do you want from me?" Sal's voice trembled.

Did I detect a small degree of hesitation? thought Rolle. *Maybe a modicum of doubt?*

"What my superiors want," Rolle said, "is for you to turn state's evidence and enter the Witness Protection Program, where neither Mendez nor anyone else can find you."

"You want me to turn rat and enter the Witness Protection Program!" yelled Sal incredulously. "Either you're a nut case or you've been smokin' up the evidence."

Rolle remained calm. "Look, Sal," he explained, "I'll be the first to admit that if it weren't for some luck, you and I wouldn't be having this conversation, but we had the luck and now we're having the conversation. You're in a bad spot and I don't think you will live the eight months to a year it will take for your trial to be completed. Not to mention, if you have to do time. You asked what I wanted from you and I told you what my superiors want. What I want from you is for you to turn the deal down."

Abruptly, Rolle changed gears, standing up and kicking his chair across the room. "I'm tired of guys like you getting off easy. Plea bargaining, turning state's evidence, technicalities, smart expensive lawyers, dumb juries. The list goes on and on. What I want is a picture of you just like this one. Lying in your own blood and someone else's urine in a filthy jailhouse toilet. I'll have it framed. No, I'll have it matted and framed so that it looks real nice. Then I'll hang it in my office so that I can start each day off with a smile and let it remind me that justice is served once in a while."

"Hold on," Sal protested, as he tried to stand up. Rolle, who was already standing directly in front of him, put his index finger forcefully into Sal's sternum and pushed him back into his chair. Rolle then looked for any protestations from O'Brian. None were forthcoming.

In a dimly lit room, with his eyes bloodshot from rage and lack of sleep and the veins of his forehead distended, Sal thought Rolle was a man possessed.

"I'm not finished just yet," Rolle said. "I'm going to cut to the chase. As loathsome as you are to me, the thing I hate most is a dirty cop. Especially one that may be in my precinct. I took you into the Booking Room and you know that it's full of Colombians. You also know that you are going to have to spend at least two nights here in custody. I want the name of the cop, who tipped you that we were coming, or you're going into the general lock up. If you tell me, I'll have you put in a private cell."

Sal felt the tiny cubicle get increasingly smaller. He felt as if some unseen force were pumping the oxygen out of the room, while rivulets of perspiration began slowly meandering down the back of his neck.

"You can't do that," Sal said. "You said you're a man of the cloth."

"Wrong again," Rolle said. "I said my father was a man of the cloth. I'm a man of the badge, but I don't care if I lose my badge, my pension or my very soul. I swear on the life of my dear seventy-two year old mother that if I don't have that name in two minutes, you're going into the general lockup." Rolle was now leaning over the still sitting Sal Roselli, with their noses almost touching. And with almost every word Rolle spoke, Sal was getting spittle on his face.

When Rolle spoke of his mother, however, the muscles in his body seemed to relax and the frightening rage seemed to dissipate. Rolle leaned to his right and spoke softly into Sal's left ear.

327

"I would rather have a stroke and be paralyzed for the rest of my life, than for my mother to be deprived of one breath of air prematurely." Rolle then calmly retrieved the chair which he had punted into a corner, and sat down facing O'Brian and Roselli. Crossing his legs at the ankles, he began to look at his watch.

Sal was relieved that Rolle was no longer standing over him. He removed a starched white handkerchief from his right front pocket and wiped his brow. His mouth felt very dry. Sal had never given anyone up in his life, but this seemed as good a time as any to start.

"Wilson," he said softly.

"What?" Rolle shouted, furrowing his eyebrows.

"Edward Wilson."

Rolle walked to the door and spoke to an unseen person. "Pick Wilson up now and bring him in." Glancing over his shoulder, Rolle gave Sal a sincere, "Thank you." Now turned fully toward the room and standing in the doorway, Rolle spoke again. "I'll give you time to consider what we've talked about. Would either of you like some coffee?"

"I'd like a glass of water," Sal said.

"Me, too," chimed in O'Brian, as he cleared his throat.

"Fine," Rolle said, "I'll send someone in with it right away."

After their heated session with Lt. Rolle, the tepid water was extremely refreshing. O'Brian and Roselli sat face to face, each waiting for the other to speak. O'Brian was first again.

"I don't think you should take the deal he's offering. I'm sure we can win in court."

"It's making it to court that has me concerned. He was right about Mendez. He'd like nothin' better than to see me dead."

"Who?" O'Brien asked.

"I'm talking about Mendez now, although Rolle made it pretty clear where he stands. Did you see the look on his face? I felt like I was trapped in a horror movie."

"How do you think he knew what was in the safe?"

"I haven't figured that out yet, but Patrice is missing and someone I thought I could trust left enough evidence in the safe to cause me a lot of trouble."

"Do you think they're in it together?" O'Brian asked.

"I don't think so, but at this point, I'm not ruling out any possibilities. What do you think about what he said about me not getting out on bail?"

"It's a certainty that you won't be out this weekend, but I'll have the bail hearing set up as soon as possible."

"It's not this weekend or this week that I'm worried about. Rolle said he would protect me until the bail hearing and he has me convinced he does what he says. I mean do you think I will get released on bond after the hearing?"

"It's hard to say. Like Rolle said, the judge may consider you a flight risk and truthfully, if they get their hands on that file or find a print in that office, not saying that either of these things exists, there is a good possibility that bail will be denied."

Sal looked, and felt, very weary. He felt as if he had been in that room for days. As he got up and began to pace around the room, O'Brian could tell that Sal was trying to sort out the possibilities. He was pacing slowly with his left hand in his pants pocket. In his right hand he held his forehead in a viselike grip.

His gaze was toward the floor and his body posture suggested that the earth's gravity had somehow increased. He had always considered himself a standup guy and despised anyone who rolled over. It wasn't, however, like he was a virgin anymore. He had already turned in Wilson. He wasn't a virgin, but he didn't want Rolle to turn him into a whore. On the other hand, there was Roberto Mendez and an army of Colombians to carry out his every wish. And the stupid charges he was up on. Armed robbery, cocaine possession.

At least if he were convicted of trafficking or racketeering, he would have the relative safety of a federal prison. He knew people in Federal pens. He had some contact in federal pens. He didn't know anyone in the county jail. If they sent him to the state prison in Raiford, which should be renamed Third World Prison, he knew he was a corpse. Not only would he have to worry about the Colombians, but any punk who wanted to get on the good side of the Colombians or Roberto Mendez. That would practically be the whole damn prison population. He was in a jam. I just hope I make bail long enough to find Vinny and Patrice, he thought.

Pacing around the room for the fifth or sixth time, he noticed something in one of the corners of the room. Had it been there all the time? How many times had he walked past it without noticing? Was it there when he first entered the room? What could it be? His mind was happy for this momentary distraction. He walked slowly towards what looked like a piece of paper folded and discarded. Maybe this was a message, a sign, a ray of hope. Somehow he felt this paper contained the answer to things, which he could not figure himself. He picked it up and walked directly under one of the bare bulbs for better lighting as he unfolded it. As he stared at what he was holding in his hand, he stood perfectly still, casting no shadow in the room.

Watching Sal, O'Brian was reminded of innumerable "B" movies he had seen in his adolescence. He actually felt as if he could only see in black and white. He studied Sal as he stood transfixed in the light, mesmerized by whatever he had found. Slowly and almost imperceptibly at first, he noticed that the paper was moving. Maybe it was just a little tremor from Sal holding it up for so long. The slight tremor then evolved into a twitch, which now involved Sal's left eye and the corner of his mouth.

O'Brian stood up and hurriedly pushed a chair behind Sal and, holding him by both shoulders, gently lowered him into it. He then took the paper from Sal. It was the picture of Alberto Santiago, and it wasn't in black and white. He heard Sal take a big breath as he pulled a chair to Sal's right side and sat beside him.

"I know things look bad, Sal, but I still don't think you should take their offer."

Looking straight ahead, Sal spoke blankly. "It won't be you in that latrine with some teenaged Colombians pissing on you while their friends stick banana knives up your ass. Tell Rolle I want to see him .... NOW!!!"

Although he had left the interrogation room over an hour ago, it seemed like only a brief respite to Rolle. He hoped it seemed like an eternity in hell to Sal and O'Brian.

O'Brian had summoned Rolle and had escorted him into the room as if they were the best of friends. He even positioned a chair opposite theirs and held it for him to sit down. After O'Brian had returned to his seat, Rolle sat cross-legged with his hands interlocked on his knee. He did not turn his head but moved his eyes from one to the other, patiently waiting to see who would speak first, this time.

It was Sal who broke the silence. "I want to take the offer you made, but I want everything in writing. O'Brian will review the papers before I say anything."

Rolle could not and did not try to hide the disappointment on his face. He stood, shrugged his shoulders and shook his head slowly.

"I'll call the District Attorney and the FBI," said Rolle as he walked toward the door. "I'm going to send out for some food. You guys want a sandwich and some drinks?"

"We would appreciate it, Lieutenant," O'Brian said.

"We'll charge it all to the Feds," Rolle said, "since you're going to be their witness, now."

* * *

The District Attorney's name was Sheila Raney. She was five-feet two inches tall, and one hundred pounds, if you weighed her with a heavy coat on. Blonde hair, hazel eyes, and the brightest smile this side of an Ultra-Brite commercial. She spoke with a Texas drawl and had been runner-up at Texas State College in Austin for Homecoming Queen. She looked every bit the former cheerleader that she was.

She had been born into a prominent Texas family. Her father was an engineer for one of the oil companies there and her mother was a former college professor, who became a full time mother and homemaker, once Sheila was born. She had an older brother, Ralph, who was a state representative, and a younger sister who was a local newscaster in Austin. She was married to one of the most successful businessmen in the state and had two perfect children. All this made it difficult, if not impossible, for anyone to understand why she was such a hard-nosed prosecutor, with the disposition of a crack-addicted snake.

The Federal Agent was Samuel Westhall, a short compact man known to all by his nickname of Glitch, which was acquired from his annoying habit of constantly repeating that everything had to go by the book without any glitches. He was only slightly taller than Sheila Raney, but considerably more muscular. He had a neck that should have had a yoke on it. He had the hard steely looks of a man with pathological determination.

He had been a Ranger in Vietnam and had volunteered for a second tour of duty to refine his skills as a killer and a survivor. In moments of reflection, it was not uncommon for him to state that it was often appropriate to liquidate an entire village of men, women, children and livestock, including pets, to make a statement to the enemy. Knowing that he was sincere when he made such proclamations, and had probably done just that on more than one occasion, made him just a bit more likable than Sheila Raney.

Raney and Westhall arrived at the precinct simultaneously. Rolle greeted them both at the door before escorting them back to his office.

"Sal has decided to play ball," Rolle said.

"Excellent," Westhall replied.

"That bastard better not try jerking me around," intoned Raney.

Rolle and Westhall shot quick glances at each other.

"Everything should be set up soon," said Rolle.

Rolle had instructed two of his men to take a desk, three more chairs, a small table and two table lamps into the Interrogation Room. He had already called for Lupe Suarez, the city stenographer that was on duty for the evening. And he had a tape recorder in his desk.

"I know that we're all familiar with the routine," Westhall said, "but maybe we should go over everything, just so that there are no glitches."

This time the glances were between Raney and Rolle.

"Let's go," Raney said. "We've got some asses to skewer."

The Interrogation Room was now not only small and uncomfortable, but crowded as well. District Attorney Raney had been to the 25th Precinct several times before and they knew how she liked things to be handled.

First, the room had to be set up properly—Ms. Raney behind the largest desk that could be fitted into the room, thereby giving her the demeanor of authority. The people to be dealt with, sitting directly across from her, behind the smallest table that was functionally adequate. A table and not a desk, so that she could observe as much of their body language as possible. The word was that she liked to see people squirm. The stenographer was always to be seated to her right without benefit of a desk or table. Just a chair and the stand for the steno machine. Everyone else was to be seated to the right of the stenographer, with them all facing the accused. A small cassette recorder on her desk, with one blank tape in the machine, ready to record, and two blank tapes on her left.

There were to be minimal interruptions as she conducted the state's business. She really preferred that no one speak until she recognized them. Only the minimum amount of courtesy would be extended to the accused and his or her counsel and everything would proceed with the utmost efficiency, until a logical conclusion, was reached.

District Attorney Raney was the last person to enter the Interrogation Room. She only had to make two or three small steps from the doorway to the desk, but she entered and sat with the air of a Supreme Court Justice, deciding a case on which the very existence of the Republic depended. O'Brian had to put a hand on Sal's shoulder to prevent him from standing up.

"Let it be duly recorded," she began, "that all participants in this room are aware that any and all proceedings are being recorded by tape recorder and by a county stenographer. I'll begin the proceedings by introducing myself. I'm Sheila Raney, District Attorney for Dade County in the state of Florida."

Sal couldn't believe his ears or his eyes. So that was Raney, in person, the ball-busting District Attorney. He had never laid eyes on her before, thank heaven, but she had caused him considerable distress over the years. If she weren't the D.A. he would have had her whacked.

Sheila Raney was still talking. "Will everyone in the room now state their name and position or purpose, starting to my right with Lt. Rolle?"

"I'm Lt. Livingston Rolle, Miami Police Department, Chief Investigating Officer."

"I'm Samuel Westhall, Special Investigator and Special Project Director, Federal Bureau of Investigation."

Raney now nodded in the direction of the stenographer.

"I'm Lupe Suarez, County Stenographer."

Raney then extended her hand and nodded in O'Brian's general direction.

"I'm Kelly O'Brian, Attorney at Law, representing Mr. Salvatore Roselli."

Finally, she made eye contact with Sal and gave him the go-ahead nod.

"I'm Salvatore Adolfo Roselli and I'm about to become the biggest whore in the state of Florida. Present company excepted," he said as he stared deeply into the eyes of Sheila Raney.

One would have thought that he had just complimented her on her attire. "Thank you, Mr. Roselli," she said calmly and without emotion, "Thank you for your anticipated and humorless comments, and thank you all for being here. The next stage of the proceedings are to ensure that Mr. Roselli, represented by Attorney O'Brian, fully understands his rights and privileges."

She reached beneath the desk and produced a brown Cross briefcase which she opened. She removed some papers and returned the briefcase to its original place. She handed the papers to Rolle, who then gave them to Westhall, who in turn, got up and gave them to O'Brian.

Raney continued, "Please let the record show that I have given Mr. O'Brian and his client, Mr. Roselli, Form 906.25B, which has been supplied to me by Mr. Westhall of the Federal Bureau of Investigation. This form basically states that we are offering Mr. Roselli immunity from all past crimes for his cooperation in an ongoing investigation. Furthermore, Mr. Roselli will be placed into the Witness Protection Program for his assistance. Form 906.25B also states that if Mr. Roselli is found to have deceived any local or Federal Government Agency by untruths or knowingly withholding information, then all protection from prosecution and his enrollment in the Witness Protection Program may be immediately rescinded."

335

O'Brian gave a cursory look at the form. He told Sal that he was familiar with that document and everything seemed to be in order. Sal signed the papers without looking at them.

Westhall then brought the papers back to Raney, who looked at the signature and handed them back to Westhall, who filed them in his briefcase, which happened to be one of those indestructible aluminum types. Much like himself.

Ms. Raney spoke, "Let the record show that Mr. Roselli, after advice from counsel, decided to sign form 906.25B of his own free will. Is that correct, Mr. Roselli?"

"That is correct, your Districtness," Sal replied. Now that he had immunity and they needed him, being a little smart-mouthed was all the dignity that he had left.

"Mr. Westhall will take you into custody and place you into the Witness Protection Program immediately. At a later time, convenient to you and to the Federal Government, he will question you about organized crime and other activities about which we believe you have knowledge.

"However, before you are remanded to the care of Agent Westhall, there are some issues which we would like you to address for us tonight. Are you familiar with one Dr. Evander Parker?"

Sal looked at O'Brian. O'Brian shrugged his shoulders, cocked his head to one side with his eyes closed, as if to say, "You might as well get started on this journey."

"Yes ... I am," Sal replied.

Rolle finally felt the clench of tension relax its grip on the muscles of his neck.

"Do you know a Sol Weinberg, also known as Solly?"

"Yes, I do."

Without any hesitation, Sue Raney continued. "Did you kill Mr. Weinberg?"

No beating around the bush with this woman, Sal thought. *Right to the point.* Sal decided to be right to the point as well.

"Yes, I did."

"Did you know a Ms. Rita Kennedy, who worked for Dr. Parker?"

This time, Sal thought he would beat her to the punch. "Yes," he replied "and I killed her, too."

Unfazed, Sheila Raney continued. "Have you ever been to the office of Dr. Evander Parker?" she asked.

"Yes, several times and on my last visit I torched it." Somehow Sal felt energized by her questions. He could actually tell the District Attorney about crimes that he had committed and they couldn't do anything about it. She was the Mother Confessor. It was a strange sense of power that began to envelop him.

"Would you mind telling us why you committed these acts?" she asked.

He was beginning to like the way she talked. Committed these acts. Blowing a guy away or crushing an old lady's skull were just acts to her. She had nice lips, too. He wanted her to talk some more.

"Would you mind repeating the question?" he asked.

"Would you mind telling us why you committed these acts?" she repeated.

"I wouldn't mind telling you anything," he replied charmingly. "I killed Solly because he was stealing from me. I committed the other acts," he said, emphasizing the word acts, "to see if I could get away with it. Well, actually, torch-ing the office and killing his secretary were to help cover the frame."

"Then why did you kill his wife?"

"Who?" Sal asked.

"His wife, Cassie Parker," Raney said.

"I didn't," Sal said calmly. "Never met her."

"Let me remind you of the stipulations in the form you just signed. You are under oath and you may confer with your counsel if you wish."

"Look," Sal said. "You say I got immunity. O'Brian says I got immunity. But only if I tell the truth. If you want me to say

I killed her, then I'll say it. It don't mean nothin' to me at this point, other than I wouldn't be telling the truth. Tell you what, you make up another set of papers that says I got immunity, if I say I killed his wife, even if I didn't do it, and I'll confess to that, too. Means nothin' to me at all."

Lt. Rolle cleared his throat.

"Yes, Lieutenant?" Raney said.

"I would like to ask Sal—Mr. Roselli—a few questions."

"Of course, Lieutenant."

"Mr. Roselli, do you know a Noel or Chandler Christian?"

"No sir, I do not."

"Did you have an occasion to rob two men at gunpoint approximately eighteen months ago and take from them a large amount of Jamaican currency?"

"Oh, yeah, that. Yes, sir, I did, but I'm afraid I never asked their names."

Sal smiled broadly, very pleased with his answer.

"That's all I had to ask," Rolle said.

"Very well, then," Raney said. "Mr. Roselli, you are now entrusted to the care of the Federal Government, represented here by Mr. Westhall. These proceedings are now closed."

Rolle escorted Raney to the front of the precinct and pulled her to the side of the front entrance before she could exit.

"May I help you, Lieutenant?" she said harshly.

"Slight problem," he said. "With the gracious help of Mr. Roselli, we have cleared two murders, but there is still the question of the wife. Personally, I believe he did it."

"What you believe personally has nothing to do with the law," she said.

"I'm aware of that, but Dr. Parker turned himself in to me and he just won't last in the county jail until his arraignment."

"So what do you want from me?"

"I want you to okay his release to my custody."

"Never in a million years."

Rolle felt his heart sink.

"However," she continued, "since he did surrender to you at this precinct over which you have jurisdiction and responsibility for the safety, as well as detention of prisoners, you may handle it as you see fit."

Rolle smiled faintly. "Thank you."

"But, in the event that said prisoner is found to be absent at the time of his scheduled arraignment, for which I can guarantee there will be no postponements, you and you alone will be held personally and professionally accountable. If there are any screw ups, for whatever reason, I can promise you that I'll serve your ass up on a silver platter on a bed of rice and that you will be forever sorry that you ever met me. Now I must say good night. My kids are waiting up for me to read them a bedtime story."

Lt. Rolle took a deep breath of the early morning air, and walked back inside the precinct. He took a small turn near the Interrogation Room and opened the door to a closet-sized room. In the room were Taylor Nash, Noel and Chandler Christian, Dr. Evander Parker and Patty Ann 'Patrice' Jessup. From this room one could look into the Interrogation Room through a one-way mirror and hear most of what was being said.

"Congratulations, all around," Rolle said, holding up a paper cup as if to make a toast.

"This wraps things up," said Chandler.

"No, it doesn't," said Rolle. "We still have an unsolved murder."

"Come on, Lieutenant, you can't believe that Dr. Parker murdered his wife," Noel said.

"Didn't say that at all, I said we still have an unsolved murder."

"I think Roselli killed her," Chandler said.

"And for what reason?" asked his brother.

"Man like that don't need a reason," Chandler replied.

"True, but why didn't he confess to it? He didn't have anything to lose."

"Maybe he's holding out. Use it later to his advantage."

"Who do you think did it, Lieutenant?" Noel asked.

"I don't know. That's why it's still unsolved."

"What's going to happen to me now?" asked Dr. Parker timidly.

"I'm placing you under protective custody," responded Rolle.

Parker's mind began to race. He had seen the pictures that Rolle had shown to Roselli. What would happen to him?

"I'm putting him in your hands, Nash."

Parker began to breathe again.

"You can check with me later to find out the date of his arraignment. You be sure he shows up. If he dies before that arraignment, you drag his dead ass to the courthouse."

Feeling a bit more energized, Parker turned toward Patrice.

"You've been awfully quiet throughout all of this."

She held her head down, with her arms folded across her chest, and began to sob quietly. "I can't believe I shared a part of my life with such a horrible person."

"Well, folks," Rolle said, "you don't have to go home, but you have to get out of here. It's already well into a new day, and I'm headed home."

Noel and Chandler were the first ones up and out. Nash told Parker that he was going to drop him off at the apartment and then asked Patrice where she wanted to go. She squeezed her purse, holding the money she took from the safe, as if for reassurance.

"Take me to the Doral Hotel. I'll check in under a different name. If I need to reach any of you, I'll call Lt. Rolle. I just need to be by myself for awhile."

Chapter
Twenty-Four

L t. Rolle was sitting behind his desk. He had phoned Taylor Nash and told him to come over to the Precinct. He also asked him to bring Dr. Parker. Less than an hour later, both men walked into his office.

"Please," Rolle said, "have a seat."

Both men sat down.

"Do you have anything new for me?" Rolle came straight to the point.

"Like what?" Nash flashed his deadpan look.

Rolle did not reply.

"Oh, you mean on the investigation into the homicide of Cassie Parker," said Nash. "If you had come to work in the past two days, you would have seen me in here with that masseuse, Mark Taylor, poring over the mug shots of every person ever arrested in the state of Florida."

"Nothing, huh?"

"Nada," Nash said. "He recognized some people he knew but none of them was the man who confronted him on the night Mrs. Parker was killed."

Suddenly, Dr. Parker got up and walked out.

"We have to remember that it was his wife who was murdered," Nash said. "Why did you ask me to bring him here anyway?"

"Just wanted to see him. I've put a lot on the line here not locking him up."

"He knows it and appreciates it. We just have to be more careful talking in front of him. By the way, where have you been for the past few days?"

"Took my kids fishing. Have to remind myself every once in a while that there are still nice people in the world and there are still good things that you can do. You ought to get married and have a couple of kids. Might do you some good. Nothing else has."

"I like my life just the way it is, thank you. But if I decide to change it, you will be among the first to know."

"Let's look at this case again with a fresh eye," Rolle said.

"Okay, teacher, teach."

"We are assuming that this guy who came to see Kelly on the night Mrs. Parker was murdered, knew her intimately or was getting information for someone who knew her intimately."

"Right."

"But before we go any further, can we assume that there was any such person? Maybe Mark Kelly made up the whole story. Maybe he killed her."

"Well, teacher, Cassie Parker was Kelly's meal ticket in a way, so it would have been stupid of him to kill her. She was worth much more to him alive. Also, the landlady confirms his story that he was there all night, plus he can produce a dozen people, albeit crack heads, who can verify that he never left the apartment that evening. I also checked his alibi for the next morning, which pans out."

"Okay, then back to the mystery man. Because of Cassie's shall we say checkered past, we also have the possibility that another one of her old acquaintances found her, tried black-mail, was unsuccessful and killed her."

"Yes, teacher, but such a person would have known her past and would not have gone to the trouble of asking Kelly to run down her history."

"Very good, grasshopper. How about a lover, new or past?"

"I checked into that. She didn't seem to date much, or really at all, before she was married. Just to double check, I got photos of hospital personnel from the time she started working there. I went over them last night with Kelly. No luck."

"So now we are faced with the proposition of a new lover."

"Get Parker in here. We're going to have to ask him some very unpleasant questions."

Nash found Parker sitting on the wooden bench in the outer office and brought him back into the room.

"I'm sorry," Parker said, taking a seat. "It's just that ...."

"You don't have to explain anything to us," Rolle said, suddenly hating his job. "We understand, and we hope you understand what we are about to do."

Parker looked puzzled. He turned to Nash, then to Rolle and back to Nash again.

Rolle plopped his flat buttocks on the cold metal table. He continued, "We are trying to find your wife's killer, as you know, and we have to explore every possibility. Some of which are going to be distasteful to you as well as to us, but we can leave no option unexplored. So, please, try not to take any of this personally."

When Parker heard that, he knew instinctively that he would.

Lt. Rolle cleared his throat. "Dr. Parker," Rolle asked very somberly, "has your wife ever had an affair?"

Don't take it personally, thought Parker. *What a joke.* How could he not take a question like that personally? He grit his teeth very hard. It was difficult for him not to walk out of the room again. This time in anger, not sorrow.

The look on his face gave them the answer, but they still waited.

"No," he said.

"How much do you know about your wife's past?" Rolle asked.

Parker looked at Nash, who was now looking at the floor.

"Not much, I guess, not much at all," he said, trying to disguise his anger and doing a very poor job of it. "We always said that our lives began the day we got married."

Rolle continued," Did you know your wife had been arrested twice in Los Angeles?"

Parker became paralyzed. Not just a slow paralysis, but he felt as if he had looked into the eyes of Medusa and had turned to stone. He couldn't move, he hoped that he was still breathing and that his heart would continue to beat.

Parker could see Lt. Rolle talking but they had a bad connection. He could only hear every fifth or sixth word. Did Rolle say something about involvement with drugs? Now, he wished his heart would stop beating because it felt as if it were going to come out of his chest. Mark Kelly? Did he just say she knew Mark Kelly previously? Impossible. He was just a masseur.

Suddenly, Dr. Evander Parker was back in the office of Lt. Rolle.

Parker's mind focused on Mark Kelly. "This was all his fault," he blurted out. "I'll kill him. He seduced my wife and then killed her, that son-of-a-bitch."

He looked over again toward Nash, who was no longer looking at the floor, but who was looking directly at him. Nash was looking at him as one would stare at a stranger, which is exactly what Nash was feeling.

Slowly, Parker regained his composure.

"It's not Mark Kelly," Nash said as calmly as he could. "Mark is not, shall we say, sincerely interested in sex from the opposite sex. Besides, he has an airtight alibi." Nash saw no need to mention that Kelly was blackmailing his wife.

Rolle was seated at his desk and had his hands clasped in front of him. He was serious and sad. "Dr. Parker," he asked, "have you ever had an affair?"

Nash knew immediately where Rolle was going with this. Maybe Parker was dallying around and his lover got jealous and iced his wife. Maybe this lover had a husband who wanted revenge.

Parker prepared himself for the worst, but he had already gone through the Medusa routine and surprisingly his feelings were only of disgust.

"No, never," he said with just enough emphasis that everyone knew he was telling the truth.

"Do you think my wife had an affair," Parker asked, taking a deep breath, "or are you just grasping at straws?" He looked directly at Rolle, who cast his gaze toward Nash.

Nash proceeded to tell Parker the story that Mark Kelly related to him about the man who came to see him the night his wife was murdered.

"That doesn't mean she was having an affair!" yelled Parker.

"We are not saying that it does, Doctor," replied Rolle. "We are just conducting an investigation, that's all."

"And destroying my wife's reputation in the meantime."

Nash released an audible sigh.

Parker and Rolle gave him their full attention.

"There's more," Nash said. "I was thinking about the note that Heather Fine left behind for you. It talked about infidelity."

"So what?" Parker sighed. "Heather was a deeply distur- bed young woman."

"Please, let me finish," Nash said softly. "I began to wonder if Heather knew something that we didn't. So I showed the doorman a picture of Heather and he said that she had been in the building asking questions about your wife. I also ran her license number through the DMV, again. This time for any priors."

"You're not supposed to do that."

Nash shrugged his shoulders and gave him a "so what?" look.

"She received two parking tickets, dating back several months before your wife's murder, not two blocks from your

345

condo. I figure she was watching your wife's every move. She may have seen her with someone."

"Well, it's a little late to ask her about it, now, don't you think?" Parker said sarcastically.

"I know it's all circumstantial," Nash said, "but it may be important."

Parker got up from his chair. "I'm going back to the apartment."

Nash got up and offered him a ride.

"No thank you, I'll get a cab," said Parker as he got up and left.

Rolle leaned back in his chair and put his feet up on the metal wastepaper basket. "Did you believe him when he said he never had an affair?"

"Yeah."

"Me, too."

Nash asked, "Do you believe his wife was fooling around?"

"Yeah."

"Me, too."

On the way home, Nash decided to stop by his apartment where Dr. Parker was now in residence. He knocked on the door, but did not use his key. Parker came to the door. He looked as if he had been crying.

"I thought it might be you," Parker said.

"Look, Doc ...."

"It's okay. I know you're just trying to do your job. Part of which is trying to keep me out of jail. I'm alright now."

Nash thought he didn't look all right. If he didn't know better, he would have thought Parker was on the tail end of a three-day binge.

"I've decided to try and help you and Lt. Rolle as much as possible," Parker said, "if only to prove you're wrong about Cassie."

Nash knew he was looking at a man teetering on the edge. He could see that he was using all of his strength to hold himself together. Telling Parker that he would call on him tomorrow, Nash was somewhat reluctant to leave him alone.

Arriving at the apartment early the next day, Nash was hopeful that he would not have to use the key. He knocked on the door and waited. No answer. He knocked again and waited. He took the key out of his pocket and turned it over in his hand. He was about to put the key into the lock when Parker came to the door. He looked as if he had not slept all night and he wore the same clothes as yesterday.

"Sorry to keep you waiting," he said, "I was in the bathroom washing my face. I've been up all night."

"It shows."

"If I can put some emotional distance between this case and myself, I may be of some help."

"Now you're talking," Nash said, trying to give him some encouragement and lift his spirits.

"I was working on a few things last night," Parker said. "If a woman, any woman, were to have an affair, it is usually with someone she has known for a while. I overheard you and Lt. Rolle saying that it is probably not someone from Cassie's past, so therefore, we are looking for someone, say from the time she moved to Miami. Statistically speaking, women and men usually have affairs with people they work with. So we should concentrate our initial efforts within that time frame and her employment parameter."

Although Nash protested vigorously, Dr. Parker insisted on accompanying him. Initially, Nash believed that this would only be detrimental to his friend, but on the way to the employment agency where Cassie first applied for work, it became obvious that this was necessary for Parker to do.

"You'll see," said Parker, "all of this time and effort will lead to a series of dead ends. You'll all be proven wrong," he said with an eerie look of determination on his face.

Nash hoped he was right.

Nash wanted to get a rundown on all of the places Cassie had been employed since her arrival in Miami. The receptionist at the office was a young black woman in her mid-twenties. She had a flawless mahogany complexion, expressive brown eyes and the prettiest smile that Nash had ever seen. Her smile was friendly but she maintained her professional manner. Her name, she told him, was Ms. Simmons and she would be more than happy to see if she could find the placement card of Ms. Cassie Smith.

"If you gentlemen would please have a seat, I'll be with you as soon as I can. The file you're requesting is quite old and I may not be able to locate it immediately."

Approximately one hour later, Ms. Simmons returned.

"I apologize for the wait but the file I was looking for was mis-referenced. It appears that your Ms. Smith was very fortunate, in that she was hired on the first job for which she interviewed. Memorial Hospital."

Nash thanked her and gave her his most charming smile. He hoped that he could get to know Ms. Simmons first name at a later date and that she would be a Miss.

He was quite handsome, she thought, and very pleasant. She wondered why she had never seen him around anywhere before. The quiet white guy with him, however, looked vaguely familiar.

Riding down the Interstate, Nash started the conversation.

"Fortunately, we don't have to check out dozens of different job sites. It seems as though she worked for the hospital from the time she moved here."

"Cassie was a very stable person." Parker sounded pensive.

"Did she have any part-time jobs that you know of?" Nash asked.

"No."

"Then we're back to the hospital. How about patients?"

"What about patients?"

"Would she have had extensive contact with the patients?"

"No." Parker shook his head. "The nurses have more contact with the patients than anyone. Unit secretaries occasionally, but rarely, have significant patient contact."

"We may have to try a new approach to find our mystery man now, since I already went over all the hospital personnel pictures with Mark Kelly."

"How about if we take one step backwards?" Parker suggested "Strong bonds are formed in school and Cassie did attend that Technical School in San Diego before she moved out here. Why don't you try contacting them? Ask them to send you photographs of her graduating class and of all the instructors that were there during her matriculation. It may be a good idea to have them send you the pictures of a couple of classes before and after hers also."

"Why, Dr. Parker, that's an excellent idea. I'll have Lt. Rolle get right on it."

"That will turn out to be another dead end, too. You'll see," he said, looking straight ahead.

Lt. Rolle called them the day the package arrived from San Diego Career Training Institute. Rolle escorted them back to the Interrogation Room where Mark Kelly was already waiting. As the days passed and Mark realized he was no longer a suspect, he began to enjoy the attention that was focused on him. He felt ill at ease when he saw Parker enter the room with Nash. He tried to avoid direct eye contact with Dr. Parker, who was looking at him with a hypnotic gaze. The last time Parker had seen Mark Kelly was when he was preparing to give his wife a massage.

Nash was glad he hadn't revealed the story of blackmail to Parker. They all sat around a square table, that looked to Mark Kelly like one of those folding high school cafeteria tables. It was. Mark and Rolle sat on one side of the table and Nash and Parker sat on the other. Kelly positioned his chair so that he would not face Parker directly.

Rolle placed the package and its contents, which had been sent Federal Express, on the table. "I looked at this earlier," he said, "just to be sure it was what we were expecting. Mark just arrived and has not had a chance to look at the pictures yet."

Rolle also wanted Parker to look at the pictures for any familiar faces.

Rolle handed half of the pictures to Parker and gave the other half to Mark Kelly. Two magnifying lenses were on the desk to facilitate their efforts.

Parker quickly shuffled through the pictures until he came back to the first one. They were all basically the same. Group shots of smiling faces. They were dressed not in traditional black caps and gowns but in all-white attire, befitting their future occupations. Most of the classes consisted of females, which was going to make this whole process much shorter. Parker studied the four group photos that he was given. In addition to the students, the picture included the instructors who were also mostly female.

None of the faces were familiar until he saw Cassie. He had never seen this picture of her. She was beautiful in white. Her smiling face, full of hope and promise. He bit his lip to try and restrain the emotions he felt welling up in him. His emotions told him that the man sitting across from him was somehow responsible, at least in part, for what had happened to his wife.

Nash was casually looking at the photos and could also see Parker in his peripheral vision. He noticed the tightness of

Parker's jaw and furrowing of his brow. The angry stranger that resided in Parker was about to make an encore appearance.

In one motion, before Parker could stand up, Nash grabbed his wrist and pulled it under the table, restraining him, and moved both chairs closer to each other. To the casual observer, it just looked as if they both adjusted their chairs. Surprised by this, Parker shot a menacing glance at Nash who closed his eyes and shook his head a few times as if admonishing a naughty child. Parker got the message.

Meanwhile, Mark Kelly was going over each male photo as if he were translating the Dead Sea Scrolls.

"No, not him. Not him either. He's cute, but not the one. I just don't see who I'm looking for in my stack."

Absentmindedly, Kelly pushed his photos in the direction of Dr. Parker. Still holding onto Parker's right wrist with his left hand, Nash used his right hand to push Parker's photos to Kelly and to pull Kelly's to them.

Rolle noticed this latest exchange and realized he made a mistake in putting the two of them together. He would make a mental note to not let this happen again.

Neither man was successful in his search and Rolle dismissed Kelly quickly but encouraged his future cooperation by telling him that he would be in touch. Kelly got up to leave the room and Rolle offered to have a squad car take him home.

"I think not," said Kelly, "Not even an unmarked one."

Several moments passed before anyone spoke.

"Another dead end," Dr. Parker said as he stood up. "Taylor, would you mind taking me to the apartment? I'm pretty tired."

"No problem," he responded.

Dr. Parker had asked Lt. Rolle previously if he could retrieve some of his personal effects from his home. The answer had been a resounding no. Rolle explained that getting objects from the house might have the appearance of collusion. He also took the opportunity to remind Parker that technically he was still under arrest.

Nash hadn't seen Parker in over two days. Certain things a man had to work out for himself and in his own time. Besides he had to work on some other cases to keep the proverbial wolf away from the door. As he drove towards Parker's apartment ... and that is how he began to think of it ... he had to admit that Parker might have been right.

There hadn't been any new leads in the case. He had talked to Rolle this morning and Rolle had told him that he had Mark Kelly review all of the photos from the school in San Diego and the hospital personnel folder again, without success.

The mid-afternoon sun beat down on his head, making sweat pop out on his forehead. He loosened his collar which was wilted from the humidity. Nash removed his sunglasses as he approached the apartment. The bright sunlight caused him to squint. He put his glasses back on and knocked on the door with no intention of using his key. He now regarded this as Parker's home. If there was no answer, he would come back later.

Dr. Evan Parker opened the door almost immediately. He looked worse than before. Nash wondered if he had been eating. He looked better when he was living on the streets.

"What in the hell is going on? Are you okay?"

"I think not," he replied. "This whole thing is getting to be too much for me. I can't eat, I can't sleep, I have no energy. If I were a doctor I would say I have the classic symptoms of depression. When I saw that photo of Cassie and the joy that was evident on her face, not knowing her tragic future, I just couldn't take any more. We had a good marriage, you know."

Looking at him, Nash decided not to leave him alone again until all this was settled.

"First thing we have to do is to get you cleaned up."

Nash told Parker to get his hygiene together and he would be back in about an hour. Parker had just stepped out of the shower when Nash knocked on the door. He pulled the towel around him and opened the door. Nash was holding a large box and had a coat hanger with a plastic suit bag slung over his shoulder.

Putting the box and the plastic bag on the bed, Nash exclaimed, picking up where he left off, "and the second thing is to get you some new clothes."

In the box were a lightweight cotton polo shirt and a pair of linen trousers. Both of the same pale blue hue. Nash took the coat out of the bag and off the hanger. It was an off-white linen and cotton blend Palm Beach sport coat. It was similar to one Parker had seen Nash wearing sometime previously.

"I didn't know your shoe size," he said, "but that's our next stop."

Overwhelmed, Parker did not know what to say. He could just make a feeble attempt at humor. "What, no belt?"

"This is a new millennium," Nash laughed, "and no belt is the way to go." After stopping at the shoe store and outfitting Parker in pale blue deerskin slip-ons and socks, they were off to get something to eat.

The lunch crowd had just dispersed at The Blue Dolphin, one of the most popular eating places on Miami Beach. They got a table right on the water and watched as some of the patrons left by boat.

"You know I didn't bring my credit card," Parker joked.

"I know," said Nash, laughing heartily. "If anybody knows, I certainly do."

They both laughed.

After lunch, of which Parker had two portions, they both walked around the ocean front pier. Some fishermen were bringing in their catch, while others were cleaning their haul and still others were preparing to go out again. Pelicans and gulls hovered around, eager for any scraps. Sightseeing boats and chartered fishing boats made their way into and away from the bay. The salty ocean breeze was subtle and refreshing, as the sun played peek-a-boo behind the clouds. It was a perfectly beautiful day.

As the two men stood staring out into the eternity of water that stretched before them, Nash spoke. "There is still a lot of beauty in the world."

"Yes," Parker said, blinking back tears behind a pair of sunglasses that he had taken from the glove compartment of Nash's car.

They lost track of time as they walked haphazardly around the pier and the surrounding area. Neither man spoke but enjoyed the other's company. The sea air revived their appetites somewhat prematurely and they returned to the same eating establishment before the heavy dinner crowd arrived. They sat at the same table and watched the moon perform its magic on the calm waters surrounding them.

Nash even persuaded the teetotaling Dr. Parker to have not one, but two glasses of dry white wine. It was a perfect complement to the fresh pompano and rice pilaf with asparagus. Key lime pie for dessert and all was right with the world.

Back in the apartment, Nash made a lame excuse about wanting to stay there because it was closer to a case that he had to get to work on early in the morning. Parker knew a poor excuse when he heard one, but was glad for the company. Nash took his usual spot on the leather recliner.

"Just like old times," said Nash.

Parker smiled and drifted off to his first good sleep in days.

The wine had the same effect on Parker as it does on most non-drinkers. He overslept. He awoke to see Nash coming in the door with two large shopping bags.

"You didn't buy anything else for me?" Parker said with the voice of an eager child.

"No, I didn't. I can't afford to."

"What's in the bags?" he asked. His voice full of expectation.

Nash unceremoniously dumped the contents of the bags onto the bed.

"Where did you get ...?"

"Don't ask," Nash said, cutting Parker off.

"How did you?

"Don't ask."

"When did you?"

"I said don't ask."

On the bed were some of Parker's personal belongings from his condo. His shaving kit, his hairbrush and comb, his bathrobe, some pullover cotton shirts, trousers, several pair of shoes, and a pair of run down corduroy slippers. There was also an old photo album.

Parker tried his old line again. "What, no belt?"

This time Nash was prepared. He reached into the pocket of his jacket and pulled out two leather belts. One black and one brown.

Nash walked over to the chaise where he had slept and gathered the bedding that he used. He folded it neatly and put it back into the closet. As he was putting it into the closet, he spoke to Parker.

"You know, Doc, it's not against the law to purchase clothes that are not black, navy blue, dark brown or grey."

Parker smiled. Until he had been around Nash he never felt that his wardrobe was so morose. He actually wanted to wear brighter colors now and had enjoyed the clothes that he had on yesterday. He had to admit they did lift his spirits. The clothes on the bed were dull and drab but somehow comforting. They were all a part of his life before he was sucked into this vortex—this nightmare.

355

He gingerly picked out a dark blue shirt and some darker blue pants and folded them over a chair. He took his shaving kit into the bathroom and disappeared for almost an hour. Nash knew Parker was alive because he could hear him singing. It was the first time that he had heard Parker sing. His voice was terrible and he couldn't make out what song it was supposed to be but Nash felt happy for him.

"What's on the agenda for today?" Parker asked, now fully dressed.

"We're on our way to see Rolle. We took the pictures over to the doorman at your building. Nothing. He wants you to look at the pictures from Hospital personnel. Maybe you'll see a face that may ring a bell. Maybe someone that you saw hanging around the lobby or just walking down the street."

"In other words, we're grabbing at straws."

Nash gave it to him straight. "Exactly."

On the way to the precinct, they stopped at a small restaurant and had a large breakfast. Nash insisted that Parker stuff himself because he knew a marathon session was ahead for them both. Nash knew that they would be in the precinct throughout lunch and he did not want them to eat anything that would be delivered to a police precinct.

Nash and Parker sat in the Interrogation Room, waiting for Rolle to bring in the hospital personnel photographs. Parker wasn't sure why Nash had insisted on such a large meal, until he saw three large file boxes filled with passport-sized photos.

They were all alphabetized and arranged according to year of employment and departments.

Rolle pointed to the boxes. "There you are," he said and left. "Call me if you want something to eat."

Nash mouthed an exaggerated "no way" in Parker's direction.

Parker had no idea that there would be this many photos to look at. It was only a one-hundred-fifty-bed hospital, but obviously those beds required a large support system and coupled with a mild to moderate turnover of employees, you ended up with three file boxes full of passport-sized photos. Also there were departments that he never gave any thought to, such as engineering, accounting, and on and on.

The search began, and continued, and continued. He saw a lot of faces that he recognized from the hospital. He saw some of their names for the first time. He actually saw some of them as people for the first time. Rolle kept them supplied with lots of room-temperature water and bad coffee. Parker only took short breaks as he was anxious to complete his task.

After investigating the last picture, Parker looked at Nash and shook his head. Nothing. All that time and nothing. Parker folded his arms on the table and gently placed his head on them, as a school child might do for an afternoon nap. He stared silently at the desk for a few seconds, before closing his eyes.

Suddenly, he sat up. "Let me see those files again."

This time, Parker went through the listings of departments. He turned toward Nash slowly, with a smile, not unlike the cat that ate the canary.

"A smart detective with all the resources of the Dade County Police Department and he overlooks something so very basic."

"And what could that be?" Nash said cockily.

"You got those photos and names from Personnel, right?"

"Correct."

"But everyone that works IN a hospital does not work FOR the hospital. Personnel would only carry the names and pictures of the people on the hospital payroll and there are lots of people that work in the hospital that are not on the hospital payroll."

"For example?" Nash said.

"How about me?" Parker said. "I've worked there for years and neither my picture nor any other doctor's picture is in any of those boxes. How about hospital trustees or ... or home health nurses or drug company representatives, volunteers? You have a lot more work to do."

Nash was embarrassed by the oversight, but was excited that they had a new lead to follow. Bright and early tomorrow he and Rolle would go to the hospital and get a list and photos, if possible, of everyone that ever passed through the hospital with the exception of the patients. You had to draw a line somewhere.

Overjoyed at being recalled to offer his help in the ongoing investigation, Mark Kelly swaggered through the precinct with an air of arrogance seldom seen in the post-Napoleonic era. He did not wait for Lt. Rolle to show him to the Interrogation Room but sauntered in and had a seat. After a few moments, Lt. Rolle joined him.

"How can I help you?" Kelly asked.

Rolle told him that they had acquired some more photos for him to look through and that his cooperation and diligence were of the utmost importance. Kelly nodded his head knowingly.

Rolle went to the door and soon after, another detective appeared with two boxes of photos from the hospital. Rolle said something unintelligible to the detective and he disappeared for a few minutes before returning with a large pot of coffee, a half dozen doughnuts and a pastrami sandwich with mayo, no mustard, the way that he remembered Kelly liked it. Rolle made Kelly feel like a crucial part of the team, which indeed he was. Rolle dismissed the other detective before speaking to Kelly.

"We're counting on you," he said giving him a firm pat on the shoulder.

After he left the Interrogation Room, Rolle doubled back to the Observation Room where he could see Kelly through the one-way mirror. Kelly was scrutinizing the photos as if he were Sherlock Holmes. As Rolle started to leave the Observation Room, Kelly turned towards the mirror and gave him a thumbs-up signal.

Rolle smiled to himself. He had forgotten that Kelly had been in Interrogation Rooms many times before, and not just to look at pictures.

After about an hour and a half, Kelly went to the door and asked a passing officer to get Lt. Rolle. When the officer told Rolle that the guy in the Interrogation Room wanted him, he was full of anticipation. Rolle figured that it should have taken at least three to four hours to review the number of photos that were there. When he got to the room, the smug look on Kelly's face told him that he was right.

"Do you have something for me, Mr. Kelly?" Lt. Rolle said, being very pretentious.

"As a matter of fact I do," Kelly responded. "This is the man who came to see me the night Cassie Parker was killed."

Rolle took the ID photo and stared at it in disbelief.

"Are you sure this is the man?"

"Look, Lt.," Kelly said, slightly offended. "I spent two years in the Q — San Quentin to you — and when a person threatens you, you don't forget their face. It's a matter of survival. If they grow a beard or shave off a mustache or if you are transferred to another prison and see them a year later with hair down to their ass you better remember. That's him."

"Thank you," said Rolle almost apologetically.

Suddenly Rolle shouted into the hall. "Sergeant Kieffer, please get a cab for Mr. Kelly and take care of the fare."

Turning back to Kelly, he said, "You know you may be called on to testify later."

"No problem," said Kelly. "Always glad to help the men in blue."

Rolle had previously asked Nash to come to the precinct later that day without Parker since Mark Kelly might still be there.

Nash arrived about three in the afternoon and Rolle immediately showed him the photo badge that Kelly had picked out.

"Was he sure?" Nash asked incredulously.

"Quite sure," Rolle responded.

"This is going to be tough."

"I'll get a warrant," Rolle said, "and pick him up. You can stay here if you like. I figure to be back at around six this evening."

"I'll see you at six," said Nash.

Rolle took two of his junior detectives with him to apprehend their suspect. He did not anticipate any trouble but this was for murder one and you always had to be prepared. Rolle decided that the best course of action would be to wait until their suspect had finished his working day. They would apprehend him just as he was about to enter his car, thus substantially reducing the risk of harm. To themselves and to the suspect.

They were now all familiar with what he looked like and the plan was carried out with ease. As he was handcuffed, Lt. Rolle read him his Miranda rights. "You have the right to remain silent. Anything you say can and will be held against you in a court of law. You have the right to an attorney. If you cannot afford one, one will be assigned to you. Do you understand your rights?"

Dr. Emerson Hitchcock nodded his head.

Dr. Emerson Hitchcock wanted a lawyer present and he could afford one. A very good one, a very expensive one whose firm had taken care of his family's affairs for over three generations. The lawyer's name was Royce Wellington and he looked as WASPish as his name sounded. He was fifty-four years of age and approximately six feet two inches tall with a slender build. His dark brown hair was graying around the temples and he had piercing bird-like blue eyes. His face possessed a generous nose and mouth with an angular chin that always seemed to be pointing skyward. Although it was after six in the evening, he had the closest shave that Rolle had ever seen. There was no sign of stubble.

Rolle did not trust a man who did not have stubble after six p.m. The name of Mr. Wellington's firm was Strother and Associates. Included in their partners was a former United States Senator and two former state Congressmen. Their firm represented corporations and people who were powerful, prestigious, influential and rich. Wellington was Princeton educated and had a remarkable record in court, which was well-known by persons in all fields of the justice system, from federal judges to beat cops.

All of this meant nothing to Lt. Rolle.

The three of them were seated in the same and only Interrogation Room in the 25th Precinct.

"As you gentlemen are aware, we are here to investigate the murder of Cassie Parker, former wife of Dr. Evander Parker, a friend and colleague of Dr. Hitchcock's." Looking at Hitchcock, Rolle continued, "Would you like to plead guilty now, doctor, or shall we proceed?"

Wellington's stately manner vanished like dry leaves in a strong wind. His face became as red as a beet and he jumped to his feet. "Lieutenant, this is an outrage. You have no right ...."

Hitchcock interrupted him. "I'm not guilty."

"Um hummm," Rolle said quietly. "We shall see."

Rolle turned on the tape recorder and announced who was present. "Lt. Rolle, Miami Dade Homicide, Dr. Emerson Hitchcock, practicing physician," and reading from the card that Attorney Wellington had given to him earlier, "Attorney Royce Wellington, Esquire, Attorney at Law representing the firm of Strother and Associates, established 1926."

As Rolle looked at the card, he remembered the one he had gotten from Sal Roselli's attorney. Compared to that one this one looked frugal. But that was, how it was, Rolle figured. If you really have it you retreated to the basics.

When Wellington stood up, Rolle took in the full extent of his attire. Wellington was dressed in a suit that he knew could not be found on the rack of any store. It was navy blue with the faintest hint of pale blue pinstripes. A white shirt that looked as if it had been starched heavily, but perfectly. His red and blue club tie blended beautifully. Rolle was tempted to look under the small table Wellington had requested to see what kind of shoes he had on.

Rolle continued, unruffled. "Do you, Dr. Hitchcock, know a Mark Kelly?"

"I'm sorry, I can't say that the name is familiar to me."

"Let me try to help you," said Rolle. "On May the seventh, which is the night that Cassie Parker was murdered, did you have an occasion to visit her masseur?"

Trying not to look too surprised, Dr. Hitchcock said, "Yes. Why yes I did."

"His name is Mark Kelly," said Rolle.

"I didn't know his name," said Hitchcock.

"Did you on that visit have a gun in your possession?"

Before he could answer, Wellington grabbed his forearm and spoke, "You don't have to answer that."

"It's okay," Hitchcock replied. "Yes, I did. He lives in a very bad neighborhood."

"What was the purpose of your visit?"

"I thought he might have been harassing Mrs. Parker."

"So you took it upon yourself to confront him?"

"Yes I did."

"And what, if anything, did you find out?"

"He told me about a lot of things, Lieutenant, but the bottom line was that he was not harassing her. So I left."

Rolle paused briefly before he spoke again. "Would any of the things that he told you have included the fact that she and he were small time con artists and that both had been arrested in the past?"

"I don't remember exactly."

"I have a sworn affidavit from Mr. Kelly that at the point of a gun, which you were holding by the way, that he did tell you these things and other not so complimentary things about Mrs. Cassie Parker, also known to him as Cassie Smith."

"Suppose he did? What would that matter to me? I was just looking out for her best interest."

Deciding to take a chance, Rolle continued. "Suppose I told you that we have concrete evidence that you and Mrs. Parker were having an affair?"

This time there was no concealing the look on Hitchock's face nor that of his attorney.

"There is no such proof," Hitchcock responded.

Just the answer Rolle was hoping for. He didn't deny the affair. He just doubted that there was proof that it existed.

"Oh, but I'm afraid there is. Dr. Parker had a patient who became obsessed with him and his wife. He is a psychiatrist, you know," he said looking at Wellington. "This patient followed his wife's every move for months quite undetected and has told us of numerous liaisons. I have, therefore, concluded that you may have gone to Mr. Kelly's apartment with good intentions thinking that Mrs. Parker was being harassed or whatever, but after your little talk, you became aware that the woman you were having an affair with was not quite the person you thought her to be. You then proceeded directly to her apartment, confronted her with the information that you just received, had an argument, things got out of hand and you killed her. Isn't that what happened?"

Wellington was quickly on his feet. "Dr. Hitchcock, I must insist that you say nothing else. You may cut the tape off, Lieutenant. This interrogation is concluded."

Rolle was very calm. He turned off the tape recorder and looked deeply into the eyes of Dr. Hitchcock. "Fine with me. See you in court, counselor. And you, doctor. As they say in Monopoly ... do not collect two hundred dollars but go directly to jail."

"I'll have you out soon," Wellington reassured him.

"He's blowing smoke," Rolle said. "There is no bail for premeditated murder and that is what we will be going for, you know. And off the record we can place you at the deceased woman's home on the night of the murder."

Since he was gambling, Rolle thought he might as well be a high roller.

As Rolle got up to leave, Hitchcock motioned for Wellington to have a seat.

"I'm advising you against this," said Wellington forcefully.

"Turn the tape back on," Hitchcock said.

Rolle pressed the record button ....

"As I told you, I am innocent. I did leave Mark Kelly's that night with the intention of confronting Cassie and to break off our relationship. I had fallen in love with her and had even asked her to marry me. To which she agreed. But everything was based on deceit. I was deceiving her husband, my best friend, and now I find out that she had been deceiving me. I drove to the condo and parked in the underground garage."

"How did you manage to do that?" Rolle gave Hitchcock a piercing stare.

"She had given me the code to the gate and I had used it several times before. As you know, Evan was on the run so we no longer felt we had to be as secretive as before. Since it was pretty safe to assume he wouldn't show up at the condo, I parked my car in his space ..." What a metaphor, thought Rolle, "... and used the tenant's elevator. It was not unusual for the tenants to see me in the building since I had been there so many times over the years. I told Cassie all of the things that Kelly had related to me, except as I told you I didn't know his name was Kelly. She didn't try to deny them. I asked her if her affair with me had been a setup from the beginning."

"'What if it had?' she said. 'It doesn't change anything'.

"I told her that it changed everything.

"She laughed and said that I didn't understand. She said, what she meant was that if I divorced my wife Beth, and married her that my financial status would provide her with more money. And that if I didn't divorce my wife, that my financial status would still provide her with more money. She said she was in a win-win situation. She would get the money from me either through marriage or blackmail. It didn't matter to her. Money was money."

"I told her that I had already told Beth of my intentions to marry her but that I was sure that Beth would take me back. That's when she asked me if I thought the medical community and my social circle of friends would take me back after they discovered that I had been having an affair with my best friend's wife.

"She asked if I thought I would get any referrals from the medical staff. She said that she would be sure everyone knew all of the depraved details. She said she would even follow me if I moved, like a woman who has been used and discarded. I asked what about Evan, and she said she only married him for his money, which was running out, and that is why she became so attracted to me. As she said this, she batted her eyelids playfully. I told her that I wouldn't be blackmailed. She said that I would either be blackmailed or ruined. She said she knew how much my medical practice meant to me and how my family had cultivated its social standing over generations. She then had the audacity to let her robe fall to the floor and try to seduce me.

"I guess I lost my head because I grabbed her hard by the shoulders and I struck her. Believe me, lieutenant, I never struck anyone in my life, much less a woman."

Rolle checked the tape inconspicuously to be sure it was still recording.

"Then she did the strangest thing," Hitchcock continued. "She calmly wiped the blood from her mouth and slowly licked the blood from her fingers. After that, she started yelling at me ...."

"'Go ahead and hit me again,' she said. 'Hit all you want. I been hit plenty in my time. For almost as long as I can remember. And by people who know how to do it way better than you. But it doesn't change one thing except now you're going to have to pay more.'

"When she said that I left. She was alive when I left. I only heard about her murder on the way to work the next morning."

"Very interesting," said Rolle. "What you told me would explain some of the bruises on her body but not the fatal ones. Would you like to tell me about those?"

"I just told you she was alive when I left."

Rolle turned off the tape recorder.

"I'd like to ask your client some things off the record, if it's alright with you, counselor."

Wellington gave him a look as if to say, "At this point what's the difference?"

"Dr. Hitchcock," Rolle kept his voice even. "What happened to your first wife?"

"She died in a motor vehicle accident," he replied.

"To be more precise, doctor, she was struck by a hit-and-run driver in front of eight witnesses who said the driver of the car swerved onto the sidewalk to hit her."

Rolle continued. "Did you receive a substantial amount of money from the insurance company after your wife's tragic demise?"

"Yes, but if you look at it in terms of my family estate it was not an overwhelming amount."

"Looked at forwards, backwards, sideways and cross-eyed, eight hundred and fifty thousand dollars is a lot of money ... doctor."

"It's all relative," Dr. Hitchcock said dispassionately.

"I see," Rolle said. "Did you keep the money?"

"Beg your pardon?" asked Hitchcock, surprised by the question.

"I said did you keep the money? As opposed to say, giving it to charity or starting a scholarship fund in your deceased wife's name. You know, stuff like that."

"No, the money was placed in the family trust fund."

"Uh huh. We never did apprehend anyone in connection with that hit-and-run," Rolle said, looking at Emerson Hitchcock very suspiciously from the corners of his eyes.

"Lieutenant ... Rolle is it?" asked Dr. Hitchcock.

Rolle nodded.

"Lt. Rolle, I was questioned in great detail about that at the time of my wife's accident."

"And the Grand Jury did not find probable cause to indict Dr. Hitchcock," added Wellington.

"Look, Lt.," continued Dr. Hitchcock, "if you are trying to make a point, I wish you would stop beating around the bush and get to it."

"Just asking a few questions," Rolle said, simulating sheepishness with a shrug of his shoulders.

The point was not lost on Royce Wellington. He had not represented Dr. Hitchcock at the time of his first wife's death. That was handled by one of the senior partners that had since retired. Wellington now had to think of defending a man whose first wife was the victim of an unsolved hit-and-run. A man who had received and kept over eight hundred thousand dollars in insurance, as the result of her death. A man who threatened another with a gun to get information. A man who was sleeping with his best friend's wife. A man who had admitted, on tape no less, that he was in Cassie Parker's home on the night that she was murdered. And that he had physically abused her. He concluded he would have to talk to Dr. Hitchcock about the possibility of a plea bargain. He noticed the twinkle in Rolle's eye as he summoned two detectives to take custody of Dr. Hitchcock.

"Don't worry," Rolle said to Wellington as they led Hitchcock away. "I'll look after him personally until the trial."

After Wellington left, and he had personally tucked Dr. Hitchcock in for the night in a private cell, Rolle returned to the Observation Room where Nash was waiting.

"What do you think?" Rolle asked.

"About what?" Nash asked.

"Do you think he killed her?"

"I would have."

Chapter
Twenty-Five

Rolle looked up from his desk just in time to see Nash flop down into the chair opposite him. Nash was wearing the silliest grin Rolle had ever seen, especially considering whose face it was on.

"I haven't seen you for almost a week," Rolle said, "Not that it hasn't been nice."

Nash just sat in the chair, wearing his ridiculous smile.

"What is it, Taylor? I'm a little busy here. So if you have something to say, say it."

"I found the murder weapon."

"What murder weapon?" Rolle asked impatiently. "We get an average of three murders a week in this precinct."

"The murder weapon in the Dr. Emerson Hitchcock case."

"That's very good," Rolle said testily. "Considering that Cassie Parker was found with an eight-inch kitchen knife buried in her chest, I'd certainly vote for you to get the Sherlock Holmes Award for this year."

As Rolle got up to leave, Nash said, "I mean the car used to kill Hitchcock's first wife. But if you're too busy..."

Rolle sat back down. "How did you manage to do that?"

"Some guys have it and some guys don't."

"I told you I was busy, so get to the point."

"You're being mighty abrupt for a man who is about to get credit for solving a murder case that's well over ten years old."

"Alright," Rolle said, "but I don't have time to play twenty questions with you."

"That's better." Nash stood halfway out of his chair and pulled out a file that he had been sitting on. "As it says here in the file ... "

Rolle reached over and snatched the file from Nash's hands. "I've told you repeatedly not to remove any official documents from this precinct. It's bad enough that I let you look at them. Where did you get this anyway?"

"The night you interrogated Hitchcock, you left it on your desk. As I was saying before I was so rudely interrupted. The file says that the car that killed Hitchcock's first wife was a dark blue or black older model Chevy."

"I know what the file says. That's the description we got from the witnesses, all elderly women, who knew nothing about automobiles. Where are those sixteen-year-old car thieves when you need them? We checked out that description car with everyone who may have been remotely related to the case. We even checked 'Stolens' and 'Rentals' without any luck."

"That's very understandable," said Nash, being theatrically sympathetic, "because the person to whom the car belonged wasn't remotely related to the case at that time."

"What are you talking about?" asked Rolle in frustration.

Nash laughed out loud, and reached inside his coat pocket. He pulled out a Florida State Car Registration and waved it playfully in the air. "By the way it was a navy blue Ford Falcon."

He slapped the registration on Rolle's desk, imitating the otherwise idle juveniles playing dominoes on the street corners. Rolle picked it up and read the name. "Well, I'll be .... "

"Easy, preacher's son. There's more. The car was sold about a year after the murder to a man in Hallandale."

"So you have his address?" Rolle asked.

"Of course."

"Well, let's go."

"I thought you were busy," teased Nash.

"I said ... let's go."

Rolle took one of the unmarked squad cars, that anyone would know was a police car, in case he had to be official.

On the way to Hallandale, Rolle began the conversation. "Unless we can tie the car to the victim all we have is circumstantial evidence."

"Sometimes that's enough," Nash said.

"In this case I don't think it will be."

There was no more conversation during the ride to Hallandale.

They were both filled with great anticipation as they pulled off the main street, onto a dirt road that led to the address of Otha Griffin.

Their anticipation was soon dissipated when they pulled in to the front of the Griffin home. Parked in a semicircular, concrete driveway, that seemed to have magically appeared from the gravel driveway of the house, was a mint condition 1964 Ford Falcon.

"We'll never get any evidence from that," groaned Rolle, sucking his teeth. "He must have restored it from the ground up. Anyone who could keep it in that condition in this dusty area must have washed it a million times in fifteen years."

Otha was not used to company, especially this type, and he came through the wooden screen door with what appeared to be a double-barreled shotgun.

He was a tall scraggly man in his late fifties, who looked like he drank and smoked too much. He had on a V-neck T-shirt, that might have been white at one time, and faded jeans with the cuffs turned up about four inches. He wore sandals, without socks, and no belt, which made Nash think of Parker. He had a face that had seen too much sun and a forehead with a receding hairline that blended right into it. There were the beginnings of innumerable skin cancers dotting every portion of his body that was exposed.

"Can I help you, boys?" he said in a stony voice.

371

Nash could see that the gun had already been cocked and he didn't like being called a boy.

"I'm Lt. Rolle of the Dade County Police Dept. and I'm here to talk to you about your car. Take it easy now, I'm going to reach into my pocket to get my I.D., Mr. Griffin."

"That's O.K.," he said as he uncocked the gun and put it on the porch that was leaning at a twenty-degree angle from the rest of the house.

"By the looks of that automobile and you knowing my name, you got to be the police." He pronounced it, "Poe lease."

"My name ain't on the mailbox and you can't look it up in the phone book cause I ain't got a phone. You say you want to talk to me 'bout my car. She's a beaut, ain't she."

"Yessir, it is," Rolle said.

"It ain't for sale," Griffin piped up.

"Oh, we don't want to buy it." Rolle tried to sound as friendly as humanly possible. "We just want to ask you some questions about the person you bought it from."

"The person I bought it from?" Otha quizzed, his face contorted with confusion. "I don't remember his name, but the dealership's up in Jacksonville."

Rolle and Nash looked at each other with puzzled expressions.

"You bought it new?" asked Nash.

"Brand new, right off the showroom floor." Griffin beamed with pride. "I was visitin' my big brother in Jacksonville just 'fore I was to ship off to 'Nam. We passed the Ford Dealership and decided to look at the new model cars. I fell in love the minute I saw it. I knew it was gonna be a classic. Figured I was gonna get kilt over there anyway, so I bought it, even though I only got to drive it a week 'fore I was called up.

"Big brother kept it for me. He didn't have to go to 'Nam on account he had polio as a kid and it left him with a gimpy leg. When I was leavin' was the only time I was ever jealous of him and his damn gimpy leg."

Rolle gave Nash a look that would have killed a weaker man. "How could you have made that big a mistake?" Rolle said to Nash.

"Don't know," replied an embarrassed Nash.

"We're very sorry to have troubled you, sir," Rolle said.

Otha could see that they were having a heated conversation as they walked away, but lately he was having problems understanding people if they weren't directly facing him.

Feeling nervous, Otha spoke up. "You can check the serial numbers if you want. Registration's in the glove box."

Otha wanted to straighten out any misunderstandings with these two policemen. He did not want them to take his cherished car away.

"That won't be necessary, sir," Nash said, turning to face him. "You see we're looking for a 1964 Ford Falcon that was purchased by someone named Otha Griffin about fifteen years ago."

Nash and Rolle saw Otha Griffin's drooping, weathered face slowly break into a smile. That is, as much of a smile, as a wrinkled, sun-weathered, hound-dog-type face can accomplish.

"Why didn't you boys say that first time 'round? That car's in the barn. Bought it to use for spare parts."

Nash didn't mind the boy quite as much this time.

Otha led them down a worn path into a barn that hadn't been a barn for a long time. "I keep it in here so's it won't be exposed to the rain and such."

Otha opened the large weathered barn door with ease and there she sat. A navy blue Ford Falcon. Nash was vindicated and Rolle felt like it just might be Christmas even though he thought Otha would make a pretty scary Santa.

Nash and Rolle circled the car gingerly as if it might disappear if they looked at it too hard. There was a damaged right front fender with a broken headlight and some smaller dents and dings along the right door. Forensics might have a good chance of getting some blood or hair from the car. Rolle would have them out first thing in the morning.

"Mr. Griffin," Nash said, "you have been a great help to us. But pleeeaase do not touch the car or let anyone else touch it."

"What's so import'nt 'bout a car I bought fifteen years ago?" Otha asked nervously. "It ain't stolen, is it? I paid good money for that car an' got a receipt and everythin'."

"No, it's not stolen and legally it is still yours, but it was used in the commission of a crime and might contain some important evidence. If this all works out you may even be on television," said Rolle.

"Don't wanna be on no television."

"Your big brother in Jacksonville might see you," Nash said.

"Never thought of that. Me on television. Don't that beat all."

"Tell us about when you bought the car," said Rolle.

"Ain't much to tell. There was an ad in the paper for a sixty-fo' Ford Falcon and I drove down to Miami to see it. The owner took me to the garage and showed it to me. Hadn't been driven in over a year. No way it woulda started. Gas had been left in, battery too. Tires was all flat but I could tell it would serve my purposes. So I had it towed here and it's been in the garage every since. I took the carburetor and the starter out and used some of the trim but other'n that it's just like I bought it."

Forensics found some blood on the broken headlight that was the same type as the first Mrs. Hitchcock's. There were also some strands of hair in the same area and on the under carriage of the car which were the same color as hers. They could exhume her body for DNA testing, but Rolle hoped that wouldn't be necessary.

* * *

Much to everyone's dismay and disgust, John Wellington had managed to get Dr. Emerson Hitchcock out on bail. It was a sizable bail but he was out nevertheless. As a condition of his release, Dr. Hitchcock had to surrender his passport and medical license until the matter was resolved.

Armed with the forensics report, a copy of the car's registration and a sworn affidavit from Otha Griffin, there was no problem in securing an arrest warrant.

Although he would never get official recognition for his work, Nash was pleased that Rolle had gotten a special dispensation from the department for him to come along, during the apprehension of the suspect.

At precisely seven o'clock a.m., Nash presented himself to Rolle at the precinct. At eight, they, along with two other officers who followed them in a squad car, proceeded to the house of the murderer of Mrs. Maureen Hitchcock.

The home was gracious and spacious and looked much as they had both imagined. Nash and Rolle walked to the door, leaving the other two officers in their car.

Dr. Emerson Hitchcock answered the door. "This is quite early for a social call, so I guess you have something else in mind."

"Yes sir, we do," Rolle said.

"Shall I call my lawyer?"

"That is your right, sir, if you wish. We have an arrest warrant here."

"Come now, Lieutenant. I'm legally out on bail."

"I understand," Rolle said, "but this warrant is for the arrest of your current wife, Mrs. Marybeth Hitchcock, for the murder of your first wife, Maureen Hitchcock."

"Who's at the door, sweetheart?" came a female voice from the rear of the house.

"It's the police, dear. They want to talk to you," he said in a crusty voice.

Under his breath Emerson said, "You know this is nothing more than harassment."

When she came to the door, Rolle gave Mrs. Hitchcock the warrant and read her rights to her. Without looking at the document, she put it in her robe pocket and walked back towards the kitchen.

"I was just making some tea for my husband and myself, would you gentlemen like to join us?" she yelled over her shoulder. Before anyone could answer, she continued. "It would be rude of you not to. Have a seat in the living room."

"Thank you," Rolle said, "I guess we will."

Nash and Rolle walked through a ten foot archway into the formal living room. Nash took a seat on an antique American Rococo carved and laminated rosewood sofa, which was flanked by two small Continental Rococo walnut banded commodes. Each commode held one of a pair of Empire patinated bronze and ormolu mounted lamps. Rolle sat opposite Nash in a Louis XV Beechwood armchair.

"Beth, these men have just accused you of murder," her husband said angrily, catching up with her in the kitchen.

"That's no reason to be impolite," she replied. "You have to forgive my husband," she shouted back to them. "You see his family's originally from Vermont. The only arguments we've ever had have been about his abrupt way with people."

Dr. Hitchcock joined the two men in the living room, and made himself comfortable in an armchair, similar to the one in which Rolle was seated.

Between the seated men stood a pair of small French tortoise-shell mounted vitrines, which held a minor portion of Marybeth Hitchcock's collection of Imperial Russian miniatures on ivory.

The room was deadly silent until Beth reappeared from the unseen kitchen, carrying an oversized silver tray, containing a silver teapot, four matching cups and saucers and a platter of assorted delicacies, including tomato on toast, just like in the Junior League book.

"May I help you with that?" Nash offered, getting to his feet.

"Goodness, no," Beth said as she sat the tray on one of the vitrines.

She poured the tea, serving Rolle, Nash, her husband and lastly herself, before settling on the sofa next to Nash. To a casual observer, it would appear as if she were hosting a small social circle of friends.

"Just help yourselves, please." Beth pointed to the assortment of tidbits attractively displayed on a Minton porcelain platter.

Rolle did just that, since he had missed his usual breakfast of coffee and Danish this morning. He picked out an unidentifiable, but tasty looking, morsel and returned to his chair. Nash and her husband both gracefully declined.

"Beth, do you realize the seriousness of the charges these officers are making?" her husband asked, assuming Nash was also with the police department.

No one corrected him.

She took a deep breath and gazed upward at the ceiling.

"I never felt that Maureen was quite right for you. I had seen her doing her volunteer work at the hospital every Tuesday and Thursday, but she didn't come across as a warm and caring person. From the first moment I saw you," she said looking directly at her husband now, "I felt that I was the only person on earth that could make you happy. And these last few years have certainly borne that out.

"I could talk to you about your cases, she couldn't. I was raised in a genteel manner, she wasn't. I wished there was some other way, but I just couldn't think of any. I was sure she wouldn't have given you a divorce." Beth rambled on.

"Heaven knows I never would have, if I were in her position. So for the both of us, I had to do something. She was so compulsively prompt that it was easy to plan my actions. Her life was so predictable that it was scary. I can still

377

remember her routine. Hairdresser on Monday. Hospital Tuesday and Thursday. Library trustee meetings on Wednesday evenings. Church every other Sunday. She must have been boring you to death."

Beth paused momentarily to take a sip of tea.

"She tried to ruin my plans at the last second by jumping back onto the curb, but my daddy taught me how to drive real good. After her ... accident, I just parked the car in the garage at my apartment. I barely drove anyway. I always walked to work. In fact everything I needed was in walking distance. After a year, I put an ad in the paper and sold it to some man in Hialeah."

"Hallandale," said Rolle.

"Oh yes, Hallandale. Why thank you. I sold it the week we were married," she said.

"Who would have thought that car would still be around after all of this time ? I mean it was old when I bought it. Just basic transportation. Some people do the most amazing things."

Dr. Hitchcock looked as if he had seen a ghost and maybe he had. His terror-stricken face was as white as bleached flour. His legs began to quiver and he became so weak, that he had to hold onto the upholstered arms of the chair in which he was seated to keep from sliding to the floor.

"But it's all been worth it," she continued. "Our life couldn't be more glorious. That is why I couldn't let Cassie Parker spoil everything. After you told me you were leaving me for her, I just wanted to talk to her and straighten things out. It just so happened that I arrived about an hour after you left. I have so many friends in the building, that getting in was no problem. They never even ask me who I'm going to see any more. It is quite a charming building."

Beth continued talking as if she was in a trance. "She was very polite, when she admitted me into her apartment. She told me that you had just left and showed me the marks you had left on her body. From passionate lovemaking, she said. I told her that I would never give you a divorce and she said that was alright with her, because she was just going to blackmail you until we were both humiliated and penniless. Well, I had worked too hard to let that happen. I told her it wasn't right for her to try and take my husband, when she had one of her own. Even if he was going around killing people, and burning buildings and such.

"She started laughing at me and said I was just a Southern belle wannabe Scarlett O'Hara and that she was going to take Rhett and Tara too. She thought herself quite witty."

She turned to her husband and said in an accusatory tone, "She said that you wanted her, Hitch, and you told her that you couldn't get enough of her. That you wanted her every day. The kitchen knife was just lying there, so I decided to put it to good use. I cut her throat, just like we used to do those hogs during butcherin'... excuse me, butchering ... season. She died instantly. Too quickly, I thought. That is why I did those other things to her."

"Which other things?" asked Rolle, still munching on his breakfast treats and sipping tea.

"Cut her up down there."

"Can you be more specific?" said Rolle between bites.

"As specific as I can, while remaining a lady. I cut her private parts and removed one of her breasts."

That cinches it, thought Rolle. That information was never made public and only the killer would have the knowledge that Cassie Parker's genitals were mutilated and her left breast was amputated and never recovered.

"Mrs. Hitchcock," Rolle began.

"Oh, please call me Beth. Everyone does."

"Alright, Beth. Would you mind telling me—us," he said, looking at Nash, and then her husband, who at this point might as well have been a mannequin, "what you did with Mrs. Parker's breast."

379

Trying to appear nonchalant, Rolle took another nibble of his breakfast.

"I have it right here in the house," she said calmly. "In the freezer. Since Hitch said he wanted to have her everyday, I have been giving her to him everyday. Usually with dinner."

Rolle grabbed his throat and coughed violently, launching the most recent portion of his breakfast across the room, where it clung to a fine eighteenth-century painting.

"I had to do it to save my marriage. It was self-defense."

Nash grabbed the walkie-talkie from Rolle, who was now pacing the room futilely pushing his finger down his throat and making sounds that should not come from a human being. Nash called for the female officer in the car outside, and for the paramedics to assist with Dr. Hitchcock, who had fainted, narrowly missing the sharp edge of one of the vitrines.

The policewoman came to the door and handcuffed Mrs. Hitchcock, placing her into custody, as Rolle ran through the house, searching for a bathroom.

Dr. Hitchcock revived long enough to tell his wife that he would call their lawyer, Royce Wellington.

"Thank you, sweetheart," she said, mouthing him a kiss as she was led away.

Chapter Twenty-Six

Back in New York, word of Sal's disappearance spread through the streets like AIDS. Sal's brother Joe asked Chop Louie to come by his home above the cleaners.

"What's up, Joe?" Louie asked. "What's the word on Sal?"

"That's the problem," Joe replied, "I don't know anything. How about you?"

"I'm kinda outta the loop on this one. Those guys in Miami are tight-lipped."

Joe became melancholic. "Louie, I'm worried about my son Vinny. With Sal missing, I don't know what will happen to him. I've tried calling him and writing to him, but I haven't gotten anywhere. I don't get any response. I guess it shouldn't surprise me ... we didn't communicate that well when he was here. Louie, if you could just ...."

"Not another word Joe, I'm on my way."

Louie was on the road to Miami the next afternoon. He would check on the kid, see if he was alright and bring him home, if he could.

He would also try to check on Sal.

Louie had agreed to go to Miami as a personal favor to Joe. He knew Joe was worried about Vinny and for good reason. *What a stupid kid.* Like most people who knew them, Louie despised Vinny as much as he loved Joe.

Arriving in Miami, Lou thought better of trying to contact Sal directly. If he went to the house, the police might be waiting to question anyone who came on the premises. He didn't even call the house because the police have a way of tracing those calls back to the source. Lou didn't know where Midge lived and he wouldn't go there even if he did, but he did know a couple of Midge's hangouts.

Lou found Midge in the third place he looked. It was a small airless bar, with just enough room to uncomfortably accommodate its regular assembly of thirty-five to forty people.

There was no neon sign outside to advertise the bar. In fact, there was no sign at all. There were no windows to invite casual glances into the interior. Only a large worn oak door with the address 1722, in large black wrought-iron numerals. This was not a place you entered by accident.

It took Louie a few seconds for his eyes to adjust to the dimly lit tavern, which was more than enough time for everyone present to observe the huge man that walked in and to determine that he belonged there. All of the patrons observed Louie, but no one looked at him. This was a place where no one really looked at each other or exchanged casual greetings. He walked directly to the booth where Midge was seated alone and stood in front of him.

Midge looked up from his scotch and soda and gestured for Louie to have a seat. Louie was glad there was an empty chair nearby that he could pull over to the table at Midge's booth, because he knew he could never squeeze his frame between the table and the upholstered booth. Louie never said a word, until Midge indicated that it was alright to talk.

"What's up with Sal?" Louie asked.

"I don't know," said Midge. "Since he was arrested, nobody's laid eyes on him. I can't get a hold of our inside man and his lawyer, O'Brien, won't return my calls."

That don't sound good, Louie thought.

"What about Vinny?" Louie asked.

"I was just about to go over to his place. I talked with Lenny and Swan and they told me that Sal had the kid pick up some things just before the cops came over. I was out of town. Just got back yesterday."

"Mind some company?" Louie asked.

"Not at all," Midge replied

Vinny was admiring his newfound treasures. He had them spread across the living room floor of his apartment. Not necessarily in the order of importance to him.

First, he picked up the folder marked John McIlvane. He could see it was some sort of medical chart. The handwriting in the chart was illegible to him and would have been incomprehensible, even if it was typewritten. He took the chart into his bedroom and hid it between the mattress and boxspring.

Vinny returned to the living room and picked up the plastic bag of cocaine. It was wrapped tightly with electrical tape and shaped like a small lumbar support. The contents of this bag, however, would not provide the user with any support, only destruction.

He sat in a chair and turned it over in his lap repeatedly, like an old lady unraveling a ball of yarn. A kilo of good cocaine, which this most certainly was, could be worth almost sixty thousand dollars wholesale and ten times that if you cut it and turned it into crack cocaine.

But this was Miami and you just didn't go around selling cocaine on your own. If you did, you could end up floating in the Atlantic Ocean towards Cuba or lying on the side of the Tamiami trail with small caliber bullet holes in your head. Trying to sell crack was even riskier. He didn't want to be killed by some thirteen-year-old kid for selling on the wrong corner. Frustrated, Vinny picked up the cocaine and returned to his bedroom, putting it in the bottom dresser drawer, under a small pile of dirty underwear.

Vinny had previously counted the money he brought home. One hundred thirty seven thousand six hundred dollars. He had placed it into several large manila envelopes. He wondered if it was real. It would be just like his Uncle Sal to have him take some counterfeit money and go to jail trying to pass it. How could he find out if was real?

If he took one of the bills to the bank and it was phony, that would lead to a lot of embarrassing questions. They might even search his house. Vinny knew passing counterfeit bills carried a long sentence. He put the envelopes in a suitcase in the back of his bedroom closet.

What was this ledger book all about? He looked through it and recognized some of the names from the local news when he had been channel surfing for something good to watch. There were numbers next to some of the names. Probably payoffs or debts, he thought, but he couldn't be sure. He needed to know how to cash in on this. He needed someone who could figure out all the angles.

Giovanni "'Johnny the Drill'" Barberossa belonged to the same drug alliance as Sal Roselli and Roberto Menendez. He acquired his nickname from a particularly nasty habit of drilling holes into the heads of his adversaries, by placing a portable Black and Decker power drill into their ear canal and torquing the bit as slowly as possible until the desired result, a slow painful death, was achieved. He was a mean-spirited opportunist, who arranged a chance meeting with Vinny, as soon as he inadvertently overheard that Sal was burdened with a "pain in the ass" nephew.

Better known as Johnny B, Giovanni hoped that an investment in Vinny early on would pay off with some type of dividend in the future.

The task of reeling Vinny in was assigned to one of Johnny B's top associates, Joey "'Joe Dogs'" Firpo. Some said that Firpo got his name for his presence at the greyhound track almost every day, while others said it was his choice of women. Vicious and unattractive. The usual greeting that Joe Dogs got from people was "How are the dogs? which he never knew how to take.

At first, Joe Dogs ingratiated himself with Vinny by introducing him to a few cooperative women. After that, he gave Vinny a small piece of some action around the city, always being careful to sidestep Sal and Midge. Neither Johnny B or Joe Dogs wanted any direct confrontation with Roselli, but if they could get something useful, so be it.

Joe Dogs was constantly telling Vinny about how generous his boss Mr. Barbarossa was and how if he liked you, he would take you in and take care of you.

After months of creating anticipation within Vinny, Joe Dogs took Vinny to meet Mr. Barbarossa, who immediately won Vinny's confidence, by asking him to call him Johnny B, even when Vinny saw that Joe Dogs called him, "Mr. Barberossa," or "Mr. B."

It did not take Giovanni Barbarossa long to discover Vinny's most vulnerable spot—his intellect.

Johnny B told Vinny that Joe Dogs had talked of him and how well he had done on the jobs they had undertaken together. Johnny also told Vinny that he had a bright future and would not be overlooked by him for future work. Additionally, he told Vinny he could contact him through Joe Dogs if he needed anything.

This was the delightful person Vinny decided to petition—for guidance.

* * *

385

Driving over to Vinny's, Midge was silent. He was racking his brain, trying to think what Sal had asked Vinny to remove from the house. Lenny and Swan said that Vinny had what appeared to be several items in a pillowcase. Sal had not asked them to inspect the bag before Vinny left, so they didn't.

Midge knew that the most vital article in the house would be Sal's ledger book. Even Midge didn't know where that was kept. Midge finally decided that Sal had just sent Vinny for the ledger and that he just took some other stuff on his own. Midge knew that he had the evil eye on Vinny and that the kid would tell him what he wanted to know when they talked.

Midge and Louie turned the corner to Vinny's apartment just in time to see Vinny pull his car out into the street. Midge flashed his lights and honked his horn for Vinny to pull over, but Vinny's car continued down the street.

"Maybe he didn't see you," Louie said.

"Maybe he did," Midge responded.

As they continued to drive, Midge got the distinct impression that Vinny was trying to lose them. His suspicions were confirmed when Vinny suddenly accelerated onto the freeway. This caught Midge totally by surprise, and Vinny was a full quarter mile away from them by the time Midge responded.

Weaving through the late night freeway traffic, Vinny had a definite advantage, in that he knew where he was going and Midge did not. Another advantage Vinny had was that Midge and Louie were both armed and did not want to be pulled over. Midge decided to follow from a safe distance.

They spotted him pulling off the freeway ahead of them and followed him into an area not totally unfamiliar to Midge. He had scouted out this area some years previously, just in case there were some problems with Johnnie B. Although they lost his car, Midge now had an idea where Vinny might be headed. Midge hadn't been in this area in quite a while and took a few wrong turns. Finding his way, he sped to the home of Giovanni

Barberossa, but arrived just in time to see Vinny's car disappear behind the gate.

Louie wasn't sure, but it looked as if that dumb kid had given them the finger. Midge gave a sigh and Louie, looking at Midge, shrugged his shoulders.

"Who lives there?" Louie asked.

"Johnny the Drill," said Midge.

"I didn't think he and Sal got along."

"They don't," Midge answered.

Back at the bar where they first met, Midge and Louie were having a drink. When they arrived at the bar, they retook their same seats, which had remained unoccupied. Midge had another scotch and soda and Louie had a ginger ale. He didn't want Rosie to think he had too good a time this evening. They had just returned from Vinny's apartment where they found the money, the cocaine and the medical folder, but no ledger.

Midge had burned the folder in an alley on the way back to the bar and had kicked the ashes into the night wind ... all the time cursing Vinny and wondering aloud where Sal and Patrice were. Louie silently observed all of this from the passenger seat of the car.

The cocaine and the money, with the exception of twenty-five thousand dollars, were in Midge's trunk. He would dispose of the cocaine and the remainder of the money—in accordance with Sal's instructions, if he could ever find him. He could not bear to think that Johnny B might have somehow also gotten to Sal and Patrice. Midge gave the twenty five thousand to Louie and told him to take five for his expenses and his trouble.

"Give the rest to Sal's brother Joe and tell him that Vinny wanted him to have it," Midge said.

Midge walked Louie back to his car and told him to have a safe trip.

They both knew that if the soon-to-be late Vinny Roselli's body ever surfaced, his head would have more holes in it than a whiffle ball.

Chapter
Twenty-Seven

He didn't have an appointment, but he was fairly confident that he would be seen. When he saw that the waiting room was empty, he became quite confident.

"Why, hello, Mr. Farouk," Ms. Johnson, the receptionist, said. "Nice to see you again." She looked past him, not expecting him to be alone.

He was pleasantly surprised that she had remembered him, even though he had only been in the office on one previous occasion. And now, he was dressed in a suit and tie, before he had appeared in all-white.

"How may I help you?" she continued.

"I'd like to speak to Mr. Wellsing. I know I don't have an appointment, but I only need a few minutes of his time."

"As you can see we're not overwhelmed with clients today," she said pleasantly. "Have a seat and I'll go back and tell him you're here."

As she got up from the desk he noticed her for the first time. In fact he noticed the entire office for the first time. Everything about his first visit was a blur.

He guessed her to be about forty-four years old, with a gracious smile, large sable eyes and a creamy complexion. Her auburn hair, pulled into a bun, somehow didn't make her look old or matronly. She was a mildly overweight woman, who you could tell had been shapely at one time. The curves were still there, but a bit exaggerated. Somewhat like a classic overstuffed couch, thought Farouk. Ms. Johnson wore a tailored

Navy blue business suit with pearl earrings and a matching necklace. She reminded him of his third-grade teacher Ms. Bolton, on whom he had had an enormous crush.

He took a seat in the sparsely furnished waiting room. Nothing in this outer area was even vaguely familiar to him. It was obvious, however, that whoever decorated this space had spent very little time and effort, and even less money. He hoped that Welsing was more conscientious about his cases.

The office was a nondescript muted brown which matched no other color in the known world. The paintings on the wall had obviously been purchased in some discount store, and preframed in plastic. The chairs were similar to those that he had seen outside furniture clearance stores, that graciously displayed their inventories on the city's sidewalks.

The only bright spot in the office was Ms. Johnson's area. It was obvious that she was making an attempt to bring some sense of style into an office that could flatteringly be described as Spartan. On her desk was a nice arrangement of freshly-cut flowers, in an art deco style vase. There were several antique silver picture frames which contained pictures of what he assumed were family members. Her desk pad, pencil holder and memo pad trays were all color coordinated and her waste paper container was a large woven leather basket. The only evidence that her area belonged to this office were her brown metal desk and chair.

She smiled as she emerged from Wellsing's office. How or why she was in his employ would be another of life's unsolved mysteries.

"Mr. Wellsing will see you now," she said as she extended her hand, signaling for him to follow her.

Wellsing stood and extended his hand. "Mr. Farouk, I've been looking for you."

"So I've heard," replied Farouk.

Farouk was sure that Wellsing had spent the few minutes that he had kept him waiting reviewing his file. He was just as sure that there was no recognition of him in Wellsing's eyes.

As they both sat, Wellsing tried to remember the face that sat across from him. "I'm afraid I haven't been able to make much progress with your case. I have contacted Dr. Parker's malpractice carrier, but I am unable to proceed any further until we can get a statement from him.

"Until recently he was a fugitive wanted for three murders and arson. He's now been released from jail and all charges against him have been dropped, but my investigator still has been unable to locate him."

"I read the paper," Farouk said, somewhat agitated.

"Of course you did," a smiling Wellsing said, doubtful that Farouk could read at all. "Parker's hiding out somewhere for now, but as soon as he returns to his home, I'll have him served with the proper documents. Then you'll see things start to move. I have all the papers in order to file against the others too. Dr. Hitchcock, the nurses, the hospital, the anesthesiologist. But Parker is the key. I don't think I'll have any trouble convincing a jury that he was unstable and incompetent at the time of your daughter and grandchild's death. We'll have it locked in place as soon as we locate him, which shouldn't be too long now."

Wellsing had managed to work himself into quite a lather. He was beginning to smell blood. And money.

Farouk sat up straight in his chair and looked directly into Wellsing's smallish eyes. Farouk paused briefly before he spoke.

"I want you to drop the suit against Dr. Parker," he said very softly.

Wellsing looked as if he was in suspended animation.

"I said I want you to drop the suit against Dr. Parker," Farouk repeated a little louder, in case Wellsing hadn't heard him.

There was still no reply from Wellsing. He didn't even blink. This was to be his biggest case. This was going to be his ticket to easy street. The big dance.

Farouk decided not to wait any longer for Wellsing to speak, figuring that he might be there all day.

"When I first came to you, I wanted Dr. Parker to feel as I felt. To suffer as I suffered. Even though I physically attacked him at the hospital, that was not enough for me. I was not satisfied. I concluded that the best way to make him suffer was to make him pay financially. I came to you to help me get my pound of flesh."

Wellsing still did not move. His mind was in an air lock. Anyone peering into the office would think that Farouk was talking to a mannequin or that Wellsing was hypnotized.

"Dr. Parker has suffered enough and the teachings of my religion have helped me to overcome the need for revenge. Dr. Parker's wife has been murdered by the wife of his best friend, with whom she was having an affair. His medical practice, as well as his life, is in ruins. Besides people who pay financially for their wrong doings often feel absolved of their misdeeds, and do not strive to remedy the mistake now or in the future, but try to avoid being caught so that they won't have to pay again.

"If Dr. Parker is at fault he should suffer because two lives were lost, not because of the threat of monetary remuneration. I have also come to the conclusion that I am not entirely blameless in this tragedy but must accept the consequences of my faith even when the results are negative."

Farouk waited. Still no response from Wellsing. He hoped that he hadn't been talking to a corpse all of this time.

Finally Wellsing spoke. "If you don't want to sue Dr. Parker, we can sue the hospital. After all he was a member of their staff and they are at least partially culpable. It wouldn't be like we were suing an actual person or anything. Just an entity with a corporate name. And it wouldn't be like revenge or anything, you could give your portion of the settlement to charity if you wanted.

"There are so many organizations that could benefit from some form of financial aid. Your group, whoever they are, could probably use more money. Everybody could use more money. If you would let me explain to you how ...."

As Farouk rose to leave, it was as if Wellsing did not notice. He remained seated, staring straight ahead and continued to talk. His brain was on autopilot.

Farouk could still hear him talking as he said "goodbye" to Ms. Johnson, and as he closed the door behind him.

Chapter
Twenty-Eight

D r. Evander H. Parker was home at last. He was sitting in his favorite armchair in his living room, pouring the remainder of a bottle of Chateau Clemens Barsac, 1988, into a crystal wineglass. Both were courtesy of Taylor Nash, who had just left, after helping him to savor the essence of such a fine vintage.

He did not know the exact time, but knew it was well past midnight. He and Taylor Nash had spent the hours talking about things, familiar and unfamiliar, with an ease known only to those who have shared a lifetime of experiences.

I'll go to bed in a few minutes, he thought, as he raised the glass to his lips.

He had slept in the guest bedroom since his return. He just wasn't ready yet.

There was a firm knock on the door.

"What do you want now? Did you forget something?" Dr. Parker said lightheartedly as he opened the door fully, happily anticipating seeing Taylor Nash again.

He froze as he stared into the somber face of Salvatore Roselli.

"I got what I want now," he replied. "And I haven't forgotten nothing."

Sal was holding a nickel plated .45 automatic in his right hand, and used it to wave Dr. Parker away from the door.

He was wearing a plaid sports coat that was two sizes too small for him, a white shirt that was buttoned uncomfortably around his fleshy neck, and a blue tie imprinted with a design of small red handcuffs. The only clothing that seemed to fit were the off-grey slacks that came over the top of a pair of black wingtips.

"How did you get in here?" Dr. Parker asked angrily as Sal quietly closed the door.

Without speaking, Sal reached into the left outside pocket of the insufficient coat and opened a black leather wallet, which contained an F.B.I. badge and picture identification of Sam Westhall. He held it at arm's length, directly in Parker's face, for him to digest.

"H-h-how did you get that?" Parker stammered.

"Westhall was so intent on protecting me from harm, the thought never occurred to him that I might take him out. All of you were so confident that Sal Roselli had rolled over. That I would be content to turn rat and spend the rest of my life somewhere in Iowa. Well, he found out the hard way, just like you will, that's not my style. The Feds were so sure they had me in their pocket, they only assigned that fool Westhall to take care of me. But to answer your question, I took this from his barely cold, but completely dead, body." Sal replaced the wallet in his coat pocket and motioned for Evan Parker to sit on the couch.

"He also involuntarily supplied me with this ridiculous outfit."

Sal sat opposite Dr. Parker on a matching sofa.

"That picture doesn't look anything like you," said Parker, struggling for something to say.

"No problem," Sal said with a broad smile, "I just put my thumb over the picture. Not many people got the balls to ask a Federal Agent to move his finger. I actually practiced it a coupla times in the mirror before I left the room in that seedy hotel where I was squirreled away. Actually it was a lot easier than I could ever imagine. With all the trouble you've been in, the people downstairs are very accustomed and accommodating to those of us in law enforcement."

"So now what?" said Parker, resigning himself to his fate. "You going to shoot me and have everyone in the building call 911 or did Westhall provide you with a silencer too?"

"That's good," Sal said, "I like a dead man with a sense of humor. For you a bullet is too impersonal ... too detached."

As he said this, Sal placed the gun on the side table next to him, and stood up.

Pouncing toward Parker, Sal felt his entire body tingle with excitement, predominately in the right places. *Where was Patrice?* he thought.

His heart racing with fear, Evan Parker looked up at Sal's menacing proximity and muttered, "Why?"

"Why what?" Sal replied, sourly, his reverie interrupted.

"Why did you rob Noel and Chandler, kill Solly ... murder my secretary ... burn my office ... frame me for murder ... destroy my life?

"Oh that," Sal said, matter-of-factly. "It made me feel young and sexy. Just like killing you now with my bare hands will."

Again distracted by thoughts of Patrice, Sal did not notice the mutation which was occurring before him, as his last words to Evan Parker became understood.

All evidence of humanity in Parker's face transformed into animal rage.

Neither Sal Roselli, the crime boss and murderer, nor Dr. Evander Parker, Ivy League graduate and eminent psychiatrist, could have predicted what would happen in the next instant.

Evan Parker sprang from the sofa, with the agility of a jungle cat, and twice as much ferocity.

"BECAUSE IT MADE YOU FEEL YOUNG AND SEXY!" he roared as he pounced on Sal, entwining his hands tightly around his throat.

Dr. Parker's attack caught Sal completely by surprise, knocking him to his back and toppling over the end stand on which he had placed the gun. The force of the two men caused the gun to slide across the highly polished, hardwood floor into the master bedroom.

Any human, without an ox-like neck, would have been asphyxiated immediately. But even with his bulky neck, Sal was beginning to feel uncomfortable, as Evan, who was now on top of him, leveraged his weight behind his hands, trying to squeeze the life out of Sal. Focused totally on the task at hand, Parker began mumbling unintelligible obscenities, drenching Sal's face with copious amounts of spittle.

Sal's outstretched hand searched for the gun to use as a bludgeon, but found the small overtuned table, which he crashed into the side of Dr. Parker's left shoulder. The blow catapulted Parker three feet to the other side of the room, but at this point he was impervious to pain.

And before Sal could recover, Parker was on top of him again with the same strangle-hold. This time Sal delivered three compact punches to Evan Parker's ribs, before he would release his hold. It was Evan who had the wind knocked out of him, but it was Sal who needed a breather.

Sal turned onto his hands and knees, and was attempting to get up when Evan yanked Sal's left ankle, causing Sal's hands to slip from under him, jamming his chin hard into the floor. Clutching Sal's leg with both arms, Dr. Evander Parker, graduate of Harvard Medical School, then proceeded to gnaw into Salvatore Roselli's shinbone.

Even a man as hardened as Sal has a tender shin. He let out a thunderous howl and looked down to see what was happening to him. What he saw were torn pants, blood coming from his leg, and Evander Parker, M.D., hooked onto his leg like a rabid ferret. It took two well-placed kicks to the top of Parker's head, before the doctor released his vise-like clench. The now dazed Parker's mouth and chin were covered with blood. Sal's blood.

397

Sal thought to himself that if he wasn't already going to kill Parker, this would have been the deciding factor.

Sal had encountered this phenomenon two or three times before in his career. The intended victim is so full of fear or anger or both that you cannot overpower them, short of death. It was at this time that Sal figured a bullet in Parker's head would save him a lot of aggravation. The neighbors be damned. If all the previous commotion had not awakened the entire building, one gunshot would not be such an overwhelming addition. After all, he was a Federal agent and could walk out the same way as he came in. He would even tell the security guard at the desk to call the police.

Parker's head cleared up in time for him to see Sal limping into the bedroom to search for the elusive gun, and came to the same conclusion Sal had. He bolted for the door, adroitly unlocked it and ran down the hall.

Parker's neighbors, who were already peering into the hallway, were more than shocked to see him running toward the garage entrance, dressed only in a tattered robe, boxer shorts and house shoes.

They would be shocked further, when five minutes later, a disheveled man with his pants leg ripped and dripping blood on the oriental carpets would lumber down the hall.

"Agent Westhall," Sal proclaimed, holding the badge for all to see. "Which way did he go?"

They all pointed toward the garage stairs.

Becoming more human again, as he ran down the stairs two at a time, Evan began to feel the pain in his left shoulder and ribs. He hoped they weren't broken. He also felt as if he had been kicked in the head. Which he had. He couldn't remember.

Entering the sweltering garage drained even more of Parker's strength. The humidity hit him like a concrete paving slab. The pain in his chest intensified with each breath and his headache zigzagged across his eyes and forehead like a chain saw.

He did not even think of trying to get into his car, which he locked diligently every night, even though it was parked in the garage of the condominium. Something made him give the car a cursory glance as he headed for the street exit. The tires had all been flattened. Somehow this made him feel better about not having his keys.

Running as fast as possible down the ramp to the street exit, he thought about Patty Hearst and how she had been kidnapped in her bathrobe, but had her wallet and keys with her. He had always thought that was strange. Now he thought it was damned impossible.

As he unlatched the wrought-iron gate, which led to the street, he could hear the metal door two flights above, which he had previously run through, slam with authority.

"PARR...KERRR!" Sal bellowed, his voice echoing. "You can't escape me."

Once he reached the deserted street, Evan wished he lived closer to South Beach where there were lots and lots of people around at three in the morning. He tried to hail a passing car, which sped up after seeing the ragged man with blood streaming from the corners of his mouth.

The teenaged driver of the car would later tell his skeptical friends that Ann Rice was right about there being vampires in Miami.

He approached a tough-looking group of adolescents, who thought he would be easy pickings, but crossed the street and ran in the opposite direction after getting a closer look at him.

The heat was becoming unbearable and his breathing was becoming more labored. After a coughing paroxysm, which pro-duced a small amount of blood, he headed toward the beach.

There has to be someone on the beach, he thought. If not, at least I can cool off in the water.

* * *

Meanwhile, Sal had little difficulty picking up Evan's trail. People were more than happy to help the kind officer, who had been harmed by the deranged maniac. They even offered to phone the police, to which Sal's prepared answer was that it was a Federal investigation and if the local police got involved it might ruin the case. A case which had been ongoing for several months now and might cost the taxpayers an additional untold amount of money. That answer seemed to satisfy everyone. No one wanted any more of their tax dollars wasted than the government was already capable of doing. And this officer, in spite of his gimpy leg, looked able to deal with the crazed suspect.

Evan Parker splashed the soothing salt water all over his body and decided to abandon his robe. To a casual observer he looked as if he had gone for an early morning swim. He also decided that he must get some help, soon. He knew that one or more of his ribs were broken, and that one of them must have punctured his lung. He was now almost constantly coughing up frothy, blood-tinged sputum.

He walked close to the water, where the sand was damp and packed tightly. Every step was agonizing, but it was better than walking on the loose sand.

He spotted a diminutive figure about a hundred yards away, walking towards him. He decided this was his last chance. He straightened up as much as possible, brushed his hands through his hair and tried to decide what to say. He knew it wouldn't be "Help me," or "Please, call the police," since he had already tried these and they seemed to be code words for, " I am a new age leper, run for your very life."

As he pondered what to say, another problem presented itself to him. It appeared that the silhouette approaching him belonged to a child. Where were his or her parents? They seemed to be the only two people on the beach, or in the world as far as he could determine.

Was this one of the many runaways that had found their way to South Florida? What could he possibly say to a runaway to get them to help him? He decided to just play it by ear.

At least this child did not appear to be afraid of a passing stranger, because he or she continued to walk directly toward him.

Evan was close enough now, so that he could see the outline of a small walking stick or a piece of driftwood.

Close enough now, to see that it was a male.

Close enough now, to see an athletic physique.

Close enough now, to make out the solemn face of Carmine Aluppi, better known as Midge.

"Hi, Doc," Midge said, as he raised what was clearly a tire iron.

Evander Parker made every effort to be quick and nimble, but those adjectives no longer applied to him.

With a full batter's swing, Midge granulated Parker's left knee. Parker felt the entire Bicentennial supply of skyrockets explode in his leg, then the pain traveled upwards, in slow motion, to engulf every cell between his knee and his brain, which mercifully lapsed into unconsciousness.

When he began to awaken, he heard Midge talking on a cellular phone.

"Yea, I got him. He's right here. No, I didn't kill him. Just like you said. No, you don't have to rush, he ain't goin' nowhere."

Parker had fallen onto his left side and now feigned unconsciousness, while he tried to determine his next course of action.

"I know you're awake," said Midge, rolling Parker onto his back, by pushing his foot into his right shoulder.

Parker responded by shielding his head with his hands.

"No need for that, Doc. I ain't gonna hit you no more."

Still lying on his back, Parker propped himself on his elbows. He continued to feel pain over every inch of his body, but at least in this position he could breathe a little easier.

"Now what?" Parker asked weakly.

"We wait," Midge replied.

"For Sal?" Parker asked rhetorically.

"Yeah, ain't cellular phones great."

"So it was you that sent him to my office."

"Indirectly," Midge said.

"What do you mean indirectly?" Parker said.

"Yeah, he got your name and number from me, but he's got a whacko nephew and I thought he wanted your number for him."

"So Sal was the boss you told me you worked for."

Midge put on his poker face and did not reply.

"You helped him rob the two Jamaicans."

Still no reply from Midge.

"You helped him burn my office and kill Ms. Kennedy."

Midge continued to stare into the space beyond Parker.

"You helped him frame me for Solly's murder and ruin my life, you son-of-a-bitch." Parker was again filled with rage.

"I said I wasn't gonna hit you no more," Midge said sedately, "but I can always change my mind."

Midge's easy manner seemed to have the same effect on Parker. As he calmed down, he realized he was taking the wrong approach. Midge was very accustomed to being confronted violently, he thought. Whatever his strategy was to be,

402

he'd better get on with it. There would be no time for shrewdness with Sal.

"You know he's going to kill me." Parker was blunt and to the point.

No response from Midge. Parker tried desperately to read his face.

"He doesn't deserve this kind of loyalty from you."

Midge looked as if he were going to fall asleep.

"Did you know he was in the Witness Protection Program?"

Midge's eyes, which were at half-mast, were now fully open, which did not escape Parker's scrutiny.

"He r..r..ratted you out," Parker said, sputtering with newfound hope.

"He ratted on you and your entire organization. I know because I heard it myself. The only reason he's out now, is because he killed a Federal Agent named Westhall. They'll never let either of you get away after that. If you were wondering why you couldn't find him in the last few months, it's because he was spilling his guts to the Feds."

"Shut up!" Midge raised the tire iron over his head, ready to charge. "You better shut up."

"Go ahead," Parker said, figuring he might as well play this hand for all it was worth. "Go ahead and kill me for the rat you've been so loyal to. The rat who's going to get you put to sleep for accessory after the fact, in the murder of a Federal Agent. An Agent who was assigned to baby-sit him in the Wit-ness Pro-tec-tion Pro-gram," Parker mocked.

Midge's hands squeezed the cold steel until his knuckles blanched as white as the sand. He looked directly at Parker, then turned his back to him and stared at the ocean. Parker thought he looked as if he would cry.

"I need you to help me," Parker said. "If you help me I'll do everything I can to help you. I'll tell the authorities how you saved my life."

"Who said I believed you?" Midge, face stark white, still faced the ocean.

Parker thought carefully before he spoke again. "Did you two do something to a Roberto Mendez?"

"So what about it?" Midge said testily.

"How would I know about it, if I hadn't heard Sal talk about it to the Feds?"

Midge turned around slowly and looked down at the helpless doctor. He walked over to Parker and stood over him ... his face contorted with distress.

"Even if I wanted to help you now, Doc, it's too late."

"It's never too late," Dr. Parker pleaded, his voice getting hoarse. "We can all change if we want to. Your sessions with me should have taught you that."

"That's not what I'm talking about," Midge said with a weak grin.

He then took his tire iron and pointed directly behind Parker.

Parker turned around, as far as his pain would allow, to look behind him.

The unmistakably plodding figure of Sal Roselli was relentlessly advancing in their direction.

"Help me, dammit," Parker shouted at Midge, which sent him into a coughing spasm that now produced bright red blood.

By the time he stopped coughing, Sal had taken his place alongside Midge, smiling at the shattered doctor that lay beneath them.

"Good job, Midge." Sal nodded approvingly. "You can go now. I'll meet you in about two hours. You know the place."

Midge shot past Parker and beelined down the beach. Parker did not turn to watch him go. His eyes were fixed on a grinning, yet menacing Sal.

After a few steps, Midge suddenly stopped and turned to face Sal, with Dr. Parker now lying between them.

"Where were you?" Midge demanded.

"I just took a coupla wrong turns getting here," Sal said. "It was my fault. The directions you gave were perfect."

"No." Midge's voice was pointed. "I mean in the last few months."

"Like I told you. I was on the run. I couldn't call nobody and nobody could call me."

"Uh-huh." Midge stared directly at Sal as if seeing him for the first time. Anger, humiliation and a sense of betrayal were written all over his face.

"Doc says you was in the Witness Protection Program."

"He's lying. You know as well as I do a guy will say anything to try and stay alive."

"Ask him to show you what's in his left outside coat pocket," Parker growled.

"Shut up, dead man," Sal said. He stomped over and stood on Parker's fragmented knee.

Parker screamed. The same fireball of pain returned, traveling upward, pursuing unconsciousness.

Parker was determined to remain awake. He used the pain to stoke his swelling anger.

"What's in the pocket, Sal?" Midge's reptilian eyes stared deeply into Sal's equally cold eyes.

"You questioning me, little man?" Sal let out a deep breath as he stepped off Parker's knee and took two steps backwards.

In the many years of their association, Sal had never made mention of Midge's height. This was the second time that Midge had been hurt tonight.

Maybe," Midge said, tightening his grip on the tire iron.

"Look," Sal said, "we're both a little tense here. Let me finish this little bit of business and then we can get everything straightened out."

Midge would normally have never fallen for this stalling tactic. But this was Sal. The man to whom he had practically devoted his entire life. For whom he had committed unspeakable acts. For whom he had risked his life countless times.

Midge relaxed his grip on the cold metal and took his eyes off Sal to look at Parker who was writhing in pain. When he looked up again, Sal was holding the nickel-plated .45 caliber automatic. It was not pointed at Parker, but at him.

"First things first." Sal sounded like a teacher patiently breaking down a math problem to his students. "Drop the iron."

Midge gently tossed the tire iron forward, without taking his eyes off Sal. It bounced off Evan Parker's neck and right shoulder, before settling into the sand.

"Now your gun," Sal said.

Midge shrugged his shoulders, as if to reply, "What gun?"

"Don't even think about pulling my chain," Sal said evenly. "And bring it out slowly. Usin' two fingers only, please."

Midge complied without resistance.

"Now toss it into the water."

With a Frisbee-like toss, Midge threw his gun into the surf.

"That's better," Sal said. "Must I remind you that you are to do what I say, when I say it? That applies to past, present and future. Do you think I let you hang around because I like being seen with a freak? The answer is, 'no.' The only reason was that you were loyal and brutally efficient. Sort of like a pit bull, only smaller."

This last statement amused Sal and he broke out in a wide grin.

"Now get moving, you puny runt."

And move is exactly what Midge did. He bolted in Sal's direction, his fists clenched in bitterness.

The bullet which exploded from the muzzle of the gun twirled Midge around like a rag doll. It entered the left side of his chest, just above his heart, ripping his aorta to shreds. He was dead before his body came to rest on the wet sand.

There was now some urgency to Sal's mission. Even in Miami, a gunshot might cause someone to call the authorities.

As he focused his vision and leveled the gun at Evan Parker, there was a sudden pain in his right hand. Evander Parker had managed to grasp the tire iron with both hands and swung with all his might at the gun hand of Sal Roselli. The blow fractured his thumb and three bones in Sal's wrist. The gun itself was propelled into the water.

Infuriated, Sal moved toward Parker, who then managed to strike him in the exact spot where he had bitten him earlier. Parker then began to flail his weapon back and forth, to keep Sal at bay, although each movement racked his body with pain.

Sal retreated and limped to the water's edge to look for his gun. A gun which twice had been knocked out of reach. His hand was swelling rapidly and becoming excruciatingly painful.

As Sal waded, ankle deep, into the shallow water, Evan Parker felt it was now or never. He managed to struggle to his feet, using the tire iron as a cane, and began to hobble back toward the street which seemed an eternity away.

Frustrated in his efforts to find either gun, Sal turned around to see Evan Parker had scrambled almost twenty yards away.

"Son-of-a-bitch," he muttered as he took off after Evan as fast as his injured leg would allow.

Evan, who had glanced over his shoulder occasionally during his flight, now tried to increase his pace, as he saw Sal pursuing him and closing the distance between them rapidly.

Soon he could hear Sal's heavy footsteps, then his heavy breathing. Too exhausted to continue and enveloped in too much pain to swing his weapon, Evan slumped to the ground and rolled on his back, holding the tire iron as a soldier would hold a rifle with a bayonet. He knew that feeble jabs were all that he would be able to muster.

Seeing Parker fall to his back, Sal thought that this was the perfect opportunity to finish him quickly. He wouldn't stand around this time, giving Parker the chance to whack him again with that iron. He would use Parker's own technique. He would pounce on top of him and quickly strangle the life out of him, or break his neck if he had enough strength left.

Just the thought of finally killing Dr. Evan Parker made Sal feel light and joyous. He sprang into the air, as if he were doing a belly flop into his pool. He came down just as Parker, whose eyes were closed with fear, made a tenuous jab with the pointed end of the tire iron.

Four inches of the metal embedded itself just below Sal's left eye, piercing the thin bones of his cheek and forcing the eye out through the socket. Copious amounts of purplish-red blood spewed from the socket that held the dangling eyeball.

Sal screamed and instinctively wrestled the tire iron from Parker's grip before he stood up. He could not, however, remove the sharp end, which had become wedged into the paper-thin bones of his sinuses. As he tried to dislodge the metal rod, Parker could hear crackling sounds, as if someone were walking on eggshells.

With the brisk loss of blood, Sal became more and more disoriented as he meandered aimlessly toward the ocean. Leaving a blood-stained trail in the sand, he zigzagged back and forth. He staggered and wobbled on jello-like legs. He was still holding onto the metal shaft with both hands when he collapsed into the shallow water.

Parker could hear him struggling to breathe as the tide came in. His head sunk down in the undertow and occasionally he would lift it and sputter out water. The noise was like a kid blowing bubbles into a soft drink with a straw.

The gasps were frenzied and erratic at first, but soon they became very slow and metered.

Before Dr. Evander Parker lapsed into unconsciousness, he was lulled by the soothing, rhythmic sounds of Salvatore Roselli's last breaths.

* * *

He awakened thirty-two hours later, in the Intensive Care Unit of Jackson Memorial Hospital. The first face he saw was that of Taylor Nash.

"How am I doing?" Parker asked weakly.

"You're the doctor," he quipped.

"Yes, but I'm on the wrong side of the stethoscope right now."

"You want the whole rundown?"

"Let's have it," Parker demanded playfully. "And in alphabetical order."

"Alright. But I'll start at the top and work my way down. I don't think I can do it in alphabetical order." Nash picked up the bedside chart, shaking his head.

They each managed weak, but genuine, smiles.

Nash read out loud. "A concussion, with multiple contusions and abrasions of the head and neck. A severely sprained left shoulder. Separation of the right acromioclavicular joint. Three fractures of the left rib cage. Multiple contusions of the left lung and a compound fracture of the left patella."

"No partridge in a pear tree," Parker said, already begining to tire.

"No partridge in a pear tree," Nash repeated softly.

"What about Midge?" Parker's eyelids fluttered like butterflies as they became heavy with a drug-induced sleepiness. "He tried to help me."

"Dead."

"And Sal?" Parker tried to stifle a yawn.

"Dead."

"Good." Parker blinked himself to sleep.

Epilogue

Nash and Parker again found themselves at their favorite restaurant, The Blue Dolphin. They arrived early, so that they could sit at their cherished table near the pier, overlooking the tranquil cerulean water. Sea gulls serenaded one another as the surf provided a soothing backdrop to the approaching twilight. A vermilion blood sunset splashed across the horizon. Like a burning star, it cast shimmers of purple and gold onto the ocean's glossy surface.

Nash had fallen into a gourmet rut, ordering the grilled Pompano and steamed vegetables du jour, as he had on their last visit. Determined not to be routine, Parker ordered the special. Grilled white shrimp and rice pilaf, with fresh mango salsa. After the waitress brought their dinners, Nash began to wolf his food down immediately and seemed to be engrossed in his own thoughts.

Looking at Nash, Parker reflected on the many moments they had shared together. How Nash had helped him through the most terrifying and depressing circumstances in his life, and how Nash had helped him with grace and style. He thought about how Nash had never been condescending and always treated him with affection and respect—even at times when he did not deserve it. Nash had been generous in lending him his strength and his ear.

A more sensitive person would have been able to convey these thoughts and feelings to Nash. To tell him that he was considered a cherished person and a true friend.

Parker looked up from his meal and stared Nash directly in the eye. "Thanks."

Order Form

Milligan Books, Inc.

1425 W. Manchester Ave., Suite C, Los Angeles, CA 90047

(323) 750-3592

Name_____ Date _____

Address

City_____ State____ Zip Code _____

Day Telephone _____

Evening Telephone_____

Book Title_____

Number of books ordered___ Total ....$ _____

Sales Taxes (CA Add 8.25%) ....$ _____

Shipping & Handling $4.90 for one book..$ _____

Add $1.00 for each additional book...........$ _____

Total Amount Due.....................................$ _____

☐ Check ☐ Money Order ☐ Other Cards _____

☐ Visa   ☐ MasterCard Expiration Date _____

Credit Card No. _____

Driver License No. _____

Make check payable to Milligan Books, Inc.

_____   _____
Signature   Date